LISA JACKSON

DEVIOUS

KENSINGTON
PUBLISHING CORP.

www.kensingtonbooks.com

KENSINGTON BOOKS are published by
Kensington Publishing Corp.
119 West 40th Street
New York, NY 10018

ISBN-13: 978-0-7582-6844-0 (ebook)

ISBN-13: 978-1-4967-2837-1

First Kensington Trade Paperback Printing: April 2011

10 9 8 7 6 5 4

Printed in the United States of America

OUTSTANDING PRAISE FOR THE NOVELS OF LISA JACKSON

Books by Lisa Jackson

Stand-Alones
SEE HOW SHE DIES
FINAL SCREAM
RUNNING SCARED
WHISPERS
TWICE KISSED
UNSPOKEN
DEEP FREEZE
FATAL BURN
MOST LIKELY TO DIE
WICKED GAME
WICKED LIES
SOMETHING WICKED
WICKED WAYS
SINISTER
WITHOUT MERCY
YOU DON'T WANT TO KNOW
CLOSE TO HOME
AFTER SHE'S GONE
REVENGE
YOU WILL PAY
OMINOUS
BACKLASH
RUTHLESS
ONE LAST BREATH
LIAR, LIAR
PARANOID
ENVIOUS
LAST GIRL STANDING
DISTRUST
ALL I WANT FROM SANTA

Cahill Family Novels
IF SHE ONLY KNEW
ALMOST DEAD
YOU BETRAYED ME

Rick Bentz/ Reuben Montoya Novels
HOT BLOODED
COLD BLOODED
SHIVER
ABSOLUTE FEAR
LOST SOULS
MALICE
DEVIOUS
NEVER DIE ALONE

Pierce Reed/ Nikki Gillette Novels
THE NIGHT BEFORE
THE MORNING AFTER
TELL ME
THE THIRD GRAVE

Selena Alvarez/ Regan Pescoli Novels
LEFT TO DIE
CHOSEN TO DIE
BORN TO DIE
AFRAID TO DIE
READY TO DIE
DESERVES TO DIE
EXPECTING TO DIE
WILLING TO DIE

Published by Kensington Publishing Corp.

Acknowledgments

When I write a book, there are many people who help me pull it all together, whether it's in editing or research, moral support, or technical advice. I trust many individuals and professionals who know far more than I about certain subjects, but any mistakes in the book are clearly my own.

I would like to thank those people who have helped me with *Devious*. There are more behind-the-scenes workers, of course, but the following people come to mind, and I can't say how much I appreciate their help and support:

Alex Craft, Ken Bush, Nancy Bush, Matthew Crose, Michael Crose, Niki Crose, Wayne Kreitz, Carol Maloy, Arla Melum, Ken Melum, Trevor Melum, Roz Noonan, Robin Rue, John Scognamiglio, Larry Sparks, and Celia Stinson. Thank you, and if I forgot someone, my apologies!

AUTHOR'S NOTE

As ever, I have made some alterations to the facts, bending the rules a bit for the purposes of story.

Also, at the time of the writing of this book, the horrific accident in the Gulf Coast occured. The oil spill was fouling the incredible waters of that part of the world and threatening the wetlands of Louisiana, probably flowing its way to New Orleans. As I write this, the spill (really an explosion like an unending volcano) is still pouring out of the seabed, and I'm sick with worry for not only the Gulf states and countries surrounding the area, but also for the entire world, ecologically, financially, and morally.

New Orleans, and all of Louisiana, is very dear to me. Though I've never lived in the South, my characters do, and I've spent many happy hours in the beauty and vibrance of that incredible part of the world.

I did not address the oil spill in this book but will in later Bentz/Montoya novels, when I know more about how this whole catastrophe plays out. My heart goes out to the people who reside and work in the area—strong, courageous people who stood on the soil they loved and fought the devastation and disaster of Hurricane Katrina only to face this new, unthinkable calamity, a tragedy for us all. It takes incredible and brave people to fight the battles of nature and man. I applaud you all.

Lisa Jackson

CHAPTER 1

"It's time." The voice was clear.

Smiling to herself, Camille felt a sublime relief as she finished pushing the last small button through its loop. She stared at herself in the tiny mirror and adjusted her veil.

"You're a vision in white," her father said.

But he wasn't here, was he? He wasn't walking her down the aisle. No, no, of course not. He'd died, years before. At least that was what she thought. But then her father wasn't her father . . . only by law. Right? She blinked hard. Woozy, she tried to clear her brain, wash away the feeling of disembodiment that assailed her.

It's because it's your wedding day; your nerves are playing tricks on your brain.

"Your groom awaits." Again, the voice propelled her, and she wondered if someone was actually speaking to her or if she was imagining it.

Silly, of course it's real!

She left the small room where she'd dressed and walked unsteadily along the shadowed corridor, lit by only a few wavering sconces. Dark, yet the hallway seemed to glisten.

Down a wide staircase with steps polished from thousands of feet scurrying up and down, she headed toward the smaller chapel where she knew he was waiting.

Her heart pounded with excitement.

Her blood sang through her veins.

What a glorious, glorious night!

One hand trailed down the long, smooth banister, fingertips gliding along the polished rail.

"Hurry," a harsh voice ordered against her ear, and she nearly stumbled over the dress's hem. "You must not keep him waiting!"

"I won't," she promised, her voice reverberating from a distance, as if echoing through a tunnel. Or only in her head.

She picked up her skirt to move more quickly, her feet skimming along the floor. She felt light, as if floating, anticipation urging her forward.

Moonlight washed through the tall tracery windows, spilling shadowed, colored patterns on the floor, and as she reached the chapel, her legs wobbled, as if she were wearing heels.

But her feet were bare, the cold stone floor penetrating through her soles.

Poverty, chastity, obedience.

The words swirled through her brain as the door to the chapel was opened and she stepped inside. She heard music in her head, the voices of angels rising upward through the spires of St. Marguerite's Cathedral on this, her wedding day.

Night . . . it's night.

Candles flickered at the altar, and overhead a massive crucifix soared, reminding her of Christ's suffering. She made the sign of the cross as she genuflected, then slowly moved forward.

Poverty. Chastity. Obedience.

Her fingers wound around the smooth beads of her rosary as the music in her head swelled.

As she reached the altar, the church bell began to toll and she knelt before the presence of God. She was ready to take her vows, to give her life to the one she loved.

"Good . . . good . . . perfect."

Camille bowed her head in prayer, then, on her knees, looked up at the crucifix, saw the wounds on Christ's emaciated body, witnessed his sacrifice for her own worldly sins.

Oh, yes, she had sinned.

Over and over.

Now she would be absolved.

Loved.

Forever.

Closing her eyes, she bent her head with difficulty. It seemed suddenly heavy, her hands clumsy. The chapel shifted and darkened, and the statuary, the Madonna and angels near the baptismal basin, suddenly stared at her with accusing eyes.

She heard the scrape of a shoe on the stone floor, and her lightheartedness and joy gave way to anxiety.

Don't give in. Not tonight...

But even her wedding dress no longer seemed silky and light; the fabric was suddenly scratchy and rough, a musty smell wafting from it.

The skin on the back of her neck, beneath the cloying veil, prickled with anxiety.

No, no, no... this is wrong.

"So now you know," the voice so near her ear reprimanded, and she shrank away from the hiss. "For the wages of sin are . . ."

"Death," she whispered.

Sheer terror curdled her blood. *Oh, God!* Scared out of her mind, Camille tried to scramble to her feet.

In that instant, Fate struck.

The rosary was stripped from her hands, the beads ripping over her fingers and flesh, only to scatter and bounce on the floor.

Camille tried to force her feet beneath her, but her knees were weak, her legs suddenly like rubber. She tried to stand, pushing herself upright, but it was too late.

A thick cord circled her throat and was pulled tight.

NO! What is this?

Needle-sharp shards cut deep into her flesh.

Panic surged through her.

No, no, no! This is all wrong.

Help me!

White-hot pain screamed through her body. She jerked forward, trying to throw off her attacker as her airway was cut off. She tried to gasp but couldn't draw a breath. Her lungs, dear Jesus, her lungs strained with the pressure.

Oh, God, what was happening?

Why?

The nave seemed to spin, the high-domed ceiling reeling, the monster behind her back drawing the deadly cord tighter.

Terror clawed through her brain. Desperately, Camille tried to free herself, to kick and twist again, but her body wouldn't respond as it should have. The weight against her back was crushing, the cord at her throat slitting deep.

Blood pounded behind her eyes, echoed through her ears.

Her fingers scrabbled at the cord around her neck, a fingernail ripping.

Her back bowed as she strained.

She fought wildly, but it was useless.

Please, please, please! Dear Father, spare me! I have sinned, but please—

Her feet slipped from beneath her.

Weakly she flailed, her strength failing her.

No, Camille. Fight! Don't give up! Do not! Someone will save you.

Her eyes focused on the crucifix again, her vision of Christ's haggard face blurring. *I'm sorry...*

She was suddenly so weak, her attempts frail and futile.

Her strong body grew limp.

"Please," she tried to beg, but the sound was garbled and soft, unrecognizable.

The demon who dared set foot in this chapel, the monster who had defiled this holy ground, held her fast. Pulling on the cord. Unrelenting. Strong with dark and deadly purpose.

Camille's lungs were on fire, her heart pounding so loudly she was sure it would burst. Through eyes round with fear, she saw only a wash of red.

Oh, Dear Father, the pain!

Again, she tried to suck in one bit of air but failed.

Her lungs shrieked.

Brutal strength, infused by a cold, dark wrath, cinched the garrote still tighter.

Agony ripped through her.

"Whore," the voice accused. "Daughter of Satan."

No!

Eyes open, again she saw the image of Christ on the cross, a film of scarlet distorting his perfect face, tears like blood running from his eyes.

I love you.

The deluge of sins that was her life washed over her, quicksilver images of those she had wronged. Her mother and father, her sister, her best friend...so many people, some who had loved her...the innocents.

This was her punishment, she realized, her hands falling from her neck to scrape down her abdomen and linger for a second over her womb.

Zzzzt. Snap! A bright light flashed before her eyes; then all was dark.

In the name of the Father, the Son, and the Holy Spirit, wash my soul clean.... Forgive me, for I have sinned....

CHAPTER 2

"Oh, for the love of St. Jude!" Valerie clicked the ESCAPE key on her laptop again and again, as if she could punch the life back into the hand-me-down computer with its antiquated hard drive and mind of its own. "Come on, come on!" she muttered between clenched teeth, then gave up, unable to turn the damned thing off without taking out the battery.

That did it! Tomorrow she'd go computer shopping despite the dismal state of her bank account. She still had a little room on her credit card, but then, once she bought a new computer, it would be maxed out as well.

The price of divorce, she told herself callously as she shoved the laptop onto the rumpled bedclothes. In her mismatched pajamas, she walked into the kitchen of the small carriage house and dipped her head under the faucet for a drink, then stared through the rain-spattered window at the uneasy New Orleans night.

The air was thick with the coming of summer, sweat dampening her skin. She cranked open the window, allowing the dank smell of the slow-moving river to roll inside. Far away, the hum of traffic could be heard on the freeway, a steady rush that competed with the song of crickets and the low rumble of toads.

Pealing forlornly, the bells of St. Marguerite's struck off the hours of midnight.

Inexplicably, Val's skin crawled. Her cop instincts went into overdrive, and she felt, again, as if she were being watched, that hidden eyes were assessing her.

"Too many nights with the sci-fi channel," she told herself. "Too many nightmares."

For a fleeting second, a splintered memory with sharp, brittle edges pierced her brain. Looming. Indistinct. But evil.

Her blood chilled with the image. Draped in black, with cruel eyes and a foul odor, the sinister creature grew larger. Threatening. A chain dangling from its clawlike hand.

No one could help her.

No one could save her.

"Husssshhh," the creature hissed, lowering the silvery noose. "Hush."

Camille! Val thought in horror. *This demon wants Camille....*

In a blink, the horrifying image disappeared, shrinking into the corners of her mind. From experience, Val knew it would lurk there until, unbidden, it would rise again.

"Leave me alone," she muttered under her breath, ignoring the hairs that had risen on the back of her arm. The fiend was a figment of her imagination, nothing more—nothing a sane, stable woman would believe.

Val took a steadying breath as the church bells of St. Marguerite's continued to toll plaintively through the night. Her insides still cold, she gripped the edge of the counter to steady herself and force the ugly apparition back where it belonged—into the darkest nether regions of her mind, into the crevices where sanity didn't dare tread.

Don't go there, she warned herself silently. *Do not go there.* Dwelling on the insidious pictures in her mind would only create a self-fulfilling and hideous prophecy.

"Everything's fine," she said out loud, though her insides were trembling. Quivering with a fear that she tried to keep hidden. No one could know. She was a strong woman. Nightmares or visions conjured by her willing brain weren't allowed to scare her. "For God's sake, get a grip!"

Willing herself to let go of the counter and her ridiculous fears, she told herself she was just stressed out. Who wouldn't be? An impending divorce, a lost career, a business teetering on the edge of bankruptcy, and a sister, her only sibling, intent on taking vows in a convent right out of the Middle Ages! And then there was the e-mail from Camille. Disturbing.

Val thought about St. Marguerite's, the historic cathedral where her sister would eventually take her vows.

That is, if they let her.

It still seemed so out of character for Camille, the party girl. Always with a boyfriend, always fending off trouble. From what she knew about St. Marguerite's, Valerie doubted that her sister's sins would be easily forgiven in that arena. St. Marguerite's Convent, with its locked gates, antiquated communication system, and strict rules, seemed more like a medieval fortress than a house of God; it was an isolated place the rest of the twenty-first century had zipped past. The people within those hallowed walls harkened back to earlier centuries where archaic conventions, cruel discipline, and antediluvian opinions prevailed. Probably because of the abbess or mother superior or whatever that old bat Sister Charity called herself. A throwback to the days of wearing dark habits, rapping the knuckles of unsuspecting students, and using threats and fear over praise, Sister Charity was as much a warden as she was a leader.

Why Camille ever decided to take her vows at an institution as rigid as Saint Marguerite's remained a mystery.

No, it's not. You know the reasons—you just can't face them.

Pssst!

A whisper of evil skittered through Sister Lucia's brain.

Her eyes flew open to the blackness of her tiny room in the convent. Her skin crawled, and her mouth tasted of metal. *Father in heaven, please let this just be the remnant of a bad dream, a nightmare that—*

Pssst!

There it was again, that horrid precursor of what was to come. She tossed off the thin covers and slid to her knees, her nightgown puddling around her as she instinctively reached for her rosary draped over the metal bedpost. She made the sign of the cross with the crucifix and began to silently recite the Apostles' Creed, her lips moving in the darkness, sweat collecting at the base of her skull. "I believe in God, the Father almighty, creator of heaven and earth...." And she did believe. Fervently. Usually she found comfort in this ritual she'd learned in her youth. In times of stress or worry or need, she sought solace by running her fingers over the glossy beads and whispering the prayers that brought her closer to God.

Pssst! Again the electric current that hissed beneath her skin brought sweat to her brow.

Not here, oh, please... not in the convent! Her prayer was interrupted and she started over, squeezing her eyes shut, leaning into the thin mattress with her elbows, her brain thrumming.

Once again she touched the crucifix to her forehead and began the succession of prayers that came so easily to her mind.

This has to be a mistake, she thought wildly as the familiar words slipped over her lips. Since she'd entered St. Marguerite's, intent on taking her final vows, she'd had no "incidents," as her mother had called them. She'd thought she was safe here.

"I believe in—"

Psssst! Louder this time.

The painful jolt cut through the darkness.

Lucia sucked in her breath and dropped her rosary, her prayer again cut short. She stood, abandoning any attempt to forestall the inevitable. Walking barefoot over the hardwood floors, she sensed the tremor of trouble brewing as surely as a hurricane off the Louisiana coast. In her mind's eye, she saw the chapel of this very parish and blinked against an onslaught of images.

An indistinct face.

Yellowed gown.

Billowing dark robe.

Twisted, deadly lips.

A heavy door clicking as it closed.

A bloody crucifix, crimson dripping from Christ's sacred wounds.

Death, a voice intoned over the raw static in her brain.

She flew into the hall, which was dimly lit by scattered wall sconces, and descended the curving staircase. Her fingers trailing along the worn banister, she followed a predetermined path. Pale light passed through the dark panes of stained glass, the heat of the June day still lingering into night.

Why? Lucia wondered frantically. *Why now? Why here? It's nothing...just a bad dream. All your fears crystalized, that's all.*

Her heart pounding like an erratic drum, she turned toward the chapel, the smaller place of worship tucked behind the huge cathedral. With a sense of darkness propelling her forward, she pushed through double doors that parted easily and stepped into God's house. The chapel was usually a place of light and goodness, forgiveness and redemption, but tonight she sensed that evil as dark as Satan's soul lurked here, lying in wait.

"Father, please be with me." She dipped her fingertips in holy water and crossed herself as she entered the nave, where all of the images congealed. Red votive candles flickered, casting shadows that shifted on the stone walls. A massive crucifix was suspended from the arched ceiling over the altar where Jesus, in his agony, watched over the chapel.

Instinctively, Lucia made the sign of the cross again. The thrumming in her brain turned into a throb.

From the corner of her eye, she caught a glimpse of movement—a dark figure in billowing robes disappearing through a door.

"Father?" she called, thinking the person running from the chapel was a priest. The door clicked closed. "Wait! Please..." She started for the doorway. "Father— Oh, no..." Her voice left her as she glimpsed a flutter of gauzy white fabric, the scallop of lace undulating on the floor by the first row of pews.

What?

Her heart nearly stopped.

The horrid, rapid-fire images that had awakened her seared through her brain again:

Yellowed gown.

Cruel lips.

A door shutting as the church bells pealed.

Just like before.

The whisper of evil brushed the back of her neck again. She

nearly stumbled as she raced forward, her bare feet slapping the cold stone floor, echoing to the high, coved ceiling.

This can't be happening!

It can't be!

Stumbling, running, afraid of what she might find, she dashed to the front of the apse, to the altar and the glorious, now-dark stained-glass windows. The crucifix towered to the high ceiling, the son of God staring down in his pain.

"Oh, God!" Lucia cried. *"Dios! Mi Dios!"*

Horror shot up her spine.

A crumpled form lay in front of the first row of pews.

"No, por favor, Jesús. No, no, no!"

Her blood turned to ice at the sight of the body, supine near the baptismal font. Biting back a scream, Lucia fell to her knees near the bride dressed in a fragile, tattered wedding dress. A thin, unraveling veil covered her face.

Lucia's stomach wrenched as she recognized Sister Camille, her face pale, her lips blue, her eyes wide and staring through the sheer lace.

"Oh, sweet Jesus..." Lucia gasped. She touched Camille's still-warm flesh, searching for a pulse at the nun's neck, where small bruises circled her throat. Her stomach threatened to spew. Someone had done this to Camille, had tried to kill her. Oh, God, was she still alive? Did she feel the flicker of a pulse, the slightest movement beneath Camille's cooling skin? Or was it only a figment of her imagination?

"Camille," Lucia coaxed desperately, her voice cracking, "don't let go, please. Oh, please... *Mi Dios!*"

The ringing bells overhead sounded like a death knell.

She looked up. "Help! Someone help me!" Her voice rose to the rafters, echoing back to her. "Please!"

To the near-dead woman, she whispered, "Camille, I'm here. It's Lucia. You hang in there.... Please, please... It's not your time...."

But someone had decided Camille needed to die, and despite her good thoughts, Lucia knew of one person who wanted Camille Renard to die.

She whispered a quick prayer to the Father, praying with all her soul; then, tears filling her eyes, she bent close to Camille's ear. "Don't let go." With her own gown, she tried to stop the spreading pool of blood coming from the wounds on Camille's neck.

Camille didn't move.

Pupils fixed.

Skin ashen. Cooling.

Blood flow slowed to nothing.

Lucia was frantic. She had to do something! Anything! *Please God, do not take her. Not now... not yet... Oh, Father!*

"Help!" Lucia screamed again, unwilling to leave the friend she'd known so closely for a year, a woman she'd known of most of her life. She couldn't be dying... couldn't be...

Lucia's mind was awash with images of Sister Camille, beautiful and lithe, with her secretive smile and eyebrows that would arch to show amusement or disbelief. A troubled woman, yes, a nun with far too many secrets, one she'd met long ago before they'd independently decided to take their vows.

Throat closing, she whispered, "It's not your time, Camille. You hear me? Don't leave... don't you..."

But the poor, tortured woman was gone, her spirit rising from the lifeless shell that was her body. Stolen from her.

"No... please... Father—"

Thud! Somewhere a door banged shut as the bells pealed again.

Lucia jumped.

Someone was coming!

Good. "Just hold on," she said to the ashen body, though she knew intuitively that it was too late. "Help is coming." Her words hung in the chill night air.

Lucia felt a shiver slide down her spine as doubt clouded her mind. She linked her fingers through those of her friend and sent up another desperate prayer as the church bells in the steeple continued to toll off the hours.

Was help really on the way?

Or was the person who had done this to Camille returning?

CHAPTER 3

Val was calmer now, the quivering of her insides having sub-
sided. She filled her favorite, chipped mug with hot water, set
it in the microwave, and watched as hidden letters appeared. The
heavy cup, bought online at ABC.com, displayed the cast members
of *Lost*, her once-favorite television show.

It had been a Christmas gift from Camille, a treasure she'd
bought before the show had aired its final episode.

Back in the days when they hadn't let anything drive a wedge
between them. Not even Slade Houston.

"Oh, Cammie," she whispered, shaking her head at their own
ridiculous fights as the microwave dinged. Gingerly gripping the
cup's handle, she scrounged the last tea bag from a box and
dunked the decaffeinated leaves into the near-boiling water.

Though it was midnight, sleep, for Valerie, was still hours away,
if at all possible. What was it Slade had always said? That her insomnia was one of the reasons the department had kept her on; she
was a workaholic who, because of her inability to sleep, could work
sixteen hours straight while being paid for eight.

Then again, Slade was known to exaggerate.

Part of his ridiculous cowboy humor.

Twisting the kinks from her neck, she closed her eyes, and for a
heartbeat, she saw her husband's face again: strong, beard-shadowed

jaw; crooked half-smile with teeth that flashed white against skin tanned from hours working under the brutal Texas sun; and eyes smoldering a deep, smoky blue. Slade Houston. Tough as old leather, all rough-and-tumble cowboy, sexy as all get-out and just plain bad news.

So why was she thinking of him tonight?

And last night and the one before that and...

"Idiot," she muttered under her breath as she willed Slade's image to disappear. The bells had stopped ringing sometime in the past few minutes. Good. Silence. Peace.

But the eerie sensation that something was very wrong tonight lingered, and she couldn't help feeling on edge.

Tomorrow.

She'd visit Camille tomorrow, regardless of the Machiavellian methods that old bat Sister Charity tried to use to dissuade her. "I'm sorry, but seeing your sister now is impossible. We have strict rules here," she'd told Val the last time she'd tried to visit Camille unannounced. "Rules we abide by, rules sanctified by the Father."

Yeah, right. If Sister Charity had any good intentions, Val had yet to see one. In Val's opinion, the reverend mother was on a power trip fueled by self-importance and a skewed view of religion.

Always a bad combination.

And one, this time, Valerie intended to thwart come daybreak.

The last tolling bell faded to the sound of footsteps emanating from beyond the chapel walls. Lucia's skin crawled as she stared at the dead girl. She tried to pray but couldn't find the words. Who had done this to Camille? Why? And the weird bridal dress, the ring of bloody drops around the neckline—what was that all about?

She glanced to the side door that had shut just as she'd arrived, and her heart hammered. Someone else had seen Sister Camille on the chapel floor. Lucia had crossed paths with either Camille's assailant or a witness to what had happened. Fear prickled the back of her neck as she wondered if help was on its way...or if the assailant was returning.

Making the sign of the cross, Lucia turned toward the doorway and screamed at the top of her lungs. "Help!"

The side door swept open, banging against the wall. Mother Superior, an imposing woman in a long black habit, hurried into the nave. Her graying hair, which was usually concealed by her veil, appeared fuzzy and disheveled. "Sister Lucy! For the love of the Holy Mother, what's going on?" she demanded. Her skirts swished against the smooth floor, and her face was a mask of disapproval, her lips pinched. Suddenly realizing where she was, she paused to quickly genuflect at the crucifix and make the sign of the cross over her ample bosom.

"It's Sister Camille..." Lucia rose, her gaze still upon Camille's body.

"What about...? Oh!" The mother superior dragged in a quick breath as she rounded the final pew. "Saints be with us." Wide skirts swooshing, she ran to the victim's side and dropped to her knees.

"It's too late. She's dead."

"But how? Why?" Sister Charity whispered, as if she expected God to answer as she fussed over the corpse and said a quick prayer. "Who would do this?"

"I don't know. Someone was here, before me," Lucia said, trying to separate fact from fiction, from the images that were real as opposed to those that had been conjured in her mind. "I saw the door to the hallway close." Yes, yes, that was right. She pointed to the door that led to a back hallway. "And...I think Sister Camille was alive at that point."

The older nun touched Camille's wrist and placed her ear next to Camille's nose, listening for any sign of life. Lucia knew she would find none.

"What were you doing here, Sister Lucy?" Mother Superior asked, addressing Lucia in her formal name—the saint's name she had taken along with her vows.

"I, uh, heard something," Lucia lied, as she had so often in the past. No one here knew her secret, not even the priests to whom she confessed.

"Heard something? From your room?"

"Yes, I was on my way to the bathroom."

As if she realized this conversation could wait, the reverend mother, still kneeling at Camille's side, ordered, "Go find Father Paul. Send him here."

"Shouldn't we call the police?"

The reverend mother closed her eyes as if seeking patience. "Do as I say. After you send Father Paul, then go to my office and dial nine-one-one."

"But the police should be alerted first—"

"Don't argue! The best thing we can do for Sister Camille is to pray for her soul. Now, go! And if anyone else wakes up, send them back to their rooms!" Her expression brooked no argument, and Lucia took off, walking rapidly through the very doorway where she'd seen someone exit. Send the other nuns back to their rooms? Cells, more likely. Or kennels. Like dogs. Oh, Lord, she knew she was *not* cut out to be a nun. Not with impure thoughts like these.

Heart pounding, she closed the door behind her and took off at a dead run—heading straight to the reverend mother's office. Let them punish her later, but right now she knew Camille was the priority. She pushed open the frosted-glass door and stormed into Sister Charity's inner sanctuary.

Everything was neatly placed on bookshelves that lined the room—books, candles, crucifixes, a healthy amaryllis with a heavy white bloom, and a solitary picture of the Pope. Lucia rounded the big, worn desk, where far too many times she had sat on one of the uncomfortable visitor chairs, her hands clenched in anxiety, as the mother superior had lectured her across the expanse of lacquered walnut. She reached for the telephone with its heavy receiver, a black dinosaur left over from the sixties or seventies, and dialed quickly, nervously waiting for the rotary dial to click into place.

"Nine-one-one. What's the nature of your emergency?" a woman's voice answered.

"Sister Camille is dead! There was some kind of accident here at St. Marguerite's Convent—no, in the chapel—and she's dead! I . . . I think she was killed. Please, please send someone quickly!" Her voice, already tremulous, was elevating with each word.

"What is the address?"

Lucia rattled off the street address and, when asked, her name and the phone number.

"What kind of an accident?"

"I don't know. Maybe...maybe she was strangled. All I really know is that she's dead, and the mother superior is with her now."

"A homicide."

"Oh, I don't know! We need help. Please, please send help!"

"We are. Officers have been dispatched. You need to stay on the line."

"I can't...I have to tell Father Paul."

"Please, Miss Costa, do not hang up. Stay on the line—"

Ignoring the dispatcher, Lucia dropped the phone, letting it dangle as she took off at a full run through the back door of the office, one only Sister Charity used.

Lucia's heart was a drum as she sprinted through the dark hallways with their gleaming floors, down the stairs, and out the double doors to a courtyard. As if Lucifer himself were chasing her, she raced through the rain-splattered cloister and past a fountain. Wind scuttled across the flagstones, kicking up wet leaves and tugging at the sodden hem of her nightgown.

She couldn't tell anyone about how she was awakened so abruptly in the middle of the night. What would she say? Anyone who heard about the voice that directed her, the beast she'd somehow unleashed, would think she was certifiable. As she did herself. She figured that voice in her head was between her and God. No one else. Not even Father Paul or Father Frank. They might think she was possessed by a demon, and maybe she was, but she just didn't want any attention drawn to her.

It's not about you! Camille is dead! Dead! Someone killed her and left her lifeless body in the chapel.

And somehow the voice knew. And awoke her.

Oh, it was all so disturbing.

Through another door and under a dripping portico, she flew to Father Paul's door, where she pounded desperately.

"Father!" she cried, shivering in the pale glow of the priest's porch light. "Please! Father! There's been...an accident!"

Over the drip of rain, she heard footsteps behind her, the scrape of leather against wet stones. From the corner of her eye, she saw movement in the shadows, a dark figure emerging through a garden gate. She gasped, stepped back, and nearly tripped on her own hem as a large man appeared, his face white and stern, his eyes sunken and shadowed in the night.

"Father Frank," she whispered, recognizing the younger priest. She had clasped her hand over her breasts and suddenly realized that the cool rain had soaked her cotton nightgown, which now pressed flush against her skin. The fabric clung to her body, hiding nothing in the watery light. "There's been an accident or...or..." She swallowed hard, aware of the secrets that Sister Camille had shared. Secrets about this tall man standing before her. "It's Sister Camille, in the chapel....She...she..." And then she saw the blood leeching from his cassock, running in red rivulets onto the smooth, shimmering stones of the pathway.

"She's dead," he said, his rough voice barely audible over the gurgle of rainwater in the gutters, his gaze tortured. "And it's my fault. God forgive me, it's all my fault."

CHAPTER 4

"Still up?" Freya's voice cut into her fantasy.

"Always." Val tried to ignore the worries about Camille. She tossed the tea bag into the sink and glanced over her shoulder toward the archway leading to the main house. When they'd bought this old inn, Val had been attracted to the small living space of the carriage house, while Freya took over the private quarters just off the main kitchen. Freya, all tousled reddish curls and freckles, appeared in shorts and an oversized T-shirt. She was cradling a cup with whipped cream piled so high it was frothing and running over the lip of her mug. Somehow, Freya managed to lick up the drip before it landed on the cracked linoleum.

Freya was five-three and still had the honed body of the gymnast she'd been in high school and the metabolism of a girl twenty years her junior.

"You look like hell," Freya observed.

"Thanks."

"Really, you should try to sleep."

If only. She turned and leaned her hips against the counter. "Insomniacs R Us." The inability to sleep was something she and Freya shared in common.

Freya toasted her friend. "Mine is decaf. Though it doesn't mean I'll actually fall asleep anytime soon."

"I've got decaf, too. Something called 'Calm.'" Val took an experimental sip. Hot water tasting of ginger and chamomile singed the tip of her tongue. "It's supposed to help you chill.... Wait a minute, let me see what exactly it's guaranteed to do." She picked up the empty box and read the label. "Oh, yeah, here it is. 'Calm's unique formula is guaranteed to ease the worries and cares of the world away with each flavorful swallow. With hints of ginger and jasmine, this chamomile blend will relax and soothe you.'"

"Sure," Freya mocked, wrinkling her nose. "Soothe *you*? No way. Anyway, it sounds disgusting."

"No, just boring to fans of triple-caramel-chocolate-macchiatos with Red Bull chasers."

"Very funny." Freya couldn't help but grin as she climbed onto one of the two café chairs near Val's bistro table.

A friend since eighth grade, Freya Martin had convinced Val to invest in this eight-bedroom bed-and-breakfast inn in the Garden District, a few blocks off St. Charles Avenue. Named the Briarstone House, the old Georgian had been minimally damaged during Hurricane Katrina, but the owners, Freya's great-aunt and uncle, had decided they weren't about to weather any more Category 5 storms. Actually, they didn't want to see any Category 1, 2, 3, or 4 storms either.

Auntie and Uncle had wanted out of the Gulf Coast, and fast.

Freya had wanted in.

She'd bought out Uncle Blair and Aunt Susie on a contract. Leaving most of the furnishings, they filled an RV and drove west, into the sunset, searching for a dry climate, new snowbird friends, and endless nights of card games and martinis.

To Val, right now, her nerves on perpetual edge, that sounded like heaven.

Valerie had been at a crossroads in her own life when Freya had asked her to become her partner. It hadn't taken much to convince her that an investment in a creaking old Georgian manor—rumored to be haunted, no less—was the best idea in the universe. Especially since the inn was barely a mile as the crow flies from Camille and St. Marguerite's.

Since Freya and her live-in boyfriend had recently parted ways,

Freya had decided she needed a business partner. She'd e-mailed Val with the details, and Val jumped on the opportunity.

A deal was struck.

The rest, as they say, was history.

Some of it bad history.

And now, with the gurgle of rain running through the gutters and the church bells now silent, Val wondered if she'd made the right decision. Again. And the eerie feeling that had been with her earlier still remained. Mentally shaking it off, she glanced at the window but, of course, couldn't see the church spire in the dark.

"Okay, spill it. Something's wrong, isn't it?" Freya asked, eyebrows puckering. "Wait a minute, forget I asked. Something's *always* wrong. Let me guess—it's Slade."

"It's not Slade," she said emphatically, and Freya rolled her eyes, not buying it.

"If you say so."

"Trust me, it's *not* Slade."

"It's always Slade. We should talk about him."

"No way." Scowling, Val skewered Freya with her best don't-go-there glare.

"Really, you should know that—"

"We've been over this ground before. I don't want to talk or think about him until I have to. In court."

"But—"

"I'm serious, Freya. Slade's off-limits." She really didn't want to discuss her ex again. Especially not tonight, when she was feeling so off-center.

Freya looked as if she was about to say something more but thought better of it. "Fine. Just remember I tried."

"I will."

"Did he do something I don't know about?"

"Probably." Val lifted a shoulder. "Who knows and who cares?"

Freya opened her mouth, but before she could bring up Slade's name again, Val said, "It's Cammie, okay? I haven't heard from her in over a week." The old timbers of the house creaked overhead, and for a second, Val thought she heard footsteps. The ghost again, she supposed. Freya thought the house was haunted; she didn't.

"Hear that?" Freya asked. Unlike Val, Freya was a believer in all things supernatural.

"The house settling."

"It settled two hundred years ago."

Val rolled her eyes.

Freya got the message. "Okay, okay. You're worried 'cause Cammie's incommunicado. So what? I don't hear from Sarah for weeks, and she's my twin. If you believe all the twin literature, we're supposed to be on the same wavelength and have some special"—she made air quotes—"spiritual connection." She rolled her eyes and took another sip. "They say we formed a psychic bond from our time together in the womb. Somehow, Sarah never got the message."

Val ran her thumb over the chipped ridge of her mug. "But Cammie is different."

"Cammie is probably just busy. You know, doing what nuns do. Praying, doing penance, good deeds, whatever." Freya wiggled the fingers of her free hand as if to indicate there were a myriad of things keeping Cammie from communicating. "Maybe she's taken one of those vows of silence."

"Cammie?" Val questioned. Gregarious, outgoing, flirty, over-the-top Camille Renard? "You do remember her. Right?"

"Oh, yeah." Freya bit her lip. "Always in trouble."

"That hasn't changed," Val admitted, the uneasy feeling returning.

"I know, that's really the problem, isn't it? Cammie just doesn't seem cut out to be a nun." Another sip. "Just like you weren't cut out to be a cop."

Val felt that same little bite that nipped at her when she thought about her career gone sour. She wanted to argue and defend herself, to tell Freya that she'd been a good cop, but the effort would have been futile. A gust of heavy wind slipped through the open window, rattling the blinds, reminding her how she'd screwed up. "Well, I don't have to worry about that now, do I?"

"Hey, I didn't mean—"

"I know." She waved a hand in the air, as if swatting a lazy fly. "Don't worry about it." But it was a sore subject, one that burned a hole in her brain and kept her up at night. She slid the window down and caught a watery image of herself: pale and ghostly skin, cheekbones high and sharp, wide mouth turned down, and worried hazel eyes. Her curly auburn hair was scraped back into a drooping ponytail. God, she was a mess. Inside and out. Rain skewed her reflection as she latched the window tight. "Anyway, you're right. I do look like hell."

"Nothing seventy-two hours of sleep won't cure."

Val doubted it.

"Anyone ever tell you that you worry too much?"

"Just you."

"Then you should take it as gospel. Quit dwelling on Cammie, okay? So she's doing the running-off-to-a-nunnery thing. It'll pass." One side of Freya's mouth lifted. "I'm surprised she hasn't already been thrown out."

If you only knew, Valerie thought, sipping her tea and glancing out the window again into the thick night where the spire of St. Marguerite's cathedral was cloaked in darkness, invisible.

Oh, God, Freya, if you only knew.

Slade Houston squinted into the darkness. The tires of his old pickup hissed over the slick pavement, and the wipers were having one helluva time keeping up with the torrent as he drove across the state line into Louisiana. His old dog, Bo, a hound of indeterminate lineage, sat beside him, his nose pressed to the glass of the passenger window. Every once in a while, Bo cast a bald eye in Slade's direction, hoping for him to crack the damned thing.

"Not tonight, boy," Slade said as he fiddled with the radio, which crackled from interference. He found a station playing an old Johnny Cash song, but the lyrics couldn't keep his mind from returning to his reason for driving in the middle of the night. A fool's mission, at least according to his brothers, Trask and Zane, who'd let him hear it while he was packing up the Ford just before dusk.

"Why the hell you want anything to do with that woman is beyond me," Trask, his middle brother, had muttered under his breath. "Only gonna bring you grief."

"More grief," Zane, the youngest, had added.

Not that Slade had asked for any advice as he'd loaded his pickup with a sleeping bag and duffel before whistling for Bo.

"Just take care of things. I shouldn't be gone long," Slade had said as the dog, with his perpetual limp and gnawed ear, leaped into the cab. Slade had slammed the door shut and felt the heat of his siblings' sullen glares.

"How long?" Zane had asked.

"Don't know yet. It depends."

"Just be smart," Trask had advised.

"Why start now?" Slade had flashed a grin to lighten things up, but the joke had fallen flat. Neither brother had cracked the hint of a smile; they just glared at him with their jaws set.

Great.

That hadn't been too much of a surprise. Neither one of them had liked Valerie before the marriage, and their opinions hadn't changed much over the years.

Slade had tried to let it drop as he climbed behind the wheel. Through the open window, he heard that crickets had taken up their evening chorus and saw the western hills had been silhouetted by the brilliant shades of orange and gold.

Trask hadn't been ready to give up the fight. "You plan on bringing her back here with ya?"

"Valerie?" he said, just to get under his brother's skin. As if there was anyone else. "Don't know yet."

"If ya do hook up with her again," Trask said, "then you're a bigger fool than I took ya for."

"She wouldn't be willing, even if I asked." That was the truth.

"She's bad news," Zane reminded him.

"Don't I know it." But he'd cranked on the engine of the dusty rig anyway, executed a three-point turn in the gravel drive without a second look at the weathered two-story ranch house he'd grown up in, and hit the gas. He didn't bother watching the setting sun light the sky ablaze behind the barns with their creaking wild-mustang weather vanes. His old Ford had bounced down the rutted lane, dried sow thistle and Johnson grass scratching the underbelly of the truck as it rolled past acres upon acres of fields dotted with cattle and horses, land he and his brothers had inherited from their father.

A red-tailed hawk had swooped through the darkening sky as he drove past the old windmill that sat solitary and still in the dead air. A good omen. Right?

He'd snapped on the radio, then turned the truck past the battered mailbox onto the county road. He drove through the small town of Bad Luck until he came to San Antonio, where he cruised onto I-10, the long strip of asphalt cutting dead east. He'd left his brothers, Texas, and the sun far behind him.

To chase down a woman who didn't want him.

He had the divorce papers in the glove compartment of his truck to remind him of that sorry fact.

CHAPTER 5

The call came in not long after midnight.

Montoya groaned as he rolled across the bed and answered his cell. While his wife, Abby, burrowed under the blankets, he kept his voice down and slid out of bed as he had a hundred times before. He was a detective with the New Orleans Police Department. Odd hours and late-night calls were part of his job.

"What now?" Abby asked, her voice muffled before she tossed the blankets off and shoved a tangle of hair from her eyes as he hung up.

"Dead woman. A nun. Possible homicide."

Abby pushed herself upright, propped her back against the pillows, and clicked on the light. "A nun?"

"According to the officer who responded to a nine-one-one call." He slid into a pair of battered jeans that he'd tossed over the foot of the bed, then found a clean T-shirt in the closet and pulled it over his head.

"Why would anyone kill a nun?" She scraped her hair back from her face, but wild curls sprang loose.

"Don't know, but I'll figure it out." He flashed his wife a humorless grin and thought back to another time when a nun had been killed—that one being his own aunt. "That's why they pay me the big bucks."

"Yeah, right." She didn't smile as she tugged at her hair. "Just be careful."

"Always am." He started for the door.

"Hey! Aren't you forgetting something?" she asked, angling her chin toward him, practically begging for a kiss.

"Oh, yeah!" He walked to the closet, found the locked box holding his sidearm, and retrieved his weapon. After strapping on his shoulder holster, he slid his arms through his leather jacket and started for the door.

"You can be a miserable SOB when you want to be," she charged.

"I *always* want to be."

"I know." But her eyes twinkled and the reddish blond curls that framed her face were sexy as hell. "You're a father now, so... don't take any unnecessary risks, okay? I want Benjamin to know his daddy."

He snapped his Glock into place, then crossed the room and pushed her back onto the mattress. "So do I." He stretched his body over hers and kissed her hard, his tongue probing her mouth, his hands splayed wide across her backside. "Wait for me," he whispered against her ear.

"Not on your life, Detective," she said, but there was a smile in her voice, and he had to keep his thoughts on the coming investigation to control the tightness in his groin and the rock-hard response she always elicited from him. One interested arch of her eyebrows could cause a reaction deep inside of him. Man, did he have it bad.

"Pussy-whipped," his brother, Cruz, had commented on more than one occasion.

In this case, Cruz was right.

"I'll be back as soon as I can. Be ready."

"Oh, God, save it, Montoya," she countered, and cocooned herself in the blankets again, covering her auburn curls with a pillow. "And whatever you do, don't wake Benjamin, okay? Otherwise I'll have to kill you." Again her voice was muffled, but he got the message. He had no intention of waking their three-month-old son.

Smiling as he left the room, Montoya nearly tripped over Hershey, their big lug of a chocolate lab who, always on guard near the bedroom door, scrambled to his big paws and stood, blocking the hallway, his tail thumping against an antique sideboard. As ever, Hershey was ready for anything, especially to take Montoya's place in the bed.

"Forget it, okay? She needs her beauty sleep."

"I heard that!" she said through the open door.

Hershey took her voice as an open invitation and galloped into the bedroom. A small dark shadow, the skittish cat, Ansel, leaped from the sideboard and followed the dog inside.

"Great." Montoya was struggling with his shoes. He didn't have time to call the dog back and figured Abby could deal with the animals. With bluish night-lights as his guide, he headed through his long, shotgun-style home, passing through the kitchen and living room to reach the front door. The night was muggy. Thick. The smell of the sluggish Mississippi hung heavy in the air. Rain was falling hard, running in the street as he jogged across his soggy yard to the driveway and slid onto the familiar leather seat of his Mustang. He closed the door, jammed his key into the ignition, and the engine roared to life.

Wondering what the hell had gone down at the conservative church, he hit the wipers, then gunned the engine. No siren. No lights. Just the windshield wipers slapping away the rain as the car's radio played and the familiar voice of Dr. Sam, a late-night psychologist, wafted through the speakers. Frowning, he drove the familiar streets and recalled another case in which the host, Samantha Walker, was the intended victim. Fortunately, Dr. Sam was still around to help the people who called in to her show.

Traffic was sparse as he rolled through the wet, muggy night. Montoya arrived at St. Marguerite's to find squad cars, lights flashing, parked at angles on the street. A fire truck dominated the circular drive, with an emergency unit idling under one of the massive live oaks surrounding the building.

Montoya double-parked and headed toward the cathedral, a looming edifice with spires, bell tower, and tracery windows reflecting the strobing red and blue lights of the parked vehicles. Gargoyles perched high on the gutters, dark, dragonlike sculptures eyeing the sacred grounds with malicious intent, their evil presence in stark contrast to the cross rising high over the highest church steeple.

He paused at the wide double doors, long enough to log into the crime scene and receive directions from one of the uniformed cops controlling the scene. Quickly, he made his way around the larger area of the cathedral proper to a side door and down a short hallway to the smaller chapel, which was tucked between the massive church and what appeared to be a garden.

He stepped inside, and a wave of nostalgia pushed him back to his youth, when his mother would take him and his siblings to Mass every Sunday. The smell of lingering incense and burning candles, their tiny flames offering a flickering, shadowed light, the hushed voices, the cavernous room with its narrow stained-glass windows.

He glanced up at the huge crucifix, and, more from habit than any lingering sense of conviction, Montoya sketched the sign of the cross over his chest.

Officers were talking in hushed tones to several people near the back of the chapel, but Montoya ignored them as he spied Rick Bentz, his partner for many of the years Montoya had been with the NOPD, standing near the altar.

Bentz was at least fifteen years older than Montoya, nearly another generation. Married to his second wife, he had a baby under a year old, and the lack of sleep showed in the lines on Bentz's wide face and the flecks of gray in his hair. He still had a limp from a previous accident, but otherwise Bentz's body was honed to that of a heavyweight boxer. Tonight Bentz wore jeans, a T-shirt, a jacket, and a dark expression, his gaze narrowed on the floor near the altar.

As Montoya hurried along a wide aisle, he saw the victim lying in front of the first row of pews. Her face was covered by an altar cloth, only tangles of dark hair showing on the stone floor. Her body seemed to be posed, arms folded over her chest, fingers twined in a wooden rosary. She was wearing a yellowed, nearly tattered wedding gown, her feet bare, a silver band around the ring finger of her left hand.

"Who is it?" he asked.

"One of the nuns here," Bentz said. "Sister Camille."

"Killed here? At the altar?"

Like a sacrificial lamb.

"Think so. There are some signs of a struggle, scrapes on her feet, a torn fingernail." Bentz pointed to her right hand. "Hopefully she clawed her attacker and the son of a bitch's skin is under her nails."

Could they get so lucky as to have a sample of the killer's DNA? Montoya doubted it.

"We haven't found a secondary crime scene yet." Bentz looked around the chapel, to the doors. "But, hell, this is a big place."

And a helluva spot for a murder, Montoya thought, eyeing the massive crucifix towering above the Communion table.

"The cathedral, convent, and grounds take up more than a city block," Bentz said, still scowling.

"Gated, right? Locked."

"Everything's locked at night, even the main doors to the cathedral. Either he snuck in before lockdown or he's a part of the community."

Montoya frowned at the draped body. The woman was slim, her arms crossed over her chest, her fingers twined around a rosary. "We got pictures of this?"

"Yeah."

Montoya yanked on a pair of latex gloves, bent down, and lifted the long, thin altar cloth to see the fixed, beautiful stare of the dead woman.

A woman he knew.

Intimately.

Son of a bitch.

Sucker punched, he drew in a sharp breath. Blood congealed in his body. For a second, he thought he might be sick.

"You said she was Sister Camille?"

"Yeah. That's what the mother superior called her. Her legal name is—"

"Camille Renard." Montoya squeezed his eyes shut for a second. Trying to gain some equilibrium. How had this happened? Why? Jesus, he didn't even know she was in the city. He had to force his eyes open again. Cammie's pale visage and glassy eyes met his. "Bloody damned hell," he whispered between clenched teeth.

"You know her?"

"Knew her. A long time ago." A flash of memory, one he'd rather forget, sliced through his brain. Camille Renard. So full of life. So fun-loving. So . . . capricious. The most unlikely woman he'd ever know to take the vows to become a nun. "I went to high school with Camille Renard."

"Oh, shi—for the love of God." Bentz's eyes darkened with concern. "Just don't tell me you dated her."

Montoya felt his jaw set even harder. "Okay, I won't."

"But you did."

"In high school."

Just long enough for him to get laid and for her to lose her virginity.

CHAPTER 6

Sister Maura slid between the sheets of her single bed and set her glasses on the tiny side table, nearly knocking over the stack of books she had positioned under the wall sconce. Her mattress, as stiff and old as the hills, creaked with her weight. She fingered her prayer book, the one she kept under the bedclothes, nestled close to her thigh, but she didn't close her eyes.

Through the small window, lights were flashing blue and red, strobing from the police cruisers parked outside and washing against the wall by the door. The white walls were now tinged with pulsing colors, the small crucifix mounted over the door in stark relief.

Her heart seemed to beat in counterpoint to the flashing lights. Good.

She smiled in the darkness, her fingers ruffling the worn pages of the prayer book, but she didn't pray, didn't offer up one psalm or hymn. Not now; not when there was so much going on, so much excitement.

Muted voices whispered along the ancient corridors and under her door.

She was excited and couldn't help herself.

Telling herself to stay in bed, to feign sleep, or if someone had seen her, say that she'd been in the restroom, she fought the urge to get up again. She could even say it was her period that had caused her to wake; no one would know.

Or would they?

She sometimes wondered if the reverend mother, that old hag straight out of the Middle Ages, kept track of all the girls' menstrual cycles. It wouldn't surprise Maura. After all, this place was rigid with a capital R, and Sister Charity was tied to her regimen as if it were truly God's word.

Seriously?

God cared about what time a person got up in the morning? Ate breakfast? Fasted? Maura didn't buy it. Nor did she believe that he cared what kind of books she read, or how she dressed, or if she cleaned her chamber spotlessly. She just didn't see God as a time keeper or a jailor.

But the reverend mother did.

It was just such a pain.

But not for Maura; not forever.

Saint Marguerite's was just a dark stepping stone to her goal, one she would soon pass. She just had to be patient and pretend obedience for a little while longer.

Angrily she tossed back the stiff white sheets. She flipped her unruly braid over her shoulder and slid out of the bed. The floor was cool and smooth against her soles. With a glance at the unlocked door, Maura tiptoed to the window to look outside. Her room had a corner window, and if she stood on tiptoe, she could look over the roof of the cloister into the garden in one direction and, if she craned her neck, to the side of the convent and over the thick walls to the street where she saw a news van rolling down the street, its headlights reflecting on the wet pavement.

She smiled in the darkness as the bells began to toll again.

Maybe now the sins of St. Marguerite's would be exposed.

Montoya's throat tightened as he stared at Camille Renard's bloodless face. Still beautiful, even in death, her skin was smooth, unmarred, her big eyes staring upward and fixed, seeing nothing. Never again.

His insides churned and his jaw hardened as he thought of how he'd known her in high school.

Vibrant.

Flirty.

Smart.

And hot as hell.

"Damn it," he whispered under his breath. What happened here?

He tried to focus, to stay in the here and now, to ignore the images of Camille as a teenager that ran through his brain.

"Hey!" Bentz was staring at him. "You okay?"

"Fine," he lied. "What the hell happened here?" He let his gaze fall from her face, to the bloodstained neckline of the tattered gown. Deep crimson drops in a jewel-like pattern.

"Don't know yet," Bentz said, his eyes still hard and assessing. "Look, Montoya, if you knew her, you shouldn't be involved in this investigation."

He ignored Bentz's suggestion. For now, he was on the case. Until he heard from the captain or the DA or someone higher up than his partner, he wasn't budging. "It's hard for me to think of her as a nun." He raked unsteady fingers through his hair.

"You hear what I said?"

"Yeah, yeah, but I'm not going to do anything to compromise the case." Montoya's gaze was trained on Cammie's still form, and he couldn't help but wonder if she'd known her assailant. Had she seen the attack coming? Or had her killer been a stranger?

It wasn't the first time he'd been at a crime scene where a member of the convent had been killed; his aunt had suffered and died at the hands of a maniac during an earlier case Montoya had investigated, the very case in which he'd met his wife.

A cold finger of déjà vu slid down his spine. He glanced at Bentz, who scowled darkly, the way he always did when he was lost in thought.

The church bells tolled.

One in the morning.

Montoya crouched beside the victim and stared at her still-beautiful face, then glanced at the bloodied lace of her gown. "What's with the wedding dress?"

"Don't know yet."

He motioned to the tiny drops of red that discolored the neckline of the old lace.

"The vic's blood? He took the time to drop her blood on the dress?"

"My guess," Bentz said.

"What kind of freak are we dealing with?"

"Sick. Twisted." Bentz's eyes looked tired, the crow's-feet near his eyes pronounced. "Aren't they all?"

"Yeah."

"Looks like our guy made some kind of necklace with her blood."

"Or his," Montoya thought aloud as his gaze ran over the tattered folds of the gown.

"Nah. We couldn't get that lucky that he left anything."

"She raped?"

"Don't know yet." Bentz frowned. "I think most nuns who haven't been married are virgins."

Montoya's guts tightened. He closed his mind to the memory of he and Camille on the short sofa in her parents' home when they were away, wouldn't think of her beautiful breasts, firm, with dark, aroused nipples. He studied the yellowed gauze of the wedding dress and shook his head. "So where are her other clothes, the ones she was wearing before she put on this dress?" He frowned. "Or did the killer dress her after the attack?"

"Doesn't look like it was done after she was dead. As for her clothes, I've got a couple of guys looking. Best guess is that she would have been in her nightgown. The convent's schedule is pretty strict. Lights-out and in bed at ten. We're not sure on time of death, but the body was discovered around midnight. The woman who found her heard the parish church bells striking off the hours."

Montoya glanced beyond the pews at the small group of witnesses gathered near the back of the chapel. The priest and one nun were fully dressed, while a younger woman shivered beneath an oversized cape. Her hair was wet, and her eyes had that hollow, glazed look of a person in shock. Something about her was vaguely familiar, and Montoya felt his nerves tighten with dread.

What the hell was this?

"The younger one, Sister Lucia, is the one who found the vic. Claimed she heard 'something,' but it was nothing she could really explain. The upshot was she got out of bed to check and found Sister Camille."

Sister Lucia.

Sister Camille.

Son of a bitch, this is getting worse and worse.

He didn't say it; instead he pointed out the obvious. "The older nun's wearing a habit."

Bentz nodded. "Not the most progressive parish."

Montoya, still crouched, took a last look at the victim. Around Camille's long, pale neck were a series of contusions and deep bruises, as if she'd been garrotted. Unbidden came the memory of nuzzling that neck, kissing the hollow behind her ear. His stomach knotted.

What kind of monster had done this?

And why? Who had Camille pissed off? Or had she been a random target?

Straightening, he shifted his attention back to the tight group of people sequestered behind the last pew. A uniformed cop was talking to the older woman in the nun's habit as Sister Lucia listened in, huddled under the cloak. The sixtyish priest with thinning gray hair and rimless glasses had a rumpled look, and even in the dim light, wrinkles were visible upon his high forehead.

"So Sister Lucia found the body. That must've been a shock." Montoya studied the shivering girl, a waif with a pale face and wet ringlets. Yep, he recognized her, too. Lucia Costa. This was damned surreal. The knot in his gut tightened.

"After Sister Lucia yelled for help," Bentz said, "the mother superior, Sister Charity—that's the older woman—she responded." Bentz hitched his chin toward the bigger nun, a mound of black fabric accented by white coif secured by a wimple. "Charity Varisco." Again Bentz double-checked the notes on his small pad. "She heard Sister Lucia screaming and came running. When she got here, she tried to revive the victim and sent the younger one to call the police and get the parish priest."

"Who put the altar cloth over the vic?"

"The reverend mother," Bentz said, and when Montoya opened his mouth to protest any alteration of the crime scene, he held up a hand. "I know, I know. Already discussed. She claims she didn't think about contaminating or altering the crime scene. She just wanted to be respectful of the vic."

Montoya cast another glance at the woman in question. Tall and big-boned, mouth set, eyes glaring at the police. "What's the reverend mother's relationship to the victim?"

"Just what it seems. She met Sister Camille two years ago when Camille entered the convent."

"What about the priest?"

"*Priests,* plural. The older one's Father Paul Neland. He's the senior priest and lives here on the grounds in an apartment next to the younger one—Father Francis O'Toole."

Montoya's head snapped up at the name. "Father O'Toole? Frank—where is he?"

"Already separated out for his statement. Doing the same with the rest of them."

Two officers were, in fact, starting to force the tight little knot apart. Sister Lucia looked at him pleadingly, then hurried off while the mother superior was ushered in a different direction.

Montoya felt a headache starting to throb at the base of his skull. Too many familiar faces here. First Camille, then Lucia, and now Frank O'Toole? What were the chances of that? "What do you know about the priests?"

"The older guy, Father Paul Neland, has been here about ten years, second only to the mother superior, who's been in charge for nearly twenty years. Before that, she and Neland worked in the same parish once before, up north—Boston, I think. O'Toole's the short-timer. Less than five years."

"I need to speak to him. Frank O'Toole," Montoya said.

Bentz let out a long whistle and stared at his partner, as if reading Montoya's mind. "Oh, Christ, Montoya. Don't tell me you know him, too?"

"Oh, yeah," Montoya admitted, not liking the turn of his thoughts. "I know him."

* * *

Sitting cross-legged on her rumpled bed, Valerie tried to turn on her stubborn computer one last time. "Come on, come on," she ordered the struggling laptop. It made grinding noises that caused her to wince as she waited for the screen to flicker to life.

It was nearly one-thirty in the morning. The rain had stopped, and moonlight filtering through high clouds cast an eerie glow on the damp bushes outside her window.

Her body was tired, but her mind was still spinning. Wired. She wanted to check her e-mail one last time before shutting off the lights and hoping sleep would come. Though it probably wouldn't. Wretched insomnia. Ever since she was a teenager, sleep eluded her if she was troubled. She'd tried everything from sleeping pills to working out to the point of exhaustion, but nothing seemed to allow her sleep for more than a night or two.

It's the divorce.

And your worries about Cammie.

As she waited for the screen to flicker on, she caught a glimpse of the single picture of Slade she'd kept, one of him riding his favorite horse, a rangy gray gelding named Stormy, their scruffy hound dog Bo trailing behind. Silhouetted against a sun that bled purple and orange along the ridge, Slade Houston looked every bit the part of a lonesome Texas cowboy. She'd taken the picture herself and had decided to keep it to remember her marriage. While she'd burned the rest—snapshots and professional photographs taken at their small wedding—she hadn't been able to destroy this one. She'd told herself it was because it was the only picture she had of Bo.

But deep down, she knew better.

"Masochist," she muttered, reaching out and slapping the photograph facedown onto the stack of bills that reminded her of the rocky financial condition of the bed-and-breakfast. She didn't want to think about her sorry bank account right now, no more than she wanted to consider her disintegrated marriage. She glanced again at the facedown picture frame. Tomorrow she'd toss the photo into the trash.

Maybe.

Her computer screen flickered to life, and she quickly went about opening her e-mail, searching through the spam until she saw it, a single posting from SisCam1. "Thank the gods of the Internet," Val said under her breath as she clicked on the e-mail to open it.

"Okay, Cammie, what's up?" Val said as the short message appeared:

Having second thoughts. Can't take it anymore. Am leaving St. Marg's. You know why.

"Oh, Cammie," Val said, her heart heavy. Of course she knew why her sister was leaving the convent: Camille was pregnant.

CHAPTER 7

"You know Frank O'Toole *and* Camille Renard?" Bentz asked, his eyes narrowing on Montoya.

"Yeah. High school." Montoya still couldn't believe it. How did so many people he recognized from a small high school end up here at St. Marguerite's, with the girl he'd dated for over six months dead at his feet? He swallowed hard as he glanced to the floor, where someone from the ME's office was bending over the body. Montoya's gaze found Bentz's again. "And that isn't all of it," he admitted, not liking the turn of his thoughts. "That nun over there." With one finger, he indicated the shivering Lucia Costa. "I didn't really know her, but for a while she dated my brother, Cruz. He's a couple of years younger than me. She was a few years behind him, I think. I was out of high school before she started her freshman year."

"So it's old home week?" Bentz's eyes thinned speculatively.

"Beats me." Scowling, stepping away from the body, he asked, "Who was the first officer to arrive?"

"Amos took the call," Bentz said.

Montoya spotted the officer talking to the shivering girl. New to the force, Joe Amos was a six-foot black man with a wide girth and mocha-colored skin accentuated by a shotgun blast of darker freckles across his face. Montoya walked in front of the first pew to a pillar where Amos was listening to Sister Lucia.

"... and so Father Paul and Father Frank and I ran back here, to the chapel and—" she was saying, but her gaze strayed to Montoya and her chain of thought was interrupted. "And... Oh, dear God." Her eyes rounded and she took a step back.

"And what?" Amos asked.

Lucia blinked, as if she couldn't believe her eyes. "You're Cruz's brother," she whispered, appearing as if she might faint.

"That's right."

Even more lines of worry showed between her eyebrows. "Raymond or..."

"Reuben. I'm with the local police department now. Detective."

Amos pinned Montoya with a glare. "You two know each other?"

Montoya shook his head. "Went to the same high school. Years ago. She dated my brother."

"You look a lot like him," Lucia said, fingers pulling the cape closer around her body. "Like Cruz."

"So I've heard." Montoya couldn't deny the obvious, having heard it for years—the family resemblance ran strong.

Amos held up a hand. "Okay, so let's get back to your statement. Let's see, you 'heard something,' you said. What was it?"

"I... I don't know." She swallowed hard. "Something sharp. It woke me and I felt troubled, like I needed to pray."

"A scream?" Montoya asked. "Or a call for help?"

"No... nothing I can really identify."

Really?

"But you left your room?" Amos pressed.

"Yes, as I said, I was upset, like I'd had a horrible dream that I can't remember. I knew I wouldn't go back to sleep, so I thought I'd go pray in the chapel. It's calming sometimes." Lucia looked frightened and small, as if she wanted to disappear into the shadows.

Amos glanced down at notes he'd scribbled in a nearly illegible hand. "So then you find the body, see someone leaving, call for help, meet up with Sister Charity, go to the office, make the call to nine-one-one, then run back to the chapel after waking the priests. Oh, only Father Paul. Father Frank was already up. Right?"

"Yes," she said, nodding slowly.

To get her story straight or because she was trying to remember? Amos scratched his chin. "What happened then?"

"Oh!" Lucia dragged her gaze away from Montoya. "Then... we, um, waited. Father Paul checked Sister Camille's pulse again. Then we all prayed for her." Lucia's voice grew husky, her nose reddened, and tears filled her eyes. "Then...then...a few minutes later, I heard sirens and you arrived." She took in a long breath, pulled the cape even tighter around her, and clammed up.

"You found the body?" Montoya asked.

"I just told him all about it," she said, looking toward Amos.

Montoya wasn't going to be put off. "So bring me up to speed."

She seemed to withdraw, as if her body were shrinking for a second. Then she gathered her breath and explained her version of the events of the night yet again. After the mother superior had answered her cries for help, she'd called the police, run into Father Frank in the cloister, awoke a sleeping Father Paul, and had returned to the chapel with the two priests.

"But you said something about seeing someone leaving the chapel when you arrived," Amos interjected.

"I...I think so."

Montoya asked, "You're not sure?"

"No...sometimes I kind of sleepwalk, so...it can be kind of"—she lifted a small shoulder—"blurry, I guess."

"Wait a second. Sleepwalking?" Montoya said. "You didn't say that before."

"No, I know.... It was different than that, but..." She looked close to tears and blinked. "Hard to explain."

"But, in the chapel, you did hear a door close over the sound of the midnight bells tolling?" Amos persisted, not one to be put off by anything, even female tears.

Lucia seemed flustered. And scared as hell. "It seems that way."

Not exactly firm testimony, Montoya thought. He'd never really known Lucia, though one of her older brothers, Pedro, had been in his class at school. What was it about her that Cruz had found so intriguing? Not just her looks, but a bit of ESP or something. But maybe Cruz made that up. Montoya's younger and wilder brother had been known to tell more than his share of lies.

They asked a few more questions to piece together the chain of events and time frame; then Montoya and Bentz left Amos to wrap things up.

"Pretty," Bentz mentioned. "What happened between her and your brother?"

"Car wreck. Cruz was at the wheel. Nearly killed them both." But there was more to the story, Montoya thought; he just didn't know it, had been off at college when the accident had occurred.

They met up with the mother superior in the hallway near the chapel, where she was being interviewed by one of the uniformed officers.

Sister Charity's voice was hushed and well modulated despite the tragedy. In the dim candlelight, her face seemed far more youthful than the sixty years she claimed to be as she responded to Montoya. "I already told one of your officers, Ms. Erwin, here, everything I know." Her words, though spoken softly, were underlaid with a thread of steel.

"We're going to need to interview everyone in the building," Officer Erwin said.

The older woman shook her head slowly. "Everyone was asleep. I can't see what good waking them will do."

"They might have heard something. Or maybe someone was up, passing through the hallway on the way to the restroom. There's a chance someone saw something," Randi Erwin insisted. "Or maybe one of the residents could shed some light on motive for killing Sister Camille."

"Oh." The mother superior crossed herself, as if suddenly realizing the magnitude of the tragedy. "I'll talk to each of them," the reverend mother offered. "Father Paul will offer them guidance—"

"It's not about guidance," Montoya said crisply as he wondered if the woman was being intentionally obtuse. "Before you speak to them, we need to interview them."

"All of them?" She seemed surprised.

Montoya nodded. "We want to talk with anyone who lives here and anyone who may have been on the property tonight. They'll need to give their statements to officers."

Erwin said, "And I'll need more information on the victim."

"We're a very private order." Sister Charity frowned. A roadblock.

"With one of your own dead? Murdered. I'd say that overrules privacy." Barely thirty, Randi Erwin was tough, a small, wiry woman who wore little makeup and kept her brown hair cut short and feathery. Once a gymnast in college, she was now a martial arts expert and took no guff, not from older guys in the department who tended to tease her and not from this imperious nun. "I'll need a list of the victim's friends. Can you think of anyone who held a grudge against her?"

"There are no enemies here." The older nun threaded her fingers in resignation, finally getting it that the police weren't just going away.

Bentz snorted. "Surely you don't believe that. People are people; they make others angry, hold grudges, seek revenge, whatever. A lot of wars have been waged in the name of religion."

She bristled. "Not here."

"Why is she dressed in that dress?"

"I have no idea."

"Where did she get it?"

The reverend mother's eyebrows drew together. "I don't know," she said, just as Officer Chris Conway approached.

"The press is here," the officer said. "A reporter from WKAM."

"Tell them to wait for a statement from Sinclaire," Bentz said. Tina Sinclaire was the public information officer. "And that's not going to happen until we notify the next of kin. They know it's a homicide if they've listened to the police band, so don't try to stonewall the reporter—just ask him to wait."

"Got it." The officer strode across the chapel toward the exit.

Montoya turned to the mother superior. "What about Camille Renard's next of kin?" he asked, barely remembering the dead woman's parents. Wasn't the dad older, a guy who worked with the railroad, the mother a part-time teacher?

"Her parents are gone. She has one sister, who lives somewhere in East Texas, I believe. A small town, I think. I can't recall now, off the top of my head."

That was right. Camille did have a sister, a year or two younger than Montoya. "Do you know her name?"

"I should, but... Veronica? Something like that. I'll check."

Veronica didn't sound right, but Montoya could picture her. Around five-seven, if he remembered correctly. Taller than Camille, with big eyes and a stare that cut right through you. Where Camille had always been outgoing and a flirt, her older sister was studious but outspoken, someone who didn't suffer fools or the stupid teenage antics of her peers. The sister was a girl Montoya avoided, but he remembered her.

"Was it Valerie?" he asked, and the nun looked at him sharply, the corners of her mouth tugging downward.

"Yes." She nodded, her wimple not moving a bit. "Valerie. That's it."

"We need her address."

"Of course." She glanced to the doors leading to the chapel and seemed suddenly saddened by the events of the night. More people had arrived. Despite Sister Charity's objections about outsiders trespassing on holy grounds, the crime scene techs went about the business of collecting evidence. Photographs and measurements were taken; the area dusted for prints; Luminol sprayed; and the floor, walls, and pews analyzed for footprints or scuff marks. The crime scene investigators worked with relentless precision.

"This is such sacrilege," Sister Charity murmured, her eyes imploring. "Really, it has to stop. The chapel is a holy place, not meant for..." She lifted a hand, palm out, almost in supplication toward the chapel where the medical examiner was examining Sister Camille's body. "We follow rules and a strict schedule of devotion, and we cannot have..." Her voice cracked, and Montoya didn't know if the emotion was grief for the death of Sister Camille, concern about the black mark a murder would make upon St. Marguerite's reputation, or simply an act. "This disruption is unacceptable," she said, but the conviction in her words was fading. "You're upsetting everyone here, making a mockery of our chapel, yellow tape and people meandering so close to the holy tabernacle."

"One of your own is dead," Montoya reminded her, letting

loose a fraction of his irritation. "Looks like a homicide. We have a job to do here, and we'll do it as quickly and thoroughly as possible, but we will do it. It would be best if no one impeded the process."

Her chin worked as if she wanted to say something, lambaste him for his impropriety and lack of respect. Instead she whispered, "So be it. I must attend to the novitiates. But please, remember this is the Lord God's house."

"And something very evil went down here."

"We don't know what happened," she said in a crisp tone that allowed no argument. "Now, if you'll excuse me, I must attend to the sisters." As she bustled off, skirts rustling and rosary beads clicking, her outfit was meticulous but for the hem of her habit, which showed more than a trace of dirt.

Odd.

Otherwise she was impeccably put together—now, in the middle of the night.

Did the old mother superior sleep in her habit? Montoya made a mental note to speak with her later, when she'd had some time to cool off.

"Sister, wait up!" Bentz said, lunging to catch up with her. "I need to see Sister Camille's room."

"There's nothing there."

"We don't know that."

She paused, then nodded stiffly. "Come along, then." She was already leading him up the stairs to the living quarters of the convent.

Yeah, Montoya thought, he'd speak to Sister Charity again. Alone. For now, he had bigger fish to fry. To Officer Erwin he said, "I think I'm going to have a talk with Father O'Toole and see what he has to say."

CHAPTER 8

Cruz's brother?
Here?
A police detective?

Sister Lucia felt the cold stone in the pit of her stomach growing heavier. She'd thought this night couldn't get any worse when she'd stumbled upon Camille's body, but she'd been wrong.

Detective Montoya made it so.

He looked a lot like Cruz—same sharp cheekbones; near-black, suspicious eyes; thick, straight hair; and white teeth that flashed against coppery skin. Too handsome. That's what her father had said about Cruz. The same was true of his older brother.

At the reverend mother's bidding, Lucia hurried to her room where she slid into her dry habit and pinned her hair onto her head. She pushed thoughts of Cruz Montoya aside as she went to rouse the other sisters, tapping on their doors, asking them to dress and meet the mother superior in the main dining hall. Several asked why, and she responded with "I don't know any details, just that the reverend mother wants to see all of us."

A lie—but just the first of many, she thought darkly. The evil voice that had awakened her was blackening her soul.

Sister Angela woke easily, popping her head out the door, almost as if she'd been waiting. Apple-cheeked, she pressed on a pair of thin glasses and blinked against the dim hall lights. "What is it?"

"I don't know, just hurry," Lucia said, lying through her teeth. Again.

"But—"

"Please, the reverend mother is waiting."

Nodding, Angela slipped inside her room as Lucia hurried down the dark hallway to rap on the next door. Sister Dorothy didn't respond. Lucia tried again, louder this time, but there was no answer.

The sinister feeling that had overcome Lucia earlier now coiled around her heart. What if Camille wasn't the only one? What if whoever had killed her had also come up here and taken the life of another? Swallowing back her fear, searching deeply for her faith, Lucia fingered her rosary and called softly, "Sister Dorothy?"

From the corner of her eye, Lucia saw another door creak slowly open at the end of the hall. Sister Maura, her perpetual scowl in place, appeared. "What're you doing?" she asked, pushing on a pair of thick glasses.

"The reverend mother has asked us to meet downstairs."

"Why?" Deep creases furrowed Maura's brow. She was a solemn woman, one Lucia didn't know very well.

"She didn't say. Please, just hurry."

Another door opened. Sister Edwina glared at the small group. "What's going on?" she demanded, flipping a thick blond braid over her shoulder. Taller than Lucia by five inches, Edwina was an athletic woman with a broad, Nordic face and high cheekbones. Her deep-set blue eyes were always stormy as she constantly needled a bad mood. "Why are you knocking at Dorothy's door?"

Lucia explained, "The reverend mother wants us all in the dining hall."

"Why? It's the middle of the night!"

"I know."

"What does she want?"

So many questions... "I'm sure the reverend mother wants to tell everyone herself."

"And why are you up?" Sister Edwina demanded, glancing

across the hallway to Lucia's small room. "Why did Mother come to you?" she asked indignantly, as if she sensed a personal slight.

Lucia had no time for perceived personal affronts. She had her own worries to attend to. First there was poor Sister Camille, and then, of all the bad luck, Cruz Montoya's brother was involved with the investigation. Her nerves were as tight as bowstrings. "Please, just dress quickly."

"You know what's going on, don't you?" Edwina charged. She was always direct, always felt somehow as if she were being persecuted.

"It's up to the reverend mother to say."

"Right." Irony dripped from her words.

The door to Dorothy's room finally cracked open just a space. "What is it?" she asked through the slim opening. Dorothy, plump and always worried, didn't sound the least bit groggy. Her voice held a whisper of suspicion.

Lucia delivered her short message. Other doors were opening as the noise in the hallway woke some of the others. Angela swept out of her room and, ignoring the sour look Maura cast her way, caught up with Lucia.

"I'll help," she offered while Edwina's door slammed shut. "Don't worry about her." Angela turned away from Sister Edwina's closed door. "She's just mad because the reverend mother chose you to be her messenger."

Lucia couldn't respond as Sister Angela fell into step with her. Not now. Lucia was too overwhelmed by the darkness in her heart that went far deeper than keeping the news of Sister Camille's death from them.

So much deeper.

Lucia, fingering the beads of her rosary, knew why she'd been awoken from her fitful sleep, understood why the breath of evil had whispered in her ear, and why Sister Camille, tortured soul that she was, had been murdered.

She knew, but she wouldn't say.

Montoya found his way down the dim hallway near the apse of the large cathedral. He rapped on the door with his knuckles, then pushed it open without waiting for an answer.

Arms folded across his chest, a uniformed officer watched over the broad-chested man in a black cassock who sat in the amber pool of light cast by a single lamp.

Father Frank O'Toole, sequestered inside this small anteroom, seemed lost in prayer, his big hands clasped together in his lap.

As the door opened, he looked up, startled.

"Reuben?" His voice held a rasp of disbelief, his eyes flickering with startled recognition.

"How are ya, Frank?" Montoya leaned over the small, scarred table to shake his old friend's hand.

Frank O'Toole's clasp was still strong and athletic. "I've been better," he admitted as he stood with a resigned smile, so different from the broad grins he'd flashed in high school. His eyebrows knitted. "So, what are you doing here?" he asked; then his eyes flickered as he made the connection. "You're with the police?"

"Detective."

"Really?" His smile disappeared. "I never would have thought..."

"Me neither. I never saw myself as a cop, and I sure as hell didn't think you'd end up as a priest."

In high school, when Montoya was flirting with the wrong side of the law, his love for athletics was one of the few reasons he'd avoided serious crime. Through sports, Montoya had the good fortune to hook up with Frank O'Toole. A star on the soccer field and basketball courts, an A student in the classroom, Frank O'Toole had seemed to have it all. He'd run with the popular crowd and hailed from a privileged background, his father a prominent attorney.

Frank had caught Montoya hot-wiring his car—a classic Mustang—when he was only fifteen and had threatened to go to the police. Montoya and he had nearly come to blows but had worked things out; Montoya had spent six Saturdays washing and waxing the damned car while O'Toole had let the younger kid cruise through the streets of New Orleans with him. Their friendship had been tenuous at best, Montoya's envy for Frank's lifestyle and popularity always under the surface, and Frank's fascination for Montoya's rebellion never quite fading. It was almost as if Frank got off hanging out with a kid who was always one step away from serious trouble with the law. Montoya had suspected that the college-bound senior had gotten a vicarious thrill from hanging out with a juvenile delinquent. The preppy and the rogue.

O'Toole let out a long sigh. "You saw Sister Camille?" His hands clenched into fists, his thumbs rubbing his knuckles nervously.

"Yeah." Montoya nodded. Camille's image, in death, was branded into his memory. At some level, it would be with him for the rest of his life.

"It's a shame," the priest said, rolling his gaze to the ceiling, as if he could literally look to God for answers. O'Toole still possessed the striking physique Montoya remembered. There were a few strands of gray in his black hair and a few more lines near the corners of his eyes, and his nose wasn't as straight as it had once been, but, in Montoya's estimation, the signs of aging only gave Frank O'Toole a more mature and interesting appearance.

"Why don't you tell me what happened?"

Something flashed in the priest's eyes. Regret? Anger? The start of a lie? "I wish I knew. I was out with a sick parishioner. Arthur Wembley. Stage-four lung cancer. I spent the evening with him and his wife, Marion. When I returned, I ran into Sister Lucia just outside Father Paul's door. She was in a panic, asking us to come into the chapel." His jaw tightened and his eyes seemed to sink into their sockets. "We followed her"—his voice lowered to a whisper—"and found Sister Charity saying prayers over Camille's body." He cleared his throat. "The first officer and the EMTs arrived within minutes."

"Why the cassock?" Montoya asked.

"The Wembleys are old school. They like tradition. I wore it for them. I usually don't."

"Why do you think Cam—er, Sister Camille was wearing a bridal gown?"

"I don't know." He shook his head, biting at his lower lip, thinking hard. "The dress looked old. Not overly expensive, I'd guess. Like the kind a nun might wear when she was taking her vows and becoming a bride of Christ."

"Seriously?"

O'Toole lifted a shoulder. "It's an old custom, and St. Marguerite's is steeped in tradition, far more than the other parishes nearby. The nuns wear habits, parishioners still abstain from meat on Good Fridays...though that's something that's coming a little back into vogue, isn't it?" He glanced away before Montoya could read any more in his expression.

"Did you know Camille in high school?" Montoya asked.

"No," he said convincingly, finally returning Montoya's gaze again. "She's...she was younger than me. I never met her back then, but I did know her older sister."

"Valerie?"

"Yeah."

"Date her?"

"No." A look passed between them. Back in the day, Frank O'Toole, athlete, hunk, and ladies' man, had cut a swath through the girls at St. Timothy's. How in the world had he turned to the priesthood, a life of celibacy? It didn't make a lot of sense to Montoya.

As if he understood, Frank said, "When my older sister, Mary Louise, was stricken with lymphoma, I made a deal with God. I'd go into the priesthood, take my vows, and dedicate my life to him, as long as he spared her."

"And how did that work out for you?" Montoya asked, trying to remember Mary Louise O'Toole.

"Mary died last year. But not from the disease. With God's help, she seemed to beat it. She was hit in a crosswalk by an old man who stepped on the gas rather than the brakes." He sighed and rubbed his face, the stubble of his whiskers scraping against his fingers. "Thankfully she died instantly."

"Do you think God held up his part of the bargain?"

"Hard to say," he whispered. "I'm not arrogant enough to believe that I'm so important that the Father would sacrifice my sister as a pawn in a faith-based version of Truth or Dare. But for me, Mary Louise's death was a test of my beliefs, of my calling."

"And did you pass?" Montoya asked.

The corner of Frank's lips twitched, though his countenance remained grim. "That's for God to decide."

"What about the victim? What do you think happened to her?"

"I wish I knew," Frank whispered fervently, though he glanced away, avoiding Montoya's glare.

"So you knew Valerie, but not Camille?"

"In high school, yes."

"And Valerie lives in Texas?"

"No. She's here."

"Here? In New Orleans?" Montoya asked, making a mental note. Hadn't Sister Charity claimed Camille's sister lived in a small town in East Texas?

The priest was nodding. "Owns a bed-and-breakfast in the Garden District, I think. I can't remember the name, but Sister Camille mentioned that Valerie had moved back to New Orleans sometime in the past couple of years." His voice was soft, far away. As if he were remembering the conversation.

"Camille talk to you often?"

"Sometimes," Frank said.

"How often?"

"A few times a week, sometimes less, other times more."

"Did she ever mention any old boyfriends?"

"You mean, besides you?" Frank cocked a dark eyebrow.

Montoya held on to his temper. "I mean anyone who might want to do her harm?"

"No."

"Enemies?"

Father Frank shook his head. "I didn't know that much about her personal life," he said. "If you're asking about her confessions, those are private, between her and God."

"And you."

"Or Father Paul." His smile held little warmth. "You might want to talk to Sister Lucia or Sister Louise. They all seemed to be close." He appeared suddenly tired, almost irritable. "Is there anything else?"

"I guess that's it for now. But if I think of anything else..."

"Of course, Reuben. Just call." He flashed a humorless smile as he rose and walked out the door, his dark cassock billowing, a stain visible near its hem.

"Father Frank?"

The priest turned, his face supremely patient.

"There's something on the bottom of your cassock." Montoya pointed at the stain, black on black.

"What? Is there?" He glanced down, saw the almost invisible stain. "I was out in the rain...."

Feeling oddly like a supplicant, Montoya bent down on one knee and touched the hem. A faint crust of reddish brown smeared his fingertips.

"It's blood," he said, looking up at Frank.

The priest frowned, his forehead furrowing. "It has to be Sister Camille's. From when I bent down over her body. Of course I hoped, prayed, that I could revive her...." His voice faded and his features twisted with the memory.

"We'll need the cassock." Montoya rose, face-to-face with the tormented priest.

Frank's face was pinched, as if he were about to object, but changed his mind. "Of course. I'll get it to you."

Montoya was already at the door. "If you don't mind, Father, I'll come with you."

"You don't trust me, Reuben?"

"This is a homicide investigation, Frank. I don't trust anyone," Montoya admitted.

CHAPTER 9

"Son of a—" Valerie bit off the last of the oath as she walked out the back door the next morning. Her eyes narrowed on the battered pickup with Texas plates. Covered in mud, with grimy arcs across the windshield showing where the wipers had slung off dirt and water, the Ford was parked beneath the overhanging branches of a willow tree on the apron of her driveway, right behind her relic of a Subaru.

The screen door slapped shut behind her, startling a couple of blue jays into flapping from their perch on a picket fence to the safety of the upper branches of a tree.

Valerie barely noticed; her eyes were trained on the damned truck.

On one side of the cab, his nose forced into the slit of a cracked window, was her dog. On the other, slumped behind the steering wheel, was her husband.

She was glad to see one.

Not so the other.

At the sight of her, Bo started barking and scratching the window, his entire rear end in motion. Slade, curse his miserable hide, opened an eye, stretched, and grinned, that wide I-don't-give-a-damn smile with teeth flashing white against a day's worth of stubble on his square jaw. No one should have the right to look so damned sexy after spending a short night sleeping in a truck.

So what the hell was he doing here?

She'd been headed for her car but angled from the path to tromp across the wet grass bordering Freya's pride and joy, an herb garden that was as drenched and beaten down as the rest of the foliage.

With a massive groan, the driver's door opened and Slade stepped onto the gravel just as Bo, unable to contain himself a second more, leaped from the cab. Whining and squirming, the big dog raced up to her.

"Hey, boy," Val said, her heart melting as she squatted down to pet the dog's sleek head and receive exuberant licks on her face and hands. "Yeah, I missed you, too." The hound couldn't get close enough to her, and for a second she remembered bringing him home from the pound, a small black and tan puppy with bright eyes and ears that nearly hung to the ground.

"And me? You miss me, too?" Slade asked as he slammed the truck's door shut and leaned against the front quarter panel. His voice, with his easy East Texas drawl, brought back memories that were better left forgotten.

Still scratching Bo behind his ears, she lifted her gaze. "You're kidding, right? Miss *you*?" She almost laughed, except nothing about their meeting was funny. "Like I miss the plague."

He squinted, his face an expression of disbelief. "You always were a pathetic liar."

"Unlike you," she said, "the master of deceit."

He didn't crack a smile.

"So what're you doing here, Slade?" Straightening, she felt the heat of the morning sun upon her back, the promise of a warm day after last night's battering storm. The jays were chattering, and from a hidden branch an owl softly hooted.

"I thought we should talk," Slade said, "just you and me. Face-to-face. No two-hundred-dollar-an-hour lawyers speaking for us."

"We tried that. Didn't work."

"Maybe we should try harder."

"Seriously?" She thought back to their marriage, the times she'd tried to communicate with him, the times he'd clammed up, the way he'd been so distant. Unreachable. The mess with Cammie. Slade's incredible ego. Her own pride and stubborn streak. "So you drove down here in the middle of the night and slept in your pickup?"

"I just got in a few hours ago, and I didn't have a reservation— didn't think you'd appreciate me waking you up."

"You got that right, but I think it's too late for any more discussion. It's over."

"Not if we both work at it."

"What?" she said, stepping closer. "Who *are* you? Where's the aloof cowboy who really just didn't give a damn about his marriage? The guy who came on to his wife's sister and when it didn't work, blamed her?"

"That's not how it happened, and you know it." He squinted at her, and she looked away.

Somewhere in the distance, the pace of the day was picking up. Val felt the change. The sun rose higher in the sky, and the hum of morning traffic, running along St. Charles Avenue a few blocks over, increased. People going about their workdays.

It was after eight; she'd slept in after a night of tossing and turning, and the last thing she needed was Slade Houston in her backyard. She had work to do at the inn. Freya was already making breakfast for the handful of guests who had spent the night, the smells of sizzling bacon, hot maple syrup, and apple fritters wafting through an open window. Val's early morning job was to keep the coffee coming and the dishes cleared.

"What I know, Slade," she said firmly, "is that if you drove all the way here from Bad Luck to convince me to give it another go, you wasted a trip. I'm not changing my mind." The hound, damn him, whined at her feet and stared up at her with big, sad eyes. Her heart wrenched. "But if you want to, you can leave Bo with me." She felt her lips twitch into a bit of a smile. She'd always been a sucker for animals. Strays to purebreds, Val loved them all.

"You can get your own dog."

"Okay," she said, not going into the fact that it was she who had made the trip to the animal shelter. She still believed the hound would be happier chasing squirrels and armadillos and jackrabbits at the ranch than cooped up here in a small yard where the gate was constantly opening and closing, strangers coming and going. "But I'll miss you, big guy," she said to the dog. As she leaned over him, she caught sight of a car in front of the main house. A squad car pulled into an empty spot at the curb.

Two men climbed out, and her heart turned to ice. "Oh, God," she whispered, knowing that whatever the two men wanted, it wasn't good. She'd been on the other side of this drama too many times to kid herself. Her stomach did a slow, painful roll as she thought of what news they were bearing, the kind of news she'd sometimes had to bring to a worried family: "There's been an accident... sincere condolences... so sorry for your loss..."

She braced herself, heard dishes clattering as if from a great, long distance away.

One of the cops, a younger Hispanic-looking guy in a leather jacket, approached her a step or two ahead of the stockier man. "I'm Detective Montoya, and this is Detective Rick Bentz of the New Orleans Police Department. We're looking for Valerie Renard."

"I'm Valerie," she said, jarred by the voice that didn't sound like her own as she accepted some kind of business card from the older guy.

Time seemed to stand still as she looked at the contours of the younger man's face. Strong jaw, sharp nose, dark eyes... The owl that had been hooting stopped, a heavy blossom on the bougainvillea near the front door silently fell to the ground, pink petals breaking apart. "Montoya?" she repeated over the buzzing in her head.

He nodded, as if expecting her to draw some sort of connection. "What's going on?"

She heard Slade's voice over the white noise that filled her ears. "Valerie?"

He was talking to her, but she was fixated on the Hispanic man with the dark goatee and thin lips.

"Who're you?" the Hispanic man asked.

"I'm her husband. Slade Houston. I think the bigger question is who the hell are you?"

Crouched near her feet, Bo let out a low, ominous growl.

Slade sent the hound a warning glare. "Hush!"

"Ms. Renard," the older guy, Bentz, was saying to her, "are you the sister of Camille Renard, known as Sister Camille of St. Marguerite's Convent here in the city?" He kept one eye on the dog.

Oh, God. Val's heart was beating a horrible tattoo.

This was about Cammie—two cops coming with unthinkable news.

"No!" she said, shaking her head slowly, refusing to believe what she innately understood, the reason the cops were here on her doorstep, their faces grim masks of resolve. She didn't want to see it, but it was there in their eyes. They were the reluctant messengers of death. "Not Cammie," she whispered, horrified. "Not Cammie. No, no, no!" Her knees started to buckle as her world exploded, splintering into jagged, ugly shards. She felt a strong arm catch her around the waist.

Slade.

"Ms. Renard?" the older, sadder cop said quietly.

"They're sisters," Slade interjected, holding her steady.

"Cammie is my younger..." Val's voice faded, her throat constricting her words to a raspy, disbelieving tenor.

Something was wrong here, very, very wrong. Cammie? No... no, it just couldn't be. So young. So full of life. Fresh-faced with a smile that could light up the world.

But then she remembered the ringing bells, the vision of a horrible black-cloaked fiend with dangling chain, the same threatening demon that cut through her mind last night, its evil, glowing eyes hungry and rabid as it slithered through the shadows, bringing death.

The ache in her heart was palpable, the ringing in her ears the knell of death.

"Do you mind if we step inside?" Bentz asked, as if from a distance. Were it not for Slade's strength, her knees would have buckled. "We need to talk."

The vision rose again, horrible and potent, so evil it reeked, the scent burning her nostrils. She heard the demon cackling in triumph, smiling wide enough to show a row of sharp little teeth....

Don't do this. Don't let go. Be strong, for Cammie. Drive that miserable harbinger of death back to its lair. You can do this, Valerie.

You've staved it off for as long as you can remember. Do not let the evil creature win. It's a figment of your imagination, nothing more. Hold on. For God's sake, hold on ...

She drew a long breath, determined not to be swallowed by the blackness and fear, though her heart was racing, her blood as cold as the demon's soul.

Bentz was still speaking, but she barely heard his inept attempt at condolences. His voice came as if through a tunnel, stronger as she brought herself back to the present, forced her legs to hold her upright.

"There must be some mistake," she said, the words tumbling off her tongue as realization, a cruel, sharp barb, dug deep into her brain. Now she realized why she hadn't heard from Cammie. The last e-mail, which she so recently read, sliced through her mind: Having second thoughts. Can't take it anymore. Am leaving St. Marg's. You know why.

Her heart cracked, but finally the vision slid away. Like the inky phantom it was, it slunk into its shadowy crevice again, to wait patiently. . . .

"What happened?" This time Slade's voice was clear, strong.

Bentz shot Montoya a glance and said, "We're not sure just yet. Maybe we should go inside where it's quiet. A little more private?"

Over the pulsing of blood through her veins, Valerie heard the hum of traffic, caught sight of a hummingbird hovering near a twining branch of honeysuckle, and was vaguely aware of the door to the main house opening to allow a couple in their fifties—guests of the inn—to step onto the broad front porch only to pause and stare in their direction. The man was adjusting a baseball cap, the woman digging through a straw purse, both sets of eyes focused on the unlikely group near the picket fence.

At that moment, church bells pealed, tolling off the morning hours, reminding Val of her sister, cloistered in the convent walls where she was supposed to be safe.

Oh, Cammie ... no ...

Images of her sister as a child with crooked teeth, big eyes, and freckles sprayed across a stubby little nose raced through her brain. In childhood, Cammie had adored her older sister. But then she'd changed, weathering the ravages of adolescence to grow long legs and breasts the boys noticed. Her face had become sculpted with high cheekbones, wide eyes, and a sharp chin. Her mouth could curve into a wide smile or turn quickly into a tight little pout that made her all the more fascinating.

Even to a boy Valerie had barely known, a dark-eyed tough who had turned into the cop standing before her: Reuben Montoya.

Val felt her jaw drop as she recognized him now. Gone was his bad-boy swagger, but there was still evidence of the rebel beneath the badge: a goatee that couldn't be department approved and a diamond stud in one ear, proof, she supposed, of his ability to go undercover, to turn, chameleon-like, into a drug dealer, a pimp, or whatever persona was necessary to make the bust.

Today he was here to pass on the unthinkable news about Cammie, a woman he'd known intimately years before.

Goose bumps chased up her arms as she glanced into Montoya's hard face and tried to read his mind. "You knew her. You knew my sister."

He nodded, his lips so tight as to show white.

"Wait a second," Valerie said, her brain coming back to life as she took in Montoya's leather jacket, T-shirt, and jeans. Street clothes. "Detectives?" She felt her insides tighten. These guys weren't the usual beat cops sent to inform the next of kin about a loved one's death. "You're *investigating* my sister's death?" Her heart was knocking wildly. "What the hell happened to her?"

"Please, Ms. Renard," Bentz said, his gaze straying to the man and woman on the porch, "let's take this inside."

"What are you saying?" Val asked. "There was some kind of accident? Where? At the convent?"

But she saw a darker answer in Montoya's eyes, and her mind raced ahead.

"No, not an accident." Her voice was hoarse, raspy. "She was killed?"

Or took her own life.

But she didn't say it, didn't want to believe any of this, including the chilling fact that the last e-mail she received from Cammie might have been a call for help or a suicide note that she received too late.

Can't take it anymore.

Am leaving St. Marg's.
You know why.
"Sweet Jesus," she whispered, shaking from the inside out.

"Val." Slade's voice whispered against her ear, and he turned her toward her cottage where the back door stood open. Guiding her, he whistled to the dog and cast a warning glance at Montoya and Bentz. "Let's just go inside and hear what the detectives have to say."

Something in his tone got to her, snapped her out of the dark folds of denial that threatened to suffocate her. She yanked her arm out of the cradle of his, gave herself a firm mental shake, and told herself to buck up. No matter what had happened, she wasn't going to fall into the trap of being the victim, of leaning on a husband she didn't trust, of ignoring the fact that some of Cammie's insecurities, her paranoia, landed squarely on Slade Houston's shoulders. "I can handle this," she said, stepping away from him, barely aware that the dog was following. "Alone."

"I'm here."

"Yeah, and why is that?" she spat. "Why this morning, huh? What kind of timing is that?"

She didn't wait for an answer.

Squaring her shoulders, she marched into her kitchen and let the screen door fall behind her. One of the cops—Montoya, who was on her heels—caught it before it slapped shut, then followed her into the kitchen and down a short hallway of ancient hardwood to the living area of the small house. She stood at the cold fireplace, her back to the blackened grate as the detectives, and Slade, damn him, collected near the front door, the toes of their shoes barely touching the bound edge of faded carpet.

She glanced at the card she'd clutched in her closed fist and, scanning the information, confirmed her worst fears. Rick Bentz was from the Homicide Division. The chill in her soul turned to ice.

"My sister was murdered?" she whispered, her gaze locking with Montoya's. Oh, God, no. Please . . . no.

"I'm sorry," Montoya said, and she felt her knees start to buckle.

No, no, no! Tears burned in her eyes as she stared at Montoya, memories of the past jarring her, rattling her soul. She remembered more about Reuben—"Diego" as he'd been called in high school—and in that split second, she thought she might get sick. "So have you arrested your friend Frank O'Toole yet?"

Montoya's jaw tightened.

"The priest? Why would we arrest him?" Bentz asked as Slade crossed the carpet to stand next to her.

She didn't hesitate a second. "Because if anyone had the motive to kill Cammie, it was that hypocritical son of a bitch." She felt tears burn her eyes. How many times had she counseled her sister to leave the church and get away from Frank O'Toole, to break it off entirely? Val's heart twisted painfully as she realized she hadn't tried hard enough. She hadn't gotten through. Camille had been so damned stubborn. Anger flooded through her, and grief clawed at her heart. "Maybe you don't know it yet, but Cammie is...was... pregnant. Guess who's the father?"

CHAPTER 10

The solitude, sanctity, and safety of the convent would never be the same. Lucia felt the loss deep in her bones as she walked briskly along the corridor from her room.

Even when the police would finally leave and the chapel would be cleaned, when poor Sister Camille would be laid to rest and the last prayers whispered over her body, when the news cameras and reporters would no longer hover near the outside gate, St. Marguerite's would forever be tainted. And Lucia would never be the same, the heaviness in her heart a constant burden she would have to live with.

Twisting the folds of her skirt in one hand, she tried to dismiss the worrisome feeling that had been burrowing deep in her soul ever since she'd awakened last night. But the feeling of evil still persisted, unaffected by the shafts of light playing through the stained-glass windows near the staircase.

The sun was out, warming the day.

Yet she still felt as cold as death inside.

She'd spent a restless night, awoken, and said morning prayers in the oratory with the rest of the nuns at five, then spent an hour meditating and silently saying the rosary. Then there had been the interruption of their daily routine, where they had all been called to the dining hall and Father Paul, Father Frank, and the mother superior had spoken in soft tones about Sister Camille and the tragedy that had happened here within these sacred walls. The outside world had invaded their piety and holiness, and the nuns were told to pray for Sister Camille's soul and find their own sense of peace in the Holy Father's arms.

"Remember," Father Paul had intoned softly, his face lined with sadness, "you are the brides of Christ. He will help you through this time of confusion and loss."

Father Frank's eyes had squeezed shut for just an instant, as if he were shutting out a private vision.

Mother Superior had bowed her head and made the sign of the cross, but Lucia had felt no consolation from God as she remembered Sister Camille's pale face and bloodless lips as she lay on the chapel floor.

She'd swallowed hard, and her eyes had met the tortured gaze of Father Frank, no longer in the cassock stained with blood. Had it been Sister Camille's? Did he know that she was carrying his child?

Did Father Frank realize what Lucia knew?

As the heat of embarrassment climbed up her neck, she had looked away quickly, though the priest's piercing gaze lingered in her mind.

She had only been vaguely aware of the rest of the meeting, though she recalled talk of the police leaving soon and the promise that the chapel where Sister Camille had been found would be cleaned and blessed.

As if prayer and holy water could cleanse the evil.

Lucia wondered if she could ever set foot on the stone floors or view the looming crucifix without the image of Camille's dead body appearing before her.

Afterward, they had been allowed to have an hour of private prayer and meditation before tackling their daily tasks.

The mood in the convent was somber, everyone caught in her own private thoughts.

Lucia hurried down the stairs, her shoes clicking upon the polished steps, her fingers trailing on the rail. She knew it was time to leave. Camille's death had started a chain of events that would be the ultimate ruin of St. Marguerite's, and she wondered if that was the killer's purpose. Was Camille's murder a public statement or a personal vendetta? She thought of sweet, troubled Camille. They had shared so much here at the convent, from having lived in the same small area of New Orleans as children to having dated brothers . . . which brought her thoughts to Cruz.

Dear Father, she never wanted to see him again.

Talking to his older brother, the detective, was bad enough, but seeing the strong family resemblance made her want to run as fast as she could from the parish. Cruz Montoya was the one person who knew her secrets, the one man who had touched her soul, the one male who had nearly killed her. Her heart fluttered a bit in her chest. Was it fear . . . or something erotic? Sometimes, when she remembered back, when she thought of Cruz and what he'd done to her, she was turned inside out, the sensual images in her memory dangerously wicked. In her mind's eye, she saw coppery skin stretched over taut flesh, dark hair thick over a muscular chest and washboard abdomen. Her blood heated when she remembered the way his jeans sat so low on his hips, how the faded denim was tight across his firm, smooth buttocks.

"Stop it!" she muttered to herself. Her scandalous thoughts were well beyond sinful. She was married to the church now, married to Christ, and she could think of no mortal man sexually. Especially not Cruz Montoya, who had so easily broken her heart. And that brother of his, the detective who resembled Cruz . . . Seeing him had started a domino effect of pictures in her mind, memories she should have buried long ago.

"Give me strength," she whispered even as she remembered Cruz's irreverent smile, the glint of the devil in his dark eyes. Her blood surged, and she silently damned herself again. "No more!"

"Your sister was pregnant?" Montoya stared at Valerie Renard as she dropped the bombshell in the living room of her small cottage.

The quaint building that looked to be a former carriage house was connected to the bed-and-breakfast by a narrow causeway, allowing Valerie Renard some privacy away from guests.

"That's right," Val said tightly, tiny white lines bracketing the corners of her mouth. "She'd gotten involved with Frank O'Toole."

As if she read his question, she added, "I know, I know. She's a nun, he's a priest, and they've taken oaths of celibacy, but trust me, she's pregnant." Something inside of her seemed to break, and she swallowed a couple of times, blinked, and leaned against the mantel of the cold fireplace. "I mean...I mean she was...Oh, God, can she really be dead?"

Her husband tried to console her, but she'd have none of it, holding up a hand before he got too close. Her gaze found Montoya's again. "You remember Frank in high school. The ladies' man? Seems like nothing much has changed despite his vestments. This isn't the first time," she charged. "Camille told me he'd had another affair with a nun, someone named...Oh, God, what was it?" She looked at the ceiling, as if trying to think, to deal with the horror of her sister's death.

"Another nun?" Bentz asked, obviously disbelieving, thinking she was in shock. Hysterical.

Valerie nodded. "I'm sure Camille said something about it once."

"Do you have a name?"

"No...oh, wait. Something like Lily or Leanne...I really can't remember." Sniffing and clearing her throat, she fought tears and asked brokenly, "How did he do it?"

The two cops didn't answer, and she said, "I want to know."

"It looks like she was strangled," Bentz offered. "We don't know the actual cause of death yet, but...that's the way it looks now."

She squeezed her eyes shut, and as she did, her face grew taut, as if she were seeing Camille's perfect face in her mind's eye, her sister's eyes bulging, her lips trying to gasp for air.

"He choked her?"

Bentz said, "We'll know more later."

"Where?" She turned from Bentz to Montoya. "Where did it happen?"

"In the chapel at St. Marguerite's, around midnight, we think." Montoya said, "We don't have any other details we can share with you."

"She's my sister." Her voice was a low whisper.

Montoya nodded. "We know, but for now, until we're certain of our facts, we can't say too much."

Valerie seemed to accept that, though she blinked back tears and straightened her shoulders in what appeared to be an attempt at gaining some of her rapidly ebbing composure.

"And you don't live here, right?" Bentz asked Slade.

So, he'd put two and two together.

"I drove in from Texas last night."

"You live there?"

Slade nodded and Valerie looked as if she wanted to wilt right through the floor.

"And you live here in New Orleans?" Bentz said to Val.

"Yeah...Slade and I are separated."

Montoya asked Slade, "So you knew Camille Renard. How well?"

"She's my sister-in-law," Slade said, meeting the detective's stare with his own.

Valerie thought of his involvement with Camille and blanched.

"You were close?" Bentz asked.

Slade lifted a shoulder. "Like family. She lived with us for a while."

"When?" Bentz pulled out a small notebook.

Slade said, "A couple of years ago."

"Before she joined the order." Bentz found a pen and was scribbling.

"Yep."

Valerie cut off the interview by saying, "So, can I see her?"

"Sure," Montoya said, though he wondered if it was a good idea. The body had already been IDed. "But first we have some questions. What do you know about your sister's friends? Any enemies? Can you think of anyone who would want her dead?"

"Besides Frank O'Toole, you mean?" she charged, angry all over again. "I'm telling you right now, no one would have more motive to kill my sister than that cowardly son of a bitch who's hiding behind his damned clerical collar. He seduced her, got her pregnant, and then, when she was trying to break it off with him, he killed her to keep her quiet. End of story."

"Wait a second," Bentz interjected. "She was breaking it off with him?"

"Yeah." She was nodding and fighting tears. He witnessed the set of her jaw. "The last time we talked on the phone, she said something like, 'I have to get out of this.' And then you know what she added?" Valerie said, her eyes filling.

Bentz and Montoya waited.

"That he wouldn't take it very well. That he'd 'kill' her." She sniffed and swiped angrily at her eyes. "And she wasn't joking, you know. She was being literal." She swallowed hard, her eyes red.

"Did he ever threaten her that you know of?" Montoya asked.

"I . . . I don't know. She, uh, didn't tell me all of the details." Val blinked hard, still fighting tears and staring at him as if he was completely dense. "I don't know what their relationship was, just that it was unethical, immoral, and God knows what else. The term 'sexual harassment' doesn't even begin to touch what was going on there!" She took one step forward, and her husband grabbed hold of her wrist, but she shook him off. "Listen, you're dealing with a sick, narcissistic psychopath who scared her to death. She said as much, thought he would kill her and his own unborn child to save his damned reputation!" Tears welled in her eyes again. "If you don't believe me, check with the medical examiner. He should be able to tell you that Camille was two, almost three months along."

CHAPTER 11

"I want to know everything you can dig up on Francis O'Toole," Bentz was saying into his cell phone as Montoya punched the accelerator, cutting through the thick traffic of the city. The windows were rolled down, and the smell of exhaust from a semi that squeezed his lane overshadowed the tinge of barbecue that hung in the air. "No, I don't know his middle name, but that can't be too hard to figure out. He's around thirty-five, maybe, the junior priest over at St. Marguerite's, and he went to a private school here in the city, St. Timothy's, about what, twenty years ago?"

Montoya nodded, then found enough room to pass the big truck, only to be stopped at the next light and have it idling, belching black smoke, beside him.

Bentz was silent for a few minutes as he listened to one of the junior detectives on the other end of the line, then said, "And find out anything you can about a Sister Leanne or Lily who left St. Marguerite's in the last few years.... No, not yet, but I'll check and see if we can come up with a last name. It shouldn't be too tough to find her, though. It's not as if convents are crawling with nuns these days.... Yeah."

The light turned, and Montoya gunned it again, leaving the semi to lumber through the light, the driver pushing the huge vehicle through its gears.

"There's a guy I want some info on, too," Bentz said as Montoya slowed for a jackass who jaywalked across four lanes of traffic. "The name's Houston... Yeah, that's right, like the city. First name is Slade. Lives in Bad Luck, Texas... What? Yeah, I know, but he swears that's the name of the town. He's married to the vic's sister, and there might have been something going on between him and the vic.... Yeah, I know, but this was before she entered the convent," Bentz said, squinting against the glare through the windshield. "Uh-huh, not exactly *The Sound of Music*. I get it. Okay... we're on our way to the morgue now. You can catch me on my cell." He hung up and swore under his breath.

"You think the brother-in-law is involved?" Montoya asked.

Bentz lifted a shoulder. "Driving all night. Alone. No alibi. On the night the vic ends up dead. There's some tension between him and his wife, and then, according to him, just after Camille Renard lived with them, she bails and gets all religious, enters St. Marguerite's. Coincidence? I don't think so."

"Maybe you're right."

"I just think we should check him out."

"Doesn't fit with the wedding dress."

"What does?" Bentz glowered out the window.

Montoya didn't see the cowboy as a murderer, but then he wasn't buying Frank O'Toole as a killer either.

"You know," Bentz said to Montoya as he scratched at the beard stubble beginning to appear on his jaw, "convents and chapels and cathedrals, they're all good places. You know, where people go to gather and worship and..." He shook his head. "A few bad apples, okay, I grant you that, but for the most part, the people involved are well intentioned and God-fearing," he said, then slid a look at his partner.

"For the most part," Montoya agreed, but they'd both seen religion and faith twisted into the very embodiment of evil. "But the hell of it is, organized religion is made up of people. That's the problem."

"I interviewed Father Paul Neland last night."

"Yeah?"

"Shaken up, of course, but I got the feeling that he wasn't a fan of the younger guy. Nothing he said so much as what he didn't say. Wonder if he knew about the affair?"

"Maybe he's the guy O'Toole went to for his own confession."

"How's that for fucked up? My guess is when the news breaks that O'Toole was having sex with one of the nuns, the church will want to cut him loose. Too much bad press as it is. The archdiocese won't want to start defending another bad seed, a priest who's messing with the novices." Bentz glowered through the windshield.

His phone rang and he answered, then listened. "Okay, got it." He clicked off and glanced at Montoya. "That was Zaroster just letting us know that the story's broken. WKAM's running it at noon. It's already on the all-news channel, and the department's getting a lot of calls."

"Sheeit. That didn't take long. We just notified the next of kin."

"I know," Bentz muttered, frowning, "but a murdered nun is news. Real big news."

Sister Lucia pushed open the swinging doors to the kitchen and realized she was late. Really late. Thoughts of Cruz faded as she walked into the cavernous room.

Several of her peers were already hard at work, preparing the noon meal. Along with the warm aroma of baking bread, she caught a glare from Regina, the lay cook who never seemed to smile. Standing at the massive iron stove where she was sprinkling herbs into a boiling pot, she managed to wordlessly convey her displeasure.

A big woman with stringy gray hair always braided and wrapped around the back of her head, she wore oversized glasses with transitional lenses that were supposed to become clear inside but always remained slightly gray. The result was to make her eyes seem shaded and dead behind the bulbous lenses.

Not far from her, Sister Irene was slicing strawberries at the sink, her knife moving quickly, its sharp little blade catching in the light.

Lucia quickly donned an apron and took her place at the smooth marble counter where Sister Angela and Sister Devota were busy kneading dough. Angela glanced at Lucia and smiled, but Devota just kept at her work, her fingers digging deep into the elastic dough.

The two nuns were as opposite as day and night. Angela with her apple cheeks, blond hair, flour-smudged glasses, and quick smile always appeared happy, if a little spacey at times. She had a tendency to forget the rules and was often in trouble for humming while she was supposed to maintain her silence or for running through the gardens when she was supposed to walk. Discipline was difficult for her, and suppressing her natural ebullience was seemingly impossible, much to the frustration of the mother superior.

Devota, on the other hand, was a tall, quiet woman who continually fought self-esteem issues, at least in Lucia's opinion. Although she possessed pretty features, thick, curling hair, and a rare smile, Devota was self-conscious of the fact that she limped, the result of some kind of accident in her youth, which she would never discuss. No wonder she offered up her time at the clinic at St. Elsinore's. Devota had no trouble following the rules and was quick to remind others, including Sister Angela, of how to be obedient and pious.

"You're late," Regina snapped as she glanced up at the ancient clock mounted over the door. "Again."

"Sorry," Lucia said to the cook.

The corners of Regina's mouth turned downward a little farther, indicating that no excuse was good enough. Her glare was positively withering, but Lucia couldn't worry about it today.

"We need more flour," Regina said curtly, then turned to a pot that bubbled upon the massive stove.

Both Angela and Devota glanced at Lucia. Angela rolled her expressive eyes and Devota shrugged, as there was still an unopened twenty-pound bag propped against the pantry door.

"Did you hear me?" Regina demanded, bringing tense silence to the kitchen.

Even Sister Irene stopped slicing berries to look over her shoulder. Tall and slim, Irene swore she'd been a ballet dancer before joining the convent, and she still knotted her straight hair into a tiny topknot, enhancing the sharp cheekbones of her pixielike face.

"Yes," Lucia said, nodding to the cook. "I'll get right on it."

"We already have an extra sack," Irene pointed out. She spoke with a small lisp but seemed fearless of everyone, including the reverend mother. She wasn't concerned about arguing with the cook. "See...it's over there." With the blade of her knife, she pointed at the bag propped near the pantry door.

Regina colored slightly but set her jaw. "We need more," she said, her lips moving over clenched teeth. "Guests are expected and I'm going to be baking all day!"

"That's no reason to snap at Sister Lucia," Irene insisted. "We're all on edge today. Upset. Worried. Heartsick over poor Sister Camille. Things might not go as smoothly as usual," Irene said, her lisp more pronounced, her head bobbing as if agreeing with herself.

Surprised that her authority was being challenged, Regina said, "No matter what happened last night, there's still work to do. The Lord's work."

"Then let's do it together. Amicably. Spiritually," Irene suggested, lowering her knife.

Angela had trouble swallowing her smile, and even Devota arched her eyebrows at the confrontation.

"No problem. I'll get it." Lucia was already stepping toward the door leading outside as Irene turned back to her bowl of strawberries. Regina, tending her stew, looked as if she wanted to spit nails. Angela and Devota turned their attention back to punching the dough for the next day's bread.

You don't belong here; you know you don't. That nagging voice in her head kept reminding Lucia that her commitment was less than most of the other nuns, that her devotion flagged by comparison. Angela, Devota, Irene, Louise, and Dorothy seemed much more devout, their faith so strong it could never be shaken. Even Regina, the sourpuss of a cook, a layperson, appeared to have an unwavering dedication and trust in God.

Not so Lucia.

"Forgive me," she whispered, making the sign of the cross as she stepped along the gravel path through the herb garden to a storage building. The scents of lavender and rosemary wafted on the warm air, and sunlight caught in a few rapidly drying puddles that had collected on the path.

It was a good day. A warm day. A day filled with God's promise.

And yet the darkness in her soul wouldn't disappear.

The door to the storage pantry creaked as she opened it. Inside, the air was cooler. Jars and cans lined the shelves while sacks of sugar and flour were kept in tightly sealed bins. Lucia opened the flour bin and hauled out a twenty-pound sack. She slung it over her shoulder and headed outside again.

Steeling herself for another round with the dour cook, she heard the crow before she saw it, a shiny black bird eyeing her speculatively from the roof of the chapel.

"Sister Lucia?" a male voice asked.

She nearly stumbled and stepped into a puddle as she rounded to find Father Frank standing at the garden gate.

"Oh...Father... ," she whispered. "I didn't...I didn't see you." In her mind's eye, she saw him as he had been last night: his hair wet with the rain, his face twisted in a dark scowl, blood running from the hem of his cassock.

"Let me help you with that," he offered, and crossed the short distance as the gate banged shut and the startled crow cawed and flapped away. Deftly, he lifted the sack of flour from her arms. "I think we should talk." A dusting of flour powdered his shoulder, and the smile he'd forced fell from his lips. "Last night I was upset, and I told you that Sister Camille's death was my fault." His expression was that of a wounded, hunted animal. "I think I should explain myself."

"You don't have to explain anything to me," she said quickly.

A cloud crawled over the face of the sun, casting an eerie gloom over the garden.

"Of course I do, Lucia." With his free hand, he touched her shoulder, the warmth of his fingertips seeping through the dark fabric of her habit. His dark eyes searched hers in a way she found far too uncomfortable.

Lucia shrank inside. She didn't want to feel his touch, nor did she have any desire to be confessor to his penance. It was his role to hear confession, not hers. The crow, bolder now, landed on the gutter over the kitchen.

An omen.

Lucia felt a chill, as if the Devil himself were watching her.

"You have to believe me," he said, his voice a strangled whisper. "I didn't kill Sister Camille. I . . . I would never do that." He closed his eyes for a second, and a breath of wind toyed with the strands of hair falling free of Lucia's braid. "God forgive me, Lucia," he said, blinking as if battling tears. "I loved her."

CHAPTER 12

Valerie had made the mistake of letting Slade drive to the morgue. His truck had been parked in front of her Subaru, and he'd insisted on being a part of this madness. After leaving Bo with a bewildered Freya, they'd taken the old Ford to the hospital.

Slade had followed the police car, and Valerie, lost in thoughts of Cammie, had barely registered the familiar scents of dust and leather inside the pickup. She'd kicked aside a tool belt that had been tossed onto the floor and stared out the passenger window, her reflection pale and wan in the glass smudged with nose and paw prints.

She hardly remembered the traffic or the drive through New Orleans, though she did hear the sound of church bells as she stepped out of the truck, their somber tolling emanating from St. Marguerite's Cathedral not a mile away.

The sun was playing hide-and-seek. Clouds were collecting, moving over the city again, shadowing New Orleans like a pall. Valerie shivered as they reached the back door to the hospital and stepped inside, where voices were hushed and footsteps were softened by a gray, industrial carpet.

In silence, she and Slade followed the two detectives down a staircase to the lowest level of the hospital. Val's stomach clenched as they made their way along a short hallway and through double doors.

Inside, the morgue was cold.

Even though she stood behind a thick glass window, Valerie felt the chill of the area beyond the pane. She braced herself but couldn't help listening to that disbelieving voice in her head: *There's been a mistake, a misidentification. Cammie is not dead. She can't be. Not beautiful, bright, high-spirited Camille. No way!*

When the attendant slipped the sheet off Cammie's face, Val's knees nearly buckled. Cammie's perfect face, bluish in death, looked upward.

Val let out a squeak of protest.

Slade's strong arm was instantly around her waist, holding her up as she stared at the woman on the slab, her only sibling, so young...

"Oh, God," Val whispered. The truth was a razor through her heart, all remnants of denial seeping from her. Tears stung her eyes and her insides trembled. For a second she thought she might be sick.

"Son of a bitch," Slade muttered. His ghostly reflection appeared in the glass, his determined, unshaven jaw, blade-thin lips, narrowed eyes overlapping the stronger image of her dead sister.

How ironic was it that Slade was here, his image superimposed over Cammie's dead, draped body?

After all they had been through. All the lies. The accusations. The heartache. Val couldn't help but wonder if Slade felt a smidgeon of guilt for Cammie's death.

He should.

As Val did. They were both integral in the contribution to her downward spiral.

"I should have done something," she whispered.

"Like what?"

"Protected her."

"Impossible." Slade nodded toward the attendant, and the sheet was pulled back over Cammie's face. He shepherded Val away from the window and through a door to where the two detectives waited.

How many times had she, in her years as a cop, been in their position, waiting to question the loved ones, trying to root out information while the family was torn by grief?

"We can talk to you here, or if you'd prefer, down at the station," Bentz said.

"Here's fine." Val found some grit.

"Okay, there's a room, just down the hall." Bentz led them along a carpeted hallway to a small room with three chairs and a dying potted palm positioned near the window, a place where doctors spoke with patients or loved ones. Outside, the sky was now a sea of gray, threatening rain.

Bentz motioned them into chairs, took one himself, and waited as Montoya closed the door behind him and stood near the ill-fated tree.

"So let's get started. Tell us what you know about the affair between Father O'Toole and your sister."

"I wish I could," Valerie said. "But I don't know all that much." She told the detectives how Camille had met with her nearly a month earlier and explained her situation, that she was pregnant, that the father was a priest, and that she was considering leaving the convent.

"But she didn't," Montoya prodded.

"No, not by the time..." She cleared her throat and told herself to "tough up" as their father had always advised whenever either of his daughters came to him with a problem. "Not by the time she'd died. She sent me an e-mail, though. It was short and said that she couldn't take it anymore, whatever that meant, and that she was leaving the order and that I know why. I guess she was talking about the pregnancy."

"When did you receive it?"

"Last night. Late. I was worried about her and..." *And you should have gone and visited her. Maybe you could have saved her.* The recriminations rolled through her mind even though she knew better. She'd been a cop, been in Bentz's and Montoya's shoes, showed family members their dead loved ones, questioned them about everyone they knew. So she tried like crazy to push her guilt aside and help the cops. She told them everything she knew, from the time that she and Camille were adopted by their mother and father, through the trials and trauma of high school. She had known of Frank O'Toole's reputation, and she recalled that Camille had dated Reuben Montoya. She admitted that she and Camille had been estranged in recent years, that part of the alienation had been her marriage to Slade, a man Camille had shown interest in.

She also reminded them of the other nun who had been involved with O'Toole, though she still wasn't certain of her name or what became of her or really if she had existed anywhere but in Camille's jealous mind.

"So..." Bentz switched his attention to Slade as rain began to tick against the window. "You were the last man she was involved with before she joined the order?"

"We weren't involved." Slade's gaze was level, his words firm. "She was my sister-in-law."

"But she... did what? Came onto you?" Bentz glanced at Valerie for clarification.

"You could say that." He glanced at his wife. "She flirted."

"Define 'flirted,'" Montoya said, and Slade had the decency to look uncomfortable.

"You know, man. She would say things, give me a look, get all pouty."

"Around you?" Bentz again, brows slammed together, eyes on Valerie.

She shook her head. "No, I never saw that."

"What did you see?"

Val sighed, glanced to the window where the rain ran in zigzagging rivulets. "I saw a woman who was confused and a man who didn't discourage her."

"Jesus, Val, that's not the way it was!" Slade scowled and shook his head. "Camille lied about me. Swore to Val that I was the one who did the pursuing." He let out a long, disgusted sigh through his nose. "That's not how it happened."

"Tell me how it did," Bentz said.

"After Val and I were married, I don't know, maybe a year, Camille came to visit for a long time, about a month. She showed some interest then, I think, but it was subtle. The next visit, not so subtle. She'd bump into me. Come up on me when I was alone working with the stock. Always said suggestive things and then laughed it off." His eyes held Bentz's. "You know when a woman's interested. Especially a woman like Camille."

"She was a beautiful woman."

Slade didn't respond.

"You tell your wife about it?"

"No." Slade frowned and Valerie wanted to slide farther away from him. "Not at first."

"Camille came to me," Val said. "She swore Slade was trying to get her into bed."

"A lie." Slade was stalwart. Didn't flinch.

"You believed her?" Bentz asked Val as Montoya's eyes narrowed on Slade.

"I did and I confronted Slade. He turned the story around."

"I just told it like it was. No, I didn't run to my wife and whine about her sister. To tell you the truth, I didn't know what to do. Everything blew up around Christmas and Camille took off."

"To a nunnery? Seriously? That sounds like something right out of the Middle Ages."

"Camille was into high drama," Slade said.

"When was the last time you saw her?" Montoya's question was directed at Slade, but they both answered.

"The day she left the ranch in Bad Luck, Texas," Slade said.

Val admitted,"I haven't seen her since last month, when I stopped by the orphanage where she worked. We barely spoke. Then there was the phone call and finally the e-mail last night."

"I'd like a copy of it, and any others you've got as well." Bentz made notes and asked a few more questions.

For the most part, Montoya allowed his partner to take the lead. They told her that Camille had fought with her attacker at the scene of the crime but that there was no other sign of a struggle, other than in the chapel at the altar. Camille, it seemed, had gone into the chapel willingly. Val felt a chill again, cold enough to turn her heart to ice as she thought about her sister's last minutes on this earth, but then all of this horror was strange. Eerie and soul grinding.

By the time they left the hospital, it was after ten and the rain had stopped, the clouds breaking apart, blue sky visible. A thick, dank mist rolled upward from the earth as Valerie walked through puddles to Slade's old Ford. Slade had insisted on driving to the hospital, and she'd been so hell-bent to get to the morgue she hadn't cared a whit how she'd gotten there. Now, as she climbed into the beat-up truck, she was acutely aware of the memories it conjured. The smell of old leather, dirt and sweat, the wreckage of a marriage.

The end of a life.

She shivered at the stark, irreversible realization that she would never see Cammie again.

It was an impossible thought. Painful.

And now, after the viewing, a cold, hard fact.

CHAPTER 13

It's been so long.
And the promise I made myself years ago, the vow, is now broken. From the Moonwalk along the banks of the river, I watch the thick waters of the Mississippi roll past, cloudy and obscure. A freighter churns upriver. The air is warm and heavy with humidity, the sky somber, yet I slip a pair of sunglasses from my pocket and onto the bridge of my nose.

"Hello, Father," a man says as he passes me quickly, catching sight of my clerical collar.

I smile.

Don't answer.

He bustles away, and I turn from the river, its dank smell caressing my nostrils. With effort, I make my way over the steep levee, my right leg dragging ever so slightly, the old pain not quite gone and never, ever forgotten.

It's a pain I can deal with.

And only in the leg.

I'm not winded, not even perspiring. I've kept myself fit. Honed.

Except for the right tibia.

Unfortunate, that.

A war wound.

I make my way into the park and keep moving, past a mime who tries silently to catch my attention. I refuse to glance his way, his sad white face of no interest to me. Instead, I stare across the park, past the statue of Andrew Jackson on his rearing horse to the spires of St. Louis Cathedral, rising upward, the cross atop the highest steeple seeming to pierce the underbelly of the dark clouds roiling overhead.

White and looming, the cathedral beckons.

And I, of course, resist.

For now.

Inside the truck, Val kicked against the tool belt near her feet and waited for Slade to slide behind the wheel.

"You okay?" he asked, closing the door.

"What do you think?"

"Okay, dumb question."

"You got that right." She stared out the windshield as he switched on the ignition and hit the wipers. With a squeak, they batted away the rainwater that had collected on the glass during the short storm.

"What about you?" she asked.

He scowled beneath the stubble of his beard. "I won't be okay until they find the bastard who did this." As he jammed the truck into reverse and hit the gas, the smell of dust from his ranch reached her nostrils.

"It's O'Toole," she said as the old Ford shuddered, then backed around an SUV taking up two spaces.

"He's a priest, for God's sake, Val. You know, a paragon of virtue—"

"He's a man, Slade." She slid a knowing glance his way and wondered if he read the silent accusations in her eyes. "No matter what kind of vows he took, how many confessions he hears, or how many times he gets down on his knees and prays, the bottom line is, Frank O'Toole is just a man."

"Not necessarily a sinner." Slade leveled his gaze at her, and in that heartbeat, she wondered if he was talking about the priest or himself.

His lips flattened as he nosed the Ford into traffic, leaving the looming hospital behind.

For a split second, she remembered a field of bluebells and Indian paintbrush, the feel of warm earth against her back, a sweet floral scent in the air. As honeybees droned and the sky stretched wide and blue above the Texas hills, she stared into Slade's eyes, gray-blue and slumberous. His pupils dilated a fraction as he stretched his long, lean frame, all muscle, bone, and sinew over her. She'd felt a sizzle of anticipation; then his lips had crashed down on hers and she'd been lost.

"Damn," she whispered, dispelling the image.

"What?"

"Everything." Silently she chastised herself for her straying thoughts. She leaned back against the cracked seat, and though her eyes focused straight ahead, the image of Camille's lifeless face was etched into her brain. Cammie was gone, and now Val was alone. No family left in the world.

Unless you counted a soon-to-be-ex-husband and a droopy-eared hound.

Slade had the good sense not to make conversation as he drove through the narrow streets leading to the bed-and-breakfast. She tried and failed to give herself a swift mental kick; no one would be helped if she shut down, sitting around and wallowing in grief. It wouldn't bring Cammie back.

"So you know the cop?" he finally asked as he turned onto the side street that ran past the house.

"Went to school with him."

"And O'Toole?"

"Yep," she said, her eyes narrowing as she thought about it. "It's like a Saint Timothy's reunion." She frowned.

"What're the chances of that?" he asked, voicing a question that had been nagging at her.

"We all grew up around here," she said, but it was odd; they both knew it. She and Cammie had left New Orleans after high school, and she'd thought O'Toole had, too. It seemed strange that he would go to seminary nearby and end up at St. Marguerite's. Usually priests moved around. Then again, maybe his father had bought him a spot near home; churches had been known to swing things for generous donors.

As for Reuben Montoya, she had not run into him since Catholic school, but it was a surprise to learn he'd ended up a detective with the New Orleans Police Department. She would never have pegged him for becoming a cop; if anything, she'd thought he might turn up on the other side of the law. And here he was, a detective. Maybe a lifelong resident of New Orleans.

Slade parked nearby in a small lot dedicated to Briarstone House. This time he had the grace not to block her car.

"It's all pretty strange," Slade thought aloud.

"Very." She didn't put a lot of stock in coincidence. She'd spent too many years as a cop to be that naive. She'd learned to see past the obvious, beneath the veneer of what appeared to be the truth.

And one of the things that bothered her now was the fact that Slade had appeared on her doorstep not long before she learned about her sister's murder.

Another coincidence.

She slid him a look as he cut the engine.

"So what's your story, Cowboy?" she asked, reaching for the door handle. "Why are you here?"

One side of his mouth curved up into that crooked smile that she'd once found so breathtaking. "I thought I already told you," he said with an irritating confidence. "I'm here to talk you out of the divorce."

"And didn't I tell you to take a hike? It's over." He started to open his mouth, and she held up a hand. "And look, I— Okay, we've been through a major shock here, but I'm not going to let you use Cammie's death as an excuse to stay. I can handle this, Slade." When he again seemed to protest, she reminded him, "I was a cop."

"This is different and you know it."

"Just leave." She opened the door of the cab. "But the dog stays. Thanks for bringing Bo." She climbed out of the truck and heard him do the same. As she pushed open the gate, he was at her side, walking with her stride for stride to the front door of the inn.

"I'm telling you. Bo stays with me." His boots clambered up the two long steps in tandem with hers.

"You're not taking the hint." She turned as they reached the door and for the first time noticed his backpack. "What the hell do you think you're doing?"

"Registering." He opened the door and held it open for her. "I've got a reservation here."

"No way," she said.

"Way. I talked to someone named Freya? She booked me for a week."

"But you said that you slept in the pickup because you didn't have a reservation."

"That was for last night. I think I'm booked in the Garden View Room tonight."

"Forget it. There's a Motel Six across town!"

"Sorry, darlin'," he drawled. "Don't want to lose my deposit."

"I'll give it back to you. Full refund!" God, he couldn't stay here.

"Too late." He was already reaching for his duffel bag.

"No way," Val said, but a sinking sensation rolled over her. Hadn't Freya pushed to tell her something "important"? Something about Slade. "Look, this isn't going to work. I don't care what happened, but you can't stay here," she said just as she noticed a television van for a local TV station turning down the street. "Oh, no." Somehow the press had sniffed out that she was a murder victim's sister. Already. "Oh, great," she muttered under her breath, and stepped inside where a few guests hovered in the lobby.

One man in his eighties with a big, toothy smile waved at her.

"Good morning," Val said, though it was anything but.

"Morning!" His wife, a little, birdlike woman who wore visors in her perfectly coiffed white hair, grinned widely and slipped a pair of pink-rimmed sunglasses onto her nose. "We're off to the French Quarter!"

"Enjoy." Val forced a smile she didn't feel as the couple walked out the front door, and Freya swept into the foyer. One glance to the front walk caused her to grimace.

"Oh, God, Val, I'm so sorry." Her face was a mask of sadness, and she threw her arms around Valerie.

"Thanks." Val fought an onslaught of tears and the need to collapse as the doorbell rang. "Oh," she groaned, assuming some perky reporter was on the other side of the vestibule.

"Don't worry, I'll handle it." Slade dropped his bag near an umbrella stand, walked to the door, and opened it, filling the doorway with his long frame.

"Brenda Convoy with WKAM. I'm looking for Valerie Renard." An evenly modulated woman's voice slid through the crack, and Val caught a glimpse of a slim, twentysomething woman with a wedge of short black hair and big doe eyes.

"She's busy," he said, not budging.

"And you are?"

"Her husband."

She brightened. "If you don't mind, I'd like to ask a few questions about a story we're following. One of the nuns at St. Marguerite's Convent was killed last night—"

Val crossed the foyer to stand next to Slade. "I'm Valerie Renard," she said, "and I'm going through a difficult time. I have no comment. Thank you." With that she closed the door, locked it, and wondered how much of the aborted interview the cameraman, standing on the front porch, had caught. Not that it mattered. The bell rang again, but she ignored it. All of the guests had been issued room keys that unlocked the back door. For once she was grateful that there weren't that many paying customers; at least she'd have a little more privacy.

Back to that.

She turned and faced Freya. "I take it Slade renting the Garden View Room was the reason you wanted to talk to me last night."

Freya was nodding, standing near the window. "Yeah." She sighed as she stared through the glass. "Now they're taking shots of the house. Great. I guess we'll chalk it up as free publicity." She turned to Val. "Anything I can do?"

"No," Val said, and with a glance at Slade said, "But the next time one of my ex-husbands calls to rent a room, hang up."

"I'm not your ex yet," Slade said.

"Soon, Cowboy."

"We'll see about that." He grabbed his beat-up duffel in one big hand. "Why don't you show me which room is mine?"

"Gladly," she mocked, and found Freya already holding out the key. "Fabulous." She snagged the key, then headed up the stairs with Slade one step behind in his dusty boots. A door on the first floor opened, and she heard a sharp bark, then the sound of scrambling paws on the marble floor of the foyer. A second later, Bo bounded up the stairs. "This is low, Slade, even for you," she said as she followed the fading carpet runner to the second floor, then turned upward again. "Calling Freya behind my back."

"Would you have seen me?"

"You know the answer to that."

"Then I guess I didn't have much of a choice."

"There are always choices," she said on the top floor.

They reached the third-floor landing where Bo was waiting, bottom wiggling, tongue lolling from one side of his mouth. Black lips pulled back, he appeared to smile as she reached down and petted his head. "I have missed you, you miserable mutt," she said with a chuckle, and the dog whined as if he understood. "Someone better be treating you right."

"Spoiled rotten."

"Just as it should be." Straightening, Val walked to one side of the landing, where an etched brass plate read GARDEN VIEW ROOM and the crystal doorknob twisted easily. She let Slade step inside the cozy room with its red oak floors, sloping ceilings, and painted tile fireplace. Double doors opened onto a private deck that did, indeed, have a view of the herb and flower garden as well as the roof of the attached cottage Val called home. It was all a little too close for comfort.

"Nice," he said, then tossed his backpack toward a closet as Bo sniffed the perimeter of the room.

"We have a no-pets policy."

"You gonna make him sleep in the truck?"

"I should. But I guess I'll make an exception. He can sleep with me."

His lips twitched."If anyone complains, let me know."

"If anyone complains, I'll handle it," she said. "And if you need anything?"

"Yeah?"

"Call Freya." She walked out of the room with Bo, then closed the door behind her. Slade's deep-throated chuckle followed her all the way to the first floor.

Freya was at the sink when Val breezed through the swinging door separating the kitchen from the dining area. Stacks of dishes rose from the sink, soaking in sudsy water, and apples simmered on the stove, the scent of cinnamon mingling with the Lysol Freya used to clean the floor earlier in the morning.

She opened the dishwasher and began loading. "You okay?" she asked, looking over her shoulder. "Hey—dog out of the kitchen!" Suds dripped from the freshly washed plate that she stacked on the lower rack.

"Definitely not," Val said, and with an authoritative snap of her finger, sent Bo to the other side of the door. He left, tail between his legs.

"Oh, God, I feel like an ogre," Freya said.

"He'll get over it."

"I suppose. How about you? Need a drink?"

"It's not even noon."

"That's why Bloody Marys were invented."

Val shook her head and heard the lonesome call of a whip-poor-will slipping through the open window. Its cry, rare now, caused a shudder to slide through her. "I think I'll pass. Or at least take a rain check." For now she had too much to do. She wanted to forward all of Cammie's e-mails to Montoya, then start her own investigation of her sister's murder. Her heart twisted again, and she blinked back tears at the realization that, along with the investigation, she would inevitably have to plan a funeral and lay her sister to rest.

If that were possible.

Would Camille find eternal peace and pass through the gates of heaven?

Or was her soul forever damned?

CHAPTER 14

"What the hell's going on here?" Bentz was agitated and didn't try to hide it as Montoya drove the Mustang away from the hospital. Leaning his elbow on the open window ledge of the sun-baked car while the air-conditioning struggled against the heat, he let fly. "It feels like I was your date at a damned high school reunion!"

"Yeah, right."

"Come on. First, what're the chances of you knowing the victim?" Bentz asked, raising his index finger. "And then the nun who found her?" Another finger shot skyward. "Not to mention the priest she was allegedly sleeping with." The third digit joined the first two. "Did I forget anyone?" Bentz groused.

"Not so far."

"Humph!" Bentz was clearly annoyed, and probably tired as hell. The case had kept them up most of the night, and Bentz, too, had an infant at home who wasn't yet sleeping through the night. His daughter, Ginny, born last Halloween and now nearly eight months old, had been colicky from the get-go.

"Christ," Bentz grumbled. "Who knows how many more will crawl out of the damned woodwork?"

"Hopefully none."

"Be sure to check the list of everyone associated with St. Marguerite's. Could be some more long-forgotten girlfriends holing up there."

"I will."

With a snort of disgust, he discovered a pack of gum in a patdown of his jacket and unwrapped a stick. He pointed out the obvious: "If Camille Renard really was pregnant, we've got ourselves a double homicide."

"Great."

"With your friend O'Toole as a prime suspect." He wadded the gum into a ball and plopped it into his mouth. "You buy him being the daddy?"

Montoya snorted. "I don't buy him being a priest."

"I don't like it."

"Neither do I."

"Nuns don't get pregnant."

"Yeah, usually the celibacy thing takes care of that," Montoya agreed, turning a corner where a lone saxophone player was playing blues to a small crowd, his instrument case open in front of him, scattered coins glinting in the sun.

"You believe he was involved with another nun, one before Camille Renard?" Bentz asked, squinting from the sun.

"Don't know what to think, but we're checking it out. Zaroster's on it."

"So what is it with this guy? Why become a priest if you're so into women?"

"Who knows?"

"Yeah, well, I just don't get the whole vow of celibacy thing. Seems to be just another way to get everyone in trouble. It's just not natural. God or no God."

Montoya didn't respond, just drove on automatic, his mind spinning as fast as the tires of his car. He wondered about Camille Renard, how she'd ended up back in New Orleans in a convent. And pregnant. He figured she must've really been carrying a child; there was no reason for the sister to lie, especially when an autopsy would reveal the truth.

"You know, the whole crime scene was wrong," Bentz finally said, staring out the window.

"Staged."

"Nuns don't wear bridal gowns or jewelry."

"Actually, O'Toole said they wear the gowns when they take their vows. And they have a ring, too. But I get what you're saying. The wedding gown. The way her body was laid near the altar with the drops of blood around the gown's neckline..."

"Ritualistic," Bentz observed.

"Sick."

Bentz's cell phone chirped. As he answered, he rolled up the window, cutting down the ambient noise.

Montoya tuned out Bentz's one-sided phone conversation as he passed a carriage pulled by a gray mule. Driving along the river, he tried to piece the disjointed bits of the investigation together. Camille as the victim, dressed in a frayed wedding dress, strangled, apparently. Who wanted her dead? Who would go to such bizarre lengths to kill her and display her body? The father of her unborn child?

Seemed unlikely.

Someone else, then. Someone who lived at the convent? An outside enemy? What about the brother-in-law, Houston? Montoya's fingers tightened on the steering wheel. Slade Houston seemed an unlikely candidate as the killer, but then, so did Frank O'Toole. As for the paternity of the unborn child—assuming Sister Camille really was pregnant—was O'Toole the father, or someone else? Montoya felt a pang of remorse, his own involvement with Camille a very painful sticking point.

Bentz clicked his phone shut as they slowed for a red light. "That was the ME's office," he said, his voice low and angry. "Preliminary report on Camille Renard. Looks likes asphyxiation due to strangulation, which we figured. And, yeah, she was pregnant. It's a double."

Montoya's hands tightened over the steering wheel again. He thought of Camille in the chapel, the way her body was displayed, the rosary beads threaded through her fingers. "So who, besides Valerie Renard, knew she was pregnant?"

"Most likely the father of the kid. Maybe a friend or two. Maybe even the mother superior or a priest, other than O'Toole. Someone like that, who she might confess to."

Montoya had already thought of them. "But the secret was probably confined to the convent and her sister."

"Unless people talked—they tend to do that." Bentz glowered out the window. "The lab's checking blood types now—Camille's and the fetus's. We'll need a sample from O'Toole, too, or rule him in or out."

"And anyone else who knew her."

"You mean in the biblical sense." Bentz slid a glance in Montoya's direction, unasked questions hovering in the warm interior of the car.

"She was a nun, for Christ's sake."

"And knocked up."

The light changed and Montoya hit the gas.

"Wouldn't be surprised if the captain yanked you off the case," Bentz thought aloud. "It's not often an investigating officer knows the vic and one of the suspects as well as the person who found the body and reported the crime." He nodded to himself. "Nah, the captain's not gonna like it."

"*I* don't like it," Montoya said.

"What about that Sister Lucy?"

"Lucia," Montoya corrected, taking a corner too fast, tires screeching. He felt the weight of Bentz's gaze, recognized the questions forming in his partner's eyes.

God, what a mess. He couldn't imagine Frank O'Toole as a murderer; then again, he'd never have guessed the soccer star would end up a priest, even with the near-death experience of O'Toole's sister.

Stranger things have happened.

"Guess you'll have to ask him." Montoya braked, allowing a slow-moving minivan filled with half a dozen kids to roll past. Balloons fluttered from the windows, catching the wind, delighting the grade-schoolers and causing ripples of giggles and squeals of laughter to rise from the van. After the noisy vehicle passed, he wheeled into the lot and pulled his car into a safe spot.

"The odd thing about this case is that it seems to center around you," Bentz prodded, and straightened his leg, wincing a little from an injury that had once sidelined him while he worked a case in

Baton Rouge, an injury that nearly cost his older daughter, Kristi, her life.

"There are lots of odd things about this case." For the first time in months, Montoya craved a smoke. He'd given up the habit years before, but when things were tense, he found himself reaching into his pocket for a nonexistent pack of cigarettes.

The hell of it was that Bentz was right about the high school reference.

Montoya felt a weird sense of déjà vu, as if he'd been thrown back in time to take a long look at his own life, the images of his youth parading by like his own personal krewe at Mardi Gras.

He only hoped that no one else he knew turned up.

"I'm telling you, he was involved with her," Sister Charity said angrily. So irritated she had to pace from one side of Father Paul's small office to the other. Books lined the shelves, stained-glass windows filtered the light, and Paul sat behind a huge desk of dark mahogany. The wood shined so glossy that light reflected off it.

"We don't know it for certain."

"I've seen them!" Sister Charity was almost trembling she was so upset. "Discretion wasn't one of Sister Camille's strengths." The headache behind her eyes began to pound. "And Father Frank... well, he just doesn't understand the meaning of celibacy!" She had only to think of the other incident... Oh, dear Father. Righteousness burned deep in her soul.

"I've talked to the archbishop," Father Paul said softly. "Told him about the situation."

Charity closed her eyes. "This is such an embarrassment for the church," she whispered.

"We'll ride it out," Paul said, and she saw the weariness in his eyes. "Have faith."

"My faith is not the issue." She sighed and shook her head. "There is a chance, Father, that Camille was with child."

He glanced up sharply, disbelief and something else—suspicion?—in his eyes. "No." He shook his head. Foolish old man. As if he could decide what was the truth.

"I'm not certain, but I overheard a conversation between her and Sister Lucia."

The lines in his face deepened. "I hope you're wrong," he said. Then his weak smile. "I don't put much faith in gossip."

He checked his watch and she understood. He was a busy man. And he was dismissing her, hiding his head in the sand, hoping that she, again, would clean up the mess. "I'll talk to Father Frank," he said benignly, as if that conversation would change anything.

Inwardly, Charity seethed as she left him and his skewed view of the "situation," as he so callously referred to it. Didn't he understand the significance of Sister Camille's murder? The ramifications to St. Marguerite's? Of course not. Whenever there had been a "situation" in the past, she'd taken care of it.

She walked briskly, hurrying through the passageway between his quarters and her beloved convent. She trailed a finger along the old walls, composed of more than mortar and brick. Years, no centuries, of history were a part of this institution; if she tried, she could almost feel the love, determination, and anguish of those who had walked before her down these hallways, which had withstood hurricanes and floods and political madness.

She reached the far end of the windowless corridor and started toward her office when she heard her name.

"Reverend Mother," Sister Zita said. She had a melodic voice and a tall, lithe appearance that wasn't hidden by her habit. Her skin was a warm mocha color, her eyes sparked with intelligence, and she had never given Charity one second of trouble.

"Yes, my child." She smiled warmly.

"I was wondering about St. Elsinore's," she said somberly. "Sister Camille and I worked in the orphanage together ever since Sister Lea left and now..." She rotated her palms upward.

"I see." Charity was nodding. "There are lots of spaces that will need to be filled now that Sister Camille has passed on. Why don't you see if Sister Maura or Lucia...or maybe Sister Edwina can go with you?" She offered a reassuring smile. "Even though the orphanage is moving to a new location, trust me, we here at St. Marguerite's will be involved. I'll see to it. Now, come with me."

She led the tall woman toward her office and, once inside, sat at her desk, unlocked a big drawer, and retrieved the staffing schedule. As Zita had said, Sister Camille was scheduled the next day at

St. Elsinore's orphanage, which was actually across Lake Pontchar-train and closer to Slidell than New Orleans. A place dear to Charity's heart. She hated to see the orphanage's venerable old doors closing, but it was already decided, the move in progress.

"Let's see... Yes, either Maura or Devota should be available. They both work there fairly regularly. Lucia... let's leave her out of it. She's been through enough in the last twenty-four hours."

"I'll talk to them," Zita said.

"Good." Then, automatically, "Bless you, my child."

Zita left, and once again, Sister Charity was alone in her office, the picture of the current Pope and the crucifix her only solace. In so many ways, these were troubling times. Much earlier, when she was a young novitiate, before Vatican II, things were so much easier to understand. Rigid, yes, but there was no blurring of lines, no question of what was expected.

Now... now nothing, it seemed, was clear.

CHAPTER 15

There was no way Val could just go about her normal life. *Nothing about it will ever be normal again,* a voice nagged at her as she walked out the back door of her little cottage and slid into her Subaru. The interior was hot; she felt as if she were climbing into an oven, and her air-conditioning was sporadic at best. She started the car, buckled up, and cranked open the window to capture any trace of cool air.

Slade was still at the house—or at least his truck was still parked where he'd left it—but she'd deal with him later.

Right now she had things to do.

She planned on dropping off copies of the e-mails she'd received from Camille at the police station. Just after she had a heart-to-heart with Father Frank O'Toole, that miserable, lying son of a bitch.

"Val!" Slade's voice chased after her as she pulled out of the short driveway and onto the street. From the corner of her eye, she caught a glimpse of him striding toward his truck.

She hesitated, then ignored him. She wasn't in the mood for a confrontation with him, nor even, for that matter, a discussion. She didn't slow down until she reached St. Charles Avenue. There, she eased into the flow of traffic, navigating around a streetcar with its cargo of tourists eyeing the gracious mansions set back from the tree-lined street, snapping pictures of the pastel Victorian with its widow's walk and gingerbread details.

Val couldn't deal with Slade now; didn't want to. Later, even though his coming to New Orleans was a fool's mission. And what was all that talk about reconciling? Ridiculous! She ignored that small feminine part of her that found him fascinating, the bit that found his stubborn determination and long drive from Bad Luck romantic.

"Pain in the neck," she muttered, reminding herself that if it weren't for Slade and the events that had unfolded two years earlier, Camille would still be alive. She set her jaw, and as she slowed for a red light, she glanced into her rearview mirror, past the traffic stacking up behind her, to the side street leading to the Briarstone House. Sure enough, Slade was waiting to turn onto St. Charles and wedge the old Ford into traffic. Behind her, traffic shifted, a sleek black convertible jockeying into the space behind her.

She was only slightly aware of the BMW, her attention focused on her husband and his beat-up truck. Was Slade following her?

No doubt.

Oh, for the love of God, why?

She felt a tug on her heartstrings and thought for a moment that he really did care, that he wouldn't have driven all the way from East Texas if he didn't still have feelings for her, that the past was the past and—

A horn blasted sharply.

"Hey, lady, it doesn't get any greener than that!" The jerk in the Beemer was gesturing at the light.

Val punched it, disgusted that thoughts of Slade had interrupted her concentration.

As the BMW found a way to pass her, the driver gunning the engine to show his disgust, she pushed the speed limit and cut through the city.

Again, her thoughts turned to Camille and her heart twisted. She'd initially thought Frank O'Toole had killed her, but now, with a little time to think about it, Valerie wasn't so sure. He was a priest who had broken his vows, yes; that much was true. But to take a life, not only of the woman he'd slept with, but of his own child, too? Was that possible? Even with human passion being what it was, Frank O'Toole was a Catholic priest, and murder was a mortal sin.

But if not Frank O'Toole, then who?

The short drive to St. Marguerite's Cathedral seemed to take forever, and as she nosed her little car into a parking space on the street, the church bells were tolling again. She realized it was noon, barely twelve hours since she'd stood at her kitchen window, worrying about Camille, sensing something was wrong but not knowing that at that very second she might have been on the verge of death, drawing her last breath. In her mind's eye, Valerie saw the image of Camille's motionless, draped body lying on a cold slab in the hospital's morgue, a picture she prayed would fade with time.

She steeled herself as she rolled up the window.

This probably wasn't going to go well.

That was just too damned bad.

After locking the Subaru, she jaywalked across the street to the looming edifice, a stone and brick building whose spires rose as if in exaltation to the heavens. The main part of the cathedral was well over two hundred years old, having withstood wars and storms and scandal. Rimmed by expansive grounds and guarded by a wrought-iron fence and gnarled live oaks, St. Marguerite's Cathedral was a reminder of ages past, a society locked away, a world unto itself.

There were no news vans parked along the street, and if the police were still on the premises, Val didn't see any of their vehicles. However, the massive doors of the cathedral were sealed with yellow crime scene tape strung through the handles, and the trampled grounds were evidence of last night's assault by hundreds of feet during the start of the investigation.

Of Cammie's murder.

Oh, God.

She followed the wrought-iron fence that guarded the church grounds, heading toward a back alley and a gate that Cammie had mentioned once, an entrance used by delivery trucks and the few nuns who occasionally left the convent.

She found it next to a solitary oak.

Locked tight.

An eerie feeling washed over her, a breeze that tickled the hairs of her neck and caused her to look upward toward the dark windows of the building. Like soulless eyes, they seemed to stare down at her, almost daring her to enter.

Being here, she had the sense that she was trespassing, that if she ever walked through these locked gates, she would be treading where she shouldn't.

So what? Could anything be worse than Cammie's murder? Pull yourself together!

A raven flapped his black wings and cawed before landing upon a gargoyle shaped like a snarling demon, and Val told herself it wasn't an omen.

Just a coincidence, imagery from too many horror movies that had terrified her as a child.

Just like the monster with hot eyes and tiny teeth who creeps through your nightmares?

She gave herself a quick mental shake, located a buzzer, and jabbed it with her finger.

Waiting, she ignored the sensation that she was being observed by hidden eyes.

No one answered.

"Oh, come on," she said under her breath, and gave the buzzer a long, hard poke. "Hey! Is anyone there?" she called.

Waiting, she felt a slight breeze as it rustled through the alley behind her, a cool breath against the back of her neck. She twisted her neck to glance behind her, certain she would find someone staring at her from the other side of the narrow backstreet.

No one.

Not even a cat slinking through the garbage bins that lined the buildings. She was completely alone, the sounds of the city distant. Squinting upward to the steep gables and turrets of the old compound, she saw no one lurking in the umbra, no hidden set of eyes following her every move. The gravel path wedged between the buildings on the other side of the gate was empty.

And yet...

Her skin crawled.

The shifting shadows from a breeze sliding through the trees caused the dappling on the ground to move, as if a ghost had passed quickly by.

Goose bumps rose on her flesh, though the temperature outside was over eighty. "Come on, come on," she said, and jabbed the button for the third time.

Within a minute, a slim African American woman in a nun's habit hurried toward the gate. Valerie watched her through the black bars.

"Can I help you?" the nun asked. Tall and regal-looking, a patient smile pinned to her lips, she peered through the wrought-iron bars. "I hope you haven't been waiting long. I'm Sister Zita."

Zita. The name rang a bell. Hadn't Cammie said she and Zita worked together, along with another nun, Sister Louise, at St. Elsinore's parish?

"I'd like to speak with Father O'Toole, and the main entrance to the cathedral is locked," Val said, offering up a little explanation, then added, "I'm Valerie Renard, Camille's sister."

"I'm so sorry for your loss," she said, but didn't move to open the gate. A glint of suspicion was evident in her dark eyes as she glanced behind Val, as if she thought there might be someone with her. "I'm not supposed to allow anyone inside. We're in mourning and—"

"So am I," Val cut in, irritated. She didn't doubt that the convent was on their own form of lockdown, that the nuns, priests, and everyone associated with the church was wary of police and reporters. Everyone within the order was probably scared for their own safety. Everyone was probably under orders to keep her mouth shut, a new twist to the vow of silence, not only because they might compromise the investigation, but also to ensure the sanctity and privacy of the parish. If Camille was right in her assessment of the mother superior, then Sister Charity would insist the convent become a fortress to avoid someone fanning the flames of scandal. "Please. I know that Father O'Toole was... close to my sister."

"I'm sorry." Again the overly patient smile along with a hint of fear. "I really don't know where Father O'Toole is. If you could leave your phone number, perhaps he will call you."

"Perhaps?" Val repeated.

"I can't speak for him."

"What about you?" Val asked, changing tacts. "You worked with her at St. Elsinore's, right?"

"Sometimes." Her face was a mask of sorrow. "I wasn't close with your sister," she said as clouds passed in front of the sun.

She was getting nowhere fast with this woman. "Fine, then, please, let me talk with Father O'Toole." Val wasn't going to be put off. She heard footsteps arriving, a heavy tread crunching the gravel.

"What's going on?" a sharp voice inquired as a large woman, dressed in a stiff habit, rounded the corner. Tall and solid, she had an imperious demeanor, with searing eyes that bored right through the lenses of her glasses. "Sister Zita?"

"I was just explaining that—"

"I'm Valerie Renard," Val interjected. She knew in a heartbeat that the authoritarian with the harsh voice was Sister Charity, the mother superior Camille had referred to as "the warden." Val met the older woman's assessing glare and noticed some raw emotion skate across her eyes, an emotion quickly disguised. "Camille's sister."

As Zita stepped aside, the older nun's eyes narrowed, as if seeking confirmation of bloodlines through resemblance as she stopped just inches shy of the gate. And there was something else in her assessment, too. Fear?

"I'd like to speak with Father O'Toole," Val pressed.

"I see." She nodded. "I'm Sister Charity, the mother superior here." Her face softened a fraction, and Sister Zita, as if hearing unspoken orders by the older nun, quietly drifted away, leaving Valerie alone with the reverend mother. Recovering slightly, Sister Charity said, "We all feel so badly about Sister Camille. My condolences. It's time to draw on your faith, child."

"And that's why I'd like to speak to Father," Val lied easily. Mother superior or not, the woman was working her.

Again that beatific, peaceful smile that didn't reach her eyes. "Right now, Father is unavailable."

"I'll wait."

"I don't think that would be a good idea."

"Why not?"

"There's a police investigation."

"Don't you think I'm aware of that?" Val tried to hide the agitation in her voice. She was tired, grief-riddled, her nerves strung tight. The older nun was really getting under her skin, though she tried not to show it. She sensed that impatience would not win points with Sister Charity. Antagonism would only make the iron-willed nun more determined. "Would you like to see my ID?"

"That's not the issue," the older nun said.

"Then what is?"

You catch more flies with honey than with vinegar, she reminded herself, a phrase Val's grandmother had told her on more than one occasion. "Look, Sister Charity, I know this is a hard time for everyone here." She reached into her purse, half expecting the older woman to stop her. When the nun didn't object, she pushed her driver's license through the wrought-iron bars for inspection.

Still scrutinizing Val as an intruder, the older nun snapped the ID from her fingers. Her eyebrows slammed together, and her lips pursed tightly as she studied the information, as if searching for signs of fraud. Did the reverend mother really think she would have a fake ID made just to get into a convent? Get real.

The seconds ticked by, but Val wasn't about to be intimidated by silence. She met the older woman's gaze without flinching or looking away.

"All right," the mother superior finally said on a sigh. "Come in." Reluctantly, she unlocked the gate and allowed Val inside. "We've been plagued by reporters and the police," she explained as she handed Val back her license. The gate clicked shut behind Val; then Sister Charity led the way along a path that cut through a garden abundant in blooms. "Come along. You can wait in my office. I have no idea where Father O'Toole is or how long he may— Oh!" The older nun stopped short near the center fountain, and Val nearly ran into her.

Charity was staring at an archway that connected to the cloister. Within the recess, a tall man was leaning forward, listening to the smaller woman standing near him.

Val's stomach dropped as she recognized the imposing, handsome visage of Father Frank O'Toole.

Bastard!

Her insides twisted, and it was all she could do to hold on to her composure as she stared at the fraud dressed in full regalia, a black cassock and stiff clerical collar.

Deep in conversation, he leaned even nearer to the young nun as he spoke, as if he didn't notice Val or the guy on the far side of the garden, a man leaning down and working with a wrench on a faucet, a coil of hose at his feet.

Nor did the young novice notice anyone but the priest. Mesmerized, the sweet-looking girl gazed up at him with adoring brown eyes. Freckles were splashed across a tiny nose, and her red hair was pulled back into a single, short plait. Smiling shyly, the girl held a single white rose.

Val thought she might be sick.

"Sister Asteria?" Sister Charity whispered loud enough to be heard.

"Oh!" The girl flinched, caught sight of the reverend mother, and then jumped back as if she'd been burned. She dropped the flower, then sucked in her breath through her teeth. White petals fell onto the bricks of the cloister floor, and a pinpoint of red bloomed on Sister Asteria's fingertip where a thorn had scratched her. "Reverend Mother, I... I didn't hear you." She started to suck her finger as the larger woman approached, Val right behind her, then thought better of it. Swallowing nervously, Asteria scooped up her wimple and veil, both of which had been left on the ground near a rosebush in the garden.

"If you'll excuse us," Sister Charity said. "Father O'Toole has a visitor."

The little nun blushed a dozen shades of red. "Of course. Yes... uh... Yes." She scurried off quickly.

Valerie watched her leave and knew deep in her gut that Sister Asteria was just another vulnerable woman caught in the allure of Father Frank—The Bastard—O'Toole.

Without comment, Sister Charity marched up to the priest, her black skirt sweeping over the fallen white rose, her shoe grinding it into the floor. "This is Valerie Renard, Sister Camille's sister. She'd like a word with you, Father."

Frank O'Toole straightened, but the sad expression didn't fade from his face as he focused on Valerie. Was it her imagination, or for just a second, did she spy a flicker of hatred in his gaze? If so, it vanished in an instant as he composed himself again.

"Valerie. Yes," he said, nodding. "I've been expecting you."

CHAPTER 16

Sliding off his jacket, Montoya sat down at his desk to answer a few phone messages and his e-mail. He'd read over the handwritten list of employees, volunteers, and residents at St. Marguerite's parish and was wishing to hell the parish had a computer. Another page listed people who had been at the convent and church the day of Camille Renard's death, but as with the computer, there were no security cameras at the parish. It was, after all, a church and a very backward one. He made a note to ask about Sister Lea, the other nun supposedly involved with Father Frank O'Toole, and was looking up St. Marguerite's parish on the Internet for background information when Inez Santiago, one of the crime scene investigators, strode inside.

Barely thirty and blessed with the body of a dancer, Santiago was a striking woman, the kind that made men watch as she walked past. Her eyes were sharp, her brown hair streaked a vibrant shade of red, her stride confident. Montoya suspected she was a wild woman after hours, but when she was working, she was all business.

"Got anything?" Montoya asked as Bentz, a couple of steps behind Santiago, wedged himself into the doorway.

"Only the basics. I already had the photos of the scene and victim e-mailed to both of you, but I thought you might want some stills, so I've printed them out." She opened the manila envelope she was carrying. "Once I get more test results, I'll send them, too. Preliminarily, it looks like there was only one crime scene, no blood or evidence of a struggle anywhere else within the convent that we found so far, and we know she went to her room around eleven."

"Nothing was found in the room?" Montoya asked.

Bentz shook his head. "Nothing that shouldn't be there, at least not that I could see. There wasn't much there, since she had only a few possessions. A few street clothes folded in a small bureau, personal items, and her shoes placed side by side on the floor of a postage-stamped-sized closet where her habits were hung. All very precise."

"Her pajamas?"

"Nightgown. Folded on a shelf in the closet."

Santiago added, "I had Marsolet get some photos of her room, too." She spread some of the snapshots out on his desk. The pictures were clear and sharp, an austere room contrasting to Camille's elaborately adorned corpse.

Montoya stared at the bloodstains on the neckline of the wedding dress—perfect, round droplets. "He wants us to concentrate on the blood," he said, pointing to the neckline. "It's there for a purpose."

"A message?" Bentz wasn't completely convinced.

"Yeah, or a distraction." Montoya eyed the unique pattern. Was the killer taunting them with a hidden message, teasing them with a clue, or trying to muddy the waters and make them look in the opposite direction? Montoya heard another set of footsteps before Brinkman, still reeking from his last cigarette and carrying a paper cup of coffee, poked his head into the office.

"That's some case you caught last night." Brinkman had been with the department for years. His houndstooth jacket was a size too small, his balding, freckled pate rimmed by hair a tad too long, but he was a smart cop. Determined. Decorated. As he himself had said often enough, he knew his shit. "You guys know your vic was knocked up, right?" His eyebrows jiggled up and down suggestively.

"We heard," Bentz said.

"Jesus, how did that happen? She's a nun, for Christ's sake." His chuckle was a rasp that ended in a coughing fit. "A little nookie in the confessional? Ya think?" He took a swallow from his cup. "What's with you guys, eh? Always with the nuns or priests."

"Father John was *not* a priest," Montoya said, referring to an earlier case where a serial killer dressed in priest's vestments had terrorized New Orleans.

Brinkman's leering grin showed he didn't acknowledge that fact, but then Brinkman never agreed with anyone. Basically, he was a prick.

"Tell us something we don't know," Bentz said, not amused or sidetracked.

"How about blood type of the fetus?"

Brinkman had their attention now.

He clarified, "B neg."

"Meaning?" Montoya asked.

"A lot." Brinkman smirked. "The mother, Camille Renard, A pos. So the nun's baby daddy gotta be negative to start with. That narrows the field."

Santiago eyed Brinkman. "Not just negative," she pointed out. "If the baby's B neg, the father's gotta be B or AB neg. Both rare types. Around two percent of the population or less, I think."

Brinkman didn't care that Santiago had one-upped him with her knowledge of biology. He was still proud of himself. "Oh, and the blood on the priest's smock or whatever the hell they're called: A positive, too."

"A cassock." Santiago was clearly annoyed. It was obvious Montoya's small office forced her to get too close to Brinkman.

Montoya didn't care. "A pos? Like the vic's? So, maybe Frank's not the father?"

Brinkman winked, beads of sweat visible on his high forehead. "Bingo! Looks like we have ourselves a winner!"

Montoya thought that over. "Wish we could speed up the DNA. Any news on the tox screens?"

Brinkman shook his head. "Too early."

"How do you know anyway?" Santiago demanded.

"Checked before I came upstairs." He grinned, loving to have the upper hand.

Montoya said, "Is that it? All you've got?"

"Not quite." Brinkman's grin widened, showing off teeth that were stained from years of coffee and cigarettes. His eyes glittered with a hint of malice. "There's a guy downstairs who wants to talk to you. Making a helluva ruckus, too."

"Who?" Montoya had a bad feeling about this. Something about Brinkman's smug attitude smelled like trouble.

"Yeah, a real rabble-rouser. He's really pissing off the receptionist. She knew you were busy but flagged me down as I started up the stairs."

"Okay, I'll bite," Montoya said, noticing that a light on his desk phone was flashing, indicating messages. "So who is it?"

"That's the hell of it." Brinkman positively beamed, enjoying the moment, stretching it out. Another warning signal. He sipped from his cup again, but his gaze was trained on Montoya. "Says his name is Cruz. Cruz Montoya."

The bad feeling that had been with Montoya all day suddenly got worse. He was already reaching for his jacket when Brinkman added, "Claims he's your brother."

Val got it.

Standing in the heat of the noonday sun in the convent's garden, she understood why women, including Camille, swooned around the priest.

Frank O'Toole was the cliché of tall, dark, and Hollywood handsome. With a self-deprecating smile, humor and intelligence sparking in his brown eyes, and a clerical collar that said "off-limits," he was the quintessential forbidden fruit.

Sexy, but safe.

Yeah, right.

"I think we need to be alone," he said to Sister Charity, who, lips tightening at the corners, hesitated, as if she were about to argue, then thought better of it.

"Of course, Father." She whisked away, causing the honeysuckle to quiver as she passed. Wide double doors clicked closed behind her.

Once there was no one else in the garden, Father O'Toole indicated a short bench under the overhang of the cloister. "We can sit here," he suggested, "or, if you'd rather have more privacy, we can go inside."

"Here's fine," she said, but didn't sit down. Instead she stood near the fountain where a sculptured angel spread her wings wide as she poured water from an urn to fill the surrounding pool. Goldfish flashed in the clear water.

Valerie and O'Toole were alone, it seemed. She gazed over the compound where her sister had lived, trying to imagine Cammie here. Though all the surrounding buildings were separate, the cathedral, smaller chapel, convent, and smaller brick buildings were connected by wide covered porches and walkways that surrounded the garden and effectively walled the parish from the city.

A few trees offered shade and privacy. Butterflies and droning bees flitted over the fragrant blooms.

It was peaceful.

Serene.

A place to meditate.

And yet, that same skin-prickling sensation that she was being silently observed stayed with her.

"So," Father O'Toole said, "how can I help you?"

This was it. "Camille told me she was involved with you." Father Frank's jaw tightened slightly, and he looked away, ostensibly to follow the path of a wren as it took flight over the garden wall.

He folded his lips over his teeth for a second, then finally said, "I have a lot to answer for."

"She told you she was pregnant?"

The priest sighed, his wide shoulders sagging as if from an invisible weight. "I...uh, we shouldn't have let things get as far as they did."

"I'll say. And you're the authority figure, the person she confided in, confessed to. You had no right—"

"I know!" he said loudly, then held up a hand to stop her from gathering steam again. "Trust me, I know what you're going to say, and I don't blame you. It was wrong and we...I knew it going in. I was the person she trusted, the man in power, the priest who had vowed celibacy." He drew in a long, soul-wrenching breath. "It... it was a terrible, terrible mistake." In that second, with the sunlight beating against his face, he looked older than he had, as if he'd aged with the admission. "But if it's any consolation to you, I want you to know that I loved her." His gaze returned to Val's, and she felt a slight stirring in the air, an undercurrent of electricity she couldn't quite name.

"And the baby?"

He closed his eyes, and pain etched his features with deep lines as he whispered, "A poor innocent."

"They both were," she said, not ready to be fooled by his act of contrition. "My sister and my niece or my nephew!" It was all she could do to keep her voice from cracking, to hold back the tears that threatened. This man, dressed in black robes and a pall of regret, was the reason Camille was dead.

"I'm so sorry. If you only knew how horrible I feel, how... guilty and sinful. I've prayed to the Father for guidance and help."

"Like you did before? With Sister Lila or Lily or...?"

She waited, saw him swallow nervously, his Adam's apple wobbling in his throat.

"Sister Lea." He closed his eyes. Sweat beaded his brow.

"What happened to her?"

He let out a shuddering sigh. "She moved away."

"To where?"

"The West Coast. The Bay Area—San Francisco, I think."

"Because of you?"

His eyes squeezed shut as if pained. "Yes."

"You just don't get it, do you? You took vows to uphold the laws of the church, and you broke them with several women."

"I do understand," he said quietly, his lips folding in on themselves. "And believe me, I've atoned for my sins. Paid for them."

"How?" She couldn't believe his egomania. "My sister is dead, Father. As is her unborn child. And you know what I think?" she demanded, close to him, her gaze pinning his. Before he could answer, she said, "I think she was a big inconvenience for you, and even though she was breaking up with you, you killed her."

"What? No!" He turned ashen in his shock.

"No?"

He held up a hand. "Murder? Are you serious? And what's this about 'breaking up'? It's not as if we were dating...." He let out another long, pained sigh. "I am truly sorry about Sister Camille, and, yes, it's true we were involved, but I didn't kill her. I couldn't... wouldn't... No. Are you serious?" His jaw slackened in disbelief.

"Deadly." She pushed, her grief throbbing through her. "How would it look for a priest of your stature to admit to an affair, to fathering a child?"

"Not good, but—"

"You'd lose everything. Stripped of your priesthood. Probably ex-communicated, right? Tossed out on the street like so much garbage!"

Anger flashed in his pitch-dark eyes, and the warmth of the garden seemed to drop ten degrees. "I didn't murder her," he said again, his teeth set, his blade-thin lips barely moving. Rage flushed his skin, and to her surprise, he grabbed her arm and leaned close to whisper, "I loved her. I swear to you and to the Holy Father, I would never hurt her. Never!" His sincerity was nearly convincing. Nearly. "On my life, Valerie, I'm telling you I would never have hurt her or the child." His gaze was intense. Fervid. The hand gripping her forearm clenching. "I loved her."

"Like you love Sister Asteria?"

"What?" His jaw slackened. "You think that I—"

"Truthfully, I don't know what to think, but my sister was in love with you and now she's dead. Another woman, Sister Lea, left because of you."

He drew in a long breath. Color began to return to his face.

"And just now I saw how that other girl was looking up at you, idolizing you, as if you couldn't possibly do her any harm."

"No. Sister Asteria and I..." He dropped her arm and closed his eyes for a second, slowly shaking his head. "I am so sorry," he said. "So very, very sorry."

"So am I."

When he opened his eyes again, he touched her gently on the shoulder. "It's not what you think, Valerie," he said enigmatically. "Not at all."

"You don't know what I think." She felt it again, that eerie sensation that she was being observed, that secretive, hidden eyes were watching her every move.

Surreptitiously, Val glanced up to the bell tower. Was someone lurking there? Or straining to see through the translucent panels in the stained glass of the chapel? Or hiding in the deep recesses of the archways opening to this private garden?

A warning breeze toyed with the hairs on the back of her neck, and for a split second, the image in her nightmares flashed before her eyes.

Dark.

Deadly.

"Are you all right?" he asked, his voice low.

No. She would never be all right.

"I–I'm fine."

Did she really think this man could have killed the woman he swore so fervently to love? Was he telling the truth? Or was she, like so many foolish women before her, beginning to trust this very mortal man dressed in priest's robes?

Slowly, she pulled her shoulder from his grip, but the action only awakened more remorse from him. Again he swore to her, "Trust me, Valerie, I would never harm Camille. Never."

"If not you, Father, then who?"

"I don't know."

Dear God, had she made a horrible mistake?

The creak of a gate on rusted hinges prompted Val to look up sharply. In a cloud of black robes, the reverend mother sped along a path that cut through blossoming daylilies and hyacinth.

Sister Charity's wide face was set in a stern expression of displeasure, her rosary beads clicking with her strides as she approached again. "Ms. Renard?" she said, her voice clipped, no breath of familiarity in it.

Val turned to her.

"Excuse me for interrupting, but your husband wants to see you."

CHAPTER 17

Cruz Montoya had never been known for his patience.
For his quick wit, maybe.

His good looks, for sure.

And his ability to slide out of trouble when he was in the middle of it—certainly.

But not patience. And right now, standing in the vestibule of the police station, a fine-looking, angry receptionist giving him the evil eye and a beefy desk sergeant with a bad buzz cut blocking entrance to the stairway and elevator leading to the second floor, Cruz was antsy. He didn't like crowds, hated being in a crush of humanity, and couldn't avoid it here. Officers, witnesses, suspects, newspeople, all coming and going, being herded through—that was shit he couldn't deal with. And he'd never been a fan of the police, didn't take kindly to authority, and felt claustrophobic in confined spaces.

"He's comin' down," the big desk sergeant told him, glancing to the next person approaching the desk, an elderly man leaning heavily on a cane. "Wait here."

Both the desk sergeant and the receptionist had mentioned Cruz's resemblance to Diego, whom they called "the detective" or "Montoya," but that's as far as it had gone. His features, so like his brother's, hadn't been the green light that had allowed him access to Robbery/Homicide.

Cruz was about to call his mother for Diego's private cell number when his brother came down the stairs, shoes ringing on the steps. Diego, a few years older, was a couple of inches shorter than Cruz, more compact, but tough as nails. His goatee was dark, an earring glittering in one ear. Of everyone in the family, Diego showed some features of the Native American ancestor who had left his mark way back in the very Hispanic family tree. Diego hadn't changed too much since the last time they'd seen each other, and he still wore his trademark black leather jacket, though it was the beginning of summer in New Orleans. Hot and humid outside.

"Hey!" Diego yelled at the desk sergeant as he jockeyed around an officer moving an impossibly thin guy through a group of people at the base of the stairs. "It's okay. I'll vouch for this son of a bitch."

With a half-grin, the beefy desk sergeant waved Cruz past and the pissy-looking receptionist didn't even glance up. She had her hands full dealing with a skinny woman with bad teeth and straggly hair who kept demanding to see "her man." Probably a guy in custody. No surprise there.

"Diego!" Cruz called him by the name his brother had used in high school.

They gave each other a quick man hug, then let go.

"Diego?" the burly sergeant mouthed, his foul mood turning to amusement. "Isn't that the real name of Zorro? So where's the mask and cape?" He made a *Z* in the air with an invisible sword.

"Or the Hispanic kid in that TV show for toddlers," another voice chirped. *"Run Diego Run."*

"It's *Go Diego Go!*" another woman added. "I should know. I've got a two-year-old. Think I've seen every episode at least five times."

"You don't know what you started," Montoya muttered to Cruz. "I go by—"

"Yeah, *Detective*, I know. I heard." Cruz walked with him up the stairs. "I practically had to sell my firstborn to get to you."

"You don't have a firstborn."

"Not that I know of," he admitted. "So what is this place? A police station or a goddamned country club? Are you here to serve the people?"

Diego snorted. "Big case goin' on."

"I heard." Cruz nodded. "The nun."

Diego slid him a glance. "You don't recognize the name?"

"Didn't hear a name. You know, just the company line about 'unidentified until next of kin has been notified.'"

"Oh." Diego hesitated.

"What?"

Frowning, he checked his watch. "How 'bout I buy you lunch?"

Lunch? What the hell? "How about you tell the yahoo of a beat cop to give me my bike back?"

"You got it towed?"

"Hell, yeah, I did. Some screwup with the title. Cops seem to think it's stolen. I bought it from a guy in Oregon last month. Clean title. But I don't have the papers, and the tags expired."

"That's pretty easy to clear up."

"Tell that to Officer Big Ass, I mean Burgess," Cruz said sourly, thinking of the motorcycle cop who'd pulled him over. At least two-fifty, with a dark helmet and bad attitude, he'd been in Cruz's grill from the get-go.

"Man, you must've really pissed him off."

Cruz rubbed the back of his neck. "Yeah, maybe."

"Speeding?"

Cruz lifted a shoulder. "Sixty-seven in a forty-five."

"And then you gave the cop lip. Not smart, bro." Diego had the gall to grin. "You're in the Big Easy now, aren't ya? And now you need my help."

"That's why I'm here."

"And I thought you just missed me."

"Yeah, right." Cruz glared at him. "Y'know, I was gonna look you up, see that new son of yours, but—"

"You found trouble first." Montoya shook his head, his black hair gleaming under the fluorescent lights. "Some things never change."

Slade had followed her? To St. Marguerite's? Seriously? Val's heart nose-dived. "He's here?"

"In the vestibule."

Great. "Thanks."

"He's waiting."

Let him wait. "I understand."

Obviously the reverend mother wasn't about to be dismissed again, especially not by someone not associated with the church.

"Ms. Renard—"

"Please, call me Val."

"Yes, Valerie, then, I would appreciate you dealing with Mr. Houston. I asked him to wait, and he's not very happy about it." Again the gate scraped open. "He isn't—" The noise caused Sister Charity to turn and press her hands to her chest. "Oh, my!"

Val followed her gaze to Slade, who stepped behind another nun as she made her way through the garden. His cowboy boots crunched on the pebbles of the path, and he seemed as out of place as a mustang in the middle of the sea.

In worn jeans and a shirt with the sleeves pushed over his forearms, he startled a mockingbird from a branch of the crepe myrtle.

Sister Charity's mouth compressed even further, bristling at the visitor's insubordination.

Father O'Toole stiffened, his jaw set as he, too, eyed the interloper.

However, the nun guiding Slade through the flowers and shrubs smiled beatifically. Tall, with a bit of a hitch to her stride, she wore an old-fashioned habit, including a full headdress. Her face was unlined, her eyes a deep shade of blue. Had Val met her earlier? She seemed familiar... but then again, no. "I'm sorry to interrupt," she said, "but Mr. Houston was very insistent."

The reverend mother was perturbed. "I was handling this, Sister Devota."

Devota's lips pinched a bit at the rebuke. "I'm sorry, Reverend Mother—"

"It wasn't her fault," Slade said, his eyes centering on the mother superior. "I was following you, and she just caught up with me."

"And opened the gate." Charity shook her head. "If you'll leave us, Sister Devota," she said to the tall woman, who looked stricken at her tone.

"Of course," Devota whispered, and bustled off, head down, as if she couldn't wait to make her way through the doors of the convent.

Once the doors clanged shut, Charity turned her frosty glare to Slade. "I asked you to wait, Mr. Houston."

"Yes, ma'am." Slade's bad-boy grin slid from one side of his mouth to the other. "But then waiting isn't something I do well."

Sister Charity wasn't fooled, nor charmed in the least. To Val, she said, "I'm sorry for your loss. Sincerely sorry. But we, too, have suffered. We need time to sort things out and pull ourselves together. It would be most helpful, in this time of tragedy, if we all had some privacy."

"I don't think the police will allow that," Val said. "My sister was murdered, Sister Charity. There's a homicide investigation going on."

"Understandably," Father O'Toole interjected. "And we're cooperating fully."

The mother superior wasn't budging. "Be that as it may, you are not an investigator, Ms. Renard. What we all need now is some time for spiritual healing."

"Sister," O'Toole admonished to the mother superior, and she stiffened slightly.

Slade said, "What we need now is the truth."

Charity's smile was weak. "And that comes only through the grace of our Lord."

"The same guy who talks about 'an eye for an eye' and 'thou shalt not kill'? That guy?" Slade demanded.

"There is no need for this," Father O'Toole said, but not before the big nun bristled, rustling the fabric of her habit, the corners of her lips tightening ever so slightly. "I hardly think of the blessed Father as a 'guy.'"

"And I'm not talking about 'the truth' in some kind of spiritual revelation," Slade pressed as a plumber packed up loops of a hose and disappeared under an archway. The double doors from the back of the cathedral opened, and two nuns, dressed in full habits, walked through the garden.

A heavy-set nun hummed softly, while the other, thin and pale, scowled behind thick glasses.

"Sister Louise!" the mother superior snapped.

Both women stopped short near the fountain. As water splashed, the humming abruptly stopped. "Yes, Reverend Mother?" the big nun asked, her cheeks flaming in embarrassment.

"You and Sister Maura need to grant us some privacy."

"I...we...didn't know that anyone was here..." Louise glanced at the small group of people as if seeing them for the first time. She looked positively stricken. "Oh, yes. I'm so sorry. Of course."

"Wait!" Val sidestepped Sister Charity. "You're Sister Louise," she said to the woman who had been humming. "You...you've worked with my sister."

"I'm sorry," Louise said, casting a worried glance at the mother superior. "I don't know what you're talking about."

"I'm Camille's sister. Valerie." She implored the nun with her eyes. "I'd like to talk to you."

Again, Louise looked over Val's shoulder. "I don't know."

Sister Maura seemed to retract into her wimple, as if to hide behind the reddish curls poking out of the edge.

"She spent time at St. Elsinore's."

"At the orphanage, yes. She liked working with children. Like me," Sister Louise said. "We were both sad that it's going to be closed. And Sister Camille, she was all about finding her birth parents."

"Wait. What?" Val said, stunned. "But she knows...knew who our biological parents were."

Louise caught a look from the mother superior. "I'm sorry. I must've been mistaken. I thought she was searching for her roots since she'd been adopted out of St. Elsinore's." Louise was stepping backward, toward the convent. "I was wrong."

Val watched as they hurried through an open archway leading to the tall building on the opposite side of the garden from the cathedral, probably the nun's quarters. As she reached the shadows, Sister Maura glanced back over her shoulder but didn't break stride; then she disappeared behind her larger companion.

Suddenly Val wondered if she'd known her sister at all. There were so many contradictions, so many things she didn't know or understand about her sister, who had never, as far as Val could remember, really enjoyed children. And yet she'd worked with them at an orphanage and gotten pregnant herself. And they knew who their natural parents were. There was no mystery there.

"What's going on here?" she said, turning to the reverend mother.

"Nothing, I assure you." Again the fragile grin. "Camille was just a very, very confused young woman."

Something was wrong here. The bells tolled loudly, ringing through the garden, and the nun who had escorted her into the garden earlier, Sister Zita, appeared.

"I'm sorry, reverend mother, but you have an appointment," Zita reminded her, almost as if on cue.

"If you'll excuse us," Sister Charity said. "We're late."

"Wait a second. I'd like to speak to some of my sister's friends and coworkers. I know she was close to Sister Lucia."

"I'll see what I can do," the mother superior said with a glacial smile.

"I do need to be at the hospital," Frank said.

Seeing that she'd run up against a brick wall, Val gave up. There was nothing more she could do here.

Today. She headed out of the garden with more questions than she had answers. She was irritated by the reverend mother, simmering with resentment at Father Frank, and still ticked at Slade for following her here.

With Slade only a step behind her, she reached the gate, which, of course, was locked. As if this were some damned prison.

"I'll get that," Sister Zita said quickly. Val turned to see Slade, followed by the nun. "Sorry about the reverend mother," Zita said as she extracted a key from a deep pocket of her habit and inserted it in the gate. "Everyone here is just so upset." She swung the wrought-iron bars open and met Val's gaze. "I'm sorry for your loss."

"Thanks," Val said, her throat growing thick. She could handle herself in anger, but kindness brought out her need to break down. Even when it came from a woman whose voice was as devoid of emotion as her eyes.

The gate clicked shut behind them.

Val took one last glance through the bars to the garden, but found it empty.

Yet, as she looked at the interior of the convent one last time, she felt that same eerie sensation that had plagued her earlier. Her eyes lifted to the buildings that rimmed the cloister, catching a flicker of movement on an upper balcony. Someone lingered in the doorway, a blurry figure dressed in black that melted backward into the shadows.

The hairs on the back of her neck lifted.

She blinked.

And all was still on the balcony. Strange...

She reminded herself this was a convent, a holy place. And yet, that eerie sense that a predator was watching...She shoved her wayward thoughts aside, told herself she was just imagining things, that she was spooked because of Camille's murder.

CHAPTER 18

Obviously disbelieving, Cruz glared at his older brother. "Lucia Costa is a nun at St. Marguerite's?" he repeated incredulously. They were seated at a booth in a small restaurant not far from the police station, Cruz on one side of the table, Montoya on the other. The place was clean enough with a variety of salads and sliced, preserved meats on display behind the windows of a long counter. The smell of an overused fryer permeated the air, the odor tossed around by a few slow-moving overhead fans. "She's here"—Cruz pointed at the tabletop with one finger—"in New Orleans?"

"Uh-huh." As Montoya took a bite of his po'boy, his gaze skated from his brother to the glass door of the establishment. People passed underneath the striped awnings, moving slowly in the afternoon heat.

"That's a pisser."

"If you say so."

Cruz had always been a wild card, Montoya thought, then decided that wasn't as strange as it sounded. All his siblings, sisters and brothers, had been known to raise their share of hell while growing up.

Over six feet, Cruz had Montoya by a couple of inches and was muscular rather than lean. His black hair brushed the collar of his jean jacket, and his eyes, dark as night, missed nothing. He'd spent a few years in the service after high school, then attended college while tending bar and driving trucks. Somewhere in the mix, he'd gotten a tattoo that was visible on his forearm and a license to be a PI. "Jack-of-all-trades, master of none," he'd always quipped. With thick eyebrows and a nose that had been broken more than once, he'd never given up his bad-ass appearance or, it seemed now, attitude.

"You know, I looked for her. Like crazy. Right after the accident. Then things got weird with her father, and I gave it up. Looking down the barrel of a shotgun can have that effect on you."

"Whoa, slow down. Start at the beginning."

Cruz snorted and wiped his upper lip and mustache with a napkin. "So we were dating. She was still in high school and I'd just graduated. You were already at the junior college."

"That much I remember."

"I'd signed up for the air force, but I had a couple of weeks before I went in, so I was basically hanging out, doing nothing, driving the folks crazy. Trying to stay out of trouble."

"And failing."

"Yeah, well... anyway, we were out one night, Lucia and me. I was driving—maybe too fast."

"Maybe?"

"Hell, I was, what, eighteen? I was probably thinking about how I could get into Lucia's pants, not paying as much attention as I should have, and a damned deer leaped over the fence and right into the middle of the road. It froze there, in the fog. Shit, I tried to avoid it. Yanked on the wheel, and the front tire hit gravel."

Montoya remembered this part of the story. When Cruz had swerved to avoid hitting the doe, the car had skidded off the road, spinning through the wire fence and into a cypress tree, the passenger side taking the hit. The side door had been crumpled, window shattering.

"God, it was horrible." Cruz's dark eyes softened. "She was screaming and screaming and then... nothing."

She'd hit her head, Montoya remembered. Cruz had suffered a broken wrist that delayed his entry to the air force, along with a few cuts from the glass of the shattered windshield. A tiny scar near his left eye was evidence of the crash.

Lucia hadn't been so lucky, as a branch of the cypress had slammed into the side of her head. Montoya couldn't remember many more details, just that she had been in a coma but had survived.

"You went to the hospital with her, right?"

"Yeah, until her old man barred me from seeing her. He convinced the hospital staff that I should be persona non grata and that he'd sue the hospital if I was allowed near her." Cruz's lips tightened. "Phillip Costa was fuckin' nuts—you know that, right? Came at me with a damned shotgun." He took a long swallow of his beer. "Christ, man, it was a mess. I tried to see her before I went into the service. I'd heard from a friend that she'd come out of the coma. But she disappeared." He snapped his fingers. "Just like that."

"Thought you were supposed to be a hotshot investigator."

"Not back then. This was when I was just out of high school and didn't know jack shit about what I was going to do with my life. And she flat out disappeared—seemed to fall off the face of the earth. Her old man did a good job of hiding her, and I didn't know how to find her. I think Mr. Costa was relieved when I finally got sent off to basic training."

"I'm sure he was glad to get the daughter away from a hell-raiser like you."

"Yeah, but the way he made her disappear..." His eyes narrowed on his bottle, but, Montoya guessed, he wasn't seeing the amber glass but a place beyond, far in the distant past. "Man, it was strange. Real strange." Another pull on his beer. "You know, I always wondered where she'd ended up, but a nun?" He shook his head, a contemplative smile twisting his lips. "Never figured that."

The door to the restaurant opened, and a couple of men took a booth nearby. They were loud, talking and laughing about the latest baseball scores.

Out of habit, Montoya gave the newcomers a quick once-over. The usual sordid lunch crowd here—gold-capped teeth, shabby graying beards, and baseball caps.

"You know," Cruz admitted, casting a glance at the two men, then dismissing them. "I thought she might be dead."

"Very much alive."

"That would've been nice to know." He finished his beer. "Real nice." Scowling, he pushed aside his basket of remaining sandwich and fries.

"And you never tried to look her up?"

"Not after I went into the air force. What would have been the point?"

"Curiosity?"

"By that time, it was water under the bridge. Ancient history. I'd moved on. And the truth of it is that Lucia, she was always a little weird." Cruz signaled the waitress for another beer. "I mean, she was good-lookin', hot and all that, but...there was something about her that seemed off. It was almost as if she could read my mind. It freaked me out."

"You mean she had ESP?"

"Whatever you want to call it; she'd get these weird 'feelings.'"

Montoya understood. Bentz's wife, Olivia, had a touch of it, had helped Bentz solve a case years before.

"And then in the hospital, when I was still allowed to see her and she was lying there, you know, in the coma. Her eyes opened for just a second and she stared at me. Her mouth moved, but she didn't talk, just tried to form words. I'm not sure, but I think she was saying 'danger.'" Cruz picked at the label of his beer bottle just as the waitress plopped another long-necked Lone Star on the table in front of him.

"Anything else?" she asked without an ounce of enthusiasm.

Montoya shook his head and frowned, and she plodded to the next table.

"She woke up to say 'danger'?" Montoya asked.

Cruz's eyebrows slammed together. "Maybe I was imagining it all." He picked up the full bottle. "Who knows?"

"Yeah, who?"

"More importantly, who cares?" After taking a long swallow, he set the bottle down and folded his arms over the table. "So now that we're done tripping down memory lane, how about you find a way to get me my bike back?"

* * *

The last thing Val wanted to deal with was her husband. "You're out of line, following me around," she said as they crossed the shaded lawn of the cathedral. "You shouldn't have come here."

"Yeah, well, that makes two of us."

When she tried to open the door, he slammed it shut with a big hand, almost imprisoning her with his body. "What're you thinking, Val?" he demanded.

She squirmed around to find him staring down at her with eyes she'd once found so disturbingly sexy, a blue that seemed to shift with his moods. "I needed to talk with O'Toole."

"It's a matter for the police. You were a cop, Val. You know that. Leave it to the professionals." His face was only inches from hers. Too damned close. Her heart galloped in her chest, her mind wandering to forbidden places. As if he felt it, too, that sudden physical awareness, he stepped away and glanced back at the cathedral where two nuns, dressed in habits, wimples, and veils, hurried around the corner. "What happened to nuns wearing regular clothes?" he wondered aloud. "I thought all the black and white getup was over."

"I think it's up to each order or diocese or whatever, maybe each parish. I don't really know. I gave up on the church a long time ago." She remembered the orphanage, the dark hallways, the grief and loneliness, then snapped her mind shut from the memories that crept through her consciousness when she wasn't expecting them, dark, disturbing images that cut painfully.

"So this place, St. Marguerite's, can be as antiquated as it wants?"

"I'm sure the archdiocese has something to say about it. Camille told me that this is the way it's always been at St. Marguerite's, and most of the nuns, especially that warm and fuzzy mother superior, prefer it that way. What she says goes."

Slade's eyes narrowed. "Throwback to another century, if you ask me."

"No one did," she reminded him, and added, "And, for the record, I don't appreciate being followed."

A smile stretched across his beard-stubbled jaw. "I figured."

"Really, Slade, you had no business tailing me here, following me inside and telling them"—she nodded toward the cathedral as a bicyclist rode past—"that we're married."

"We are."

"Not for long."

"Marriage is something the Catholic Church takes very seriously. I figured it would open some doors and it did."

"Well, they're closed now," Val observed, glancing back at the main doors of the cathedral with the yellow crime scene tape fluttering in the same breeze that was causing the Spanish moss in the gnarled oaks guarding the place to shift and sway. "The hatches battened down tight."

"Makes you wonder what secrets the old cathedral hides."

"Amen," she said, though she didn't blame anyone at St. Marguerite's other than Frank O'Toole.

He snorted, a humorless laugh. "You going back to the inn?"

"Not right away." She shook her head as she slid into her car's sweltering interior. "I have to drop some things off at the police station." She pulled the door shut and switched on the ignition. The old engine sputtered, then caught. To make certain he understood, she rolled down the window. "I really don't need an escort."

He hesitated, then gave a sharp nod. "Fair enough. I'll see you at home."

Home? "Oh, God, Slade, don't you have better things to do?" she asked, unable to stop needling him a little as the air-conditioning kicked in, blowing warm air throughout the car. "Isn't there a steer to brand, a doggie to round up, or some fence to mend?"

His grin stretched wide, white teeth flashing against his tanned skin. "Well, darlin', that's exactly what I'm doin', now, isn't it? Just here to mend fences with my wife."

"Save me," she said, finding a pair of sunglasses in the console and slipping them onto her nose. "You know, you're on sacred ground here, Cowboy. You'd better watch how much b.s. you're peddling. God might not like it and strike you down right where you stand!"

The minute the words were over her tongue, she thought of Camille's body, positioned at the altar, her young life cut down.

"I gotta go," she said. Before he could engage her another second, she shoved the car into gear. As he stepped away, she pulled into the empty street, leaving him standing beneath one of the trees that shaded the cracked asphalt.

Slim-hipped with his old jeans riding low, his forearms tanned from the sun, he looked every bit the Texas rancher he was.

And you're still in love with him, that horrid little voice in her head nagged.

"No way," she said aloud.

Loving Slade Houston was borderline crazy after what he'd done. She wouldn't, couldn't, go there.

CHAPTER 19

"So tell me again what your problem is with Slade?" Freya suggested as she bent over the stove, pulling freshly made blond brownies from the oven. The kitchen smelled like heaven with the scent of warm vanilla wafting through. Val's stomach gurgled, reminding her she hadn't eaten anything all day.

She found a glass and dropped some ice cubes from the freezer into it before finding the pitcher of lemonade in the refrigerator. "Can I get you some?" she asked Freya, who shook her head, then motioned to the counter where a large opaque cup sat near the window.

"Already got iced coffee." She set the pan of blondies on the top of the stovetop's iron grate. "And you're avoiding the issue. I asked about Slade."

"Yeah, I know. I've got lots of problems with Slade," she admitted. "Too many to count."

"Hmmm."

The back door was open, and through the screen door, Val could see the lump of fur that was Bo, sitting quietly on the porch, looking inside the kitchen. So intent was he that he didn't notice the stray cat slinking across the yard. Merlin, a black tom with a long tail, disappeared around the hedge.

"You're losing your edge," Val confided in the dog. At the

sound of Val's voice, he cocked his head and hoisted himself to a sitting position for a better view.

"I see you," she said, smiling.

God, she missed the old hound.

He thumped his tail on the painted floorboards as she walked outside, the screen door slapping loudly behind her. "You're a good guy," she admitted, scratching the hound behind his ears. "You know that, don't you?"

From inside the house, Freya said, "He misses you."

"I suppose."

"I wasn't talking about the dog."

"Oh. Slade?" She shook her head. "I doubt it." Val couldn't imagine Slade missing anyone, especially not a suspicious wife who was intent on divorcing him.

"I know the signs." Freya appeared at the other side of the screen, her oversized cup in hand.

"This from a woman who's had two husbands."

"And an extra fiancé."

"And a live-in boyfriend."

"Don't remind me." She walked outside and hoisted herself onto the railing. "But I know what I know, and I see how that guy looks at you."

"Enough! I get it, okay?" Val placed her cold glass to her forehead to fight the headache that was beginning to form. She closed her eyes, blocking out Freya, Slade, and the whole damned world for just a few minutes. "Didn't we have an agreement when I moved in that we wouldn't put our noses in each other's love lives?"

No answer.

"Freya?" Val prodded. "I distinctly remember—"

"Okay, okay, I'm just sayin'—"

"I know what you're saying, and I hear you." Opening her eyes, she sighed, then took a long sip from her glass.

"Want a vanilla brownie?"

"In the worst way. You?"

"Absolutely. I'll be right back, and you can tell me what happened this morning." She hopped off the rail and walked inside while Val, drained, thought about what she'd accomplished. It all added up to a great big zero. Father Frank had given her nothing, the mother superior hadn't wanted to talk, and she'd missed Detective Montoya when she'd left the e-mail with his partner, who had been mum on the subject of Camille. And then there was Slade.... Oh, hell, how did she even begin to deal with him?

The pain and humiliation she'd felt two years ago came back in a wild rush with its own brand of familiar heartache. Now, looking back, she realized it had been a matter of "he said/she said," and she'd trusted her sister that Slade had not just come on to her, but also had actually, at Christmastime, slipped into her room and her bed. According to Camille, "nothing had really happened," but she'd said it so hesitantly, Val had doubted it. Seeds of suspicion had been planted and had quickly taken root. Slade had always liked Camille, and they had flirted. Oh, God, what was the point? It was over now. She was divorcing her husband and her sister was dead. Twisting her glass in her hands, watching the ice cubes dance, she wondered if she'd been too harsh on her sister, too rash with her husband, too damned ready to believe the worst.

The cop in you.

Yeah, well, that part of her life was over, too. She'd quit being a detective when she'd left Texas. At least officially. Until now.

Old habits die hard. Especially when your own sister is murdered.

Frank O'Toole had to be the killer.

Who else?

Her gut instinct told her to look no further.

Her head reminded her to see past the obvious.

She thought of her sister. Cammie had been troubled, no doubt about it. Though she hadn't heard all the details of her sister's death, she'd been told enough to convince her that Camille's murder hadn't been a random act. The bridal gown—had that been Cammie's idea? Had someone else dressed her? Someone close to her? Her nightclothes had been in her room. Everything she knew about her sister's murder made her think that someone close to Cammie had killed her.

She just needed to figure out who and prove it. Fast. Hours were ticking by, and it was a known fact that if a homicide wasn't solved in the first forty-eight hours after commission, the chances of solving the case were cut in half.

Which meant it was time to pin down O'Toole. Though she had almost believed the priest when he'd said he'd been in love with Camille, she still felt as if he could have killed her.

An act of passion.

There had been signs of a struggle, the cops had told her, but they'd said nothing else about the crime. She knew from her own experience that the police withheld evidence to weed out the real killer, the only person who would have intimate knowledge of the crime. All she knew was Camille had been strangled in the chapel around midnight, nothing more. She still felt O'Toole was the most likely suspect for the crime, but she needed concrete evidence to tie him to it.

Or prove him innocent.

Was it possible?

If so, then who would hate her so badly to kill her?

Let the police handle it. Isn't that your motto? When she was with the sheriff's department, she'd hated it when novices got involved in her investigations.

But that was different. She wasn't a novice, not by a long shot. She had investigative experience, and now her sister was the victim. She couldn't sit around and wait for the likes of Montoya and Bentz to plod through their job.

No, Val had to take charge.

"I say fresh-baked goodies can cure just about anything," Freya called through the screen door as she appeared with a small plate of blondies, which she set on the short table beside her chair.

Although Val appreciated the gesture, both women knew there was no way to soothe the loss of a sister, the end of a life. And when murder was involved . . .

Freya bit into a square and declared, "Oooh. Maybe my best batch ever."

"Modest, aren't you?" Val took a bite of the warm confection, and immediately bits of chocolate melted in her mouth, pecans crunching between her teeth. Bo, with his big, sad eyes, began to drool.

"Here ya go," Freya said, and reached into her pocket for a dog biscuit, which Bo licked with an obvious lack of enthusiasm.

It was so like Freya to have something to appease everyone. "So now, Val, all old, ridiculous promises aside, let's hear it. Why the hell is it that you think the hunk you're married to is evil incarnate?"

A few blocks off the river at a watering hole in the French Quarter, Slade worked on his second beer. He'd spent some time familiarizing himself with the city, figuring it was good to avoid the bed-and-breakfast for a few hours and give Val some space after their last confrontation at the cathedral.

He'd even driven as far away as St. Elsinore's, the parish on the other side of the bridge that spanned Lake Pontchartrain. Built of stucco, its once-white exterior had darkened from years of grime. Giant willow trees draped over the walls guarding the orphanage, convent, and parochial school attached to the church. Not an inviting place, it looked deserted, closed for the day.

But there had been one door left ajar for a maintenance man, and Slade had slipped into the cool, dark interior and walked the mostly empty hallways, acquainting himself with the layout. A few doors were locked, of course, and he avoided areas where he heard voices, but he did get a general feel for the place, had taken note of the office for the parish and the orphanage. He'd seen evidence of children, a few toys and artwork on the cracked plaster walls. He'd seen a flyer taped to the windows announcing a charity auction and the fact that the building was about to be condemned, the orphanage moved. The disrepair was palpable—cracks in the walls, stains near the ceiling, the smell of mold beneath the stringent odor of disinfectant. Like St. Marguerite's, St. Elsinore's appeared antiquated and dark, in its death throes.

He'd climbed the creaking stairs to the second floor, then hurried down an outdoor stairwell, studied the sorry playground and layout of rooms, the connections between the buildings. He'd even tried a few locked doors but hadn't taken the time to try and break any dead bolts.

At least not yet.

He hadn't stayed at St. Elsinore's long, hadn't wanted to be confronted and forced to answer awkward questions about why he was there. He really couldn't explain it. Yes, there was a need for a glimpse of the crumbling building and grounds, the place where

Valerie and Camille had lived for a short while before the Renards had adopted them, but there was more to it than that. Camille had worked at St. Elsinore's recently, had taken a job with the children in the orphanage, a place Val had rarely spoken of.

What was the deal with that?

After the trek across Lake Pontchartrain to St. Elsinore's, Slade had returned to the city and driven straight to St. Marguerite's, clocking the miles and time. He couldn't put his finger on it, but he had a gut feeling that whatever Camille had been doing at St. Elsinore's had been important. What had the big nun who'd worked with her—Louise—said? That Camille liked to work with kids? That she'd been searching for her roots?

When she supposedly knew all about her life.

Val had been stunned.

Worth looking into.

Once he'd checked the mileage to St. Marguerite's, he'd driven through other parts of New Orleans, some still scarred and abandoned, as empty as an evacuated war zone, the resulting destruction of Hurricane Katrina years before.

He'd taken the time to familiarize himself with the city where his wife had grown up and now called home.

That thought stung like a bitch, and he wondered, in light of Camille's murder, if Val would ever return to his ranch near Bad Luck.

Probably not.

Once he was finished with his tour, he'd wound up here in the Plug Nickel, a honky-tonk that was about as glamorous as its name.

The bartender swabbed down the scarred bar, revealing tattoos that seemed to be inked on every inch of her exposed skin. Her overprocessed hair was piled high on her head and tied with a red scarf. A tank top and shorts gave ample view of the body art that was scrolled on her arms, legs, and neck. So far, the spiderweb that climbed up her throat hadn't reached her face.

A good thing, in his estimation.

"You need another?" she asked, offering him a bright smile as she replaced his nearly empty bowl of salty Chex Mix with a full one.

"Still workin' on this one."

"Just let me know." She took a drag on her cigarette, then

jabbed the filter tip out in an ashtray near the soda gun and moved down the bar to wait on other customers. Two women in their twenties laughed over a couple of glasses of wine. Farther down, another single guy nursed a scotch while surreptitiously watching the female patrons' reflection in the mirror that ran along the wall behind the bar.

Bottles glistened like jewels in the soft light, and pool balls clicked as a couple of guys in jeans and T-shirts played a game of Nine Ball at one of the two pool tables.

A television mounted high in the corner had been tuned to a local station. The five-o'clock news was just airing the big story: nun murdered at St. Marguerite's.

Oh, hell.

Every muscle in his body tensed.

The volume on the television was set too low to hear much over the conversation in the bar, but Slade caught the drift. A male reporter stood in front of the cathedral, explaining details of the crime. A close-up of the crime scene tape around the doors of St. Marguerite's gave way to an image of Camille. In the photograph, she wasn't dressed as a nun. It was a photo Slade recognized, a posed senior portrait, which was over five years old. The same photo Valerie had displayed on the mantel at the ranch when they'd lived there together.

Slade's jaw slid to the side as the screen changed to a series of black-and-white photos of nuns as the reporter quickly went through some of the history of St. Marguerite's.

The barkeep saw him watching the screen.

"A helluva thing," she said, scooping ice into three empty glasses, the small cubes rattling loudly. "Who in their right mind would want to kill a nun?" She poured healthy shots of vodka over the ice. "I mean, really."

"No right mind was involved," the single guy at the end of the bar interjected, then added, "She sure doesn't look like any of the nuns I had in grade school." He smiled, hoping to engage the women sitting near him.

They ignored him, as well as the TV.

Slade didn't say anything. That Camille was beautiful wasn't an issue in her death.

Though it had been part of her undoing in life.

In his mind's eye, he saw her again as he had the last time he'd been with her—long, perfect neck, dark hair falling in thick, coiling waves that skimmed the tops of her naked breasts—full, round, with large pink nipples standing at attention, begging for the touch of his fingers and tongue.

A long, knotted rope of pearls had fallen between those breasts, and the electric blue of her eyes had sizzled with the promise of an erotica that had teased at his mind. That girl had opened doors to dark alleys that should have stayed closed forever.

It had been Christmas Eve, rain battering the windows, the East Texas wind blowing cold. With candles lit and the sound of a choir singing "*O Holy Night*" whispering through the ranch house, Camille had been set on seduction.

And Armageddon had ensued.

Damn it all to hell.

Now the news story changed, and Slade drained his beer. He left some cash on the bar and, with a nod to the tattooed barkeep, strode outside to the heat of late afternoon.

The image of Camille followed him outside, and though he tried to shake it, she hung close, as she had in life. A shimmering ghost. Death had only exacerbated the feeling that she was nearby, that she would never let him be.

Slade walked a few blocks toward the river, striding with purpose. He hardly noticed the people he passed, teenagers in groups, each plugged into an iPod or talking on a cell phone; a jogger, sweating and intent on getting in her predusk workout; two homeless men with beards, backpacks, and watch caps, asking for spare change. Local color was lost on him; his mind was anywhere but here.

The air was heavy, the sultry heat that pressed against his skin thicker than what he was used to in the hill country he called home.

At the top of a levee, he paused to watch ships and boats churn up the murky water of the wide, muddy Mississippi River. The sun hung low in the western sky, promising to dip below the horizon within the next few hours.

Shadows lengthened, but the warmth of the day remained,

seeming to ooze from the ground as he walked back to his truck and climbed into the sunbaked interior.

Earlier, despite all his adverse thoughts, he'd given Val some space. She'd been furious with him for following her to the convent, but there was something else in her eyes as well, something that gave him a bit of encouragement.

And just what is it that you want?

A marriage without trust?

A separation?

Maybe a divorce would be the best thing—a clean slate. You both could start over.

Their romance and wedding had been like fire in a tinder-dry forest. Quick. All consuming. Destined to burn out.

They'd met when he'd gone into the local sheriff's office to report some cattle that had gone missing—stolen, he'd expected. When the dispatcher had told him politely that someone would come out to the ranch to look things over, he'd expected a silver-haired deputy with a bit of a paunch and years of experience. Instead, Valerie Renard had stepped out of the department-issued Jeep, all five feet five of her. Her uniform had fit snugly, showing off her athletic body and hinting at her curves. Reflective sunglasses had covered the upper half of her face, a hat shading her forehead, auburn hair pulled back. She'd worn little makeup, but he'd found himself fantasizing about her, as if she were one of those cop-impersonator strippers. He'd figured his brothers had pulled a practical joke on him.

But when she had not whipped out her cuffs to "arrest" him and had settled down to business about the missing cattle, he'd had to accept the fact that she was a cop doing her job. She'd been thorough, but the twenty head were never found, most likely victims of a rustling ring that had swung through the hill country.

Nonetheless, he'd been intrigued with the deputy who was quickly promoted to detective. And when he'd gotten up the nerve to ask her out, she'd surprised him with a quick "Sure, Cowboy, why not?"

There had been dozens of reasons why not, but they'd ignored them all. She'd slept with him on the third date, moved into the ranch house the next month, and said "I do" six weeks later. Their affair had burned hot, rash, and straight into trouble.

Which had come in the form of her baby sister: Camille Renard, a younger, wilder version of Valerie and a woman who had been determined, it seemed in retrospect, to break up their marriage.

In the end, even in death, Camille was the pall that hung over their relationship.

Valerie had chosen to believe her sister rather than her husband. What the hell was that all about?

And now Camille was dead.

He squinted into the dying sunlight, watching as a tugboat pushed a barge upriver. It looked like an impossible task, yet the tug was making progress. Sure and steady.

He only hoped he'd be so lucky.

CHAPTER 20

After explaining to Freya that she didn't really think Slade was the devil, just Lucifer's right-hand man, Val spent the next hours compiling all the information she could about her sister. Though she'd already left copies of Camille's e-mails with the police, she had made other hard copies that she slipped into a file.

She made a timeline of Camille's life, starting with her birth, moving to their natural parents' deaths, their short stint at the orphanage, their subsequent adoption, and every address where they'd lived. Val included the schools they'd attended and a list of Camille's friends and boyfriends, at least the ones she remembered. At first she could recall only first names, but after looking on the Internet and through old school records, the list became fairly complete.

One person on the list she wanted to meet was Camille's ex-fiancé, a law student at Tulane University named Brandon Keefe. Val didn't know all the details of the relationship and the breakup, except that Keefe had dumped Cammie and married an old girlfriend within the year.

Cammie's best friend throughout high school had been Georgiana Pagano, who had gone off to California for college and, as Val recalled, had gotten married to someone she'd met in L.A.

As for enemies, none of the names on the list popped for Val.

No doubt Cammie had wronged more than her share of people, but in the past year or so, she'd attempted to turn her life around. She had even joined a convent for God's sake. She should have been safe.

But really, how hard had Cammie tried to turn things around? She'd managed to get pregnant.

By a priest, no less.

Which reminded her to add the staff of St. Marguerite's to the list, starting with Sister Lucia, the best friend. Cammie had said Lucia was "interesting" and "different," that she possessed some kind of ESP, which Cammie had found fascinating. She'd commented once that she suspected Lucia had joined the convent because she was running from her secret past.

Just like Cammie.

But Camille's crime had been no secret: an affair with her sister's husband. Inwardly, Val cringed as she remembered screaming at her sister to "Get out! Just leave us the hell alone!" upon finding Camille in her bedroom with Slade. Soon after that, she'd packed up and left the ranch, knowing in her heart that her marriage was over. Even now, the thought of Slade with Cammie—her sister, for God's sake—tore at a raw wound in her heart.

"Son of a bitch," she said under her breath, and tried to concentrate. She could not let her mind wander to the "what ifs" of life....

What if Val had never married Slade?

What if she hadn't offered Cammie a place to stay over the holidays that year?

What if she hadn't been called to the accident that night?

What if she'd never learned about her husband's infidelity with her sister?

What if she'd swallowed her pride, tried to talk things out reasonably?

What if Cammie had never left Bad Luck...

"Stop it," she warned herself. This was getting her nowhere. She shook off all the old, melancholy memories, forced herself to push past her grief and think like a cop again.

She thought of nuns Cammie had mentioned: Sister Edwina, whom she thought was "the ultimate ice princess," and Angela, who was "a silly goose. A Goody Two-shoes." The statement would have been odd if it hadn't been issued from Cammie, with her wicked sense of humor.

"Aren't all nuns good?" Val had asked during one of Cammie's first visits to Briarstone House, and Cammie had smiled, a naughty glint in her eye. They'd been standing in the herb garden, near a trio of birdhouses sitting atop poles of differing lengths, the sun so intense they were squinting.

Cammie had emitted a low chuckle. "Of course most nuns are good. Very good. It comes with the territory. Angela falls into that category, but Sister Edwina?" Cammie had held out her flat hand and tilted it back and forth, indicating that she was wavering on her opinion of the tall nun. "Not so much. And Sister Devota?" Cammie had rolled her eyes. "The perpetual victim." Nodding to herself, she added, "There are still a couple I can't figure out. Irene sometimes takes on the world and doesn't care. If the meek are going to inherit the earth, then Irene's going to end up broke. She's like a Russian soldier one minute, and then kind and calm the next. That Irene's an odd one."

Cammie had thought for a second. "And Sister Zita is so . . . quiet. She's always watching everyone. It's a little creepy. Ever so silent until it's time to play yes-woman to the reverend mother. It's like she's trying to earn points with Sister Charity, or maybe the priests or God. Who knows? It just doesn't seem authentic, but then I should talk." She'd walked over to one of the birdhouses and peeked inside the hole. "No one home, huh?"

"Not yet. So, do you have any friends?" Valerie had asked.

"From that group? Just Lucia, and that's probably because we went to the same high school, you know, had kind of a 'shared history' "—she made air quotes—"even though we really didn't know each other back then." She'd admitted, "I get along with Angela. She really is just plain sweet, I think. Pretty impossible not to like."

"The Goody Two-shoes?"

"Yeah. Well, I guess I was just being a little catty."

"You?" Val had teased.

"Yes, *moi,* believe it or not. But Angela seems real. Genuine. I'm not so sure about Maura."

"Why not?"

"I don't know. Just a feeling. Maura's a bookworm. Quiet. Wears thick glasses and never, I mean never, smiles." She slid a look at Val. "I sometimes wonder if she's really filled with the Holy Spirit. Doesn't seem to have much joy in her life."

"Maybe she's just an introvert."

"Maybe," Camille whispered. "But the one I can't really get a bead on is Asteria. She seems like a ditz—you know, the kind of dreamer who believes in fairy tales and frogs turning into princes, all that romantic junk."

"And she became a nun?" That seemed odd.

"Go figure. Sister Edwina told me that Asteria had been engaged to a guy who committed suicide, so Asteria joined the order. Edwina said it was commit herself to God or to a mental institution."

"Sounds a little overly dramatic."

"Everyone's story is. Except for Sister Charity, who says that she knew she wanted to be nun from the time of her First Communion. Can you believe that?"

Camille had stopped herself and sighed loudly. "I guess I shouldn't be gossiping about any of them. I'd hate to hear what they had to say about me."

"St. Marguerite's is starting to sound more like a high school than a convent," Val had observed.

Cammie had laughed without a whole lot of humor. "You don't get it, do you?" she'd said. "Of course the convent is like high school. The whole world is like high school. Take a look around."

What? "Maybe in your world."

"In everyone's world," Cammie had insisted, "and, trust me, the convent is no different. There's the same pecking order, the same authority figures, the same cliques. It's just that it's like an all-girls' school." She'd looked away then, her face puckering into a frown.

Val could still see her sister as she'd been that day, dressed in plain street clothes, a simple pair of gray slacks and a white blouse, without a touch of makeup, her black hair pulled back into a thick rope and shining blue in the sun. Camille had walked to a bench and sat down. She'd seemed unbearably sad.

"You don't have to go through with this," Val had said. "Maybe you're not cut out to be a nun."

"I know." One side of Cammie's mouth had lifted into a sad, self-deprecating smile. "In for a penny..."

"It's not you."

"I get it. I know I went into the convent for all the wrong reasons." She'd lifted her ponytail and readjusted the band holding the thick hank of hair away from her face. "I'm just kidding about the other nuns. Some of the women there are so devout, their faith so secure, it makes me wish I had that same trust in God. I pray every day that I find it, but...I don't know." She'd shaken her head, a few lines evident between her eyebrows. "Sisters like Louise and Angela and Dorothy, they belong. Even if they're all half in love with Father O'Toole—he's the young, hot priest, and all of the sopranos seem to be under his spell." She'd grinned. "Maybe even me." She'd picked off a piece of chipped paint from the pole of the birdhouse.

"Seriously," she continued. "But they're good people. Take Louise, for example. She's one of those terminally upbeat people I just don't get. Musical, too. Always singing or humming, which bugs the reverend mother. Big-time." Camille had smiled, as if amused at the thought. "She works with me at St. Elsinore's sometimes." She'd cast her sister a look. "I know, you think we should avoid the place, but I think it's a good spot to start giving back."

"Really?" St. Elsinore's wasn't a place she liked to think about too much. A parish far outside New Orleans and built on higher ground, St. Elsinore's worked hand in hand with St. Marguerite's, and together the two convents staffed the orphanage.

"Really." Camille had flashed a bright smile. "See, I'm trying. But"—she'd shrugged, her grin fading—"the truth is, it's a struggle to belong."

"More than the others?"

"Who knows? Lots of the others don't seem like typical nuns. Take Irene. I mean, she was a ballerina. Go figure. Athletic and strong and not particularly even-keeled."

"I don't think there's such a thing as a diva nun," Val had said.

"There shouldn't be."

"Meaning?"

"She has a dark side, I guess." Camille's face had turned pensive. "Maybe we all do." She'd squinted and watched a hawk circle high overhead. "But the thing is, they all seem to think they're doing the right thing—fitting in."

"But not you?"

"Uh-uh. Not me."

"No one's put a gun to your head and said you had to stay. There's plenty of time to change your mind."

"And where would I go?"

"Anywhere, Cammie. You're young and beautiful and smart as a whip. If you want to take your vows, fine. If the convent life is for you, great. But if you think you don't belong there, then leave."

Camille had looked away then, gazing across a fragrant clump of rosemary to a place only she could see. "Well, now, that's the problem, isn't it? I don't think I belong anywhere...." She'd pulled out a pair of sunglasses and slipped the dark lenses over her eyes.

Val had felt her heart rip. "I'm so sorry," she'd said, her throat thick as she recognized her own culpability, how she'd played a part in her sister's decision. "I shouldn't have thrown you out that night. I should have talked to you, listened to you."

"No, you shouldn't have." Camille had scoffed at the thought. "I was with your husband. And that's something that the mother superior probably shouldn't know. I've confessed my sins to the priest, but..."

"You lied to Sister Charity."

"Omitted some information is all." Camille had sniffed loudly, as if fighting tears, though when Val had checked to see if she were crying, her eyes were hidden by sunglasses.

"It was all a mistake."

"The story of my life," Camille had said before hurrying out the garden gate.

Now, nearly a year later, Valerie's heart squeezed painfully at the thought of how she might have saved her sister's life. If she had responded differently that day, would it have changed what happened to Camille?

Probably not. But the guilt stayed with her, hanging close, never completely disappearing.

Val wrote a few notes to herself about Camille's comments on everyone at St. Marguerite's and added her own impressions of the people she'd met earlier in the day. Then she skimmed the other names she'd previously jotted down: Father Paul Neland, Regina St. James, Terri Sue Something-or-Other, people Camille had mentioned at one time or another. Laypeople who worked at the parish. There were other people on staff, as well as volunteers, but she didn't know their names. While making a mental note to obtain a complete roster, she caught a glimpse of Frank O'Toole's name on the legal pad where she'd scrawled it earlier.

Conjuring him up, she decided Father Francis O'Toole was an enigma. He was too handsome not to attract notice, too strong to forget. She wondered what it was like to make a confession to him, and the thought was unsettling.

She circled his name with her pen, around and around, dark lines of ink, as if she were physically zeroing in on him.

Well, she was, wasn't she?

Who else would want her sister dead?

Who else had so much passion?

Valerie didn't know.

But as she stared at his name on the legal pad, she vowed that she'd find out. And soon.

CHAPTER 21

Hours later, Montoya was at his desk, having reunited his brother with his bike. Cruz had brought up Lucia Costa again before starting the Harley, but Montoya hadn't said much more, not wanting to compromise the investigation. It was dicey enough that he was investigating Camille Renard's homicide. If the department wasn't stretched thin, he was certain there would be talk of reassigning him.

For now, though, he was on the case.

But what were the odds, he wondered, that two of the women he and Cruz had dated in high school had ended up at St. Marguerite's as nuns?

Long.

Very long.

Fewer and fewer young people entered the convents, seminaries, and monasteries around the country, and yet both Lucia and Camille had joined an order of nuns that was, even by convent standards, antiquated.

All afternoon outside the doorway to his office, phones jangled, keyboards clicked, and the hum of conversation was interspersed with an occasional burst of laughter. Although the air conditioner rumbled quietly, the temperature was well into the seventies, with heat from bodies, lights, and electronics at war with the cooling system.

At one point, Lynn Zaroster, one of the smarter junior detectives, had flown by his open door, footsteps full of spring, her mop of black curls bobbing with each stride. One hand held a cell phone to her ear; in the other, a bottle of Diet Coke sloshed with each step.

"I know, I know. Look, I don't care what that lowlife son of a bitch claims," she'd said into the phone. "I'm telling you his ass was Mirandized. That jackass was read his rights—by me—and he said he understood them. Talk to Deputy Mott. He heard it all." She'd hurried down the hallway, her heels clicking until she was out of earshot.

But now things had quieted, only a few day-crew detectives still logging in hours.

Montoya pulled his concentration back to his own case. He tapped his pencil on the desktop beneath the glow of his computer screen, where photographs of the Camille Renard murder scene had been posted. Scrawled on a legal pad were his notes—questions that needed answers:

Who killed her? Who had motive and opportunity?

Who was the last person to see her prior to her death?

Why was she wearing a damned bridal dress?

What was the significance of the drops of blood around the neckline of the dress?

Why did he feel that he was being stonewalled by the mother superior and everyone else at St. Marguerite's?

He had some vague theories, half-baked ideas, but nothing concrete other than the notion that Father Frank was the number-one suspect.

Frank O'Toole.

Closing his eyes, he tried to imagine the guy he knew from his youth squeezing the life out of his lover, garroting her until she couldn't breathe, keeping up the pressure until her heart stopped in the middle of the chapel, dropping her body near the altar where he often led prayers.

Then what? Slip outside to the driving rain to have Sister Lucia find her a few minutes later? It didn't make sense, but then most murders were not well-planned events.

He decided to concentrate on what he did know, realizing that answers might be buried in his notes or those taken by other officers. He had statements from everyone associated with the convent and church, along with a few more from people in the neighborhood who had been out at midnight. One man, Mr. Sylvester, had been walking his dog. There was another statement from two teenagers who had been making out in a car in the driveway at a nearby house. The kids—half dressed and the windows steamed—had been freaked when confronted by the police, and they hadn't noticed any unusual activity on the church grounds.

There were statements from all the nuns and staff, most claiming that they were asleep and had heard nothing. The few whose stories were different were Lucia Costa, who had "heard something and gone down to investigate," and the reverend mother, Charity Varisco, who had been leaving her office when she'd heard Sister Lucia's cries for help. Sister Louise admitted to going to the restroom about that time, and Sister Irene had been awake but in bed, worrying about her ailing father. She'd heard nothing, though her room was close to Sister Lucia's. Father Paul had been reading, and Father O'Toole had been visiting with the ailing Mr. Wembley. A groundskeeper, Neron Lopez, the only other man who lived at the convent, was in his room over the garages. He, an energetic seventy-year-old, was watching a late-night talk show on one of only two televisions in the compound. The other TV belonged to Father Frank O'Toole.

Only three people admitted to knowing of Camille's pregnancy: Father Frank, Valerie Renard, and Lucia Costa, all of whom mentioned the unborn child in their statements. She hadn't confided in the mother superior, or so Sister Charity claimed.

Was the baby the reason Camille was killed? Or was there some other motive that had yet to be uncovered? Some other secret yet to be revealed?

He read Lucia's statement one more time. She'd been the one who had found Father Frank outside in the rain when she'd gone searching for Father Paul. According to her statement, O'Toole had told her he was responsible for Camille's death, saying something like, "It's all my fault, God forgive me."

Looked like a confession to Montoya.

Putting the statements side by side, Montoya realized he'd have to interview some of the nuns again, especially Lucia Costa. What was the "something" she'd heard that had awoken her? A scream? A cry for help? Someone walking in the hallway? And was she certain about Frank's admission of guilt? It was something to take up with the priest, along with a dozen other questions. The neighbors hadn't produced anything, but it was worth another shot with them. And he would need to go another round with Mother Superior and Father Paul. And the sister—Valerie—he'd want another word with her. She'd forwarded a batch of e-mails that Camille had sent her, then dropped by with hard copies. Pretty conscientious, but then she had good reason to be, with her sister murdered.

Reading the e-mails, he'd felt like a voyeur. The relationship between the sisters was obviously strained, for a reason that wasn't spelled out in their words. The last communication from Camille was the most damning; the girl seemed totally depressed.

Having second thoughts. Can't take it anymore. Am leaving St. Marg's. You know why.

Obviously she was doubting herself and her decision to become a nun.

No surprise there.

She'd obviously felt pressured enough to want to leave the order. Was it just the affair and pregnancy, or something more? The obvious answer was the fact that she was going to have a baby, and her sexual relationship with O'Toole would be exposed, damning her in the eyes of many who believed that the vow of chastity was sacred.

However, he thought, twisting a pen between his fingers, the pregnancy might have been a smoke screen.

Thinking hard, he scratched at his goatee.

The e-mails bothered him, as there was no computer at St. Marguerite's, which really was a throwback to another century. According to the information on the printouts, most of the e-mails from Camille had originated from a BlackBerry, another item that would have been taboo at St. Marguerite's. A few had come from a library not far from the convent.

Montoya was checking to make certain the BlackBerry was registered and paid for by Camille Renard. He'd like to take a look at the activity and billing records for the nun who had ostensibly given up all worldly goods, which, he assumed, included computers, cell phones, BlackBerries, and the like.

So far, the BlackBerry hadn't been located.

Another little secret.

He made a note of all the anomalies of Camille's life, those things that didn't mesh with the archaic institution where she lived and the daily routine that she was supposed to follow. Her pregnancy. The wedding dress in which she'd been killed. The e-mails to her sister. He figured convents weren't known for being high-tech, but St. Marguerite's was more antiquated than most. Yet Camille was e-mailing, maybe texting. To Valerie, he knew, but who else did she send messages to?

The phone records should be arriving soon. He double-checked his computer to see if they'd been e-mailed.

Not yet.

He was trying to piece the last few days of Sister Camille's life together but wasn't making much progress. She spent her hours much like the other nuns—on a strict schedule that included prayers and praises, sermons, meditation time, meal preparation, and partaking of meals. There was some light housework involved, and Sister Camille also worked in the convent herb garden. According to the mother superior, Camille also ventured outside St. Marguerite's walls to the orphanage at St. Elsinore's, on the other side of Lake Pontchartrain.

As far as Montoya could tell, her visits to St. Elsinore's were about the only times she left the convent grounds.

Could she have met her killer on the outside?

Or was it someone she knew intimately, someone she saw often within the gated walls of St. Marguerite's?

And what about the orphanage at St. Elsinore's, the aging institution from which Camille and Valerie had been adopted? According to his notes, Camille had been there as an infant, but Valerie had been five years old. The older sister would have remembered, but for Camille, it would be a blur in her memory. Was it significant that she'd been volunteering there lately, or just a coincidence?

He glanced down to his desk where Frank O'Toole's statement was piled on top of the others. On the surface, his alibi had checked out, but it deserved another look. Especially in light of his emotional confession to Sister Lucia.

Down the hallway, he heard some scumbag protesting his innocence while demanding the removal of his cuffs.

Some things never changed.

Montoya's cell phone rang, and he saw his home number, as well as Abby's face, appear on the small screen.

"Hey," he said.

"Hey back atcha."

Just the sound of her voice was enough to calm him. He leaned back in his chair. "What's up?"

"Only the usual: diapers, spit-up, laundry, and never enough sleep, thanks to you and Ben."

He chuckled, then yawned. It had been a long night and day. He was starting to feel the round-the-clock hours in his neck and back.

"So," she continued, "I was just wondering if you were coming home for dinner—you know, since it's already getting dark?"

Was there a bit of resentment in her question?

"Oh, and by the way, your son has sprouted a full set of teeth and started walking while you've been gone."

Uh-oh. Full-on sarcasm.

Montoya chuckled despite a trace of admonition in her words. "Funny lady."

"I can be if I have to."

He checked his watch. "Yeah, I'll be there."

"Fabulous! Think you can manage to pick up a bottle of wine and a loaf of bread? French, maybe, or Italian."

"If you twist my arm," he said, then added with a low chuckle, "Real hard. Or any other body part you prefer."

"Like your nose?" she quipped back.

"Tell ya what, I'll let you decide tonight."

"Promises, promises, just give me a call when you're leaving the office, and I'll adjust dinnertime accordingly."

"You're on."

"I'd better be." She hung up and he was left smiling. Yeah, he'd gotten lucky with her. Real lucky. He glanced at the small photo on his desk of Abby, her shoulders bare as she held a swaddled Benjamin close. She gazed down at the baby, her eyes full of love. In the shot, little Ben was sleeping, dark eyelashes sweeping over his chubby cheeks, black hair framing his serene face.

Montoya's heart swelled with an emotion he'd never thought he would feel.

"Hey!" Bentz popped his head into the office. "I'm going to have another talk with Father Father. Thought you might want to come."

"Now?" He glanced at the clock on his desk.

"He's a busy man."

"Aren't we all. Is that what you're calling O'Toole? Father Father?"

"Yeah, premature, I guess. We don't really know yet."

Montoya rolled his chair away from his desk and reached for his jacket. "Guess we'll find out soon." The blood work was being processed. No DNA results back yet, but the blood sample Frank O'Toole had reluctantly deigned to give would soon reveal whether he was a potential candidate.

And if he wasn't, Montoya thought, checking his sidearm and sliding it into his shoulder holster, they were back to square one.

In the darkness, with candles burning, a solitary window open to allow in a breath of night, I hang my robes on a peg. I take my time, heat the oil, then slowly rub the silky liquid upon my nakedness, anointing my body, feeling my hands run over my own muscles. Solid and sinewy beneath my skin, the muscles work smoothly as I massage them.

Shoulders and abdomen, rigid and strong.

Hips and thighs, muscular and glistening in the candlelight. Buttocks round, flexed.

I see my reflection in the narrow mirror.

Tall.

Handsome.

Nearly perfect.

But there are flaws.

One in my shoulder where a bullet had lodged, buried in the tissue until I had the strength to extract it. There is still a depression, a dimple marring the skin, but it is small, barely visible now. No real damage had been done.

The other imperfection was more severe.

My right leg.

Beneath the kneecap, where calf muscles should bulge, there is a tangle of flesh and scarred skin. I smooth oil over the battered flesh, reminding myself that this is my battle scar, a war wound for a greater cause.

The reason I suspended my mission.

I spent years rehabilitating my leg, determined that I would walk flawlessly, run smoothly, hide my imperfectness from the world.

Until the time is right.

I run my fingers along the jagged scar, kneading the tortured flesh below my knee, oiling the old wound.

I have waited.

Been patient.

But now I know I am being rewarded.

God is calling.

The waiting is over.

I kneel, facing the mirror.

Taking a deep breath, I think of the women.

All of the women with their flirty smiles, come-hither glances, glistening lips, and dirty talk. Seductresses and whores, sirens and harlots, all thinking they would be the one special enough that I would break my vows....

If only they knew.

Would they tingle with excitement?

Pursue their need to baptize themselves in murky waters?

Of course they would.

Smiling in the darkness, remembering their sins, carnal and warm, flesh pulsing, the scent of want mingling with perfume and sweat simmering in the air.

I feel a tightening in my groin.

Warmth slips into my blood.

My maleness rises, beginning to throb.

I think of all those glorious rounded mouths, surprise and desire flickering in their long-dead eyes.

And then I pray.

CHAPTER 22

Father Frank was conveniently MIA.

And Bentz was burned. Montoya saw it in the set of his jaw as the older detective stared through the gate at Sister Charity.

Then again, the reverend mother, who had answered the buzzer herself, wasn't pleased. Not at all.

"Father Frank is at the hospital," she said, her lips tight, her eyes, magnified by her glasses, filled with quiet scorn as she stared through the wrought-iron bars. "You should have made an appointment."

"I did," Bentz insisted.

Her gray eyebrows knitted. "He was called away to the hospital." She tucked her hands into the sleeves of her habit, as if waiting for them to leave.

Bentz stood his ground.

"Since we're here, we might as well talk with the other people on our list."

"But it's late, at least for us here at the convent, and you can't speak to Father O'Toole. So why don't you come back tomorrow, at a time that's more convenient?"

"Now is better," Montoya had persisted. "When things are still fresh in people's minds."

Bentz agreed. "Besides, maybe Father O'Toole will show up."

She seemed ready to argue, until Bentz started reeling off the names of staff they needed to interview.

"Fine," she finally agreed. With a scowl, Sister Charity unlocked the gate before walking off stiffly to locate the people who needed to be questioned again.

Montoya had decided to talk directly with Sister Lucia, despite their connection. He wanted to see for himself her reactions when questioned about one of her friends. Now they were seated opposite each other, in the same room in which he'd interviewed Frank O'Toole less than twenty-four hours earlier. Same dim wall sconce and scarred table, same disturbing feeling that the truth was hiding in the corners just out of touch and skittering away from the light.

"You don't remember what it was that woke you?" Montoya asked, checking his notes.

Sister Lucia shook her head as she nervously braided her fingers together. She was pale and looked as if she wanted to be anywhere but in this small room talking to the police.

The door to the outer hallway was ajar, a bit of cool air from the darkened corridor seeping inside. Montoya wanted to close the door, suspecting that the reverend mother was still prowling nearby, and her presence had an icy effect on the rest of the nuns.

On the other side of the chapel, Bentz was in a similar room, questioning people who resided in the convent—nuns and lay staff—whose statements needed clarification.

"No," she said now, "I don't remember a specific sound waking me. It was just a feeling I had." She bit her lip anxiously, and he could see that she was a really bad liar. "Maybe I, er, heard a noise in my sleep, a dream or something, but nothing I can really name."

"A scream?" he prodded.

She shook her head violently. "No." She blushed and looked away.

"A cry for help?"

"No!"

"Footsteps?"

She met his eyes, her gaze miserable in her grief. "I'm sorry," she whispered.

They were getting nowhere. He tried a new direction. "Okay, then. Let's talk about Father O'Toole. You found him in the courtyard that night?"

"Yes. Or he found me. I was knocking on Father Paul's door, and Father O'Toole stepped into the light. He startled me," she said, explaining again how she had suddenly found the younger priest behind her.

"You were Sister Camille's closest friend," Montoya suggested.

"Maybe." She lifted a shoulder. "At least one of them. We're all friends here."

He doubted that. "You were the one she confided in about her pregnancy, the only one."

Lucia's eyes slid away. "Yes," she said faintly, obviously uncomfortable. "Well, you know, we went to school together, though we never hung out much then."

"Did she tell you the baby was Father Frank O'Toole's?"

Lines formed across her smooth forehead. "She never mentioned him specifically."

Montoya took note.

"But she did say that she and the baby's father were, uh, 'involved'—that's the word she used. Which was pretty obvious since she was pregnant," Lucia said.

"But she didn't mention Father O'Toole?"

"No." Lucia swallowed hard. "Not in so many words, but I, um, saw them together a couple of times. You know...embracing... kissing. When they thought no one was looking."

She avoided his eyes, embarrassed.

"And others saw them?"

"I suppose." She lifted a shoulder, her body stiff. As if she wanted to jump out of her own skin. "They tried to be discreet, but, you know, there's always someone around."

"How did Sister Camille feel about her pregnancy?" Montoya asked.

"She was...scared, I guess. She said she didn't know what she'd do but that she'd probably have to leave the convent."

"But she was intent on having the baby?"

"What? Oh!" Her eyes grew round when she understood that he was asking about the possibility of Camille terminating the pregnancy. "Oh, she was absolutely going to have the baby and raise it. She wouldn't do anything to stop it. I mean, no, oh, no way." Lucia was shaking her head violently. Passionately. Now she wasn't hedging. "Sister Camille was adopted herself, and she was all about finding her birth parents. She didn't believe they were dead, I guess. Because of this baby and...Oh, no, she would never do anything to hurt it. She wanted to raise the child." Lucia's little chin lifted defiantly, as if she felt she needed to save her friend's reputation.

"Did she pressure Father O'Toole?"

"I...I don't know. She talked to him, but she didn't really say anything other than that she told him she was going to have a baby. If you're talking about asking him to leave the priesthood and marry her, I don't know about anything like that."

"How did he take the news of her pregnancy?" Montoya asked.

"She said he was upset."

"How upset?"

She shook her head. "I don't know. You...you should probably ask him."

"We will."

"Look, he didn't kill her," she insisted. "He swore to me that he didn't!"

"You asked him?"

"No, of course not. He just told me later." She explained her conversation with the priest, but as she did, she seemed to shrink away, as if she knew she shouldn't have blurted out anything, that somehow she was betraying both Camille and Father Frank.

Montoya realized he'd made a mistake by questioning her himself. Sister Lucia was intimidated. Nervous. Maybe because he was a man, probably because he looked so much like Cruz. There was a chance Lucia might have opened up more to a female officer.

He asked about a BlackBerry or cell phone.

"I don't know about anything like that, but she did have a diary, I think, or maybe it was just a notebook," Lucia admitted reluctantly.

A diary. Could be revealing...though Bentz hadn't come across it when he searched Camille's room.

Montoya asked Sister Lucia what she knew about the diary, but she had never read it; she knew only that it existed.

Another dead end, Montoya thought, ending the interview with more questions than he had answers. "Thank you," he finally said.

Lucia's shoulders seemed to sink in relief; she was obviously glad that the interview was over.

Outside the small room, they found Sister Charity pacing the hallway, her fingers running over the beads of her rosary, her lips and jaw tight.

"Are you finished?" she demanded. The penetrating eyes magnified by her glasses were trained on Montoya.

"Not yet."

She shook her head, the hem of her wimple brushing the back of her habit. "This is the Lord God's house," she said softly, "not an interrogation chamber. I realize you are doing your job, but we really cannot stand for these disruptions." For a moment her spine of iron seemed to melt a bit, her eyes pleading with him. "Of course, we want you to locate Sister Camille's killer. He needs to be brought to justice. But at what price? All my sisters are on edge. Suspicion slithers down our hallways. Gossip, speculation, and fear have replaced hope, love, and faith." She let out a long, world-weary sigh. "I trust in Our Almighty Father, as well as the Son and Holy Spirit, to carry us through this crisis. But as you do your job, please grant the house of God the respect it is due."

"We're just trying to conduct an investigation."

"I realize that, Detective, but at what cost?" The lines in her face seemed more severe today, her usually fierce spirit defeated.

Montoya felt a twinge of compassion for the sister, but he stood his ground. He couldn't back down...not even for Jesus Christ himself. "These things take time, Sister. I know you want us to do a thorough job."

"Thorough?" Her lips pulled into a knot of annoyance. "Come with me," she said, and with clipped, determined steps, her skirts billowing, she led him to the chapel and swung open the door. "Is this what you call thorough?" She lifted one disbelieving eyebrow and then grandly gestured to the interior of the little nave.

Fingerprint dust covered most of the surfaces, coating the wood of the pews and the upholstery of the kneelers. Hymnals and prayer books were scattered. The entire place was in disarray.

"We have to spend our time with the investigation."

"Again, Detective, this is God's house. No matter what atrocity was committed here, this place is holy. Sacred. Remember that."

With a look of disgust, she left, walking swiftly away before he could ask any more questions.

He decided to let her cool off a bit and went to find Bentz, whom, he was told, had gone to reinspect Sister Camille's quarters. Sister Devota escorted him to the dormitory area of the convent, down a narrow, windowless corridor dimly lit by wall sconces that looked like they may have been stolen from a dungeon. Was the eerie atmosphere caused by the musty smell and shadows or the fact that a woman had lost her life at the hands of a still-unidentified assailant?

Sister Devota pointed him to Camille's room, where he found Father Paul and Sister Edwina, the tall nun with Scandinavian features, standing guard in the hallway, keeping watch over Bentz.

Inside the cell-like room, darkness battled the meager light of a small lamp. All the charm of a tomb. The bedding had been stripped to be analyzed by the crime lab.

His partner moved the cot aside to check the floor underneath. "Thought I'd take another look," Bentz told him as he flashed his cell phone on the floor for light. Even with the single lamp lit, the room was dark as a tomb.

"You didn't happen to find a diary, did you?" Montoya asked, leaning close to Bentz so the others couldn't hear.

"Oh, that's how it works. We find a diary and it spells out who the perp is. Happens all the time," he said sarcastically as he glanced up at the bare, cracked ceiling. "Haven't come across that yet."

"Yeah, I thought so." Montoya straightened as his eyes moved over the blossoming clouds of fingerprint powder on the flat walls.

His gut told him they weren't going to find anything here. Nothing. Nada.

He stepped around the small, bony cot. Surely this tiny bed wasn't where Camille and Frank O'Toole had made love? It seemed unlikely, but anything was possible. When passion ruled, all bets were off. Common sense had a tendency to fly straight out the window.

But as he studied the mattress, he noticed something. One of the buttons pinching the stuffing beneath it together was missing. No big deal. Hardly noticeable. Yet, he found an evidence glove and yanked it on, then felt near the tiny hole where the button's threads had raveled.

The tip of his finger encountered a bump, the tiniest of imperfections in the ticking. "What's this?" he said, and saw that the mattress had been mended with tiny little stitches. Carefully, so as to disturb as little as possible, he withdrew his Pomeroy 5000, a utility knife with several blades, and sliced through the hand-sewn seam.

He felt inside the slit, and his fingertip touched the edge of something made of paper. Carefully he retrieved a long, slim envelope, wrinkled slightly from being wedged beneath the sheath covering the mattress.

No address on the outside, but the envelope had been sealed, a red-brown stain over the flap where it was glued down.

"Blood?" Bentz asked.

"Looks like."

Bentz said, "Could be a print."

"Got it." Montoya wasn't messing with the seal. Saliva, the blood, or fingerprints could be on the envelope. Using the thinnest blade of his utility knife, he sliced one thin end of the envelope and flexed it open to retrieve a single sheet of paper, a letter, written only to "My Beloved" and signed by "C."

The paragraphs between the greeting and single-letter signature were written in a cramped, seemingly hurried hand, and they described in graphic detail what the writer, a woman, wanted from her lover. Rather than flowery and sickeningly romantic, this letter

was a demand for sexual favors, specific in their intent, all indicating bondage was involved.

Even Montoya, a seasoned veteran, was surprised.

"Is this Sister Camille's handwriting?" he asked, and the mother
superior, her lips drawn together as if by purse strings, scanned the
note with disgust.

"It could be," she admitted. Then her veneer of revulsion gave
way to pity, and she made the sign of the cross over her chest.
"Camille was a tortured soul."

CHAPTER 23

Val sat in her favorite chair, her legs tucked beneath her, notes about Camille on the nearby table. A solitary lamp burned as the night encroached, and the television, tuned to an all-news station, was flickering quietly while Bo lay snoring in a tight little ball on the floor at her feet. She'd just hung up with Detective Montoya and was still processing the information when the dog, lying near the French doors, lifted his head and growled low in his throat.

"Stop it," she said, but Bo climbed to his feet and pressed his nose to the paned glass. Again he growled, a deep, warning rumble.

"Hey!" she said. "Knock it off."

But the hound's gaze was glued to the window, and the hairs on the back of his neck rose, his lips curling.

"What is it?" she asked, and snapped off the light beside her so that she wasn't backlit as she walked to the window and cautiously peered outside and into the darkness.

The grounds were illuminated by the porch light and a few dim landscape bulbs that cast bluish pools over the walkways that spanned the grass. Oak trees cast weird shadows, but nothing seemed out of place. Warm lights glowed in the windows of Freya's rooms and the main hallway, even one of the guest rooms, though the uppermost floor, where Slade was staying, remained dark.

"It's nothing," she told the dog, and tried to convince herself that he'd only caught the scent of a marauding possum or raccoon or maybe a neighboring cat.

And yet she, too, was a little jittery, her nerves still on edge as she snapped on the lights and made her way into the kitchen where she heated water in the microwave, then found a tea bag.

She'd just settled back into her chair and shaken off her case of nerves when Bo's ears pricked, and he let out a soft little bark.

"Enough," she said. "Okay?" Then she heard the low rumble of a truck's engine. She knew before she glanced out the window that Slade was back.

Great. Just what she needed on top of everything else. Ever since her phone conversation with Detective Montoya, she'd been second-guessing herself. Reexamining her life.

She closed her eyes for a second and fought that tiny little urge deep within, the absolutely ridiculous feminine part of her that Slade still touched.

Quit fighting it. Be glad he's with you. He might be able to help you find Camille's killer. If not, at least he's moral support.

She scoffed at herself. *Moral* support? From the man who'd tried to seduce her sister?

What a joke.

Then again, Cammie might have lied about what really happened. Hadn't Val already considered that as a very real possibility? Either way, dealing with Slade would be difficult.

Bo was going nuts, wiggling and whining at the door. Sure enough, through the crack in the blinds, Val watched Slade get out of the truck and, instead of heading for the main house, turn and make a beeline for her cottage.

"Here we go," she said, walking to the door just as he rapped on it. Bo was beside himself as she unlocked the dead bolt and tugged open the door.

Slade stood under the porch light on the other side of the screen. His face was all shadowy planes and angles, his jaw set and beard-shadowed. He offered her the hint of a smile, a crooked twist of his thin lips. "So did I give you enough space?"

"You're still here, aren't you?"

There was no denying Slade Houston's presence. His shoulders nearly filled the doorway, reminding her of how solid and wide his body was. "Be nice," he said.

"I'm always nice."

His grin widened. "Right. Nice people invite people standing on their porch inside."

Bo yipped, then quieted with a sharp look from Slade.

"Fine," she said, opening the creaking screen door and stepping aside. "Come in. I've got something for you." She walked to her small desk where she noticed a few past-due notices in the stack of bills she'd been ignoring. She picked up a large envelope from her attorney. "This is what I'd been working on," she said. "Preliminary." She handed him the envelope, and he glanced at the return address. "Still some details to hammer out, and since you're here..." She shrugged, trying to summon her outrage, her need to sever all ties with him, her desperate desire to let him know that she wasn't going to let an ill-fated marriage ruin the rest of her life. But she couldn't. All of her hot emotions had run cold with the loss of Cammie.

"Already got a copy in the truck." He tossed the envelope onto her coffee table. "This isn't a good time."

He was right about that. "Just so you know where I stand."

"Oh, I've got it." His face had gone hard. "But right now, we've got bigger fish to fry, don't ya think?"

She nodded. "Okay. Sure. Truce, for now." She waved him into a chair. "I just wanted to make things clear."

"Crystal."

"Good." Walking into her small galley kitchen, she called over her shoulder, "I've got tea or coffee or a soda." She opened the refrigerator door, then peered over it as she looked into the living room where he was bending over and scratching Bo behind the ears. Her heart tugged a bit at the familiar sight. How many times had she seen him in just that position on the porch of the big old rambling house at the ranch? With the setting sun throwing him into dark relief, Slade had leaned over and petted the hound before kicking off his dusty boots and padding into the kitchen hundreds of times.

Once inside, he'd always taken the time to kiss her. He'd either quickly buss her cheek or, more often than not, sweep her into his arms and press hot, hungry lips to hers. "I think we have time for a quick one," he'd whisper against her ear, only half joking. The scent of hay, horses, and dust had clung to him, and in that first year of their marriage, she'd usually take him up on his offer. "A quick one *what?*" she'd teased. And then, laughing, would find herself lifted from her feet and carried into the bedroom, where he'd made love to her, and not in a hurry.

Other times she had come home from work to find something barely edible simmering on the stove while he tended to the pots. At the sound of her footsteps, he had looked over his shoulder, then, in mock surprise, threw his hands high into the air. "I'm innocent, Detective," he would say, appearing guilty as sin, his eyes flashing dark.

"I doubt it," had been her usual response. And, as if on cue, he had always turned around, hands extended behind his back, his neck twisted so that he could pin her with a wicked gleam in his eye and suggest, "Cuff me anyway."

Again, they had ended up in bed.

So how had they gone from that lighthearted crazy-in-love banter to this—total mistrust and simmering fury?

The answer was simple:

Camille.

Val met his gaze and wondered if he, too, was tripping down the painful cobblestones of memory lane. "There's a beer in here, too."

"That'll work." He followed her into the kitchen, took the bottle of Coors from her outstretched hand, and twisted off the cap. He took a long swallow and followed her into the living room where he landed on the small sofa, she in her chair. Tucking her legs beneath her, she decided that it was probably safe to confide in him about Cammie.

"I talked to Detective Montoya a little while ago."

"Any news?"

"No answers," she admitted, "just more questions." She told him that the police were looking for a cell phone or BlackBerry and a diary or notebook. "I know she had some kind of phone, and I guess I never really thought it was odd, but I have no idea where it is. And I don't know anything about a diary." Ignoring her rapidly cooling tea, she added, "The oddest thing he brought up again was that Camille had been looking for our birth parents. I heard it earlier but couldn't believe it. We've always known that our parents were killed. They were relatives of Nadine and Gene, our adoptive parents, who took us to visit their graves."

"You never questioned it."

"Never." She was shaking her head slowly as she picked up her cup. "We were adopted out of St. Elsinore's when we were really young, and I never had a reason to doubt they had really died."

"But Camille did?"

"I guess." Valerie was still processing the information. "But that's crazy. I mean, it was never hidden from us. We knew we were adopted and where we'd come from all our lives," she said.

"You sure of that?"

"Of course."

"How can you be so sure?"

She took a sip from her tea, not liking the conclusions she was drawing. "From everything I've been told . . ."

"And you never considered that Gene and Nadine Renard may have lied about the truth?" he asked, lifting a skeptical eyebrow. "People make up stories all the time, especially when it makes them look better."

She saw the doubt in his eyes and quickly turned away as denial swept through her. This had to be wrong. It *had* to be! How many times had her mother, Nadine, told her the story of their adoption, the red tape that they'd fought to claim Valerie and Camille as their own? She remembered her father, at the kitchen table, recounting the story of talking to the parish priest, demanding that he be allowed to adopt his "blood kin."

"I was there today," Slade said, and she snapped back to the present.

"Where? At St. Elsinore's?" she asked. "Why?"

"I had time to kill."

"A lot. That's miles away," she thought aloud, remembering the whitewashed church and high wall surrounding the playground of the school where church bells never rang. The empty bell tower had been as run-down as the rest of the buildings.

He lifted his shoulder. "The parish office was closed. But I did find this." He handed her a flyer for the upcoming charity auction that was advertised as a gala event for the express purpose of raising money for the new orphanage.

"And the reason you went up there is...?" She knew it was no coincidence that he had visited the orphanage today.

"First of all, you made it pretty clear that you needed some space. So I decided to back off and see some of the places you mentioned, places from your past. I went by your old house, and the schools, too."

Her skin prickled with uneasy goose bumps. She tried to conjure a kind face or a tangible memory, but all she came up with were blurred images of confusion and fear, of not understanding what had happened to her parents, of worrying for her baby sister. There had been hands touching her, trying to calm her as disembodied voices tried to explain that her parents were gone. She remembered strangers' blurred faces filled with compassion and worry, soft whispers and words that were used to placate her when she'd been scared and alone.

"Everything will be all right," an elderly woman had whispered, patting her shoulder.

"It's not up to us to question God's will," a man in embroidered robes had cautioned.

"God moves in mysterious ways," yet another woman with curly bluish hair had intoned.

But all Valerie had known was that her life would never be the same. And then, out of nowhere, Gene and Nadine Renard had appeared, saviors who would adopt not only her, but her baby sister as well. "This is all so surreal," she admitted now as she stared into her cup, where the tea settled dark against the white enamel.

Slade asked, "Do you remember your biological parents at all?"

"Of course. I was four when they died. Almost five."

But did she?

Of course, she had images of a couple, but nothing concrete. There had been a backyard with an empty concrete fish pond and a battered picnic table and chairs. She remembered her mother—wasp-thin and dark-haired—lounging in short shorts, the end of her cigarette glowing beneath the drooping, shifting branches of a willow tree. Her father always seemed to be working in the garage, hammering noisily, and there had been a basement, right? Stairs twisting down to a dark, dank-smelling vestibule with a locked door...or had those images been dreams, conjured memories that had never really existed?

Her throat went dry.

"Do you remember your adoptive parents ever talking about visiting them?"

"No. They weren't close..." Her voice faded as she glanced up at him. "You know all this." They'd discussed it once or twice during their marriage.

"I don't remember ever seeing any pictures of your biological parents."

"It was before computers and camera phones and the like. Any pictures were lost...." Or so she'd been told. She wanted to argue with Slade, and her stomach knotted at the thought. This whole new scenario, that her adoptive parents had lied to her, shook her to the core.

"But you know your parents' names? Your name?"

"Yes. Mary and Michael Brown."

"Common names."

"Yeah, I know. But why would they lie? Mom and Dad—Nadine and Gene—what would they be hiding?"

"Maybe that's what Cammie was trying to find out."

"Oh, God," she whispered, thinking about her sister. Cammie always did have a flair for the dramatic, an overactive imagination.

Slade tilted his head back, and she watched his throat move as he took another long pull from his bottle. "Maybe that was why she was killed."

"But it doesn't make any sense. It happened so long ago...." She tried to pin down the facts, the details of her parents' deaths. She'd been told that a plane crash had taken her parents' lives. A day trip. Valerie and Camille had been left with a family friend when tragedy had struck and the plane had gone down. With both sets of grandparents already dead, the small, grief-ridden family had to scramble to find a suitable home for the children. Valerie and Camille had been sent to St. Elsinore's until the family could sort things out.

The end result had been placement with the Renards, as Nadine was a third cousin to Mary Brown, the only relative with the means or desire to take in a preschooler and an infant.

"Cammie didn't tell you she was looking into your biological parents?"

"No." Val shook her head.

"Why not?"

"I don't know. Maybe because I would have told her she was nuts, that she was chasing ghosts." A dry, penetrating wind swept through her soul, upward through the cracks in the foundation of her life, sweeping aside all the memories she'd held as true. Her throat closed in on itself as she met Slade's gaze. "Because if it's true, if Mary Brown wasn't our mother," she whispered, the flyer crinkling in her fingers, "then my entire life has been a lie."

"Bless me, Father, for I have sinned. It has been one day since my last confession," Sister Asteria whispered the words that were so familiar while making the sign of the cross. On the other side of the screen, deep in the shadows, a priest was ready to listen. Father Paul, thank goodness, rather than Father Frank. She tried to ignore her trip-hammering heart as she folded her hands and took in a steadying breath.

At the whispered encouragement from the priest, she closed her eyes and began to unburden her heart. "I was once in love with a man who turned out to be married, and as soon as I found out, I left him."

His face was hidden, unrecognizable in the semidarkness, but she knew she had his full attention. He sat, rapt, as she continued.

"I was determined never to make that mistake again, to never fall in love with a mortal man, to follow Jesus as my savior, as my strength, as ..." She felt tears fill her eyes. Her voice caught as she let out a shuddering breath.

"Slowly, my child. Gather your thoughts and confess."

She did, pouring out everything that had been torturing her for the past few weeks. "My thoughts have been impure," she admitted, "and my actions—" Her voice caught, and she steeled herself. Whatever the penance, surely it would be easier to bear than the burden of her private, sinful secrets.

Asteria thought she heard another sound, a quiet footstep outside the door to the confessional.

Her back muscles tensed.

Surely no one would be hovering nearby or listening in. No, her confession was between herself and the priest...

And yet, she was certain she heard someone, or rather sensed someone, nearby. Wasn't that the sound of a gasp being stifled?

Her unease intensified, and she could almost feel the presence of another person nearby.

Friend or foe?

She swallowed hard.

"Go on, my child," the priest encouraged in his soft rasp, and Asteria reined in her wild imagination. Her fantasies and dreams and nightmares had always been her undoing, getting her into trouble.

Now, in the wake of poor Sister Camille's death, her worries and her own sins loomed large in her mind, scratching at her nerves.

She needed to release herself from her secrets, from the sins that had enslaved her.

She ignored the hairs rising at the back of her neck, the nervous beads of sweat that collected along her spine.

She was alone with Father Paul in the house of God, here for the sacrament of penance. She let out a long breath and began speaking again as she told herself she was safe.

No one could harm her here.

Or so she vainly tried to convince herself.

CHAPTER 24

"The dog can stay with you," Slade said as he carried his empty beer bottle into Val's kitchen. This cozy little cottage, so different from the rambling ranch house in Texas, still felt like home. Because of Val, he realized.

"I can keep him?" she called from the living area, where the television still droned on, the volume low.

"For the night."

Bo lifted his head but didn't alter his position on the rug near Val's feet. She pushed herself out of her chair, and the hound was instantly on his feet, ready to follow her anywhere.

Like you? he silently asked himself, and hated the fact that he was weak where she was concerned. His brothers were right—he was whipped with a capital *P.*

"Maybe I'll keep him," she said.

"Fat chance."

She was teasing, a spark of humor in her hazel eyes. God, he'd missed that, the way her face could change from pensive to amused in a heartbeat.

"We'll work it out in the doggy-custody hearing."

"He stays with me, on the ranch. End of subject." Slade walked to the front door, and the damned dog didn't so much as look at him. Bo, it seemed, was as pathetically hung up on Valerie as he was.

"Gee, I love when a man tells me what to do," she quipped. "Or how it's gonna be. Like I can't figure my life out for myself."

A smile tugged at the corner of his mouth as she snapped off the television and walked up to him, the angle of her chin definitely defiant. "Sassy, aren't you?"

"Sassy. Is that the new PC term for bitchy?"

"Hey, if you want to fight, we can. Your call." But he was grinning by now, and there was a part of him that wanted to meet the challenge in her eyes, yank her off her feet, and haul her into the bedroom he'd noticed just on the other side of a short hallway. He'd seen the foot of her bed through the open doors, noticed a familiar area rug covering the hardwood floors. But he figured the surest way to push her into going through with the divorce was to move too fast. When she didn't respond to his challenge, he opened the door, though the screen was still latched.

"You'd lose any fight," she said.

Man, she was asking for it. "Careful, Valerie."

"Of what?" Again with the arched brow and angled chin.

"I could go—how did you used to phrase it?—'all Neanderthal' on you right now."

She groaned. "Oh, God, and what? Show me who's boss? Save me."

"As I said, you can keep Bo tonight, but"—he sent the dog a warning glare—"he still belongs at the ranch."

"Sure. If you say so," she said, her eyes belying her words.

"And as for tomorrow, I think we should go to St. Elsinore's when the place is open."

" 'We'?" she repeated.

"Yeah, 'we.' Like it or not, I'm here and involved."

"You don't have to be."

"I know, but I want to be."

She hesitated. "Look, Slade, you don't have to feel obligated, okay? Just because we're still married doesn't mean that you have to jump in or be my advocate or protector or whatever might be in your head. I can handle myself. I was a cop. A detective. Remember?"

"One with nightmares."

"Everyone has them. Comes with the territory."

Slade wasn't so sure. Val's dreams, though infrequent, terrorized her. He knew. He'd woken up to her screams, to her night sweats, to her body trembling in fear. He'd tried to give her comfort, to hold her, to whisper that everything would be all right, but she'd always insisted upon rolling off the bed and going into the living room where she'd curl up on the couch with an old afghan and stare at the dying embers of the fire with Bo beside her.

She'd never objected to him joining her and the dog, but she'd needed a few minutes to compose herself first. She'd refused to tell him what the dreams were about and dismissed them as "stress from the job."

He'd come to suspect she'd been lying, placating him. He thought her night terrors might have been triggered by a horror she'd witnessed while performing her duties, but they ran much deeper than what she'd admitted.

Now she was so close he could reach out and touch her, brush the wayward lock of auburn curls from her cheek, wrap his fingers around her nape and draw her closer. But he resisted. Instead he asked, "So are we on for tomorrow?" Of course, he thought they should leave the investigation to the police, to try and keep their emotions out of it, but he knew Val wouldn't be able to back off. With her temperament and experience tracking killers, she wouldn't just let her sister's murderer get away without a fight. He figured together they might be able to find out something that might help the authorities, though he knew that if he said so much to the detectives in charge, they would not only laugh but also tell Val and Slade to back off in no uncertain terms.

Tough.

This was the way Val was determined to play it.

He saw the hesitation on her face; then her eyebrows pinched together.

"Come on," he urged. "I have some experience myself. And I have questions. About Frank O'Toole and about your adoption—

why Camille was looking into it. We're assuming she was killed because she was pregnant, because it's so bizarre that she broke her vows, that she got herself into that kind of mess with a priest, no less. But what if the pregnancy didn't have anything to do with her murder?"

"What?"

"I mean, it's likely, yes. It's the one thing that's so big and different, so out of whack that we think she had to be killed because of it, but that's only an assumption."

"But the bridal gown?"

"Yeah, what does that mean?" He inched a little closer to her. "What I'm saying is that we have to keep an open mind here, look at all the possibilities. And I think I can help with that." She was about to argue when he added, "I'm not as emotional as you are about all this."

"I'm not..." She let out a long breath. "Okay...fine," she finally relented, though she didn't seem too pleased about the prospect of working with him.

"But you have to agree that anything we find, we give to the police immediately."

"Of course." She closed her eyes for a second. "I just can't believe this happened. Even though I know it does, I always thought it was something that happened to other people, you know. Not Cammie." She sighed and wrapped her arms around herself. "I can't believe I'll never see her again."

God, he wanted to wrap his arms around her, to hold her and whisper ridiculous platitudes into her ear. As if she knew where his thoughts were taking him, she added, "We'll work together, but if you bring up the divorce or separation or marriage, the deal's off. You know where I stand on that."

He wanted to argue.

Badly.

Instead, because he knew she was still trying to work through her pain and grief, he inclined his head. "Deal."

"Good."

To the dog he said, "Good night, traitor," then opened the screen door and walked across the small stoop and into the cool of the night. He didn't look over his shoulder, didn't even wait to hear the click of the lock behind him. He'd try to play by her rules.

For now. Until they found out what happened to Camille.

Montoya figured Abby would be pissed.

He didn't blame her.

He was late. Really late, he realized. But finding the letter in Camille's mattress had set off a chain of events in which the forensic guys came out again, the mattress was taken into the lab, and another round of questions begun. He'd talked to Father Frank, in the priest's office, a book-lined room filled with volumes on philosophy, history, and religion. In a quick glance, Montoya saw the names of Friedrich Nietzsche, Sigmund Freud, Mao Zedong, and Thomas Jefferson on the spines of those closest, though there were hundreds more.

The priest's desk had been bare save for a few pictures of members of his family, some of whom Montoya recognized. A crucifix was mounted over the door, another behind his desk, and a print of Jesus and the Sacred Heart framed upon one wall.

Upon being shown the letter, Father Frank had closed his eyes and pulled back as if he expected the words to twist and form into Satan incarnate.

"Yes," he had said, he'd thought Camille had penned the letter.

No, he didn't think it was intended for him, but he had no idea who that might be.

Who, indeed?

Was Frank O'Toole lying, trying to lay blame elsewhere? Or was Sister Camille was involved with a second lover? Was he the kinky guy—into handcuffs and dominance? Or was that Father Frank? After they had left the building, Bentz had admitted he thought the man was "lying through his orthodontically straightened teeth."

Again, if Camille had another lover, who was it?

The question had plagued him ever since discovering the letter. The conversations with Father Frank and Sister Charity hadn't been enlightening. When questioned about Father Frank's alibi of visiting the sick old Arthur Wembley, Charity had looked away, as if embarrassed to lie, but she had verified the priest's story.

Charity Varisco was nothing if not loyal.

Now, Montoya tried to put the case aside. At least for a few hours.

The beams of his car's headlights washed over the single-story shotgun house as he wheeled his Mustang into the drive and cut the engine. Scooping up the items in the passenger seat, he locked the car, then jogged across the patch of front yard. Similar homes lined the street. The neighbor's dog, a friendly dalmatian, bounded over the row of boxwoods separating the yards.

"Hey, boy," Montoya said, stopping to pet the animal, when the door to the house next door opened.

"Apollo?" the neighbor, a middle-aged woman wearing a bathrobe and slippers, called from her front porch. The red tip of her cigarette glowed in the night. "Come on, now! Come on home! It's gonna rain soon! Git in here!"

"Better go home or you'll be in as much trouble as I am," Montoya advised the dog. Apollo cocked his head, then took off like a bullet, leaped over the shrubbery effortlessly, and galloped onto the porch to his waiting owner.

"What do you think you're doing, leaving the yard?" the neighbor reprimanded, chuckling as she gently scolded the dog and held the screen door open. Apollo shot inside as the woman waved at Montoya. Then she shoved her cigarette into one of the potted plants positioned around a porch swing and shut the door firmly behind her.

Time to face the music.

Montoya's house was dark, not even the porch light left burning for him.

Not a good sign.

He opened the door and caught the thin smell of smoke from candles recently extinguished, hovering over the aromas of cheese, garlic, and fish.

He snapped on the overhead light and saw that the small dining table was still set for two. Shiny white plates sat empty and waiting upon gold chargers and bold, striped place mats. Beside a small glass bowl of rose petals, three once-tall white candles, their wicks blackened, trailed wax that was still warm.

No doubt he was in deep trouble.

"Oh, hell," he muttered.

He set the keys, bottle of merlot, and loaf of bread on the counter, then headed toward the back of the house. It was double sized, as Montoya had bought the property next door and combined the two buildings. Of course, he'd had to gut and renovate the place after Hurricane Katrina, but he was happy with the result.

A line of flickering illumination was visible under their bedroom door. The television.

The dog whined and scratched.

Great. More trouble.

He opened the door slowly, and Hershey burst through, a tornado of clicking paws, brown fur, and wet tongue. The dog sniffed wildly, probably smelling Apollo's lingering odor. "Hey, hey, hey," Montoya said, giving the dog some attention before poking his head into the bedroom.

"A little late," Abby said from their bed. Propped by several pillows, she didn't take her eyes off the television. Yep, she was ticked off. Her hair was piled onto her head, and she was wearing an oversized T-shirt. Her cat, Ansel, was curled into a ball near her head. On Montoya's pillow. Abby hit the PAUSE button and finally glanced his way.

"Yeah, sorry."

"Don't apologize to me," she said sharply. Man, was she burned. "Tell it to your son the next time you see him, hopefully in this millennium."

"It's work."

"It's always work."

"That's how I met you," he reminded her, sliding onto the bed and leaning close enough to kiss her neck. She scooted away, leaning back to look at him dead-center, straight in the eyes. "I remember," she agreed, some of the starch leaving her spine. "Yeah." Her voice softened a bit. "Believe me, I'm not trying to be a bitch, but, you know, you've got a family now." Her gaze touched his with the same intensity it always had, but there was something more. Though she was struggling to mask her hurt with anger, he saw it.

"This was the deal when we got married."

"I know."

"So you can't be mad now."

"Sure I can. The rules changed. We have a child."

"Speaking of whom..." Montoya scooted off the bed and headed out the door.

"Oh, no, you don't! Reuben! If you wake him up, I swear I'll kill you," she called after him in a stage whisper.

Montoya didn't pay any attention. The door to the baby's room was ajar, and he stepped inside, where the night-lights gave off a soft glow. Benjamin was sleeping, but Montoya didn't hesitate to pick him up and carry him into the master bedroom, where Abby had unpaused the television. A laugh track was softly playing for a sitcom he didn't recognize.

"I told you—"

"Shhh."

Cradling the baby, Montoya slid onto the bed. Ansel meowed in protest, then hopped to the floor and slunk out of the room.

Little Ben yawned, showing off his gums, not opening his eyes. He had a head of dark hair, some of which seemed to be rubbing off, and pudgy arms and legs. He looked more like his father than his mother, but that could certainly change over time. Montoya hoped so.

Abby hit the MUTE button and the TV went silent. "Okay," she said, "apology accepted."

"Good."

"But I still don't like it."

Theirs was an argument that had been brewing for months. "What do you want me to do? Hand in my badge? Become a security guard at the mall?"

"Don't be silly. I just think you can get a safer job with the department, one where you have more regular hours." She shoved a stray piece of hair out of her eyes and gently touched her son's cheek. "What about a desk job?"

"I'd go nuts in two minutes."

She sighed through her nose and rested her forehead against his, the baby between them on the bed. "Yeah, you would."

"This is what I do, Abs. I get the bad guys."

"And you love it."

"Yep." He saw a question forming and cut it off. "Don't ask me to choose. That's not fair. Apples and oranges. You and Ben, you know what you mean to me."

"But—"

"No buts. That's just the way it is. I believe we can have a family, and I can still do my job."

She smiled but there was a trace of sadness in her eyes. "You know I love you, and, yeah, I bought into the whole rebel-cop thing, fell for you hard. Okay, I admit it, but, damn it, now it's not just you and me. Ben needs his dad. I need my husband. The game's changed." She rolled her eyes. "Oh, God, now I sound whiny and needy, a wife who's trying to manipulate her husband. I hate that."

"Then stop." He kissed her gently, then changed the subject. "I brought bread and wine."

"Such a hero."

"Maybe we can eat whatever you made tomorrow night?"

"Seafood Alfredo?" She wrinkled her nose. "Not so great on the second day."

"Sorry."

She nodded. "Anyway, I offered some to Cruz."

Montoya's head jerked up at the mention of his brother's name.

Abby explained, "He stopped by to see Ben earlier, but he couldn't stick around."

"There's a surprise."

"Must run in the family."

Montoya said, "So okay, you're pissed. I get it." He turned his palms to the ceiling. "What do you want me to do, Abby?"

"I don't know."

"Tomorrow. We'll go out. Get a sitter for Ben."

"Oh, right, in the middle of the case." She knew him better than that. For the first time that night, she actually smiled with some humor. "I don't think I'll hold my breath."

"Oh, ye of little faith—"

"That's me. Okay, let's not fight. You're forgiven," she said, rolling off the bed. That was the great part about her; she never stayed mad for long. Oh, she could get white hot and fast, but it always dissipated quickly.

Her feet hit the floor. "I guess this is where I play the part of the doting wife."

"Yeah, right."

"You take care of your son and I'll heat up your dinner."

"You don't have to—"

"You got that right. I don't." She stopped at the doorway, barefoot, one hand on the door, her gaze skewering his. "But I know you were out bustin' crime, tryin' to make the city safe, right? So I'm offering you an olive branch here, because I know I came off like a world-class bitch. You know I do understand that your work is important, that you're trying like crazy to find out who killed that poor nun."

Folding her arms under her breasts, she leaned against the doorway with her shoulder and added, "Look, I know being a cop is in your blood, okay? But sometimes I can't help myself. What you do scares me to death. There are nights when it's really late and you're not home, and I go quietly out of my mind. My imagination goes into overdrive. I get scared that something's happened to you and I'll never see you again and . . . and Ben won't know his father and . . ." She met his gaze, her eyes filled with a quiet, dark fear. "I can't help it, Reuben," she admitted. "That thought scares the hell out of me."

CHAPTER 25

The room was dark, just a hint of moonlight shafting through the tiniest of windows. The heat of the day had settled beneath the rafters, humid heat trapped in the small space.

As a night bird cried, its call plaintive over the quietness of the city, Edwina let her nightdress fall into a puddle at her feet, then kicked off her underwear.

She turned and stared at her reflection in the cracked mirror propped against the wall of the attic. She was naked, her skin white and bare, her body half in shadow, half catching the weak light of the moon. The crack in the mirror split the light and dark halves of her image imperfectly, reminding her that she was but a servant of God, that she was ultimately flawed—a sinner.

Her pale braid fell over one shoulder, the end of the plait brushing the tip of her small breast. Her body was still muscular and athletic, her waist small, her shoulders wide, her hips slim. Her nipples were tiny and dark, one visible, the other hidden in shadow. Her nest of blond hair at the juncture of her legs, too, was cleaved in the mirror's distorted image.

Swallowing back any doubts, she reached forward, her fingers exploring the back side of the mirror, finding the nail protruding from the thick wooden frame surrounding the glass and the smooth leather crop that hung hidden there.

Her fingers curled over the worn handle, pulling free the whip with its nine leather straps.

She fell to her knees in front of the glass. She said a prayer under her breath, then lifted the wicked little whip high over her head, its nine tails with their hard little knots dangling high.

"Forgive me," she whispered, thinking of all her sins. So many. So deep. A lifetime of wickedness, until she had come here, until she had learned how to receive ultimate absolution.

"You must overcome pain and fear," she'd been told. "You must transcend the mortal and atone...."

As she had so many night before, she stared at herself in the mirror's reflection, then cocked her wrist.

"Welcome the pain, the remission of your sins."

She did. Bravely, she flicked her wrist.

Snap!

The whip flicked.

SSSST! It hissed through the air.

Slap!

Like hornets stinging, the strips of leather bit.

Sharp.

Quick.

She sucked in her breath.

Didn't flinch.

Didn't cry out.

Didn't dare close her eyes.

Because she knew, deep in her soul, she was being observed, her actions noted.

Who was watching?

She didn't know.

One pair of eyes? Two? A dozen?

She couldn't begin to guess.

It didn't matter.

She let her breath out and squared her shoulders.

Then she raised the whip again and snapped her wrist.

Its sharp hiss echoed through the room.

It was far too late to call in favors tonight, Val thought, but come the morning, at the crack of dawn, she would be on the phone.

What she couldn't find out for herself on the Internet she'd have her ex-partner look into through police channels. One of his room-mates from college had worked for the FBI for years, so there would be ways to find out their true identity. Find out who Mary and Michael Brown really were.

Since her truce with Slade a few hours before, she'd been dig-ging for information on the Internet, but every search produced no results. Then, because she couldn't completely ignore her obliga-tions as Freya's partner and owner of the inn, she'd forced herself to attack the bills, paying the most pressing, then updating the cal-endar on Briarstone's Web site.

Here, in the office of her little cottage, she took care of the busi-ness end of running the bed-and-breakfast. When she wasn't help-ing Freya with the guests, she checked the reservations, maintained the Web site, paid the bills, kept up the calendar of local events and sites of interest, and corresponded with other bed-and-breakfasts in the area.

The wireless system in the cottage was accessible from the rooms in the main house, so guests could use their own laptops. However, the inn did not provide computers or a business center, and the only televisions were in Freya's suite and here, in Val's bed-room. Freya's vision for the bed-and-breakfast included keeping Briarstone as authentic to the period in which it was built as possi-ble without sacrificing a few modern conveniences, like individual bathrooms and electricity. In general, they tried to keep electronics to a minimum.

Fortunately, tonight, her computer had only lost its connection a couple of times, far better than usual. Val closed her laptop and stepped out to the porch, where the moist air smelled of river and night. Clouds blocked out the moon and stars again, a storm brew-ing. Leaning against the railing, she glanced over to the main house, where Slade had been helping Freya clear a backed-up drain in the kitchen that had required not only emptying the P-trap but also renting a snake and unclogging the pipes.

He'd also managed to replace some broken face plates on elec-trical outlets and fix a temperamental light in the foyer. In so doing, he'd ingratiated himself to Freya.

"Handy as well as handsome," Freya, pushing a vacuum cleaner into a nearby closet, had remarked when Val had stopped in during a break from her research.

Wanting to avoid any further conversation about her soon-to-be ex, Val had ducked into the kitchen, which was filled with the odors of cinnamon, bacon, and apples for the next morning's bread pudding.

But there'd been no escaping Freya. Wiping her hands on a towel, she'd returned to the kitchen to peer into the oven. "Yeah, I understand why you're set on ditching him," Freya had said.

"Don't start with me." Val hadn't been in the mood.

"Ouch! Touchy, aren't we?"

"Ouch! Nosy, aren't we?"

Freya had laughed and held up her hands in mock surrender. "Okay. Okay. I get it. Talking about Slade is off-limits. I remember the agreement."

"Good." Val had walked into the laundry room, taken the last of the towels from the dryer, and folded them before retreating to her cottage again.

Now Val walked to a corner of the porch that allowed her to look up at the uppermost floor of the house. Lights still burned bright in the room Slade was renting.

She'd told him to get out of town, and he hadn't listened. In fact, he'd seemed all the more insistent upon staying. She should have been angry that he was still here.

Instead, stupid as it was, she felt safer, more secure.

But then, she decided as the first drops of rain plopped against the porch's roof, she'd always been an idiot where men were concerned.

The news reports have it wrong.

All wrong.

Of course.

Then again, why would I expect anything more?

With only candlelight illuminating my small, hidden room, I watch an ancient television. It's disturbing, really, that the reporters are so incompetent.

As bad as the police.

At the thought of the detectives assigned to the case, my stomach turns. Reuben Montoya and his partner Rick Bentz. Suspicious men with narrowed eyes and pointed questions. Men without faith. I turn away from the screen so that I only hear the report of what happened to Sister Camille: the unfortunate victim of some sadistic killer.

That makes me smile to myself, and I send up a quick prayer of thanks to the Father for granting me a superior intelligence.

If they only knew.

Facing the TV, I glare at the reporter's plastic face.

"Come on," I whisper between my teeth, desperate to see the images, to hear the reports. I have no patience for the sad tone of the reporter's words as she aggrandizes the deceased.

Camille the beautiful.

Camille the liar.

Camille the condemned.

Did "Sister Camille" understand about conviction?

No.

Did she take her vows seriously?

Of course not.

At last the newscast shows a picture of Camille in her full habit, appearing pious, a rosary draped through her fingers.

Such incredible blasphemy.

Watching those angelic images of her upon the screen, I can barely tolerate the perfidy. And yet the wanting stays with me, and I remember her body against mine, the torturous but sweet warmth of her whisper against my ear, the sly smile and bright bit of wickedness in her gaze.

Oh ... to touch her again.

To lay with her in sin ...

I close my eyes. Feel her breath upon my face. The back of my throat turns to dust with the wanting. "Camille," I whisper, and my fists curl in frustration. I consider self-flagellation—the smooth whip with its sharp bite—but not tonight. There is no time.

For now the wanting is enough of a punishment.

But there will be more.

A reckoning.

As my eyelids open, I see the fuzzy screen again.

The report of her death makes my insides churn. I could throw up at all the accolades bestowed upon Camille, as if she were truly holy, on her way to canonization—a saint.

Which is the ultimate profanity.

She was as far from saintly as Jezebel.

And just as tempting.

Her smiling, beatific visage is such a sham. I can't stand the ignominy any longer. Angrily, I turn off the television.

"Rot in hell," I whisper as the image fades to black.

But Camille's face stays with me, haunts me as I blow out the candle. A pain as hot as the fires of Hades tears through my soul.

Then I hear her laughter, as surely as if she were still at my side.

My stomach curdles as I walk out of the room, and in a vain effort to keep her ghost from chasing after me, I lock the door.

CHAPTER 26

Gracie Blanc needed cash. She was late on her rent again, and that creep of an apartment manager Harold Horwood, who had the balls to call himself McHorny, like a character on a popular television show—oh, sure—was pressuring her, offering to be her pimp for special privileges. "You're a whore, and I've got a woody. Get it? Horwood?" he'd said, thinking he was super clever.

Gross.

He wasn't even bad-looking, with his straight, near-black hair and ever-tanned complexion, but his attitude made her stomach churn. She needed to get another place.

All his attempts to enter pimpdom were a waste of time. Grace was independent. She didn't need some man "managing" her career, as McHorny had put it so often. As if turning tricks was her lifelong ambition.

She needed a new place to live and a new job. The trouble was her current apartment was cheap, and she was good at what she did; she just couldn't make the same amount of money tending bar or pouring coffee at an all-night diner.

She walked along Bourbon Street, the lights flickering, the crowd jostling her in her platform shoes and shorts. Here, she didn't get a second look, nearly blending in with the crowd that filled the street, so she turned toward the river and walked a few blocks away, where there was less noise, fewer people, and the cops didn't patrol as often.

Here, cars could actually pass and identities were hidden in the shadows.

She paused under a streetlamp, lit a cigarette, and made her way to her favorite corner. Sometimes she had to share the territory, which was all right; she felt safer just knowing another working girl would notice her. And she had her cell phone if anything got a little too kinky or rough.

The night was warm but thick, the rain threatening to start in earnest. Even so, because she was desperate and couldn't go back to her apartment without some cash, she let her jacket slide off her shoulder.

In a tube top and black leather skirt, she knew she looked her best. She kept herself in shape, her waist small, her ass a "bubble butt" that wasn't too large, just big enough to attract attention. Her hair was still thick and lustrous, falling nearly to her waist in loose red curls. The johns loved her hair. Oh, they were into her breasts, too, but it was her fiery, tousled hair that really caught their attention.

Go figure.

She leaned up against a light post and took a deep drag on her cigarette as a few cars rolled slowly past. She gave each one an interested eye, but no one stopped and no windows were down. It wasn't worthwhile to call out.

A bunch of teenage boys drove by. Their car, a black Lexus two-door, throbbed with music, the bass heavy even through the closed windows. On the second pass, they stopped and a cloud of marijuana smoke drifted out as the driver's window was eased down.

She sauntered up to the driver's door. A pimply faced kid who didn't look old enough to have a license, his hands gripping the wheel so hard his knuckles showed white, could barely look at her.

There were four other boys crammed into the car.

"How much?" the driver asked nervously, and the kid in the passenger seat had the brains to turn down the rap music.

She eyed the group, thought of her younger brother in Duluth.

He was older than these punks, but not by much. "Five hundred a piece," she said, because she had her standards. Underage horny boys, especially a pack of them, were off-limits. Big trouble.

"What?" In the lamplight, the driver looked like he'd just peed himself.

"Fuck! No way!" an African American dude in the backseat called. "That's highway robbery, man."

"Going rate."

"Like hell."

"That's the going part of it. You'd better get going."

"That bitch tryin' to rip us off!" said another kid, one in the shadows of the backseat, his face hidden.

She wasn't into playing games.

"Gang bangs aren't free," she said.

"You ain't seen what I got, baby," No-Face purred. As if he were God's gift.

The rain was coming down hard now, so she said, "So let me show *you all* what *I* got, okay?"

"Yeah, baby," the guy in the passenger seat said.

Gross.

She whipped out her cell phone. "If you don't want me to call my pimp, then you'd better get yourselves out of here. You know he's pretty badass."

"We...we got fifty bucks," one kid offered up. Jesus, had his voice even changed? "Don't that buy a blow job? It's my bro Jesse's birthday."

"Happy birthday, Jesse," she said. "How old are you?"

A kid with red hair pressed his face to the window of the backseat.

"He's eighteen," No-Face insisted.

She almost laughed. Jesse couldn't have been more than fourteen, fifteen tops. The fun was over. She threw her cigarette onto the street, mashed it out with the toe of her platform, then dialed a fake number into the phone. When a male voice answered, thank God, she said, "Yeah, Big Len, I got me a little problem down here...Yeah, my usual corner. Some punk kids are hassling me...Yeah, bring Ralph along. And make it quick."

"She's just fuckin' with us, man." No-Face again. The wise one.

"I wish she was fuckin' us," the black dude said. "Check out her ass."

Gracie glanced down the street, as if expecting someone. That did it for the driver. His mouth opened and closed like a fish out of water. "I'm outta here. My dad will kill me if I get into any trouble with his car."

"What a pussy!" No-Face wasn't impressed, but the driver hit the gas, tearing out and nearly running a stoplight.

She was about to give up when a silver sedan, one that had driven around the block a couple of times, showed up again. This was it, her last chance. The rain was playing hell with her hair and makeup.

The car eased up to the corner, and a guy with dark glasses rolled down his window. No marijuana. No group of testosterone-driven teenagers. No rap music, just the quiet banter of a radio talk show.

"You lookin' for a good time?"

"Always." His smile was enigmatic.

"It'll cost ya," she said, but he was nodding; he knew the drill. He didn't even flinch when she upped her standard fee twenty bucks.

Man, the rain was really coming down now. His windshield wipers slapped it wildly off the glass.

"It has to be my place," she was saying.

"Of course. I'll drive."

She hurried around the back of the car and slid into the passenger seat. It smelled clean, no lingering smoke, so she didn't light up, just rattled off the address as he, dressed all in black, his jacket zipped to his neck, drove calmly, not talking. The swish of the wipers and hiss of the tires over the wet pavement underscored the drone of the radio. He drove the speed limit—no hurry—and they arrived at the old apartment building where she resided. Her two rooms were on the first floor, near the back entrance. She dashed through the rain with him on her heels, and though she thought it odd that he didn't remove his sunglasses, Gracie was used to all kinds of freaks, some of whom didn't even want sex; they just wanted to talk or watch her fondle herself, or... well, whatever. If she'd learned anything in this business, it was that she couldn't guess what made a john tick.

Damn, the hallway reeked of Mrs. Rubino's old-world spaghetti sauce, meaning there was enough essence of garlic to keep even the toughest vampire at bay. And her television was cranked to the max, the noise from one of her favorite late-night game shows echoing down the corridor. Mrs. Rubino, nearly deaf and overly friendly to the point of being downright nosy, was Gracie's only neighbor on this side of the building. The maintenance room, elevator, and stairway to the upper floors separated the two units.

Gracie didn't apologize for the odor and knew that it would stop at her doorway. She always made sure her rooms smelled of vanilla and musk, the scents of the candles and incense she burned in her tiny quarters.

Quickly, she unlocked her door and stepped inside.

The john followed after her, and as she lit the candles, she heard him shrug off his jacket.

"I get paid in advance," she said gently, touching the end of her lighter to the charred wick of a tall, fragrant taper.

"I know." His voice was low, nearly melodic, and she felt rather than saw him withdraw his wallet, open it, and leave the money on the small kitchen table near the window. Then she heard the venetian blinds snap shut.

She set down the lighter. The ambiance was lost on so many of her johns, but she liked the soft light and warm scents. Shrugging out of her jacket, she turned and her heart nearly stopped when she saw the clerical collar that had been hidden under his coat.

"You're a... priest?" she asked, though it didn't matter. Men of God were still men, and the john might not even be a priest. How many "doctors" had she met who didn't know one end of a stethoscope from the other?

He didn't reply, just removed his clothes, taking off his pants and folding them, doing the same with his shirt and collar. Candlelight showed off his muscles, hard and sinewy, a strong man and handsome, though she couldn't see his eyes through his dark glasses.

He could have been a male model, she thought, but for the

wicked scar on one leg, a jagged, red gash that seemed to pulse. She tried not to think of what might have caused it. A horrid motorcycle accident?

Maybe something worse.

Shuddering inwardly, she caught a glimpse of the bill he'd tucked under the empty vase on the table. A C-note...but it was off— Ben Franklin's eyes blackened. Her skin crawled a little; then she told herself to get over it. So the hundred-dollar bill was marred? So what? It would spend as easily as a crisp new one. And it would make a good dent in the rent she owed, get Harold off her back.

She turned her attention to the job at hand.

His cock hung limp.

"Wear this," he said, and as he walked closer to her, she caught a glimpse of something sparkling in the candlelight, little glass beads oozing through the fingers of his right hand.

A rosary?

What was this?

Did he expect her to kneel and pray with him?

Talk about kinky!

"You haven't said what you want," she told him. He was close enough to kiss her now, to yank off her tube top or push her skirt over her hips.

If he wanted to.

"Submission," he said softly, and leaned forward, nuzzling her neck. "Total and complete submission."

"Whatever you want," she whispered back, smiling, her hands reaching upward to circle his neck, her breasts pushing through the flimsy knit fabric of her top to rub suggestively against the hair that was thick upon his chest. "Everything's for sale...even submission."

"I thought so." His smile twisted a bit as he walked her backward through the open bedroom door.

Was there something in his hands? She'd felt something... more than the rosary.

"Take off your clothes."

"No prob." At least he was getting down to business. She did a quick little striptease for him, hoping to see some life come to his dick, but the damn thing didn't so much as twitch, not even when she held her breasts in her hands, letting her nipples peek through her fingers.

Wouldn't you know?

"You look good," she cooed, working on his male ego.

He didn't respond, just set a small radio on the bed and turned it on, back to the talk show that had been playing in the car. Then, almost methodically, as if it were a ritual, he slid the rosary over her head and let it dangle against her breasts, the beads warm from holding them in his hand.

To get the show going, she let him kiss her. And fondle her a little roughly.

As they fell onto the faded quilt on her old mattress, she tried to ramp up the heat, licking him, purring against him, rubbing all those places she knew usually guaranteed an immediate and hard reaction.

Not this time.

Oh, great. She'd really have to work for her money tonight. Wouldn't you know. But at least the guy was good-looking. She reached up to remove his glasses, and he caught her wrist.

"Don't touch them!"

"Oh, wow. Okay."

"I mean it." His voice was rough, and for the first time she felt his cock twitch.

"I said okay."

Wow, this was getting a little weird. Better get him off and fast, then kick him the hell out. She began kissing him again, working her magic, but he pulled back and stared down at her through the shaded lenses. "You're a whore," he said.

She played along. Whatever fantasy turned him on. "And you like whores, don't you, Father?"

"I detest them." His dick was actually coming to life.

"So you want to punish me?" she asked. God, was the guy into spanking? Well, she could handle a little of that. She rolled over, pushing her ass into the air; then she looked over her shoulder coquettishly, through a veil of wild red curls. "Have I been bad?" she asked, playing into his fantasy. "Have I sinned? Do I need a spanking?" She let her lips roll into a pout.

His mouth curved into a wicked smile. He slapped her hard, right on the ass.

She yelped.

"A spanking is just the start," he said, pulling the rosary tight, the beads sharper than she'd expected as they cut into her throat.

"Hey!" she tried to scream, but her voice was silent. Only little gurgling noises erupted, and he was pinning her down, his weight pushing her into the mattress, her face forced into the pillows.

Panic tore through her.

She struggled. Kicking upward. Trying to push him off. Feeling his erection grow stiffer, harder, fatter the more she fought.

Oh, God, he was a freak, a murderous freak!

Her lungs were on fire, her strength fading, his breathing rough against her ear, the radio whispering into the room that grew darker by the instant.

NO! NO! NO!

Gracie thought of her brother in Minnesota, the last time she'd seen her mother, and then wondered why she'd trusted this sick priest.

God help me, she thought.

And then there was nothing.

CHAPTER 27

"Your boy's lawyered up," Brinkman said as Montoya walked into the lunchroom the next day. It was not the news Montoya wanted to hear this early in the morning, never the type of news to be received from the guy who put the "dick" in *detective*.

Irritated, Montoya moved away from Brinkman, the soles of his shoes squeaking on the floor, which was shiny from the previous night's cleaning. The lingering odor of some pine-scented cleaner mingled with the aroma of brewing coffee.

Several cops were grabbing their morning cups; a few others leaned over the tables cluttered with newspapers and magazines. While sipping from their steaming mugs, they scanned headlines and exchanged barbs before heading to their desks. On one of the round tables, a box of cupcakes lay open, crumbs and wadded, used cupcake papers surrounding half a dozen remaining cakes decorated with white frosting and chocolate sprinkles.

When Montoya didn't respond, Brinkman added, "You know, the priest. Seems as if his daddy is some hotshot attorney."

Montoya remembered Frank's old man. Tall, lanky, always well dressed in a suit or polo shirt and slacks with a perfect crease down each leg. Even if he was just going to one of his kids' basketball practices or a football scrimmage, Raymond "Buzz" O'Toole looked the part of the successful attorney. A scratch golfer with a taste for scotch, he'd been disappointed when his son had preferred soccer to football.

Montoya imagined that Buzz was nearly apoplectic that his son, a man of God, was involved in a sordid scandal.

Montoya said, "I thought Buzz O'Toole was an estate attorney. Never touched criminal stuff."

"Yeah, well, he's got friends in low places." Brinkman scowled at the near-empty coffeepot. "Someone over at that firm where your brother-in-law used to work."

Technically, Cole Dennis was Abby's brother-in-law, not his, but Montoya wasn't in the mood to split hairs. Especially with Brinkman, who was always looking to bring up something uncomfortable.

What a jerk.

"The upshot is that I talked to the attorney, who's claiming his client's innocence because good ol' Father Frank has B-positive blood."

"Then he's not the baby's father."

Montoya felt a flash of relief. He'd found it impossible to believe that Frank O'Toole had killed anyone. At least not the Frank O'Toole he remembered.

"Doesn't mean he didn't do her," Brinkman said. "And I'm not talkin' in the biblical sense; we know he did that. But he could have found out she was bangin' someone else and went off. Killed her."

"After making sure she was wearing a wedding dress?"

"Whatever turns him on." Brinkman's smile was smarmy.

"Nah. Too premeditated."

"Ya never know. Just a theory."

"We need facts," Montoya said.

"I gave you some. You don't even have to wait for DNA to start lookin' for another guy as the kid's father. Man, nuns weren't this hot when I was growin' up. I had to get off on the girls in their uniforms—y'know, with the knee socks and pleated skirts—"

"Oh, God, please, stop now," one of the female officers said. She cast Brinkman a pained look as she placed a sack lunch in the refrigerator. "Let's be grown-ups."

Montoya agreed. He didn't have time for Brinkman's sexual fantasies. He had his own to deal with. Last night, he'd been able to patch things up with Abby, which had included the kind of love-making session they'd shared before the baby had been born. If he let himself, he could get a hard-on just thinking about it, so he didn't. At least he'd woken up in a decent mood, one Brinkman seemed intent on ruining.

"Back to O'Toole," he said, interrupting Brinkman's sleazy train of thought.

"I'm just sayin', we have to get his attorney involved." Edging over to the near-empty box of cupcakes, Brinkman added, "Pain in the ass," before snagging one of the treats. He crossed to the coffeepot, picked it up, and scowled. To the few cops still hanging out in the lunchroom, he said, "If anyone else wants a cup of Joe, they're SOL." Even though he obviously hoped someone would take the bull by the horns and brew another pot, no one jumped up to take over.

Lynn Zaroster, one of the youngest female detectives, walked into the kitchen at that moment and saw Brinkman holding up the empty pot. He offered her a wink and smile.

Charming.

She wasn't buying it. "Oh, yeah, zero in on the woman because all this kitchen stuff is women's work, right? Give me a break, Brinkman!"

"Hey, I'm just talking about making a fuckin' pot of coffee."

"Got it." Lynn did a quick one-eighty out of the lunchroom, her short, black curls swirling indignantly behind her.

"It's not about being a woman. It's because you're better at it than I am," Brinkman called after her.

"Yeah, right."

The female cop who had taken on Brinkman earlier sent him a look guaranteed to send his soul straight to hell and then walked out of the lunchroom.

Louis Brounier, who had observed the whole exchange, shook his head as he stood and gathered his paper. A big, burly African American with a fleshy face and silver hair, Brounier couldn't move as fast as he once had, but his dark eyes caught everything, including Brinkman's ridiculous self-imposed predicament. "Ya know, Brinkman, you might have to break down and make your own coffee."

"Bite me, Brounier."

"You wish."

"Look, I got a case to solve," Brinkman complained.

"Just one? Lucky you."

"You know, Brounier, you can be a real douche bag."

"I'm just saying we're all busy." Brounier tucked his newspaper under his arm and sauntered out of the lunchroom, muttering, "Pansy ass," under his breath.

Brinkman called out, "I heard that!"

"Good."

Brinkman snagged a second cupcake and motioned toward the box. "What's the occasion anyway?"

"Peggy's, in Missing Persons, birthday," Del Albright said out of the corner of his mouth. He was leaning against the counter, perusing the Sports page. "Rita brought 'em in. You might want to save one for Peg."

"Why?" Brinkman bit off half the cupcake and said around a mouthful, "She's always on a diet."

Montoya had had enough. He left the conversation behind and went to his desk to start reviewing files and double-checking the timeline for the last hours of Camille Renard's life.

Her last twenty-fours hadn't been that out of the ordinary. She'd spent most of her day at the convent, only going out for about six hours to where she worked in the orphanage in the preschool.

If she'd hooked up with O'Toole or any other man, she'd been discreet.

And she'd never sent the letter tucked inside her mattress. The lab was still processing that kinky bit of unsent correspondence. There had been a desperate, almost pleading tone in her demands for sexual favors.

Why the hell was she a nun? Montoya believed there might be some unfulfilled sexual needs in most members of the clergy. Hell, celibacy was a bitch. Abstinence nearly impossible.

People were sexual creatures.

To take a vow of celibacy, one's convictions had to be so much stronger than natural animal attraction. He really believed most members of the Catholic clergy pulled it off. But there were a few who couldn't.

Sister Camille was obviously one.

And she knew it, was thinking of leaving the order.

"Too late," he whispered, caught up in the enigma that was Camille Renard.

He took a few calls while he waited for the autopsy report, but in the back of his mind, he wondered who the father of Camille's baby was. A parishioner? Maybe a father of one of the kids she worked with? Or workers at the convent? Clifton Sharkey was the maintenance man for St. Marguerite's, fifty-four, the father of six and a grandfather twice over. Elwin Zaan a forty-two-year-old janitor. Both with airtight alibis for the time of Camille's death.

Nothing was making any sense, he thought, finishing his coffee just as the autopsy report came in through his e-mail. Setting his cup aside, he viewed the photographs and read through the notes. He wasn't surprised that the coroner confirmed what the prelim had suggested: Camille Renard, eight or nine weeks pregnant, had died of asphyxiation due to having her air supply cut off by a garrote that was uneven in texture. The cuts and abrasions on her neck were deeper in some spots, a pattern clear.

But there was an oddity, too. The ME had discovered scars on Camille's back, tiny lines crisscrossing her shoulders and lower, mostly healed, certainly not part of the attack that killed her.

He frowned, made a note, and kept reading.

As he perused the report, ugly memories assailed him, gruesome images from another case where victims were killed in a like manner. He typed the name of that killer into his computer, just as his partner paused in the doorway.

"Father John," Bentz said, eyeing the screen.

Montoya froze at the mention of a serial killer who had terrorized the city years before. "He's dead. You took care of that. Remember?"

He pointed to the computer monitor where a picture of the first victim of the serial killer, known as Father John, appeared. Cherie Bellechamps, a local prostitute, had had the misfortune of meeting the twisted psycho masquerading as a priest, only to come to a horrifying, grisly end.

"Maybe."

"Holy Christ, Father John has to be dead." Montoya thought of the madman, a tall, good-looking man with a sordid penchant for killing. Bentz had shot him dead in the swamp. Right?

"Same weapon." Bentz had come to the same conclusion as Montoya: Camille Renard had been killed with a rosary used as a garrote.

"Jesus, don't even go there." Montoya didn't like the dread crawling through him. "It's been years. What, ten? Twelve?"

"About that." Bentz's brow furrowed.

"But Father John killed prostitutes, or people he thought were whores." Montoya was still shaking his head.

"Maybe a nun who got herself pregnant qualifies."

"He's dead, man!" Montoya thought Bentz was definitely barking up the wrong tree.

"Never found his body."

"Well, shit, so what? It was the goddamned swamp. You nailed him!" Montoya felt his blood pressure rise. He wanted that son of a bitch dead. Forever. "Besides, in this case, the MO is way different. The killer didn't leave any C-notes with Ben Franklin's eyes blacked out sitting around, the way that other sick bastard did. Nobody's complained about a priest running around in sunglasses. And the biggy—Camille Renard wasn't raped. No sign of sexual trauma, according to the autopsy report. Father John got off on raping his victims as well as killing them."

"You're right," Bentz said, "but still—"

"I'm tellin' ya, this isn't the work of a serial killer," Montoya said. "This murder"—he tapped Camille Renard's autopsy report with one finger—"it's personal. The killer knew her."

Bentz tugged at his tie. From his pinched eyes and washed-out face, he looked as if he hadn't slept in days, which was probably right on. Bentz's infant daughter was colicky, kept Bentz and his wife, Olivia, up at all hours. "Just a thought."

"Yeah, well, a bad one," Montoya said. To prove his point, he opened the computer image of Camille Renard as she'd been found in the yellowed wedding dress, lying near the base of the altar. Then he put the two photos side by side, Camille beside the battered body of Cherie Bellechamps spread-eagle on the dingy sheets of a cheap motel room bed. There were other photographs as well, and he clicked through them, searching for any link to the other victims of Father John, a nutcase if ever there was one.

"I hope he's dead," Bentz said fervently, then, dragging his gaze from the computer screen, added, "I've got one lead. Found the wireless service Camille Renard used and got the records for her BlackBerry. The cell phone company sent them over this morning."

That was a start. "You have a chance to go through them?"

"Uh-huh."

"And?"

Bentz laid the list of telephone numbers on Montoya's desk. "Most are what we expected—calls to her sister and to O'Toole, of course. To the orphanage, where she worked, and even a call here"—he pointed to one number in the list—"to the parish." He slid his finger lower, to another number. "The only one that is a question mark is to a prepaid cell phone. Get this, I already talked to the store where it was purchased, by cash, of course, but the person who bought it was none other than Camille Renard."

"So she had two cell phones?"

"Unless someone posed as her or she bought it and gave it to someone else," Bentz said. "They've got security cameras in the store and keep the tapes for several months. Later today I'm gonna review the tape for the day it was purchased, just to make sure Camille was the buyer. If someone else was impersonating her, we've got ourselves a lead to follow. And if it was Camille Renard, where the hell are the damned phones?"

"Probably with her BlackBerry and diary." Montoya scowled and shoved a hand through his hair. "For a person who's supposed to give up worldly possessions, Sister Camille had quite a few."

"And then there's the baby. I double-checked, and Brinkman's right about the blood type. We're looking for a man with B-neg or AB-neg blood as the father."

"Apparently not Frank O'Toole."

Bentz nodded.

"Should narrow it down."

"Yep. We just have to find out who else Camille was sleeping with." He looked back at the nun's image on the monitor. "She had a pretty busy social life for a nun. No wonder her last e-mail to her sister said she was having second thoughts and planning to leave the convent."

Montoya tapped a pencil against the desk. "So who the hell got her pregnant?"

CHAPTER 28

"I'd just like to talk to her," Cruz said, flashing his most winning smile as he shifted on the uncomfortable chair in Sister Charity's office. The place gave him the creeps, reminding him of all the times he'd sat for hours in dim hallways with shiny linoleum floors that smelled of disinfectant, mold, and his own nervous sweat while waiting for the principal to mete out some form of cruel punishment on Cruz Montoya, forever the miscreant.

Today, in this tomb of an office, the old nun wasn't buying into Cruz's attempts at charm.

"This isn't a sorority house, Mr. Montoya," she said, tiny lines of disapproval evident around her lips. "It's a convent. With duties and obligations. We live a simple life of devotion, and we adhere to a strict schedule. If Sister Lucia wants to contact you, I'm sure she'll write you or call you during her free time." Sister Charity's face was glacial, the eyes behind her glasses as observant as a hawk's. She folded her hands over the desktop. Blue veins were visible beneath her skin, and yet the fingers appeared strong enough to snap a ruler in half. "If you leave your telephone number, I'll see that she gets it."

Cruz didn't believe it for a second. Sister Charity was definitely old school, more of a warden than a loving mother figure.

No way was she going to pass on his info.

They both knew it.

The lie simmered between them.

She was right about one thing, though—St. Marguerite's, with its stiff wooden chairs, crucifixes adorning the walls, and quiet, somber hallways was a far cry from any sorority house he'd ever set foot inside.

The reverend mother finally broke the silence. "You know, I find it interesting that you have come to visit Sister Lucia now, after our recent loss of Sister Camille. Your brother is investigating the case and now, poof," she said, her fingers lifting swiftly as if from a small explosion, "you show up."

"I came to visit my brother. When I saw him, he mentioned that Lucia was here. No crime there, sister."

Her keen eyes were sharp with intelligence, her mouth edged in cruelty. "So why do you want to see her?"

"It's personal."

"Is it?" She offered him an impassive smile that didn't touch her eyes. Growing up in a very Catholic family, Cruz had been around his share of nuns. Some had been stoic, some fun-loving, some seemed to be filled with the Holy Spirt, and some, drill sergeants like Sister Charity, were all about rules, obedience, and punishment. Cruz couldn't help but wonder what made the woman tick, what her story was. Where'd she come from? How had she ended up here, at St. Marguerite's, with Lucia?

"You can confide in me, Mr. Montoya."

Seriously? "I said it's personal."

With a long-suffering sigh, she stood, signifying the meeting was over. "Then I guess we're finished here. I'll be certain to let Sister Lucia know that you stopped by."

Another lie.

Cruz rose just as there was a series of soft raps on the door.

Little lines of irritation pinched the corners of Sister Charity's mouth. "If you'll excuse me," she said. "I'm a busy woman. You know what they say about God's work? That it's never done? Well, it's true, Mr. Montoya."

Another rap, then the receptionist, a laywoman with frizzy blue hair and a suit of olive polyester, poked her head inside. "I'm sorry to bother you, Reverend Mother," she said, glancing nervously at Cruz, "but there's a call for you. Sister Simone from St. Elsinore's."

"Thank you, Eileen, I'll take the call. Mr. Montoya was just leaving."

That was his cue.

As the receptionist retreated, Sister Charity moved back to her desk and reached for the receiver of the black telephone, a behemoth that looked like something straight out of the sixties. "God be with you," she said softly as Cruz left.

He walked past the impossibly thin receptionist and wondered why a church and convent, a house of God, could seem so evil.

Just your imagination.

He started for the main doors, then paused as he heard voices lifted in song. He knew he shouldn't intrude—as the reverend mother had reminded him, this was a place of worship and solace—but he tossed her warnings aside.

What was the worst that could happen?

He'd be tossed out on his ear?

So what?

The police would be called?

Nah. What would he be charged with? Trespassing? No way.

Quietly, feeling guilty of some nameless sin, he followed the sound of a hymn from his youth. Around a corner, the music was much louder.

It came through a door that was slightly ajar.

Accompanied by a pianist, the voices sang a rendition of *"Ave Maria"* that filled the small music chamber and flowed into the corridor. Women's voices rising in faith and song.

He peered inside.

A group of twenty or so nuns, all in black habits, were singing in harmony from their spots on risers. Their gazes were locked on the woman leading them, a tall nun with her back to the door.

Lucia Costa was front and center, her voice bright and clear.

Cruz's chest tightened. She hadn't changed much, still small and petite, her face without lines. Her eyes were large, with thick lashes and arched eyebrows, set above pronounced cheekbones that angled to a pointed chin.

In his mind's eye, he saw her trapped in the twisted metal that had been his car, blood streaming down the side of her face. Her black hair had been matted and lank, her eyes rolled upward in her head. Later she'd awoken for just a second and whispered in pain, "Danger . . ." then blacked out.

Guilt overtook him, and the scar splitting his eyebrow pulsed.

At that moment, Lucia's gaze strayed from the choir leader to the door, and she missed a note, her eyes rounding at the sight of Cruz. The two nuns next to her, a tall African American and a shorter woman with big glasses, shot her a look at the sour note.

Lucia blanched, tried to pay attention to the choir mistress who rapped her baton on the music stand in front of her. The music stopped, voices fading as the piano's notes ended abruptly.

Tap. Tap. Tap.

"Sisters, please!" the leader said sharply. "Sopranos? Is something wrong? Sister Lucia?"

"No," Lucia answered, her voice so familiar, as if he'd been with her just yesterday. "I . . . I just lost track of where we were."

"Then pay attention!" Again there was a rapping. "From the refrain," she said. A piano chord echoed through the hallways, and the female voices rose again.

He decided to wait.

Why not?

Again, the worst thing that could happen was that they'd toss him out. Well, so be it. Sister Charity might be an authority figure, but she wasn't exactly the Gestapo. She was a nun, for crying out loud.

He folded his arms over his chest and settled in near the door, one shoulder propped against the wall.

Some twenty minutes later, the singing stopped, giving way to the shuffling of feet. Suddenly nuns spilled into the hallway, a small parade of black habits, veils, and white wimples. Really, with them covered in those gowns and veils, Cruz could barely tell them apart.

Several stopped dead in their tracks at the sight of him.

"I'm Sister Irene. May I help you?" a tall woman asked, her gray eyes curious.

"I'd like to speak to Sister Lucia," Cruz said, his gaze traveling to Lucia, who looked as if she wanted to be swallowed up by the polished floor.

"This is highly irregular," a bookish nun in large glasses said.

"Shhh! Sister Maura," another tall one said. She was pretty, with even features and a pleasant smile. "I think Sister Lucia can handle herself. I'm Sister Devota."

"But no one's supposed to be in this part of the convent!" Sister Maura insisted.

A chubby nun with rosy cheeks giggled. "Oh, Maura, give it a rest."

"I will not, Sister Angela!" the bookish one said, blushing.

Lucia, white-faced, stepped forward. "I'll talk to him. He's.... uh, an old family friend. Cruz Montoya"—she shot him a look guaranteed to cut through steel, then said through tight lips—"this is Zita," as she motioned toward a black girl standing nearby.

"I'm Edwina," said an athletic woman with strong, Norse features and deep-set blue eyes that regarded him with suspicion.

Others, some of whom he'd heard called by name, introduced themselves quickly. As she introduced herself, plump Dorothy wrung her hands, and a nervous tic appeared at the corner of her eye. Louise, who was carrying sheet music, offered him a kind, if questioning, smile.

"Come with me," Lucia said to Cruz. "We can talk in the garden." She led him down the stairs, along a back hallway, and through double doors to a garden where a fountain gurgled.

As soon as the door closed behind them, Lucia whirled on him. "What the devil are you doing here?"

"Looking for you."

"After all this time?"

"You disappeared."

She stared at him. "I know. On purpose."

"Why?"

"Why?" She rolled her eyes. "Because I didn't want to see you again."

"You could have just said so."

"And you would have just walked away?"

He hesitated, remembering the guilt he'd felt after the accident, remembering how much he'd loved her. If that was the right word. Back then, guilt, desire, and love were all tangled up in his mind.

"See?" She touched him lightly on the shoulder. "Go away, Cruz. I'm taking vows to live the rest of my life as a servant of God."

"Seriously?"

"Yes." Her voice was firm, and though he noticed a sliver of doubt in her eyes, she stood tall, her chin up. He felt as if a cloud had passed over the sun, though no shadow stretched across the flowering shrubs. "Go," she added more urgently, as if she, too, had sensed the anomaly.

"Just one question."

"What?"

"Why did you decide to become a nun?"

"Isn't it obvious, Cruz?" she said. "I did it because of you."

His throat tightened, and he felt the ridiculous urge to kiss her. She tried to retreat, but he grabbed the crook of her arm, spinning her around. "And what did you mean when you said 'danger' the night of the accident?"

"That's two questions."

"Okay, I lied." His fingers curled over the heavy material of her habit. "What was the danger?"

She licked her lips nervously, making him groan inwardly. "Lucia?"

"You and me, Cruz, we're dangerous together, and—"

He saw her swallow.

"And we were flirting with danger just by dating." Now she was lying; he could tell by her polished movements, by the high pitch of her voice. She looked at him with those dark, intelligent eyes. "Now, let me go and leave me alone. I never want to see you again! Got that, Cruz? Never."

He didn't buy it for a second, and to his shock, he yanked her close and kissed her hard on the lips. Warmth invaded his blood, and she sighed into his mouth, hers opening under his.

He closed his eyes for a second and felt her release, the gentle pressure of her lips, the flick of her tongue, and for just a second she leaned into him. Surrendering to the fire that had always been there.

He groaned, hands splaying.

In a heartbeat, it was over.

She stiffened in his arms. "No!" she whispered, pulling away, staring at him in horror. "This can't happen." She backed up quickly as if stricken. "Oh...no..." She was shaking her head so quickly her veil trembled.

"Wait!" He wasn't going to lose her again. Not when he still had so many questions, so many unresolved feelings. "Lucia—"

"I mean it."

He grabbed the crook of her arm. "Then call me."

"No."

He rattled off his cell number, anyway, an easy one to remember, ending with the digits of the year she was born. "You won't forget."

"I will," she said, and pulled her arm back, forcing him to release her. "Go away, Cruz, and don't ever come back here! Never!" She nearly tripped as she scrambled away from him, running through heavy doors.

Cruz, his blood still pounding in his ears, turned to spy Sister Charity glaring down at him from an upper balcony. Her face said it all. Chalk-white against her black veil and twisted in disapproval...no, something more.

The paragon of virtue's features were set into an expression of disgust, as if she'd just seen something so vile and repulsive she couldn't speak.

As her eyes held his, she made the sign of the cross over her chest, leaving Cruz to wonder why the benign action seemed like a threat.

CHAPTER 29

It was late afternoon by the time Val and Slade headed to St. Elsi-nore's convent. The sun, hidden partially by clouds, was hanging low in the sky, threatening rain again as Slade drove toward the parish where Valerie and Camille had been adopted.

Most of the day had been filled with taking care of paperwork, guest registrations, and Internet reservations and helping Freya in the kitchen and with the laundry and guest rooms that the part-time maid couldn't get to. Though they didn't serve lunch, there were evening displays of wine, cheese, and crackers, along with something special Freya baked. This afternoon, she'd whipped up batches of her signature pralines and ginger cookies. The aromas of ginger and vanilla seeped through the airy rooms.

Any other time, Valerie would have been tempted by the scents and tasted the warm cookies, but today she hadn't been interested, and a part of her still couldn't believe the world just kept on turn-ing, people going about their lives, while Camille was now lying in a morgue, waiting for Valerie to make arrangements.

She just couldn't go there yet, hadn't totally accepted that she'd never see her sister again, never hear her laugh, never catch her eye at a private joke.

"Get over it," she'd told herself, but the sadness was still with her, lying in wait on the fringes of her consciousness, ready to play havoc with her emotions.

So she'd kept busy.

Today, as she'd worked, her cell phone had been near and she'd kept checking, hoping Montoya had called to tell her that Cammie's murderer had been caught.

But that was more complicated than she'd originally thought.

When she'd first heard about Camille's murder, Val had been certain Frank O'Toole had taken her sister's life, but the more she thought about it, the less likely she thought him capable of murder. She'd seen it in his eyes when she'd talked to him, his abject despondency at Camille's death.

The priest had vowed he'd loved Camille with such fervency that though she hated to admit it, Valerie almost believed him.

Almost.

But if not Frank O'Toole, then who had hated Camille so intensely as to kill her in the chapel, dressed in a wedding gown?

Someone with intense hatred.

Someone with a point to make.

Someone with access to and knowledge of the parish buildings.

Someone who could make Camille do his bidding.

Someone strong enough to control her.

"Damn it all to hell," she whispered as she considered the fact that with each passing minute, she believed the killer was getting farther and farther away. She couldn't let it happen. She had to be proactive in finding Cammie's killer.

Now Slade drove his truck out of the city on I-10, heading northeast, across the smooth waters of Lake Pontchartrain. Seagulls skimmed the water and wheeled in the sky where the hazy clouds hovered, diaphanously blanketing the sun.

Val's stomach was tight as they drove; her palms itched with her case of nerves.

The chapel came into view first, whitewashed bricks and stained-glass windows, a steeple rising high into the hazy day. Upon closer inspection, she saw that there were cracks in the steeple and that some of the glass panes had been covered in plywood, the whitewash dingy and streaked.

Through the fence, she saw a few children playing on old equipment as Slade pulled into a potholed parking lot. Val told herself that she was being ridiculous, that St. Elsinore's was a parish with an orphanage and the people who worked here were God-fearing and well intentioned.

High-pitched voices, squeals, and laughter rang through the play yard and into the quiet neighborhood surrounding the parish. Large trees, their leaves and gnarled branches creating a thick canopy, allowed sunlight to dapple the ground and the cracked sidewalks leading to the old, scarred doors of the orphanage.

Telling herself she was being an idiot, Val made her way up the broad steps and into the vestibule where the smell of warm bread and cinnamon invaded the dark hallways. She saw the office door with its pebbled glass window and pushed it open to find a woman sitting at a desk in front of a glowing computer screen. She looked up as they entered. "May I help you?" she asked, rising and extending her hand. "I'm Sister Philomena, the receptionist here." Her eyes were bright, her smile wide, her handshake firm. She was wearing slacks and a light sweater, her hair cut in a stylish bob.

A far cry from the black-draped, somber nuns Val remembered thirty-odd years earlier.

She introduced herself and told the nun that Slade was her husband, not bothering to try and explain her complicated relationship with him. "My sister was Sister Camille Renard, and I was told she worked here."

"Oh, yes. I'm so, so sorry for your loss." Sister Philomena seemed sincere. "Camille was a delight."

Tears threatened the back of Val's eyes at the compliment, surprised at the nun's kind words and her own reaction. With the new, emerging image of her sister, she was grateful that someone besides herself had seen the good in Cammie. "Thank you," she said, not so much as glancing at Slade.

Clearing her throat, she added, "I'd really like to talk to some of her coworkers."

"Or the priest?" she asked. "You know, Father Thomas is extremely understanding and can help you through your grief."

She wasn't here for grief counseling, but, of course, Sister Philomena didn't understand that. "Maybe later. For now, I'd like to speak with her friends. I know she worked here often."

"Of course." Sister Philomena was nodding. "We should start with the reverend mother." She turned, then rapped gently on an inner door, slipped inside, and within seconds, she returned, a tiny woman bustling after her.

Barely five feet, with curly brown hair shot with gray, the mother superior wore a navy blue skirt and a matching jacket over a white shell. Energy seemed to radiate from her. Her face was creased and tanned, as if she spent hours in the sun, and a gold crucifix dangled from a tiny chain around her neck, while reading glasses were perched upon the end of her small nose.

"I'm so sorry," she said, introducing herself as Sister Georgia and taking Val's hand in both of hers. Her face was a mask of concern. "This is a hard time for all of us. Come on into my office and we'll talk."

They followed her into a small room where they were motioned into worn chairs positioned at the front of Sister Georgia's desk. The room was compact but filled with light from several windows, one of which looked over the enclosed play area, now empty of children. Books lined one wall, and an antique globe was suspended in its own carved, wooden stand near a pot containing a burst of dark-throated orchids.

"How can I help you?" the reverend mother asked after everyone was seated.

"I'd like information about my sister," Val explained. "I know she worked here some of the time, and I heard that she was looking into our birth parents."

"Ah, yes, she was obsessed with finding out who they were."

"But we knew. I remember my birth parents!" Val said, and repeated the story she'd been told about her adoption. The reverend mother listened patiently, not interrupting, only once in a while glancing at Slade, who sat in the chair next to Valerie.

Once Val was finished, Sister Georgia said, "Of course, all the adoption records were sealed long ago. I couldn't help Camille except to counsel her, as I do with a lot of the people who come here searching for answers." She frowned slightly. "As for the validity of the story you were told..." She shrugged.

"But you could find out."

Georgia nodded. "Yes, but I've taken an oath. As I said, the files are sealed."

"Then find a way to unseal them," Val insisted, realizing that this kindly nun was just as rigid in her own way as Sister Charity was in hers. "This is my life"—she jabbed her thumb at her chest—"and I think there's a chance my sister was killed because of what she was looking into!"

The reverend mother's face remained impassive.

"Please. You can understand. I need to know the truth."

"Of course. It's just that I have responsibilities. Obligations, if you will—"

Slade's cell phone rang just as he was reaching into his pocket. "Sorry," he said quickly as Sister Georgia's lips tightened. "Excuse me," he said quickly, and made his way out of the office. Val heard him say, "Hello? Oh, damn. Which horse?...Look, I'm still in New Orleans. Call the vet..." And then his voice faded, cut off by the door as it closed behind him.

"How are you dealing with your loss?" the reverend mother asked, her composure once again intact. Concern etched her features. "It's difficult. I know."

"Yes," Val said, but she wasn't in the mood to talk about grief or pain or funeral arrangements. She'd come here for answers, and though this mother superior was a warmer, kinder person, she was as much of a road block as Sister Charity. She toned it down a notch, calmed herself, and said, "I really would like my birth records, and I would like to speak with the people Camille worked with, anyone who might have some idea of what happened to her."

"Isn't that what the police are doing?"

"Of course, but..." Val's hands clenched and opened as she tried another tack to get through to the woman. "Sister Georgia, do you have any siblings?" Val asked, tired of being stonewalled.

Sister Georgia nodded. "Five, actually."

"And what would you do if one—the baby?"

"My brother Patrick."

"What if Patrick was murdered in cold blood? Wouldn't you try to do anything in your power to bring his killer to justice?"

Georgia's lips turned into a wan, patient smile. "I understand your need to do something, to find answers, to seek retribution, but sometimes it's best to make your own peace, through God's counsel." Sister Georgia reached across the desk and took Val's hand. "Sometimes that's the only way we find answers. I would try my best to trust in God's wisdom."

Val drew her hand away; she was tired of the placating, the sincere, helpful words meant to appease her rather than offer any real answers.

"I'm not asking for much." She held the older nun's gaze and tried like hell not to cry or scream or rail to the heavens in frustration; instead she managed to keep her cool, the same calm she'd used when she'd been a detective in Texas. "This is a personal tragedy for not only me, but for the church as well. I'm only looking for answers, trying to understand my sister's death. I'm not trying to get in the way of the police or in any manner thwart the authority of the church."

Georgia heaved a long sigh and tapped her fingers on her desk, then seemed to come to terms with Val's request. "I do understand," she said, seemingly sympathetic, "and I'm certain some of the people who worked with Sister Camille would love to talk to you." She wrote a few names on a notepad, then stuck the note onto a flyer that was identical to the one Slade had taken earlier. "I can't open our records for you, and even if I wanted to, it would take time. Those records are a quarter of a century old, before we were on computer. They're stored in the basement, I think. I'm not even sure."

Val thought that was a lie, but she wouldn't call the reverend mother on it—not yet.

Georgia offered a kind smile. "I do hope you're coming to the auction. As someone who was adopted out of St. Elsinore's, you have a special connection here, and we're encouraging everyone associated with the orphanage to participate." Her lips curved into a smile that didn't reach her eyes. "It'll be, well, I hate to say 'fun' in this time of your sorrow, but let's just say it's a worthwhile project. We'd love to have you join us. In fact"—she reached into the top drawer and found an envelope from which she withdrew two tickets—"I just happen to have a couple of complimentary passes. Please come as my guest." She gave Val the page, flyer, and tickets, then even went so far as to walk her through the hallways and paths that connected the church, playground, and gardens.

Being inside the walls of St. Elsinore's was difficult. Though the buildings had changed a bit, she still couldn't shake the feeling that she was walking backward to her past and the terror she'd felt as a preschooler who'd just lost her parents and was brought here.

The orphanage itself, a two-story building with rows of long windows, caused her skin to crawl. She remembered the ward, just vaguely, a bright, gleaming white room by day that became dark and frightening when the lights had been turned off. Above each metal cot was a crucifix, and the sheets were scratchy and stiff, smelling of bleach. She recalled all too vividly lying in bed, the covers pulled over her head as she heard the sound of footsteps pacing the hall, crepe soles squeaking, dark shadows passing, and cried softly for her parents.

She'd been scared to death, and the girls in the ward had only stared at her with wide, haunted eyes. Most of the nuns, who then wore habits, had been kind, if busy, pushing her through her day, but there had been a few who had seemed ill-suited to tend to children.

The playground, too, was a place she remembered feeling left out and awkward. The other kids had their own cliques, a caste system where she, as the newest member, was ignored or made to feel alien.

Today, as clouds gathered overhead, blocking the sun, she glanced at the slide, a corkscrew of twisted metal, and remembered one bossy girl barely older than she was who had blocked the ladder. "This is mine," the girl had said with a sneer; then, once Valerie had backed down, she'd climbed up awkwardly, dragging a foot in a cast signed by most of the older kids.

Even Val's infant sister had been separated from her, and it had been Valerie's worst nightmare that she would never see little Camille again. Thankfully, the Renards had adopted them both.

And now, even that was under suspicion.

Lucia dropped the small package into the postal slot and automatically made the sign of the cross over her chest.

There. It was done.

She almost heard Sister Camille's low laughter. "I knew you couldn't keep a promise," she would have said, her eyes glinting with a quick intelligence. "Some friend you turned out to be."

Oh, dear God.

Lucia was such a failure!

"I'm sorry," she whispered, nearly running into a boy of about three who had strayed too far from his mother, a woman holding another baby while juggling a diaper bag and three boxes. The boy slid behind his mother's legs, staring up at Lucia with round eyes. She offered the child a faint smile. "God be with you," she said to his mother, and hurried out of the door feeling like the fraud she was.

The glare and heat hit her full in the face. Though clouds threatened the sun, the humidity was high, and she was sweating. From the weather, or her own case of tangled nerves?

"You know what your problem is?" Camille had asked her one day while they'd been walking from the chapel, through the cool dark halls.

"My problem?"

"You don't have any real sense of conviction." Camille's sky-blue eyes had darkened like an angry sea. "You're afraid, Lucia. If I had to guess, I'd say you were running from something . . . or someone."

"No, I—"

"Sure you are," Camille had insisted, leaning closer, whispering into Lucia's ear. "But I'll let you in on a little secret. We all are." She'd straightened and grinned then, her lips twisting into that little, knowing smile. "Anyway, I trust you to keep this," and she'd dropped her prized possession into Lucia's hands. "Don't lose it."

Now, Lucia's stomach twisted. She'd been lying to herself, trying to convince herself that she wasn't a coward. But Camille had been right.

Seeing Cruz Montoya, talking with him, had only driven the point home. Even now, in broad daylight, walking swiftly down the crowded street, she felt her cheeks flush, her pulse race just thinking of how his dark gaze had drilled into hers, silently prodding her, reminding her of what they'd shared. And he'd given

her his phone number, one she'd stupidly seared into her brain.
As if she would ever call him!

"Help me," she whispered as she stepped off the curb.

A horn blasted.

She jumped, catching a glimpse of a huge, speeding SUV.

"Watch out!" someone yelled as she stumbled backward, her
heel hitting the curb.

Immense tires screeched over the thunderous rumble of an
engine.

As if in slow motion, she started to fall. Caught sight of the
metallic beast with its grinning maw of a grill and headlights like
chrome and glass eyes.

Strong arms surrounded her and jerked her back to the sidewalk. The dirty SUV flashed by only inches from her. It swerved
and veered, cutting across traffic in a blur of dirty side panels and
smoked glass windows.

Heart thudding inside her ribs, adrenaline and fear chasing
through her blood, Lucia felt the strong arms slacken a bit. Just as
she caught a whiff of a familiar aftershave.

"Oh, no," she whispered, and found herself staring into the
dark, assessing gaze of Cruz Montoya.

CHAPTER 30

At St. Elsinore's, slightly bugged that Slade hadn't returned, Valerie tried to shrug off the dark memories that clung to her. She met a few of the nuns and lay teachers at the orphanage, those who had worked with Camille, none of whom wore habits. When she mentioned the wardrobe to Sister Georgia, the older woman nodded. "We're not as steeped in tradition as St. Marguerite's," she said. "Our priest, Father Thomas, is fairly progressive, and I, for one, was glad to see the habits and wimples and antiquated dress go. To each his own, of course, but here, I hope, we're more modern and have more flexibility, in keeping with the congregation. Our mission is to serve God, of course, but I don't think he minds if we're a little more comfortable as we do it."

Val kept up with the energetic mother superior, walking swiftly but on the lookout for Slade, who had seemed to disappear with the phone call. How odd. From his end of the conversation, she assumed that one of his brothers had called from the ranch to discuss a problem with the livestock, but that should have been easily handled. Unless he, too, needed to talk to a vet or the ranch foreman or someone . . .

She did look through the windows and spotted Slade's truck, parked where he'd left it, so she decided whatever had happened he'd deal with it and catch up with them.

She was introduced to several people, two nuns and a cook, none of whom could offer her more than a few words of comfort and kind thoughts about Camille.

"A lovely woman who enjoyed the children," the tall, impossibly thin cook had said as she'd tossed a dirty apron into a hamper and hung up her hair net.

"Helped me in the infirmary whenever I needed it," Sister Rosaria, an older nurse, agreed when they'd found her checking stock in a locked medications closet. She was frowning as she counted the vials and jars but paused to offer Val some encouragement. "I could always count on Camille to help with the kids." She glanced up at Valerie over the lenses of her thin glasses. "No matter how you sugarcoat it, kids hate shots." She offered a weary smile. "I'll miss Camille, and I'm truly sorry for you and your family."

Val fought a tightening in her throat as they walked from the infirmary to a hallway she knew, from memory, led to the chapel.

"Oh, here we go," the reverend mother said as they passed a window with a view of the playground. "Sister Simone was very close to Camille." She walked rapidly toward a doorway leading outside, where a woman, Sister Simone presumably, was gathering some balls and a Wiffle-ball bat that had been forgotten during cleanup.

With coffee-colored skin and curly black hair, Simone was nearly five ten, big-boned with dark, slightly suspicious eyes. She'd been humming to herself, a pop song Valerie couldn't quite name, but stopped abruptly as they approached.

When Sister Georgia introduced them and explained that Val was Camille's sister, Simone's face fell into sadness. She offered her condolences, then said, "I'm really going to miss Camille. She was never late, always had a smile."

"Sister Georgia?" the receptionist called from a doorway. "There you are! You have a phone call."

"I'm sorry," Sister Georgia said quickly. "No rest for the wicked. Isn't that what they say?"

"Or weary," Sister Simone said. Her curly black hair was unruly, her smile a wide slash of white against her smooth skin. "Works either way."

"Of course it does." The mother superior was distracted. "Would you mind showing Valerie around?"

Before Simone could answer, the reverend mother bustled off and through the doorway.

"I guess you're on," Val said, "whether you want to be or not."

"Sister, are you all right?" a blond woman asked Lucia, who was still stunned from the near accident and the fact that Cruz, still holding her, had probably saved her life.

She realized that people were still looking at her—no, make that at *them*. She in full nun's habit—wimple, scapular, veil, and all—and Cruz in his T-shirt and jeans, his arms lingering a little too long around her as he yanked her from the street.

"I'm fine . . . fine," she assured the woman and a few others who had gathered—two black teens who cast suspicious glances her way, the blond woman with her two children, and a group of young girls, each with a cell phone attached firmly to her ear. There were a couple of businessmen as well, and, as luck would have it, a priest speaking to a homeless guy pushing a shopping cart. Lucia wanted to die a thousand deaths. "I, um, I guess I was lost in thought." She forced a smile to the blonde and felt the heat wash up her face.

The light changed, and most of the pedestrians crossed, the worried woman clutching her children's hands as they hurried across the street to the park where playground equipment was visible through the stands of live oaks and hedgerows of vibrant crepe myrtle.

Lucia didn't follow but took a deep breath, then turned her attention to Cruz, her erstwhile savior. "So what are you doing here?" she demanded, casting a nervous glance at the post office. "Following me?"

"Yep."

Oh, dear Mother, this was not what she needed! Not now. Well, not ever.

His mouth was that insanely sexy slash of white, and she mentally kicked herself for noticing.

"Why?"

"To save you from deadly SUVs?"

She almost laughed. Almost. "The real reason?"

"Because the last time we talked, you told me to stay away, something like forever."

"You're impossible."

"Part of my charm."

"Right." Still shaken from nearly being run down, she started walking along the sidewalk, away from the corner and the few remaining people who still cast curious glances her way. Quickly, she walked along the storefronts, and as she did, she told herself her nerves were stretched tight because of the adrenaline still racing through her bloodstream, that it had nothing to do with Cruz. But, of course, she was lying to herself again.

This lying, it was becoming a habit. Not healthy.

To her consternation, Cruz fell into step with her. "I think we're even now, right?"

"Even?" She shook her head. "I'm not keeping score."

"Sure."

She wasn't going to be baited by him. "You still haven't said why you were following me." She thought of the package she'd just mailed, and her palms began to sweat. Mother Mary, she was a horrible liar. "I thought I made myself pretty clear that we couldn't see each other."

"I know, but I thought you were a little on the melodramatic side."

"So what? I was serious."

"Don't believe it."

She'd forgotten how irritating he could be. "Believe what you want to," she said, mentally scolding herself for kissing him, for giving him the slightest glimpse that she still cared. "Just leave me alone."

She stopped under the overhang of a little dress shop and caught their reflection in the glass. Faint, as if a superimposed negative over a display of sundresses, was the image of a man and a woman; he in battered jeans and a faded T-shirt, and she in her voluminous habit and veil. An odd couple, and yet, there was more. A glimpse of hidden emotions in the blush of her cheeks, the intensity of his gaze.

The memory of a forbidden kiss.

His gaze caught hers, and her heart began to throb, a pulse beating at her throat. She looked away, blinking, catching a glimpse of something else in the panes, something as disturbing as the clouds collecting overhead.

The wavering image of a man of the cloth—a priest wearing sunglasses. She froze. Something was off about the guy.

"What?" Cruz asked, and in that flicker of an instant, when she turned her attention to him, the image of the priest was gone. She turned to look over her shoulder to the park.

"Did you see him?"

"Who?"

"The priest."

"What priest? The one helping the homeless guy on the corner?" Cruz's gaze followed hers to the empty park.

"I don't know," she said, thinking maybe she'd conjured up the image, and yet it burned in her brain. Cold as dry ice and just as foggy.

Like the night so long ago.

She had been in Cruz's car, the radio playing loudly. As if it were yesterday, she remembered that last night of their youth, of the exhilaration of being with him, of doing something dangerous, of defying her father . . . They'd been kids then, teens, and the world had been a big, vast, exciting place where their future had seemed to stretch out endlessly.

Until the moment she'd seen the deer in Cruz's headlights, the spindly legged animal frozen in fear in the rising mist, twin beams mirrored in the doe's glassy eyes.

A voice as rough as sandpaper gritted in her ears. "Lucifer's son is the harbinger of death."

She'd screamed as the tires spun out of control, the axle twisting, metal groaning. Glass shattered. Panic and pain sizzled up her spine. . . .

Now, looking at the empty park, she felt the same chill, the flesh on her arms pimpling at a dark, unknown danger.

"I have to go," she insisted, glancing up at Cruz to the cleft in his eyebrow, evidence of that night.

He grabbed her arm. "Lucia, please..."

Knowing she would be damned in hell forever, she stood on tiptoes and brushed a kiss across his cheek. He tried to catch her lips with his, but she pulled away. "Cruz, if you love me, please...don't follow me." And with that, she pulled away, dashing across the street and into the park.

She didn't look back, but she felt the weight of Cruz's gaze, heavy against her back.

CHAPTER 31

"So you're Cammie's sister," Sister Simone said to Val in the playground. She shoved her hands into the pockets of her slacks and nodded, as if agreeing with herself. "She said you two were close."

Until Slade Houston came between us. "We were."

"So sad that she's gone," Simone said. "And I mean it. I loved Sister Camille. She was blessed with a thoroughly wicked sense of humor. I didn't understand why she stayed at St. Marguerite's." Her gaze caught Val's for a second before she looked away. "I wouldn't have thought she would fit in there."

"Why?"

Sister Simone lifted a shoulder, noncommittal as she watched a paper wasp work on a tiny nest under the eaves. "Camille didn't strike me as the traditional, by-the-rules-at-all-costs kind of nun. She seemed more...independent than that. A woman with her own mind."

Amen.

Simone seemed to be the first one who actually understood Cammie. Val thought about keeping Camille's secret, then realized that was ridiculous. The truth would soon be spread through the press and run through the parochial community like wildfire. Val decided she'd more likely find out the truth if she was forthright.

"Did you know she was pregnant?"

Sister Simone's eyes widened a bit. "Oh, Holy Mother," she said, shaking her head. "I...I was afraid...No, I didn't know."

"But you knew she was involved with Father Frank O'Toole."

"I'd heard she was...taken with a priest." Simone's dark eyes glanced to the ground. "I don't think I really wanted to know. Once, Camille tried to talk to me but changed her mind, and I saw her leaving with a priest."

"Father O'Toole?" Val asked, making certain.

Simone shrugged, seemed uncomfortable. Biting her lip, she looked up at the bell tower where swallows were flying erratically, backdropped by gathering clouds. "I don't know. It was dark, and he was turned away from me, but he was tall, built like Father O'Toole."

"Did he, Frank O'Toole, come here often? Meet with her?"

"I'm not sure. He's...he's been here, with Father Thomas for Mass, of course, and he's visited the orphanage and the clinic, just as many others have. St. Elsinore's is unique, you know, a real community."

Valerie's gut twisted. She did know. She did remember. She'd lived here, if only briefly.

"Sister Camille said that you were her only living relative," Simone said as they walked across the empty playground where a solitary swing, its hinges creaking mournfully, moved with the breeze.

"Yes, our parents are dead and there are no other siblings or close cousins. However, Camille was looking for our birth parents."

Simone blinked and her expression tightened. "You knew that? I thought she was keeping it to herself."

"She and I were in this together," Val said, stretching the truth more than a little. "I know she was checking the records here and using the computers to find out if the people who we were told were our biological parents really were."

Fingering the cross at her throat, Simone nodded.

"Did she tell you anything?"

"No." Simone shook her head. "But"—she glanced over her

shoulder, and her eyebrows drew hard together—"I, uh, I helped her with the computer, and I know she kept a notebook."

The diary! Val's heart nearly skipped a beat. Finally, Valerie felt as if she were getting somewhere.

Simone cleared her throat, as if nervous that she'd said too much.

"Do you know where it is?"

Simone hesitated, as if she were fighting an inner battle, but finally said, "We have private cubicles here. It's a relatively new practice because of some theft, but the school decided the few personal items we have and the equipment we need to teach should be locked up." She led Val past the slide with its corkscrew turns and depression in the sawdust where thousands of tiny feet had landed.

Just not hers.

A gust of wind blew, rattling the chains on the playground again, and it was all Valerie could do not to fall back into the darkest period of her life in this place where she felt forever frightened.

"This way," Sister Simone said, breaking into Valerie's reverie.

Telling herself she was being ridiculous, Val realized the nun had stowed the bats and balls in a basket on the porch and was holding the door open. She followed Sister Simone along the old familiar hallways where the art and paint color were different, but the worn tiles on the floor were the same and the doorways hadn't moved in over thirty years. At the gym doors, there was a flurry of activity, volunteers already working on the auction that would be held in a few days. While the dinner was going to be held in a hotel three blocks away, tours of the orphanage, before it closed its doors forever, would be allowed. Hence, the volunteers were converting the gymnasium into the display area for the donated items that would be auctioned.

Valerie had never spent much time in the gym, as she'd been so young when she'd arrived at St. Elsinore's.

Today, as Sister Simone led her down the halls, her heart began to drum a little faster. She remembered the kids staring at her on the day that... What was her name? The woman who'd brought her here? Theresa... or... Tonia... No, that wasn't right, but she remembered the nun who had been assigned to settle Valerie into the orphanage.

Sister Ignatia had pulled her along this very corridor. Sharp fingernails had dug into Valerie's upper arm as she'd been propelled along. The corridor had seemed endless, dark and scary.

"Hurry up, now, child!" the old nun, dressed in a full dark habit, had urged, her heavy dark skirts rustling as she'd sped foward. Ignatia, who to Valerie had resembled the old lady pedaling the bike in the tornado in *The Wizard of Oz*, had swept Valerie along these dark hallways so quickly that Val had been forced to run to keep up with her. "Didn't anyone ever tell you that sloth is a sin?"

Val had been pulled past so many closed doors, and, even though she had been not yet five, she had wondered which one baby Camille was behind. What were they doing to her? Would she ever see her sister again?

Eventually, Sister Ignatia had deposited Valerie in a room with Sister Anne.

Unlike Ignatia as day is to night, Sister Anne had welcomed a frightened Valerie with open arms, a kind face, and extreme patience. She'd been kind and gentle, read stories and allowed the children, including Valerie, to sit on her lap. None of the children had ever been rebuked for playing with her scapular, coif, or rosary.

"God blessed the little ones with curiosity," Anne had told a disapproving, sour-faced Ignatia when Valerie had fingered the bloodred beads.

"Cursed is more likely," the older nun had huffed, but hadn't challenged the younger nun. Ignatia had suffered Anne's serene authority where the children were concerned. It seemed to Valerie that Ignatia was only too happy to get rid of the responsibility of dealing with the "urchins."

That had been thirty years ago.

Now, Sister Simone pushed open a door and frowned. "Odd," she said. "This is one of the few rooms we lock. Hmmm." She moved past a conference table to a counter under which were storage cupboards. She paused in front of one, then, almost to herself, said, "It's not locked either. Weird."

She swung the door open and Valerie peered inside.

The cupboard was empty.

Just like Mother Hubbard, she thought, her throat thickening when she recalled Sister Anne reading the nursery rhyme to the boys and girls spread at her feet in a room just down the hall.

"I don't understand," Simone said.

"Does anyone else have keys?"

"Yes, of course. Sister Georgia, Philomena, and the maintenance man and some others."

"Father Thomas?"

"Of course."

So much for privacy, Valerie thought. "Is anything missing from your cupboard?" she asked.

"I don't think so. Why? Oh. Let's see." She unlocked another cabinet, and Val saw a couple of books and a small box of markers within. "Just as I left it." She tried another, and sure enough there was a couple of skeins of yellow yarn and two sets of knitting needles along with what appeared to be the start of a baby blanket.

"What about Father Thomas?" Val asked.

"Oh, he doesn't have a cubby," Simone said as she straightened. "He's got his office."

"Is he in?"

"I don't think so. He had a conference that starts tomorrow; I think he flew out early this morning."

"But do you have a key?"

"What? To his office? Oh, no." She seemed startled at Val's suggestion. "No, of course not."

Val wanted to ask Simone if she would show her the priest's office and unlock the door if it was bolted, but she thought better of it. Besides, if it came to looking through Father Thomas's things, she'd rather do it alone. Not that she had any reason to suspect the priest of anything, but maybe, just maybe, if Camille needed to talk to someone about her relationship with Father Frank, she might have turned to someone outside Frank O'Toole's parish for counsel.

Something to think about.

"It's odd," Sister Simone said as she ushered Valerie toward the front of the complex again.

Val wondered what had happened to Slade. It had been over an hour since he'd taken the call that had propelled him from the office.

"What's odd?" Val asked. Everything was odd to Valerie; there wasn't any one thing she could put her finger on.

"I'd just called St. Marguerite's and spoke with Sister Charity today about Sister Camille's things, and now they're gone."

"When did you make the call?"

"Just a few hours ago." Simone's perfect brow knitted. "She said she'd send someone for them, but no one spoke to me."

"Maybe we could look on the computer and see what she found."

"I don't know."

"They were my parents, too," Val pushed.

"The parish computers are private, for parish use only, but... I'll have to check with Sister Georgia."

At that moment, Val finally spied Slade, walking swiftly along the hallway as he tucked his cell phone into the pocket of his shirt.

"Ready to go?" he asked Val, then extended his big hand to Sister Simone. "Slade Houston, Val's husband."

"Nice to meet you," she said as Val introduced her.

"Sister Simone was a friend of Camille's and showed me around."

"Sorry I missed it," he said with that crooked smile that she found so irritatingly endearing. "Now, if you'll excuse us, we really have to go."

She caught his look and didn't argue, even though she didn't think she was finished here—she was certain that somewhere in these dark hallways was the answer to her sister's death. "Would you please let me know if you find out what happened to Camille's things?"

"I'm sure the reverend mother will," Sister Simone said as Slade walked swiftly to the front doors, Valerie at his side.

"What's wrong with you?" Val demanded once they were outside. With storm clouds brewing, dusk was soon settling over the land. "Is there something wrong at the ranch?"

His lips twisted as they reached the truck. "Everything's fine."

"But I thought you got a call...."

"Yeah, well, that was an excuse. I called myself." He climbed in behind the wheel as she slid into the passenger seat.

"You what?"

"You were getting nowhere with the reverend mother. The same old runaround, and I decided I needed an excuse to leave and snoop around again. So I faked the call."

"You're downright devious," she said as raindrops fell, pinging against the roof of the old Ford.

"I'll take that as a compliment."

"Do." She was surprised at his deception. "So did you find anything?"

He flicked the ignition, and the truck's engine rumbled to life. "Yep." Checking his mirror, he pulled into the street.

Her heart raced just a bit. "Okay, what?"

He slid her a glance. "Look in my jacket pocket," he said, turning off the side street and into heavier traffic heading south.

She was already reaching into the space behind the seats where he'd tossed his jacket. Digging into the pocket, her fingers brushed against a plastic bag, and inside, the spine of a book. In her mind's eye, she saw Camille's empty cupboard. She felt a second of regret as she pulled out the slim bound pages, the cover as plain and black as a prayer book. "Camille's diary?"

"Looks like."

"*You* stole it?" she said, disbelieving. She'd been certain the killer had taken the diary to hide his identity.

"Borrowed. We'll have to give it up to the police once we're done with it."

"Have you read it?"

"Only enough to confirm it was Cammie's."

"And you had an evidence bag with you?"

"I found some ziplocks in a drawer. Figured we didn't want to destroy any evidence."

Valerie swallowed hard. Through the plastic, her fingers caressed the soft leather binding, and she had the distinct feeling that when she opened the first page, she'd catch a glimpse into her sister's private thoughts, maybe even her soul. She hesitated, afraid of what she might find. "This seems wrong. Like we're trespassing."

He slid her a glance. "I thought you wanted to find out who killed her."

"I do."

"Then?"

She stiffened her spine. "Yeah, I know." As the wheels of his truck reached the bridge over Lake Pontchartrain, rain began to spit faster from the sky.

"There are gloves in the box."

"Really?"

"It is called a glove box."

"Yeah, I know. But for you . . . Oh, never mind." She opened the compartment, and sure enough, along with a flashlight, a wrench, pliers, a pocketknife, and a bag of dog biscuits, there was a box of latex gloves.

"I do examine livestock, y'know. Give 'em shots, clean 'em, help pull calves and foals." He shrugged. "It's just better to be prepared."

"Besides, you never know when you're going to steal evidence and hope to convince the authorities that you didn't taint anything."

"Yeah." He nodded.

They both knew the police would be ticked off, but she didn't argue, just pulled on a pair of oversized gloves and gingerly opened the cover to her sister's private world as the rain began to pour and the waters of the lake frothed wildly.

"You're going to hell, you know."

He cranked the wipers up a notch and grinned. "Oh, ya think?"

"Yep. When the Devil finds out what you've done, he's gonna take your soul. No doubt about it."

"Let him come." Slade slid her a wicked little glance that caused her pulse to jump a little. "Somehow I think he'll be lookin' for you, too."

"So it's going to be you and me, together in hell?"

"Yep." He winked at her as he hit the gas. "Consider it a date."

CHAPTER 32

The baby was fussy.

Again.

"Teething," Olivia said, and Bentz believed it, walking his tiny daughter around the house, jostling her as she cried. "Here, let me take her," Olivia said as she put aside her book, a paperback guide to the first year of a baby's life. She walked into the kitchen where, from his cage, Chia, the parrot she'd inherited from her grandmother, Virginia "Ginny" Dubois, the baby's namesake, squawked.

"Hey, there, sweetie," Olivia whispered. "It's okay."

It was definitely not okay, and Ginny let her mother know it. But Olivia was calm, though this was her first child. Bentz had another daughter, a grown woman now, from his first marriage. Kristi was a quarter century older than her half sister, and Bentz had the battle scars to prove it.

Kristi was a firecracker—trouble from the get-go. Just like her mother. Bentz loved her fiercely, despite the fact that Kristi had taken years off his life with her antics, everything from teenage angst and rebellion to life-threatening injuries... Oh, God, he hoped Ginny's life was calmer and easier.

Now, Kristi was married to Jay McKnight, who worked for the state crime lab and taught classes on criminology at All Saints' College in Baton Rouge, the place he and Kristi had met again after being high school sweethearts.

The baby stopped crying and began to coo in her mother's arms, and Bentz's stupid old romantic heart swelled when he witnessed Olivia holding Ginny; their gazes locked.

"See, it just takes the right touch," Olivia said, and Bentz couldn't help feeling a wave of happiness. God, he loved this woman and this child, even thought he knew any kid was going to put him through the emotional wringer. It was humbling how much he cared for this tiny, new little person.

Funny, he thought now, how he'd been against having another child, how he'd argued with Olivia, but when she'd ended up pregnant, his life had changed for the better. Now he couldn't imagine a world without little Ginny, fussy thing that she was. Blond, like her mother, her scalp visible through her wisping pale curls, her eyes wide and interested in the world, she was crawling all over the place, terrorizing Hairy S, their aging little dog—another animal inherited from Olivia's favorite grandmother's menagerie.

Bentz saw years of happiness on the horizon.

"Okay," he said, "you win. You *are* the better parent."

Olivia laughed and he walked into the den where he picked up the phone to dial his son-in-law. Maybe Jay could push things through a little faster on the Camille Renard case. They still needed a tox screen, and Bentz wanted to double-check the blood work on the unborn child against that of Frank O'Toole's again, just to be safe.

An uncharacteristic pang cut through him as he settled into his worn desk chair. He thought of Camille and her baby, the child's life cut off before it drew its first breath.

Little Ginny, free of her mother's grasp, had made her way in that speedy crawl of hers into the den. She looked up at him and grinned, showing off two bottom teeth, obviously proud of herself to have located him.

Behind her, standing in the doorway, stood Olivia.

"Come here, you," he said. Bentz grabbed his daughter again, kissed her tiny head, then plopped her onto his lap. While she was busy shredding a small notepad, he dialed Jay.

It was time to find out more about Camille Renard's condition at the time of her death. Were there drugs in her bloodstream? What about the marks on her back?

And who, of all the men she knew, had a blood type that was consistent with that of her child's father?

"Kinky stuff," Slade said. He sat across the table from Valerie as they read the photocopied pages of Camille's diary.

"It should be burned." Valerie, her glass of wine untouched, flipped over a page and sighed. "Too personal."

"The police will need it."

"I know, I know." She was resigned to the contents of her sister's life, of her most private thoughts, being reviewed, studied, and noted, but it was difficult. He understood. Camille Renard was the antithesis to everything a nun should be. At least in his opinion.

He'd carefully photocopied the pages on Val's clunky printer and had left the original diary intact for the police. Though he'd expected the pages to reveal some of Camille's inner thoughts, he hadn't been prepared for the graphic nature of her affair. There were a few names scattered throughout the pages, but none of them were connected with her romantic or sexual relationships, at least not directly. And there were what appeared to be initials, maybe just notes, indecipherable, at least to him.

Val finally took a sip of her wine. Her countenance was troubled. "Some of the notes are in code." She frowned, then pointed out a note. The quickly scribbled line read *C U N 7734, RM CV.*

"What? Is that part of a phone number?" he asked. "Or a license plate?"

"RM CV—Room 105?" she thought aloud. "Is it partly RM—room, then CV like in Roman numerals?"

"Maybe. They could use them at St. Marguerite's. At least more often than on the outside."

"You talk like it's a prison."

"Isn't it?"

"Not according to Camille. She told me that no one forces them to stay inside, just their own conscience and commitment." Frowning, she shook her head as she read the notes. "But who knows?"

she said, disturbed. Then, flipping one of the copied pages, she said, "Here's another: 'TOM BF 2 M and M.'"

"BF—isn't that 'best friend' in kid jargon?" Slade asked.

"Seriously? You've been keeping up with teen-speak? How do you know this, Cowboy?"

"We do have computers at the ranch, you know. I do have a cell phone. I have heard of Facebook." He winked at her. "Even in Bad Luck, Texas, kids text. Sometimes, I think, adults do, too."

"Wise guy!"

"Everyone who's conscious on this planet knows the whole BF and BFF thing. Even nuns in St. Marguerite's, despite its archaic facade."

"It's not a facade—trust me." She rolled her eyes, but at least she scared up a smile. "Okay, Mr. Text, then if *TOM* is 'Thomas' someone, like the priest at St. Elsinore's, what's the rest of it? Best friends to M and Ms? The candy?"

"A lot of people are," he deadpanned.

"I know. I think I qualify." She thought hard. "Tom . . . Do you think?"

"That she was involved with the priest from St. Elsinore's?" He shook his head. "What are the chances that she found two priests who were willing to break their vows? What's that say about them?"

"Or her?"

"We already know about her," he said, and instead of arguing with him in the no-win battle, she sipped from her glass, found no answers to the cryptic notes, and saw another—a doodle really. A heart shape, with a message inside: *CALLED.*

Val studied it. Had someone—her lover—called? Was the heart meaningful? And why no name? She sighed, seeing how the heart was outlined over and over again, surrounding the single word.

Oh, Cammie, she thought. Was this a message, or just the idle musings of someone who was dreaming of phoning her lover; or had the lover called her? Who knew?

And finally, there was a note that only said *Reverend Mother,* with half a dozen little arrows pointing at the word, like angry arrows, as if Camille truly hated Sister Charity.

Without any concrete answers to the cryptic notes that really could be no more than idle doodles, Val flipped another couple of pages. "Uh-oh. Even you made mention in the hit parade." She twirled the stem of her glass of Pinot between her fingers, and her smile slowly disappeared. "Looks like I owe you an apology."

In the diary, Camille had admitted to trying and failing to seduce a "particularly stubborn rancher who took his vow of marriage as seriously as he did his long Texas heritage."

"Unless there's another cowboy out there."

She leveled her gaze at him. "Like who? Trask? Zane? Last time I checked, they were both single. She definitely mentioned the marriage vows." She took another sip, and he was caught again by her beauty, made more so by the simple fact that she didn't realize how breathtaking she was. Never as flashy, flamboyant, or outwardly sexy as her younger sister, Valerie Renard had been and still was blessed with a more subdued and classic beauty and a sensual intelligence he'd always found fascinating.

"What if she'd lied in this diary?" he asked, leaning back in his kitchen chair, hearing the wood squeak as he reached for his beer. "What if she'd said that I'd gone after her, that she'd just not been able to say no to me? Would you have believed it? Or condemned me?"

Val didn't answer.

"She's still running the show, Valerie," he said, the quiet fury that had been pushed aside rising again.

"What are you saying?"

"That you should have trusted me. Known that I was telling the truth, but you didn't. You believed her, and now you're believing her again. Her handwriting says it was a lie, and you believe her."

"I'd think you would be happy that I understand. Thrilled, even."

He held her gaze. Recognized the fire in her hazel eyes. Felt himself weakening, a crack slowly splintering his determination to work this thing out between them on his terms, not terms dictated by a dead woman.

"These pages," he said, pointing to a particularly vivid sexual scene, "could be pure fantasy."

"You're saying she's lying in the diary."

"I'm saying she could be. That's all. Don't take anything at face value."

"Including your innocence."

"Yeah." His chin clenched so hard it ached. "You need to trust me, Val. Just because I'm me. Because I've proved myself. I never lied to you. Never."

Valerie's throat worked. Her gaze wavered, then slid away, and it was all he could do not to cross the few feet of battered hardwood floors to take her into his arms.

"Okay...so you're right. This diary could just be her imagination. Pure fantasy." Val's eyebrows drew together, and she bit at the corner of her lip. "But I don't think so." She was shaking her head as she thought aloud. "First of all, she talks about all her lovers. The first one?" She set down her wineglass in disgust. "In high school? Who do you think that is?"

He lifted a shoulder. "Don't know."

"Athletic. From a large Hispanic family."

"Could have been anyone."

"Reuben Montoya," she said, and when she recognized doubt in Slade's eyes, she pushed. "I know it."

"You said they'd dated."

"They damned well did more than that!" She tapped a finger on the copied pages. "According to this, he was her first, still in high school. Then a string of boyfriends, a one-night stand or two, all without names; then you're so conveniently mentioned and finally a priest. And we know who he is."

"Frank O'Toole."

"Bastard," she said, scooting out her chair and walking to the kitchen where she poured the rest of her wine down the sink in a quick, angry motion. Bo, ever the traitor, tail wagging slowly, followed. "Montoya shouldn't be on the case. It's too personal. And Frank O'Toole should be behind bars."

"You're sure he killed her?"

"Yes! Oh...God. No, not really." She shook her head, and the light over the sink caught reddish glints in her hair. How many times had he left their bedroom, seeing the summer sunlight as it streamed through the window to cast fiery sparks in her tangled hair? How many times had she opened a sleepy eye, caught him gazing at her, and slowly grinned, an open invitation that he'd never refused? If he tried, he could smell the scent of their sheets, dried in the hot Texas sun and smelling of her perfume and sex. He felt a tightening in his groin and denied it.

This was definitely not the time.

"That's the problem," she was saying. "Frank O'Toole doesn't seem capable. Hell, I believed him when he said he loved her and I can't...I just have trouble thinking of him with her. At least like that." She glanced at the pages on the table, and her lips tightened.

He knew what she meant. The sexual acts, more dark than loving in Camille's descriptions, didn't fit with the man who helped the sick in hospitals, spent time with children in St. Elsinore's orphanage, gave of himself to help build homes for the needy here in New Orleans after Katrina and in other places as well. Her lover had been strong. Sexual. And, it seemed, had a sadistic bent that was more cruel than kind.

Frank O'Toole?

But who really knew what a person was capable of?

Outwardly normal, inwardly twisted and dark.

He'd once seen a picture of a prim little churchgoing woman in her fashionable skirt and suit jacket. Her hair had been a blondish white and perfectly coiffed in the little-old-lady helmet style, her smile as sweet as Georgia peaches. She had to have been pushing eighty. But the next shot was of her naked, tattoos and piercings over every inch of her skin, her nipples pierced, her pubic hair shaved, her look turned raggedly sexual. It wasn't her placing body art all over her body that he found so odd; it was the fact that she'd allowed the picture to be taken and placed on the Internet.

Maybe it had been Photoshopped.

Maybe she hadn't allowed it.

Maybe her head had been put on someone else's body.

It didn't matter. The image stayed with him and reminded him that no one really knows what goes on in someone else's head. Otherwise, why would there be so many confused neighbors who couldn't believe the man next door had been a wife beater, a pedophile, or a murderer? Too many times he'd witnessed people convinced that the accountant next door had been the perfect neighbor.

So Frank O'Toole, priest or not, could certainly be the man who liked to bind Camille's wrists to an iron bed as he poured oil over her body and the man who had found ways to keep her aroused far into the night with objects that tickled, delighted, and caused just a tiny bit of pain. O'Toole could be the lover who had spread her arms and legs and flogged her back, getting hard before thrusting into her from the rear, waiting as she arched up to him, her desire more acute with the threat and sizzle of torment. He could also be the man who would ultimately be proved to be Camille's killer.

"Sick son of a bitch." Valerie rinsed out her glass, absently patted Bo's head, and walked into the living room, where she sat in her favorite chair. She looked up at Slade still seated at the table. "I'm sorry," she said, her voice thick. "For doubting you. For taking her word over yours." She laced her fingers and unlaced them again. "I was wrong." Her voice was an awkward whisper.

He should walk across the room and pull her to her feet. He imagined tipping her head back, brushing the hair off her cheek, and kissing her eyelids as he murmured platitudes and accepted her apology, but he couldn't. Not yet. Not when everything between them was raw and unspoken.

The easy thing would be to pull her body next to his, lift her off her feet, and carry her into the bedroom. In his mind's eye, he saw her naked beneath him, anxious and hot, lifting her hips to his as he thrust into her. Her hair would be wild on the pillows, dark with sweat, her breasts full, dark, incredible nipples erect and waiting for him to take them into his mouth and kiss and nip at them.

Her legs would wrap around him, and she would gasp with an ache so deep that her throat would catch as he grabbed her buttocks and forced her tighter against him.

He knew that making love to her now would be a wild, frenzied act intent on washing away the pain, of reaffirming their lives while Camille would never again wake to a warm June morning.

He drained his beer and climbed to his feet.

"I think we both need to get some sleep," he said, leaving the bottle on the table, not taking a step closer to her. "We should be at the police department around eight." He walked to the door and hesitated. "We both have a lot to think about."

Bo was on his feet, tail swinging slowly, head cocked. "Stay," Slade said to the dog but ignored his own compelling urge to remain in the cozy little cottage. With his wife.

Oh, hell.

With one last look at Val, Slade managed a bit of a smile, then opened the door and screen before stepping into a night as thick and dark as an oozing pool of warm, black tar.

CHAPTER 33

"It's time," the voice prodded. "Hurry."

Sister Asteria slipped out of the room, a giddiness running through her bloodstream at the thought of what was to be. She picked up the folds of her long dress, lifting the hem so that her bare feet could hasten down the hallway, through pools of blurred light from decrepit sconces.

Elated, almost drunk, she stumbled a bit but caught herself and made quick tracks down the back stairs, where she'd been steered.

"He's waiting."

Yes! She hurried forward, feeling a sharp prodding that kept her moving. At the doors, she stopped, suddenly unsure.

"Now!" The voice was insistent. Demanding. "Go on!"

Deep inside, beneath her odd, fast-ebbing elation, she felt the first tremor of fear, a worry scratching at her brain, a tiny reminder that what was happening was wrong, so very wrong.

Remember Sister Camille, the voice warned from somewhere in the nether-reaches of her mind. But she ignored it, concentrated on staying upright as she shoved open the doors and burst into the night. Here the moon was bright, the night close, the scent of gardenias mingling with the heavy smell of the earth. The pebbles of the path were rough under her bare feet, but she didn't care, couldn't really feel pain. It was almost as if she were floating as she proceeded through a gate that was open, as if someone had been waiting for her.

Her groom. Of course.

Joseph!

She conjured up his handsome face, imagined what it would be like to kiss him again...

No, wait. Not Joseph. That wasn't right. Or was it? She was confused for a second, the moonlight suddenly off-kilter. Why wasn't she in the church? And if she wasn't marrying Joseph, who would be waiting for her at the altar?

Christ! You're marrying Jesus, the Son of God. You're a nun!

Of course.

She tried to reclaim the feeling of well-being that had captivated her earlier, but it was fast escaping, leaving a sudden dawning realization that she'd been duped, probably drugged, in its wake.

But how?

"This way." The disembodied voice nudged her around a corner and through another gate that was also ajar. When it creaked on rusted hinges, she realized she had entered the cemetery, where tombs, stone sepulchers that rose from the ground, loomed around her. A sinister breeze skittered through the whitewashed tombs, tugging at her dress and rattling the branches of the surrounding trees. Spanish moss danced ghostlike from the gnarled branches, and she heard a voice hiss against her ear, "Your sins have come to bear...all your sins, Sister Asteria."

"No!" She tried to scream but made no sound.

Terror raked its claws across her soul.

"You've made a mockery of your vows."

Oh, dear God.

"Wait," she tried to say, but her voice was hushed, mute.

"Move."

Stumbling forward, Sister Asteria prayed for mercy as fear consumed her. The blood in her veins was like ice. Frigid. Congealing. Reminding her that she deserved this punishment.

The memory of poor Sister Camille's fate seared through her

brain as a crow cawed his plaintive, mocking cry before flapping off to the dark heavens.

Asteria trembled, her skin scratching against the tattered fabric of the bridal gown, her fate sealed. Tears streamed from her eyes, and she thought of escape, of turning around and dashing through the tombs, of screaming out for help.

But she couldn't.

Her voice was silenced.

By her sins.

This was what she deserved.

She knew about Sister Camille, had heard that she had died wearing the same kind of dress. Camille's death had been a warning, one she hadn't heeded.

Father, help me, please, she silently prayed, tripping again. When she caught her balance, she felt the knife at her back, prodding her forward through the crypts and tombs. She knew her attacker, or thought she did, though the figure draped in black was unclear.

Her heart thudded wildly, bidding her escape. She wanted to run, but her legs would hardly do her bidding. It was all she could do to stay on her feet.

As the oldest daughter of seven, Asteria had always done what she was told.

Had never questioned.

Never balked.

From the time of her first Communion, her faith had been supreme, and throughout her life it had wavered only once, for a short while. She cringed at the memory.

Joseph.

She'd been a silly girl, barely sixteen and swept away by an older man, twenty-four at the time, or so he'd claimed. What Joseph Allard hadn't mentioned was his wife and daughter.

To think she'd fallen in love with a married man . . . Her own sin made her sick. When the truth had come out, she had rebuked him mercilessly. She'd been horrified that he'd lied to her and wouldn't hear any of his lame excuses about being "unhappy" or "trapped" in a loveless marriage.

She had refused to see him again. Within the week, while his wife and infant daughter had slept, he'd slipped into the garage with the doors shut, sat in his car, and turned on the engine.

Having learned of the affair, Joseph's wife had blamed Asteria for making her a widow, and a penniless one at that without his income. Even his small life insurance benefits had been invalidated because of the suicide.

Asteria had felt vile. Upon graduation, she had reaffirmed her decision to enter the convent. She'd put all her romantic fantasies aside and dedicated her life to Christ.

But she hadn't realized she would meet someone like Father Frank O'Toole, a man of God. Her heart wrenched as she thought of him. So handsome, so virile, so...everything.

And so, so, wrong.

Had Satan tempted her again?

Oh, no, no...not with Father Frank.

And yet here she was, slightly dizzy, wearing the bridal gown, knowing she was going to have to pay for her sins in this cemetery, here among the boxlike tombs that stood like hulking beasts aboveground.

Her heart pounded, threatening to explode in her chest. As her fingers twined in the beads of her rosary, she felt her veins throbbing in fear.

How had she come to this?

She let out a sob and felt the tip of the knife slice through the flimsy dress to prick the skin at her side. Cold steel against her hot, frightened flesh. She tried to scream but failed and felt warm blood oozing down her rib cage. "No," she whispered, her heart pounding in her eardrums.

"Scream and I'll condemn your soul to hell!" the voice assured her. "Now get moving!"

She hurried forward, picking her way through the tombs, obeying as she'd been taught. Her thoughts sped to her mother and father, still young by most standards, in their early fifties and still tending to her youngest siblings. Images of all six of them flitted through her mind, but it was Marie, the youngest, whose face came to her. Barely eight, with freckles, curly hair, and eyes a deep, somber brown, she and Asteria were the most alike in appearance and conviction to God, even though Marie was still too young to really understand her faith.

"On your knees," the rough voice ordered as she reached a grave where a sculptured angel, wings spread wide, scowled down at her from atop a tomb. Blocking the moon, the statue's face was shadowed, its expression hidden. "Here!"

Asteria was pushed hard.

She fell to the ground, gravel cutting through the dress, slicing into her knees. "What are the wages of sin?" the voice demanded.

What? Fear skated on tiny blades over her skin.

"For the wages of sin are..."

Oh, God! "Death," she squeaked as terror screamed through her body. Silently, her voice now having abandoned her completely, she began to pray.

Our Father who art—

A noose was cast over her neck.

No!

Fight, Asteria! You have to fight! There's no one to help you!

She tried to rise, but the thin, strong loop around her throat tightened quickly, cutting deep into her flesh.

Panic surged through her, a screaming redness flashing before her eyes.

Fight! Run! Get the hell away from this psycho!

She tried to scream. To breathe.

Her fingers clawed at her neck, searching for purchase, trying to yank the vile garrote free.

Oh, please, Father, please, save me, she thought wildly, all the while struggling. She flung one arm through the air while the other dug at her throat, trying to loosen the cutting noose. Her lungs were on fire, her brain screaming in pain. Blackness pulled at the edges of her consciousness, and, as if from far away, church bells began to clang.

Oh, no...please...Savior, please...

She was spinning, pinned down by the crushing pressure in her chest. Her soul clung to her body for a last second before, as if rising above her body, she saw her attacker twisting the garrote, forcing the sharp, steely cord into her flesh. From above, she watched as spots of blood bloomed at her throat, small garnet gems that glistened and spread. Her body bucked, then went limp.

Zzzt! Snap!

In that instant she slipped away, floating upward, thinking in dissociated, fragmented thoughts that the bright flash that exploded before her eyes was the one so many people spoke of, the light that leads upward. Oh, God... The blackness came over her again, a thick, murky cloud that absorbed her pain, quieted the terror.

She was dying.

She knew it... brokenly, her thoughts random.

But one question cut through her brain like a hot knife through butter.

Would the gates of heaven be open to her?

Or, as she feared, would she be cast into the very bowels of hell for all eternity?

Psssst!

Lucia's eyes flew open.

No! Not again!

Not before she could leave...

Her heart clamored, and despite the cool, slight breeze wafting softly through her open window, she was sweating, her scalp wet from perspiration. She clutched the sheet and thin blanket covering her body and prayed she was mistaken, that she hadn't heard the unearthly voice, the rasp of a demon against her ear.

"Please, Father," she whispered, her body so tense she could hardly draw a breath. In her mind's eye, she saw the image of an angel, arms uplifted as if reaching for heaven. "Not another..."

But she knew in the very primal part of her, the thin slice of her brain where fear and hope collided, that she was being forced again into a new and dark horror.

The midnight bells were tolling, soft and plaintive in the night. *Oh, God. Oh, God. Oh, God.*

With a feeling of panic, she rolled to the side of the bed, grabbed a habit from her closet, then tossed it over her head. The second the skirt hit the floor and her arms were through the sleeves, she snagged her rosary off the bedpost with trembling fingers and, praying softly, followed the preordained path.

She could almost smell the evil that lingered, the scent of demon spoor as repugnant as it was earthy and seductive, as she hurried out the door of her room and down the dark tunnel of a hallway to the stairs.

She didn't expect to meet anyone, but as she rounded the corner, she nearly collided with Sister Edwina. "Oh!" Lucia said, clutching her chest. "What're you doing up?" The communal restroom and showers were in the opposite direction.

"Couldn't sleep," Edwina said. "And you?"

"Come with me. It's too hard to explain." She tugged on the other nun's habit and kept moving, not wanting to think too hard, not daring to try and confide in Edwina. "I . . . I think something's wrong."

"You think?" Edwina repeated skeptically. "Why?"

"I don't know. Come on." Down the stairs she flew, without a glance behind her. "Hurry!" The slap of the taller nun's footsteps on the stairs told her that Sister Edwina was following. Vaguely she wondered why Edwina, fully dressed in her black habit and veil, was wandering through the hallways, but she didn't have time to dwell on it. Nor did she want to consider all the possible reasons.

"Where are we going?" Edwina demanded.

"I'm . . . I'm not sure."

"Wait a second. You don't know what you heard, where you're going but—"

"Just follow me, okay?" Lucia snapped. She wasn't usually bossy, but tonight, oh, sweet heavens, she had to be. As for her sanity, even she was beginning to doubt it. But she kept hurrying forward. She hoped she was wrong—oh, please, let her be mistaken—that the voice she'd heard was only her imagination, but the hairs lifting on the back of her arms told her differently.

"I don't know about this," Edwina said, her voice wavering as Lucia shouldered open the double doors and stepped outside. A stiff wind smelling of the Mississippi hit her full in the face. Clouds scudded over the moon, dimming the stars.

Lucia didn't wait for the other nun but hurried along the pathway, through open gates and into the cemetery.

Please God, be with me.

She tried to reach out to the Lord despite the evil whisper that prodded her along.

Edwina, who had been lagging behind, caught up with her just inside the cemetery gate.

"Are you out of your mind?" Edwina's pale eyes drilled into hers as the tombs and crypts impeded their paths.

Maybe, Lucia thought, but didn't have time to consider her sanity. She didn't answer, just picked up the pace, running now. Although the voice of the demon no longer propelled her, she knew precisely where she was going, and she was afraid of what she might find.

Please let me be wrong, she thought wildly, her heart racing as the night wind teased her hair. *Let this be a mistake!*

Lucia's steps didn't falter as her eyes locked upon the angel statue from the vision. An unworldly gray, her wings were spread wide, her arms uplifted, dirt and grit trailing from her eyes like the tracks of her tears.

Just like in the vision.

And at the statue's base, in front of the tomb, lay the still form of a dead woman.

Sister Edwina turned the corner behind her and let out a skull-shattering scream.

Thin moonlight shimmered over the corpse. This woman, like Camille, was dressed in a tattered wedding gown, its gauzy folds lifting with the gusts of wind that scraped through the cemetery, rattling the branches of the trees, moaning softly.

"Holy Father, no!" Edwina cried as Lucia bent down to see if there was a breath of life in the small body. Edwina let out a low, grief-filled moan. "Not Asteria..." She wrapped her arms around her midsection and fell to her knees, weeping.

Sister Asteria stared up at them, her gaze fixed on the night sky.

Lucia's hands flew to Asteria's wrist, searching for signs of life... hoping... praying.

But Asteria had no pulse.
She didn't breathe.
She lay motionless.
Her soul, presumably, already rising.
Tears rained from Lucia's eyes.
A prayer came to her lips, its cadence broken by her sobs.
And the midnight bells were finally silent.

CHAPTER 34

"Don't tell me, an old classmate of yours?" Bentz said as Montoya crouched beside the body and stared down at the cold form of Sister Asteria. In death, her skin had taken on a bluish tint, and her fixed gaze was as lifeless as all the tombs surrounding them in the graveyard.

"Funny," Montoya snorted.

"Well?" So Bentz was half serious.

"No, Bentz," he said as he straightened, relieved. "The first time I met her was during the interviews." God, had that been only a couple of nights ago? It seemed like a lifetime.

"Good."

More than good. Knowing so many people involved in a homicide was beyond surreal; it caused him to think that he might be the common denominator. But now, with Asteria McClellan's death, that had changed.

"This is a damned nightmare," Bentz said under his breath as they walked away from the spot where the ME was quickly examining Asteria's body before stuffing it into a body bag and hauling it away.

Giving the crime scene a wide berth, Lynn Zaroster approached. She flashed Montoya a humorless smile. They'd been partnered up recently, while Bentz had been on leave recuperating from the injury that had nearly cost him his job as well as his life. Once Bentz was reinstated, Zaroster had been partnered with Brinkman, whom she detested. Zaroster was the one person in the department who wanted Bentz to retire so she could partner up with Montoya again.

Now she said, "The press is wanting answers. Pronto. They're talking serial."

"Already? Jesus." Bentz shook his head.

"A little premature to label the killer as a serial," Bentz said, but Montoya didn't agree. Just because the texts suggested at least three vics with a cooling-off period between the murders didn't make it so. Who really knew the mind of a true psychopath? They couldn't be pigeonholed. Two nuns killed in the same method screamed *serial* to him, either the start of a rampage or, maybe, the killer had struck before.

"Brenda Convoy is pretty persistent," Zaroster said, surveying the scene and frowning, her face illuminated by a few flashes from cameras and the pale, watery light from a shrouded moon. Montoya frowned. He'd never liked the pushy reporter with WKAM, but then he wasn't too close to anyone in the press.

"I told her to wait for a statement from the PIO," Zaroster said, "and she looked like she wanted to spit little green apples."

"That's shit little green apples," Brinkman said, correcting her.

Zaroster's jaw clenched.

Brinkman didn't notice. "And that's just too damned bad. Even Convoy knows she can't get anything without talking to Sinclaire." Tina Sinclaire was the latest in a string of public information officers with the department.

"What've ya got?" Montoya asked.

"So far nothing." Even Brinkman looked perturbed, some of his smirk having disappeared. "This is a bad one," he admitted.

"Hey, do you mind?" Bonita Washington, the head crime scene investigator, demanded. "We got a scene to work." She was big and black and didn't take lip from anyone. Her hair was scraped away from a face shiny with perspiration, and she was carrying a clipboard in one hand and a small toolbox in the other.

"Sooorry," Brinkman said with a condescending sneer, his attitude clearly back in place. "We were just trying to do our job."

"So do it already," Washington said, her green eyes snapping, "and let me do mine." She turned away to confer with Santiago as the photographer snapped pictures, flashes pulsing eerily, lights splaying for milliseconds on the crypts and statues of the graveyard.

Brinkman pulled a face. "Someone got up on the wrong side of the bed."

"I heard that, Brinkman, and yeah, I don't like being jerked out of the house in the middle of the night." Washington eased her way closer to the statue under which Asteria had been found.

"Yeah, well, you're not the Lone Ranger, here," Brinkman muttered. When he elicited no response, he gave up trying to needle her and turned his attention back to the case.

"So what's the deal? Again the same nun finds the body?" Brinkman asked Montoya as he nervously searched his pockets for a crumpled pack of Marlboros. Deftly, he shook out a cigarette and jabbed the filter tip between his lips as they walked through the cemetery with its sun-bleached tombs rising from the ground. Here in New Orleans, the dead were buried aboveground, as most of the city was at sea level or lower. No one wanted dead grandma coming back to visit in case of a flood that could wash away the ground and cause previously subterranean caskets to float away from their final resting places. "What's up with that, the same person finding the corpse before it's even gotten cold?" The unlit cigarette bobbed as he spoke.

"Don't know yet," Montoya said. "I'll find out. I'm questioning Sister Lucia first."

"Seems like she knows more than she's saying."

They reached the gate to the cemetery and walked through. Brinkman snapped his lighter open and paused to light up, the scent of burning tobacco tantalizing, the red tip of his cigarette burning like a tiny beacon in the night.

"What about the priest?" Brinkman asked.

"I've got him. As soon as his lawyer shows up," Bentz said.

Brinkman let out a plume of smoke. "You been to the vic's room?"

"Not yet. Zaroster's got it."

"I'll go with her," Brinkman said. "That way the mother superior won't give herself a coronary to think a man's alone in the bedrooms of the sacred virgins." He turned away, leaving a trail of smoke in his wake.

"Insufferable," Bentz said as they headed inside.

"Beyond." Montoya wended his way along the path to the wide double doors leading into the hallway connecting the cathedral to the convent.

Any sense of propriety or decorum at St. Marguerite's had fled when the 911 call had come into the department and cops had been sent to the scene.

Now the staid old cathedral and grounds were a madhouse.

Not only the cemetery where the body had been discovered, but also the chapel, cathedral, outbuildings, and convent itself had been roped off, on lockdown. Police were crawling over the old brick buildings. The press, ever alert, was on hand, reporters standing in front of the cathedral, with camera crew and lights, alerting the city of another homicide at the nunnery.

The circumstances were almost identical to Camille Renard's murder.

Another nun.

Another bridal gown.

Another altar cloth placed over her face by the reverend mother.

Another ring of jewel-like beads of blood in the fabric around her throat.

This time, though, the killer had struck in the cemetery rather than the chapel.

Why?

Already the interviews were being set up, the parish sealed off, everyone within the walls being questioned. Other cops had been dispersed into the neighborhood, still more patrolling the streets, all hoping to find someone suspicious, something out of the ordinary that would help them nail the son of a bitch.

Of course, the killer could already be long gone, having made good his escape before the police arrived.

Montoya walked along the hallway to the reverend mother's office. Once again, the body had been found at midnight, the chapel bells still ringing. The first officer had arrived eight minutes later, just long enough for Sister Lucia to phone the police and wake the reverend mother, in that order, much to Sister Charity's dismay.

Sister Lucia.

Again.

What was that all about? Brinkman was right—her discovery of both bodies put her under suspicion. Along with all the "how did that happen?"

Montoya had arrived at twelve twenty-seven. He'd parked near the cemetery as a news van from a local station had rolled down the street, nosing into a spot near one of the emergency vehicles.

There was a surreal and chilling quality to this murder, another layer.

He, and the rest of the department, had believed that the murder of the first victim, Sister Camille, had been an isolated case. He'd thought she was killed because she was pregnant, involved with a priest, or because of some other personal reason. He'd believed her to be a target, not a random victim, because whoever had killed her had taken time with the crime, ensuring that she was wearing a wedding dress, killing her at close range, feeling her life ooze from her body.

But he hadn't suspected there would be other victims, that Camille might just be the first trophy of a serial killer. Man, he didn't want to go there. Didn't want to think that someone off his nut was into picking off nuns.

Not just nuns, but sisters who lived here, at St. Marguerite's.

Unless there was another connection between the two women.

His shoes rang down the old hallways as he made his way to the rooms set up for interviews. Once again, he was going to spend the wee hours of the morning talking with the inhabitants of St. Marguerite's, and it would probably be worse than before.

This time they knew a killer was in their midst.

And, apparently, he wasn't going away.

"Wake up, sunshine, let's go!"

Somewhere, as if far in the distance, Val heard Slade's voice.

"Hey, Val!"

Her eyes flew open, and she noticed sunlight streaming through the windows. Slade, dressed, his hair wet from a recent shower, was towering over her bed. Bo, who had climbed onto the foot of the iron four-poster, lifted his head and thumped his tail wildly as Slade scratched his ears.

"What time is it?" she said, rolling over the bed and looking at the clock. "Six-thirty?" She felt as if she hadn't slept a wink.

"Get a move on." Through the blankets, he slapped her on the butt.

"Hey! What's the rush? I thought you said eight o'clock or nine or…" She blinked her eyes open, the bleariness receding. "How did you get in here?"

"Freya gave me a key."

"Remind me to wring her neck."

"Run through the shower. I'll make the coffee."

"Or maybe I'll just shoot her. Easier."

"Come on!"

"I don't like to be bullied."

"I remember." His voice held a note of nostalgia, but before she could pin him in her gaze, he walked out of the room.

What was his rush?

Not that she didn't feel the urgency to find out what happened to Camille, but she'd spent all night and most of the wee morning hours studying Camille's diary, trying to understand the sister she now felt she'd never really known.

She rolled off her bed and started stripping out of her oversized T-shirt. She caught a glimpse of her reflection in the antique mirror on the counter and cringed when she saw her wild hair and red-rimmed eyes. Her lips were devoid of any color, her eyes had huge circles under them, and the skin beneath her freckles was a sickly white. Rather than linger on the image, she walked to the shower, taking a few seconds to wash and rinse her hair, then snapped it back into a wet ponytail. A dash of lipstick and blush, a swab of mascara, and her makeup was complete. She threw on her clothes and walked barefoot into the living room to the smell of brewing coffee. In the living area, the television was on, the volume low on the local news, and Slade was just coming into the kitchen through the back door with Bo at his heels.

"Dog's been fed and let out. Grab a to-go cup and let's roll." He'd already grabbed Camille's diary within its plastic bag.

As she poured a cup and added a splash of cream, she saw Slade pause behind the sofa, sipping coffee, his eyes focused on the television screen. "You'd better come see this," he suggested.

She walked up to stand next to him just as the camera panned over a scene she recognized, the double doors to St. Marguerite's Cathedral. A reporter stood before the edifice, eyes staring straight into the camera's lens.

Before she could tune in to what the report was saying, Slade said, "This isn't an old tape. This is live, Val."

"What do you mean?"

"I heard it on the radio. Your sister's murder isn't an isolated case any longer. Another novice has been killed at St. Marguerite's."

CHAPTER 35

"Just don't tell me she was pregnant," Montoya said to Lynn Zaroster the next morning as he poured himself another cup of coffee in the small lunchroom at the station. He was talking about the latest victim at St. Marguerite's: Sister Asteria McClellan, all of twenty-two.

"Too early to know. Autopsy's scheduled for later today; they put a rush on it."

"Good."

"Anyone talk to the family?"

"Parents and six siblings, younger, most of whom still live at home, all in Birmingham." She glanced down at her notepad. "Jacob and Colleen McClellan are the folks. They're being notified this morning." She glanced at her watch. "Should be happening now."

Montoya gritted his teeth. Notifying next of kin was a hard job, necessary and oftentimes informative, but giving out the news that a loved one had died was hell.

It was eight o'clock in the damned morning, and he was powering up on coffee and a couple of cigarettes he'd snuck on the way into work, a sure sign that he was running on empty. Yeah, there was the adrenaline high of being on a big case, one that was now attracting national attention, but today, after less than four hours of sleep, he was at the end of his very short rope.

He'd been at the cemetery until after three, interviewing all the novices and nuns again, but Sister Charity and Father Paul were stonewalling him, putting up roadblocks. They'd outwardly cooperated, answering questions, allowing access to all the people who lived within the confines of St. Marguerite's, but there had been several mentions of "talking to the archdiocese" and "keeping the bishop" informed. Montoya's translation: Attorneys for the church were about to be called in, even though, as Sister Charity had said, "we will do everything in our power to help find the tortured soul who is doing this."

Father Frank had been stunned, nearly apoplectic, to the point his face had faded to a sickly color of white and he'd held on to the wall so that his knees wouldn't buckle. "No," he'd whispered, and closed his eyes to say a silent prayer, his lips moving, no sound escaping from his throat.

Had the two dead novices been close?

No one could really say; they hadn't seemed to hang out together any more than anyone else.

Had they both been involved with Father Frank? There had been no evidence of that, though a few of the nuns had blushed at the thought. Edwina, Devota, Charity, of course, and Maura had all nearly squirmed in their chairs.

This time Lucia was not alone when she found the body; Sister Edwina had been with her. Lucia had been awoken by something, not a noise she could or would name, and Edwina had said she'd gotten up to use the bathroom, though that story didn't quite jive with Lucia's.

He settled behind his desk while the sounds of the department buzzed around him. Phones were already jangling, voices rising, the antiquated air-conditioning system kicking on with a familiar growl. The wheels of the investigation were turning. More cops talking to anyone associated with Sister Asteria, her last few days scrutinized, any anomalies in her life noted, even the smallest connection to Sister Camille put under a microscope. The lab work was being done, collected evidence sorted and studied, Asteria's body being prepared for the first incision of the autopsy. Two detectives had been sent to St. Elsinore's, where Camille had worked, though it seemed Asteria's daily routine didn't include the orphanage on the other side of Lake Pontchartrain.

He thought of Asteria with her freckled face and red hair, and his gut twisted. Another short life cut off mercilessly. Hideously.

All he had to do was figure out who had gotten her into the old wedding dress, then overpowered her and garroted her, only to leave a pattern of blood drops at the neckline and ensure that her rosary was threaded through her fingers.

Sick prick.

He turned his attention to his computer screen and began checking his e-mail, hoping that the phone records for Camille Renard had been sent, when his office phone rang.

He snagged the receiver before the second blast. "Montoya."

A female voice said, "This is Officer Joan Delmonte, SFPD. I've been looking for Lea De Luca, that novice who left St. Marguerite's Convent a while back?"

The other nun supposedly involved with Frank O'Toole. "Right."

"So here's the problem. I can't locate her. Checked all the nunneries around here and no one has heard of her. Even called the archdiocese but got nowhere there, too."

"Wait a second." He checked his notes, found the date, and offered it up.

"Yeah, I know. But I'm telling you, so far Sister Lea De Luca doesn't exist, at least not anywhere in the Bay Area."

Montoya felt his skin crinkle in apprehension.

"You got the name of any relatives? Someone we could talk to other than anyone connected with the church?" she asked.

"I'll get it to you."

"Be a big help, if this is that important."

"It is," Montoya assured her, his stomach twisting the way it did when things didn't add up, when he felt that he was being manipulated. "Keep looking and go beyond the church, if you can. If she's not a nun, she could be a layperson, a teacher maybe. I think she had her credentials, at least here in Louisiana."

"Will do."

"Thanks. I'll get back to you later about the relatives."

He hung up and stared at the phone a second, then called the number he had for the SFPD and asked for Joan Delmonte. Just in case. There was a log of all the calls that came into the department, but he wanted to hear the woman's voice, to convince himself that he wasn't being played.

"Delmonte," the same woman answered after he'd gone through an operator.

"Montoya, NOPD, just thought you might want my cell number."

"Sure." She laughed, deep and throaty that ended with a smoker's cough. "Don't kid a kidder, Montoya. We both know why you called. Just in case I was some nutcase yanking your chain. Sorry to disappoint. I'm the real McCoy. But give me that number anyway."

He rattled it off and hung up.

Zaroster appeared in his doorway. "Next of kin for Asteria McClellan has been notified, and the press is all over the story."

"Tell them—"

"I know, I know. To talk to the public information officer. Sinclaire's preparing a statement."

"Good."

"Won't stop the likes of Brenda Convoy."

Montoya scowled. "Yeah, I know. Thanks." He felt the electricity crackling within the department, the second homicide at St. Marguerite's so quickly on the heels of the first creating a newfound urgency. Nerves were strung tight, and no doubt the Feds would be calling.

So what was the connection between the two victims, other than the obvious that they were two novices at St. Marguerite's Convent here in New Orleans? Were they close? Closer than other members of the cloister? He ran a hand around his face, felt the beard stubble surrounding his goatee. His eyes burned.

He finished his cup of coffee and turned toward his computer monitor again where he'd put up the two pictures of the victims on the screen. Both lying supine, rosaries clutched, dressed in ancient bridal dresses, with the distinctive pattern of blood dropped around the necklines.

Both scenes were staged.

The altar cloth on the first placed by the mother superior.

One in the chapel, under the looming figure of Christ upon the cross, the other in a cemetery, near a tomb where a sculpted angel rose high into the night sky.

Was there more of a link between the two victims?

Why were they culled out of the habited flock?

"Come on," he said, as if the two images on the computer could hear him and talk. "Come on."

From the corner of his eye, he noticed Bentz appear in the doorway. His partner held his favorite old coffee cup in one hand and a plastic ziplock bag in the other. Inside the bag, a book was visible. "We've got company," Bentz announced. He looked ragged around the edges, freshly showered, his hair still wet, but the creases near the corners of his eyes more pronounced.

"Hopefully not a reporter."

"Nope. Better. Vic one's sister and her husband. They brought us a present." He handed Montoya the plastic bag.

"What's this?" Montoya asked, but he knew. Before Bentz told him, he realized he was looking at Camille Renard's diary.

"The book we've been looking for."

"Where the hell was it?"

"St. Elsinore's. In her locker or cubby or whatever. The husband lifted it yesterday."

"He did what? Oh, for the love of God, what an idiot." Outraged, Montoya was on his feet, the bag still in his hand. "What the hell was he thinking? He should have just left things alone, called and let us handle it. Now there's no evidence chain—we can't prove that someone else didn't get a hold of the diary since it was put in the locker." Montoya was furious. Fuming. The frustration of the case that had been building inside exploded white-hot. "A defense attorney will have a heyday with this. Even if Slade Houston swears it was with him from the moment he pulled it out of St. Elsinore's, it creates doubt, no police record. Shit!" He kicked his chair back to the desk. "He probably contaminated evidence and compromised the whole damned case." Raking fingers through his hair, he forced himself to calm a bit. "Where are they?"

"Interrogation room one."

"Let's go!" Hauling the plastic bag and diary with him, he was out of his office in an instant, impotent fury propelling his long strides. "Wasn't she a cop or something?"

"Detective with a county in Texas."

"Detective? Yeah, that's what I thought. I don't know how they train 'em in Texas, but she should have known better!" Montoya was striding down the short hallway. "Son of a bitch," he muttered under his breath. "Son of a goddamned bitch!"

Val knew she'd be hung up by her hamstrings for taking the diary, and she wasn't disappointed. Detective Montoya was rabid in his anger as he stood in the interrogation room, the plastic bag and Camille's diary on the table in front of her. "This is a police matter; there are rules that we have to abide by so that our case isn't compromised, so that all parties are protected."

"We found it and brought it in," she said, her hackles already raised as she sat in the stiff, uncomfortable chair next to Slade. So far they hadn't split them up; that was probably coming, but who cared. Their stories would match. They were only telling the truth. "Someone else was killed last night, another nun from St. Marguerite's," she said. "It was on the news this morning."

Montoya hesitated for a second, slightly derailed. "Sister Asteria McClellan."

"Oh, God," Val whispered, her hand flying to her mouth as she remembered the fresh-faced girl with the red hair and freckles, the one who, in the garden, had gazed up at Father Frank O'Toole with such open adoration as she'd held out a single white rose to the priest.

Val felt sick to her stomach. "Oh, no." She shook her head.

"You knew her?"

"No, but I met her." She told Bentz and Montoya about running across Asteria in the garden with Father Frank.

"I couldn't judge his reaction," she admitted, though just the thought turned her stomach. "But it was obvious she was in love with him. She handed him the flower and seemed to bathe in just being around him." Hearing herself, she shuddered. "Sorry. I may be way off, but that's the way it appeared to me."

"You were the only one there?"

"The mother superior, Sister Charity, she'd let me into the garden where they were meeting. And probably Sister Zita; she was the first one I talked to."

"She's the African American nun."

"One of them—maybe the only one," Val said, nodding.

Montoya didn't appear to like the connection to O'Toole again. Val read the disbelief in his dark eyes. Frowning, he asked, "Was Asteria close to your sister?"

"I...I don't know."

Montoya persisted, "Did she ever mention her?"

"Maybe...but just in passing." She shook her head, honestly perplexed.

"They weren't close?"

"I don't think so," she said, then glanced at the bag in his hands. "But then there are a lot of things I didn't know about Cammie."

"You should have left this where you found it," he said, indicating the ziplock and diary. "Take anything else?"

"That's all there was," Slade said.

"Have you looked through the diary, Detective?" Val asked. "You might be interested in the fact that it pretty much lists all of her lovers, starting with her first. Not hard to figure out."

To her surprise, Montoya flinched a bit, almost imperceptibly, but it was there just the same.

"Does it list O'Toole?"

"Camille was discreet—didn't name names."

She noticed Montoya's tense shoulders sag a bit at the news. For that, she didn't blame him. They all hoped that the book would be key, that it would point out the person who had killed Camille.

"I didn't recognize him, if that's what you're getting at, but I'm sure he's there along with a list of others."

"So you went through this page by page?" Montoya accused.

Slade said, "We used gloves."

Montoya's lips were white as they flattened over his teeth. He was trying and failing to rein in his anger.

Bentz, from his spot near the door of the small room, asked, "Did you recognize anyone in the pages?"

"Not really. Just put two and two together." She swung her gaze back to Montoya and saw a tired, angry man. "You know, you're pretty good at pointing fingers and telling me what I shouldn't do, but do you really think you should be investigating Camille's murder since it's pretty clear that you were lover number one?"

Beneath his swarthy skin, Reuben Montoya colored, but he didn't miss a beat as he leaned over the table. "Since you looked through the pages, I would appreciate knowing if you saw anything that might indicate who her last lover was."

"I already told you: Frank O'Toole."

"And he admitted to it, but here's the kicker," Montoya said without an ounce of satisfaction. "There's no way he could be her baby's father. Not according to the laws of science. So, if not him, who do you think it might be?"

Sister Charity had been struggling for hours. Sitting at her desk, she was bone-tired, her muscles ached, her eyes felt as if they'd been rubbed in grit. She'd dozed twice, there at the desk, with her open prayer book beside her and poor Eileen hammering away at the typewriter when she, too, was beside herself.

"What happened?" she'd asked earlier, then held her thin fingers over her mouth and squeaked in disbelief as Sister Charity had explained what she could about Sister Asteria's horrid demise.

"Dear, dear. Poor sweet girl." Eileen, eyes brimming, had held her hand and they'd prayed; then, tissue box next to her little angel mug often filled with peppermints, Eileen had tried to go about her work.

Sister Charity was beyond exhausted. After dealing with the police in the predawn hours, she'd spent the rest of the night talking with Father Paul and Father Frank, not trusting either man completely. Both were weak. Paul unable to stand up to the archbishop or some of his more domineering parishioners, especially those with large wallets, and Frank . . . well, because of his weakness.

At the first sign of his true nature, she should have called him out, put an end to things, but she hadn't.

And now two of her darlings were dead.

Guilt tore a hole in her heart as Eileen's fingers tapped their irregular cadence beyond the slightly open door, and Charity knew, deep to the center of her soul, she'd been at least partially to blame for Asteria's death. She squeezed her eyes shut hard at the admission to herself.

She should have been more forthright with the police, less secretive and protective. She felt the scars on her back, long healed, and knew she had to pay her own penance for her sins. "Forgive me," she whispered for the hundredth time since Asteria's body had been discovered and realized dawn was casting its brilliant rays over the city.

She'd spent the early morning hours kneeling on the cold floor of the chapel, praying to the Father for guidance, clasping her hands together so hard her old knuckles showed white, the bone so close to her pale skin.

She had to be strong, she'd told herself, and had slept so very little since the horror of finding another one of her flock, the women she sincerely considered her charges—no, her children—had been murdered.

Her muscles ached as she pushed back her desk chair and walked through the back door of her office and through the halls she'd loved so deeply. This, St. Marguerite's, was as much a part of her as the family home she'd never had.

Few people knew that she was an orphan, that she had grown up at St. Elsinore's, never adopted out. She found her calling into the service of the Holy Father. The nuns at St. Elsinore's had both frightened and inspired her, and she'd never thought twice about taking her vows.

Until now.

The halls of the convent were quiet now. The police had once again created chaos here, but, for the moment, it had passed, most of the police officers having left but the cemetery was still cordoned off.

Most of the nuns were spending the day in contemplation, the rigidity of their daily routine interrupted until this evening when they would all gather together in the chapel and Father Paul and Father Frank would conduct a special Mass.

Charity should rest—her body was reminding her of that very painful fact—but she couldn't, not yet. She walked through the doors to the garden and the fountain she loved so dearly. In the shimmering water, she caught a glimpse of her reflection distorted by her own shadow, rippled by the water's movement and the glints of gold when the fish darted through the pool's tiled depths.

She was a relic in her habit and veil. Archaic. Clinging to the old order that was becoming a distant memory. And yet she knew deep in her heart that she was following her true destiny, that she had helped so many like herself, those abandoned, for reasons both good and evil, by their families.

"Sister?" A male voice brought her up short, and she nearly gasped, so deep was she in her reverie. On the other side of the fountain stood that incorrigible Detective Montoya. She didn't trust him for a second. "May I have a word?"

At least he was being respectful.

"I'm sorry, Reverend Mother," Sister Devota said, and looked truly rueful. "We"—she indicated her companion, Sister Irene— "were returning from the orphanage, and he was waiting at the gate."

"It's all right," she said to the worried novice. Devota bit her lip, then hurried off, her gait slightly unsteady. She was a difficult woman, full of impassioned faith that concealed her own doubts about herself. Irene's faith was just as solid, and she was the antithesis of Devota. Tall and lithe, with an almost regal possession of her body. Her fluid movements made Devota's awkwardness more pronounced.

All so different; all the same.

"What can I do for you?" she asked the detective, surprised to find him alone. They usually talked to her in pairs, but then, the police department was probably stretched thin with these recent horrors. "I thought I answered all your questions last night." Her voice was dry and sounded weak.

"It's something that I found out today," he said, jumping right in. "You told me that Sister Lea De Luca left New Orleans and joined a convent in San Francisco."

"That's right."

"Where?"

"I don't know, but I do know that she decided against taking her final vows." Montoya seemed surprised as he rounded the fountain. "I don't know the details, but I got a card from her last Christmas saying that she'd decided to become a teacher. A lay teacher. She didn't say why. She'd left the order."

"Do you have the name of the parish?"

"St. Dominique's...No, no, that was someone else. Oh! Our Lady of Sorrows?" she said in a question, scouring her memory. "Yes, that was it."

He shook his head. "The SFPD checked all the parishes. No one remembers Sister Lea."

Charity felt her lips purse. "I said she gave it up."

"They were specific. No one named Lea De Luca in the last decade."

"But..." Charity felt the very foundations of her faith begin to quiver. What was the officer saying? "I don't understand. As I said, I've gotten correspondence."

"But she hasn't called or visited?"

She pinned on her overtly patient smile, the one she knew to be intimidating, the one that silently called the person asking her a silly question an idiot. But she was certain Detective Reuben Montoya was no one's fool, even though, as he squinted against the hard sun, the ridiculous diamond in his earlobe glinted in ostentatious flamboyance and that small beard of his—a vanity. Her lips pursed. "This is a convent," she reminded him. "One with certain values and decorum, but you know that. We've had this conversation before."

"The correspondence," he said. "Do you still have it?"

"The latest was a card at Christmas, but I'm not certain," she admitted. "Come with me into the office and I'll look." He walked with her along the path and through the cool, dark hallways to her office where he waited while she opened the drawer in which she kept her personal correspondence, a pitifully slim folder.

She sifted through the few envelopes and found it, a white envelope and inside a card, showing the blessed Virgin Mary holding a perfect little Christ child, halos glowing around them, a lamb at Mary's feet. The message was a simple Bible verse and the card was signed "Peace be with you in this holiest of seasons. Sister Lea" in her perfect, Catholic school cursive scrawl.

"May I have this and the envelope?" the detective asked, and when she answered, "Of course," he slipped them both into a plastic sleeve, as if the card were of some great importance.

There was a knock on the open door, and the receptionist with the frizzy blue hair poked her head in. "I'm sorry, Sister, but there's someone here to see you...Oh!" Her eyes rounded at the sight of Montoya as he and the reverend mother entered through a small back doorway.

"Thank you, Eileen. Detective Montoya and I are almost finished."

"Detective?" Her graying brows drew together behind the glasses that made her eyes appear owlish. "But the man who's here says he's—"

Montoya's partner, the heavier-set fellow, appeared behind Eileen.

"It's all right," Charity said, waving him inside. "I think I need to talk to both detectives."

Eileen had shifted slightly and Bentz entered.

"Please, close the door," Charity said to Eileen, and as it closed, she motioned to the two chairs facing her desk. "I'm glad you're both here," she said, finally ready to unburden herself. "You see, I haven't been completely honest with you."

CHAPTER 36

"It's as if I didn't even know her," Valerie said as they walked into the mausoleum. Slade's boots rang against the polished marble floors, and, as always when she visited here, Val felt cold, her skin chilling as if the ghosts of the dead haunted the wide hallways of the mausoleum where the ceilings rose twenty feet and the walls were polished stone. Tall windows on either end of the edifice let in natural light, today a filtered sun. She had the feeling she was walking through a long tunnel, the walls of which were inhabited by the dead.

Her parents' ashes were sealed here, on the east wall, along with dozens of others who had died. Gene Richard Renard and his wife, Nadine Lynne Bates Renard, held permanent residence in a vault on the fifth row from the bottom in a wall of veined marble.

Val ran her fingers over the etched letters while Slade leaned against a tall ladder that was used to reach the higher spaces. She'd come here often after they'd died, first her father of throat cancer and less than two years later, her mother of a brain aneurysm, just after Christmas, the very year that Camille decided to live with Val and Slade in Texas for a while, then left to join the convent. Though Gene had been nearly seventy when he died, Nadine had been much younger, only fifty-eight when she'd died. Val had sometimes wondered if the aneurysm had been caused by the stress her daughters had put Nadine through, though every doctor she'd talked to had dissuaded her of the idea.

God, that was a bad time for all of them.

Val shook off the memory and said, "I mean...it's almost like Camille was two people. Or...something."

"A split personality?" Slade asked, but she shook her head.

"No, not really. I've heard that people have public lives and personal lives and private lives. Everyone sees the public life, the family and close friends are part of the personal life, and then there's the secret life, the one no one but you knows about. Camille's secret life, that's what I'm talking about."

"Someone knew about it," Slade pointed out, walking closer to her, touching her on the shoulder in a way that was intimate and caring—a bridge between them.

"Yeah, someone did." Whoever she was sleeping with surely did, the man Cammie had referred to only as "Beloved." Whoever the hell he was. Frank O'Toole? Or the unknown guy who had impregnated her.

If only Cammie had confided in her. Told Val about the other lover.

Maybe she thought the kid was fathered by Frank.

Sighing, Val studied her parents' inscription. Gene and Nadine, names that rhymed. A joke between them. Her father had sworn that if she and Camille hadn't already been named, he would have called her Valdine and Camille would have been Camdeen. He'd winked as he'd said it, and Val had rolled her eyes.

They'd been good parents. Gene, a welder who worked for the railroad, and Nadine, a substitute teacher for the public schools, though they'd enrolled their daughters in St. Timothy's.

"Doesn't hurt to get a little religion with your ABCs now, does it?" Gene had said, usually over a long-necked bottle of beer in front of the television.

But the two had shared a look, and Val had overheard an argument once. She'd been hurrying down the hall, almost at the head of the stairs, and her parents' voices slipped through the bedroom door that hadn't been quite closed.

"You can't get behind with the tuition!" Nadine had whispered harshly. Tiny and thin to the point of being bony, she was a strong woman whose convictions were matched only by her faith.

"We're not. It was a screwup. I took care of it." A dozen years older, Gene Renard was a foot taller than his wife, his hair in gray tufts around a significant bald spot, the smell of tobacco and smoke forever clinging to him.

At her mother's words, Val had stopped, her hand on the newel post, her gaze riveted to the crack between the door and the jamb. From her vantage point, she saw her mother's full-length mirror and the reflection of her father stepping out of his dirty work jumpsuit.

She had nearly turned away but couldn't. "Look, Gene, I promised Mary, okay? Private school. Catholic. So we can't mess this up."

His legs were white but muscular, his jockey shorts black as night. A once-athletic man who had developed a bit of a paunch in his later years, he was about to yank off his shorts. She'd blushed at the sight of him; then, when his gaze caught hers, she'd hurried quickly down the stairs.

Neither of them ever spoke of that moment again. She thought then that it was odd, as many times as she'd been here, she'd never once visited the graves of her biological parents, those two people who were but wispy memories. Where the hell were they buried? The woman who'd been their friend, who had supposedly brought Val and Camille to the orphanage, she might know. Again, the woman's kind face came into view, but her name... Wasn't it Thea? No... but she was married or had been and that guy's name was... Oh, damn. Steve...no! Stanley! That was it. Stanley O'Malley!

"Let's go," she said, not really knowing why she'd brought Slade here, why she'd felt an urgency to touch the tomb of the parents who had raised her. It seemed they, too, had secrets they'd taken with them to the grave.

"Where to?" They were walking through the oversized glass door and into the bright sunlight of the afternoon. The air was thick, the sky a sharp, brilliant blue as they followed a brick path across a carpet of lawn to the parking lot.

"First I want to go to the library and the local newspaper, check the old files, anything I can't find on my own over the Internet. I think it's time to look up that 'friend' of the family. I think her name is O'Malley. She's the woman who supposedly was watching Cammie and me when our biological parents were killed. I'd like to see what she has to say for herself."

"Okay."

She'd unlocked the car, and he was sliding into the passenger seat.

"And then I need to go back to Briarstone and look in the attic over the garage," she said, thinking for the first time of the boxes her sister had stowed up there as she slid into the stifling heat of the Subaru. She started the engine, then quickly rolled down all the windows. "When Camille went into the convent, she left a bunch of her stuff with me. I didn't want it, as we weren't on the best of terms, but I finally relented when she said she'd get rid of it as soon as she could, give everything to charity or something, once she'd gone through it." She pulled out of the lot and nosed her Subaru into the traffic leading to the Pontchartrain Expressway.

"I thought it weird at the time, didn't know when she'd ever get away from the convent for something so trivial, but she hauled the boxes into the attic, and no one's touched them since." She slid a glance his way. "You game?"

"Sure." He grinned slightly. "It'll be just like Christmas."

"Right," she said without even the trace of a smile. "Just like."

From two of the most uncomfortable chairs on the planet, Montoya and Bentz listened while the reverend mother unburdened herself. Montoya watched her transformation, from bristling, secretive mother hen to a penitent, an aging woman slowly losing her grip on the reins of control over her spiritual fortress.

"I probably shouldn't be talking to you, not without a lawyer from the archdiocese or someone of authority to witness what I'm saying, but I think that's wrong. Father Paul and I are in disagreement about it, of course, but then we often are and...and sometimes I think it's important to do what you believe to be the correct course in your heart. I believe in rules and discipline and structure, but sometimes...well, as I said, as much as I trust authority, I know I was given my own free will to pray, to seek the Father's counsel, and then do what I believe is best.

"I know there is a lot of darkness surrounding the church right now, but there is so much good that is forgotten. Here, we help the sick and the hungry, offer counseling and guidance and love. Did you know that St. Ursuline's has been in the city since the seventeen hundreds and provided medical care for a disease-riddled, new-found city? I believe the first pharmacist in the United States was a sister from St. Ursuline's, and the nuns there helped educate girls and...Oh, there's no use telling you the history of convents and trying to prove to you our worth. You already know it. But, with all good comes the capacity for evil, I suppose."

For someone so rigid, Montoya thought, this was a surprising admission. The fine lines across her face seemed more pronounced today, her spine having lost much of its starch. "It's not as God in-tended, to speak through attorneys. I know the church, which I love with all my heart, has been battered in recent years. All the ugly scandals coming to light." She looked pained, her graying eye-brows drawn in consternation and sadness. "But all that is Satan's work, and we do God's work here, so I just want to tell you the truth before anyone else, another of my novices, gets hurt."

She stood and walked to the window, where she looked out to a courtyard. "You're asking about Sister Lea, and I'm not surprised. I knew her name would come up."

"Why?" Bentz asked.

"Because she, too, was enamored with Father O'Toole." Charity sighed through her nose. "The girls who come here, for the most part, are barely women. They're young and full of life and filled with joie de vivre and the Holy Spirit. They're often giddy and naive, some even rebellious, but they are good-hearted and willing to serve God and come here to learn. I'm strict with them, yes. They often need structure and discipline, but in the end, they can be trained to be angels of mercy here on earth....Oh, listen to me go on. The point is, they're impressionable, and they are women. They have hormones and dreams, and many are romantic, caught up in youth and..." She pulled a hand from the pocket of her habit and waved off whatever else she might say as fluff.

"Anyway, I saw that Sister Lea was treading in dangerous water, falling in love with Father O'Toole. He's handsome and fiery and virile." She slid a glance at Montoya. "As I said, nuns, even this old one, are women. We notice though we try not to." She cleared her throat, her hand disappearing into the black folds of her habit again. "I wasn't the only one who witnessed the, uh...attraction. I heard the younger nuns talking, and Father Frank...well, just as the nuns are women, he's a man. It was a difficult situation.

"I talked to Lea. Actually, she came to me and though she wouldn't discuss what had happened between her and Father Frank, she agreed to leave, but only on her terms. She'd lost her spirit of conviction and wasn't certain she wanted to be a nun any longer. I let her go."

"And you didn't check on her?" Bentz asked.

The older woman turned and skewered him with a gaze meant to cut through granite. "No, Detective, I didn't. I asked her to contact me when she was settled, and I received a postcard saying she was leaving the church.... Here, maybe I can find that one, too." She walked to her file drawers again and searched through several files before she found what she was looking for. She handed him a postcard of St. Paul's Cathedral in San Francisco, the twin spires cutting upward through the fog. On the back was a handwritten note stating that she'd arrived, was "excited" to be in "the city" and was still working on her spiritual issues.

"Can we take this?" Montoya asked.

She nodded. "Of course."

"Have you talked with any members of her family?" Bentz asked as Montoya carefully slid the postcard in with the Christmas card in the plastic evidence bag.

"No," she said sadly. "Lea's parents were divorced. Her mother died a few years back, car accident I think, and her father and Lea were estranged. He remarried shortly after the divorce and moved out of the country." Her brow wrinkled beneath her wimple. "Yes, I think so. Mexico maybe?"

"What about siblings?"

"None, but I thought you knew." She seemed genuinely surprised. "Sister Lea was an only child, adopted years ago."

Montoya's muscles tightened. He felt that little sizzle in his blood, the rush of adrenaline as it spurted through his veins when he knew he'd found something important to the case.

"From St. Elsinore's?" Bentz asked.

"Of course." She acted as if this was common knowledge. "Most of the women who come here are from St. Elsinore's, sisters in spirit, yes, but also sisters because they grew up in the same place, the orphanage." The corner of her lip trembled a bit. "Just like me."

Montoya wanted to make certain he'd heard right. "You were adopted out of St. Elsinore's?"

Her smile was forced. "No. I never was adopted, though my brother was." She sighed sadly. "I grew up at the orphanage. A lot of us did. The older ones, harder to adopt, you know. It breaks my heart that it's closing...."

Montoya felt a little buzz in his bloodstream. "Sister Camille was adopted from St. Elsinore's, right?" He'd read that in his notes.

"Yes." She was nodding.

"But Asteria, she was from a large family in Birmingham."

"No, Detective." The mother superior's face was thoughtful. "She was adopted from St. Elsinore's as well." Her smile held a bit of sorrow as well as irony. "It was a case of the parents struggling to conceive, and then when they adopted Asteria, Mrs. McClellan, Colleen I think her name is, had another child within twelve months. After that, Asteria's siblings came along quite steadily."

"None of the others are adopted."

"Not that I know of."

Montoya's mind was racing. Could this be it? The connection they were looking for? St. Elsinore's orphanage rather than St. Marguerite's convent? "Can we get a list of anyone who resides here who came out of St. Elsinore's?" he asked.

"I . . . suppose. But now we're stepping into matters of personal privacy."

"Easy enough to find out through public records," Bentz pointed out, and she nodded.

"All right. Let me talk to the women first, and then I'll get a list for you."

"One more thing," Montoya said. "Was Sister Asteria involved with Father O'Toole?"

"What? Oh, no! This is a convent, Detective, and though, yes, there have been some...well, indiscretions, it's not as if it's the summer of love here. Everyone, the priests, nuns, novices, we all practice celibacy, and before you interrupt, yes, I know about Sister Camille and Father O'Toole, and of course I'll admit that Sister Lea was...tempted, as was Father O'Toole, but not Sister Asteria...." But her voice faded, and for a second she turned her gaze from the detectives, staring off to the middle distance. Denial flared in her eyes but quickly died. "There may have been some flirting or, uh, fantasies on Asteria's part, I suppose, but nothing serious, I assure you."

Montoya nodded, though he wasn't convinced. He had to ask something that had been nagging at him. "Sister Camille's body had some odd marks on it," he said, testing the waters.

The old nun stiffened slightly in her habit, but she didn't ask what, just waited him out.

"Kind of crisscross marks."

"As if she'd been flogged," Bentz added, and the reverend mother whispered something under her breath.

"Excuse me?" Montoya said.

She closed her eyes for a second, and when she opened them again, they were focused, clear behind the lenses of her glasses. She stared at him with the intensity of an entomologist dissecting a newfound species of insect. "Sometimes, Detective, when a sinner atones, she takes it upon herself to punish herself physically, for clarity and purification. Though this isn't a practice I urge, I know it's done here."

"You don't require or urge it, but you condone it?" Bentz said, his eyebrows slamming together.

"I believe that each individual must do what she feels is necessary as penance. It's between her and the Holy Father."

"Sister Camille practiced self-flagellation?"

"I don't know for certain. As I said, there are some practices that might appear archaic such as corporal mortification, but I assure you, Detectives, it's not something we practice as a whole, or even suggest. Do some practice it?" She nodded slowly. "I suppose. As I think I said before, Sister Camille was a tormented soul."

She cleared her throat, scooped an excessively large key ring from a desk drawer, and said, "Now, please, if you come with me, there's something I want to show you." She waved them to their feet, and they followed her through a private door and along the quiet hallway to a staircase. Holding on to the rail, her steps quick, she led them to the third floor. Once there, she located a small doorway that opened to a musty attic. She snapped on a dim light, hiked up her skirts, and walked inside, passing by old desks and dusty lamps, candle holders and cots, artifacts and picture frames.

Mouse traps were scattered on the floor, and spiderwebs and dust covered the few small windows that let in a dim, watery light. At the end of the littered pathway was another door that reached to the sloping rafters. The reverend mother paused before it, ran her fingers over the grainy wood, then found a key on her enormous ring and inserted it into the lock. With a click and a jangle of the other keys on the ring, the lock sprang open and she pulled on the knob. Creaking as if in protest, the door swung open to reveal a dark empty space.

The reverend mother snapped on a light and stepped inside. Wooden dowels ran the length of the closet. Clothing sheathed in plastic hung on wire hangers from one rod.

To Montoya, it looked as if this was where all the old vestments—cassocks, albs, habits, robes, and items he couldn't name—hung; all covered in plastic. The other rod was empty.

Sister Charity stared at the dowel from which nothing was suspended and shook her head. "But they can't be gone. They just can't be," she whispered, crossing herself.

"What?" Montoya asked, trepidation plucking at the hairs on his nape.

"The bridal gowns. They're missing. All of them." She shook her head in worry, obviously distraught, then turned to the side of the closet holding the vestments and began rifling through the plastic bags. "I was afraid of this," she admitted, pushing one plastic-encased robe after another to the side, the hangers' hooks scraping along the rod. She peered between each separate sheathing, as if willing the dresses to appear, then shoved the offensive bag aside. Faster and faster. One heavy vestment after another whipping past.

"You're talking about gowns like the ones the victims were wearing?" Bentz asked.

She sent him a glance that called him a fool. "Of course! They're the wedding dresses that were worn in the ceremony for becoming the bride of Christ. We haven't used these particular gowns for a long, long while. They've been stored up here for years. Forgotten, I'd thought." She turned back to her search.

Zzzip!

Another plastic-covered cassock flew past her, nimble fingers on to the next.

Zip! One more cassock.

Zip! Zip!

Two habits flew by and then there was none.

"They were all in here." She was at the end of the dowel and beginning to show signs of panic, a tic evident near the edge of her wimple, just under her eye.

Backing out of the closet, she pushed aside an old table that rolled on squeaky castors; then she scoured the cloth-covered artifacts with her eyes.

"How many were there?" Montoya asked, a cold stone settling in the pit of his stomach.

"A dozen," she said swiftly, her cheeks infused with scarlet.

"Was that before or after the bodies were found?"

"After, of course!"

"When did you notice them missing?"

"They were here yesterday...." She closed her eyes so tightly her jaw clenched. Her hands, too, fisted, one around her key ring. "I checked just yesterday, and there were eleven dresses hanging right here." Eyes flying open, she jabbed a long finger toward the empty rod. "Eleven." The last word was weak. "Only eleven and now all gone."

"Only eleven?" Bentz repeated.

"Yes." She made the sign of the cross over her chest. "But there were twelve up here that I remember. I double-checked my notes, and one was missing yesterday."

Montoya felt a chill as cold as a north wind whisper through his brain. "Sister Camille was wearing the twelfth," he guessed.

"Yes."

"And Sister Asteria the eleventh," Bentz said, his gaze meeting Montoya's. "Meaning that there are ten left."

Montoya said, "Ten dresses, ten more victims?"

"Oh, please, no!" Charity gasped, but Montoya could tell the idea had already come to her; he was only reaffirming her worst fears.

"We'll need that list of names," he said. "Of anyone who once was an orphan at St. Elsinore's."

"And also the nuns who work there now. Some work with the kids and at the clinic, right?" Bentz asked as the reverend mother, in the sweltering quarters of the attic, nervously fingered the cross dangling from a chain at her neck.

"Yes, yes, of course," she said, still shaken. Then with more conviction than he would have expected, she added, "I'll get what you need right now." She blinked and sniffed, as if tears were burning the back of her eyelids.

Anger?

Righteous fury?

Or guilt?

Who knew? And did it matter?

"Come along, then." Some of the stiffness had returned to her spine, the determined, no-nonsense set of her jaw back again. "If Father Paul gives me any grief, any talk of legal issues, I'll tell him to take it up with God!"

CHAPTER 37

It was late afternoon by the time Slade helped Valerie carry boxes down from the attic. Shadows were stretching long over the grounds of Briarstone, evening fast approaching.

The day had gotten away from her. She'd had some paperwork for Briarstone that couldn't be put off any longer while Slade had called his brothers, checked on the ranch, then repaired a clog in the sprinkler system and worked on Valerie's computer, debugging it, adding some memory, cleaning out files with her permission, and getting the damned laptop up to speed. She'd done some digging on the Internet when the computer was up and running and had found several O'Malleys in the phone book, looking for the elusive Mrs. Stan, but so far had struck out.

All the while, she'd been thinking about Camille's disturbing diary—the images it had evoked and the cryptic messages she'd left for herself.

Which were probably nothing.

Yet they nagged at her, kept scratching at her mind, an itch that couldn't be relieved.

Now she was at her desk, hanging up her phone after a call from a woman who apologized profusely for canceling her trip to New Orleans and her reservation at Briarstone for the weekend because her husband had been rushed to the hospital for emergency gall bladder surgery.

Slade had spent the last hour working on her laptop at the small table she'd tucked near the kitchen. A warm summer breeze drifted through the screen door, and Bo, making the weird high-pitched whine he always did while sleeping and dreaming, was lying just outside on the porch.

"This should work a lot faster," Slade said, screwing the computer's case into place.

"How do you know how to do this?" She motioned toward the laptop.

"What?"

"Fix the damned thing? Add memory? All of it?"

His grin was lazy and amused, his thin lips twisting. "You don't think we have computers on the ranch?"

"Yeah, I know, but, I mean—"

"I told you that Bad Luck's in the twenty-first century, right? And I've been a closeted geek for years," he teased, glancing up from the screen. He slid his chair back and stood, still holding the screwdriver, stretching his arms high enough over his head to nearly touch the ceiling while listening to his spine pop.

"Really?" She tried not to notice that his shirt hiked up as he stretched, exposing those lean, hard muscles of his abdomen, the trail of dark hair that slipped beneath the waist of his jeans.

"You don't remember?" He cast a surprised look down at her, one of his eyebrows arching.

"That you were into high tech?" she asked. "No."

"I said 'closeted.' "

She rolled her eyes up at him. "So it's true. The wife is the last to know."

" 'The wife' hasn't been around much lately," he reminded her, and the barb was as sharp as the Pomeroy utility knife she was planning to use on the wide tape that sealed the five boxes she'd found in the attic over her small garage.

There it was between them.

The marriage.

The impending divorce.

She didn't want to think about that, not right now. "So you really are the computer-genius cowboy?"

"Yes'm," he drawled, twirling the screwdriver like it was a six-shooter, then holstering it into his jeans pocket. "Here at the BS Ranch—and that *BS* stands for Briarstone, don'tcha know—we do it all. Everything from pulling calves to restoring laptops." His crooked, decidedly sexy smile stretched wide.

"BS is right," she said, and laughed for the first time in what seemed like eons. She also remembered why she'd fallen so hard and fast for him. *Oh, Slade,* she found herself thinking, *if only we could start over—wipe the slate clean.*

She realized then that she'd never stopped loving him.

Her throat caught for a second. What an idiot.

You can never go back. Didn't she believe that old axiom? Her smile faded as she saw the empty years stretching out before her. Her parents and sister dead, her husband an ex and living at the Triple H, far, far away in a long-distant past. Oh, God, now she was getting maudlin.

Fool!

She felt her cheeks burn and prayed Slade had no idea what she was feeling.

"Let's see what you think." Slade carried the laptop to her desk, where he set it down. He was standing so near her she smelled a hint of his aftershave, and it brought back memories of lying in bed, his scent still lingering on the pillows long after he'd gotten up to feed the livestock. Irritated, she pushed the wayward memory aside.

He was standing half behind her, one shoulder nearly brushing her back, his face even with hers as he pushed a few buttons on the keyboard. "Try something."

"Such as?"

He slid a glance at her from the corner of his eye. "Well, I was talking about a program on the computer, but if you have something else in mind..." His voice was low and suggestive.

"In your nightmares, Cowboy."

"And yours, I'll bet."

"I'm not having this discussion with you!" She sounded tough, but inside she was melting.

His laugh was low. Mocking. As if he knew what she was thinking. She turned her head and noticed his belt buckle, right at eye level, the faded fly of his jeans, right above the top of her desk and slightly rounded.

Oh, great!

He was getting aroused, too?

Not good! Not good at all.

Quickly she turned her attention back to the computer screen. "Okay, hotshot," she said, hating that she sounded slightly breathless. "Give me a demonstration."

There was a pregnant pause, and she felt her cheeks burn.

"You can be such a bastard!" she said.

"And you love it." His laugh was deep and rich, the timbre familiar.

"God, what an ego!"

Ignoring his amusement and his eye-level, jean-covered crotch, she reached for the computer's mouse, plugged it in, and with a few clicks located the program she used for booking reservations at the inn. "Let's see if I can cancel Mr. and Mrs. Miller's rooms for the weekend." She turned her mind away from the slight bulge at the front of Slade's jeans and began working.

"You're a tease, wife," he said.

That makes two of us. "And you're always thinking with your—Oh, never mind."

"You were gonna say 'heart,' right?"

"Yeah, that's it," she joked.

He leaned closer and whispered into the shell of her ear, "You're right. I am." His breath was warm against her skin. Inviting. A second later, he brushed his lips across the crook of her neck, and she shivered inside, feeling a little tingle deep inside, right between the juncture of her legs, that sweet itch that always signaled the start of her sexual arousal, the beginning of a pulsating, hot throb.

Trouble.

If she turned her head, he would kiss her. And from there . . . oh, sweet God . . .

"I don't think this is a good idea."

"You're right."

"Slade..." She closed her eyes. *Don't do this!*

She turned her head and felt his lips against hers, but he didn't kiss her, didn't press his mouth more urgently to her own suddenly willing lips. She opened her eyes and found him staring at her, pupils dark with desire, blue irises so thin they were barely visible. The pores on his skin, the stubble of whiskers starting to grow, all so close, and the scent of him, of aftershave and desire almost palpable.

She swallowed against a mouth as dry as an East Texas canyon in August.

Slowly he pulled his head away. "You know, Val," he said, his voice a low whisper, his expression as serious as death, "I would never have cheated on you. Never."

Tears sprang to her eyes.

"Not with Camille. Not with anyone."

Her throat closed and she fought the urge to break down completely.

"I was tempted. Oh, man. I was tempted. But it wasn't worth it." He let out a long breath. "Nothing was. Because I knew that I'd lose you. If I would have done it, slept with her, it would have been just sex. Maybe even good sex. But with you..." He looked away, to the doorway where Bo was now standing on the other side of the screen. "Well, you know. We both do."

"Oh, God, Slade..." A tear tracked down her cheek, and she dashed it away with the back of her hand. She couldn't go down this path right now. She was too broken inside. Dealing with Camille's death—no, her *murder*—learning that her parents might have kept secrets of her birth from her, that her entire life might have been built on stones that were crumbling, and having Slade return now, it was all too much.

Pull yourself together! Don't be a whimpering, simpering weakling!

"I, uh...I think we should look in the boxes now," she said, reaching for her utility knife and kicking back her chair. Trying to calm her wildly beating heart, she walked to the stack of boxes they'd brought into the living room from the garage.

Covered with a fine sheen of dust, taped and labeled, the five cartons represented all that was left of Camille's life.

Of course, her sister had gotten rid of most of her things when she'd entered the convent, but still, these few boxes seemed a pitiful legacy for Camille's vibrant life.

She knelt beside the first carton, noticed Camille's bold, whimsical scrawl on one side, and read *Bedroom.*

"This looks like a good place to start," she said, and flicking open the razorlike blade, sliced through the tape.

In her apartment, Constantina Rubino hung up the phone on her no-good daughter, then crushed out her cigarette. Ever since Giovanna—oh, excuse me, Jean—had taken up with her sorry excuse of a husband, her fifth, no less, and the worst in a long, unending line of pathetic excuses for men, she'd had little time for an aging, arthritic mother. At least this one had some money, or so Giovanna insisted, and the way she was flashing around gold and diamonds the last time she'd visited, maybe she was telling the truth.

For once.

At least she had Enzo and Carlo, two of the most wonderful sons in the universe, neither of whom had changed their names. And though they were married to gold-digging Protestants, they had both borne her grandchildren, a total of five, the precious darlings! It was true Enzo had divorced and married again, but who could blame him? His first wife was nothing better than a fancy-priced whore. If only he'd had the marriage annulled. She worried about that, the getting into heaven part. With a sigh, she made the sign of the cross over her ample breasts.

Unfortunately, Enzo and his wife lived in that hellhole New York City, and Carlo sold real estate in the desert, Scottsdale, Arizona.

Only Giovanna—well, whatever she wanted to call herself, the ingrate—was nearby.

With a groan, Mrs. Rubino hefted herself from her favorite chair and, using her walker, headed slowly into the kitchen where her sauce was simmering. Her bad hip pained her, but she ignored it and refused to take any of the drugs that the doctor prescribed. She didn't want to get hooked on any of that poison. Oh, she took an Aleve now and again, and sometimes washed it down with a drop of wine, but nothing more.

Wincing at the pain, she stopped by the mantel of the electric fireplace Carlo and that wife of his, Misty—what kind of name was that?—had sent last Christmas. On the vinyl mantel—oh, it looked good enough to be real walnut—she had pictures of the darling grandchildren, and she smiled at them all. Of course, there was the 8 x 10 of her wedding day and her beloved Silvio, rest his soul. She was dressed in a white gown with a handmade lace veil, and he wore his dark suit. His eyes had been such a rich, rich brown, and his mustache, trimmed to perfection, had been as black as night in the photo. She touched his face and told him, in Italian of course, how much she loved him.

"Io l'amo per sempre."

One husband, one love, one marriage.

Never five.

She saw the picture of Jesus, his halo bright, and she smiled, again making the sign of the cross and whispering a quick Hail Mary. Then she made her way to the kitchen, using her walker, taking more time than she liked.

She turned off the stove and thought of the young woman who lived down the hallway. Yes, she was a whore; that much was evident by the amount of men who frequented the hallway between their doors, but Constantina was starting to believe the woman might be making a change.

Why, just last night, through her fish-eye peephole, she'd spied a priest leaving the apartment.

A good sign.

Maybe the woman was seeing her sins for what they were.

If so, it was up to Constantina to be a good neighbor, to help her leave her sordid life behind her. Yes, it was up to her to reach out to the young woman.

Humming to herself, she found a mason jar and filled it with her steaming sauce. It was so good that her friend Donna-Marie Esposito had told her over and over again at their Saturday afternoon gin rummy marathons how Constantina should market it, just like Paul Newman did. When Constantina, blushing, had remarked that she didn't have Mr. Newman's money, nor his fame, Donna-Marie had shooed off her arguments with her plump, beringed fingers. "So what? Your sauce is better than anything I've ever tasted, and that includes my dear departed aunt's. I tell you, *Zia* Rosalia's and that Mr. Newman's can't hold a candle to yours, my friend. Oh, wait!" She lifted her hands as if she'd just received a message from God himself. Hands clutched tightly around her cards, her rings caught in the light from the huge chandelier that hung over her dining room table. Her cigarette, an unfiltered Camel waggled between her fuchsia-glossed lips. "You could call it 'Rubino's Pure Old Country Italian' and give that Newman a run for his money, I don't mind saying. Newman? Definitely *not* from the old country. You could make a fortune. And by the way, 'gin.'" She slapped her cards onto the table.

Blushing and smiling now, Constantina screwed on the top of the jar and paused to light another cigarette. She sat down and smoked it to the filter—waste not, want not, her mother, God rest her soul, had always warned her nine children to remain frugal. Constantina would take that advice to her grave. She ground her Salem Light into an ashtray, washed her hands, and placed the jar of sauce into the handy basket attached to her walker; then headed to the front door.

It took a while. She wasn't as young as she used to be, and that hip, oh, my, but she hitched her way to the woman's—Grace, her name was—apartment, where music was blaring.

She rapped her large knuckles against the door, but it swung open. Unlatched. No wonder the music—something popular and definitely *not* Frank Sinatra—was so loud. What was it called? Hip-hop? Like a rabbit?

Young people today!

And what was that girl thinking leaving the door open in this neighborhood?

"Hello?" Constantina called. "Hello, Gracie?" She adjusted her walker and started into the room. "I brought you some of my spaghetti sauce...." Where was she? Still in bed? The door was open, and Constantina had never seen a woman of ill repute's boudoir. "Hello?" she called again, not wanting to startle Gracie or catch her dressing. "Gracie?" She angled her walker toward the door, and beginning to perspire, wishing she'd brought her pack of

Salems with her, she pushed onward, through the opening to the room and—

She stopped short.

Saw the naked girl on the bed.

Grace's lean body was a pasty gray color, her eyes open and bulged, the skin around her throat raw. Spread-eagle. Her breasts sliding to the sides, her muff of reddish hair shorn into some weird pattern. But she was dead.

Dead as dead.

Revolted, Constantina screamed as she'd never screamed in her life.

Obviously the girl had been strangled.

Murdered! Her life of sin coming back to her.

Oh, Mother Mary.

Making the sign of the cross wildly, her gnarled fingers shaking, she was certain Lucifer was lurking, snarling in the corners, taloned fingers ready to rip out Constantina's jackhammering heart.

She tried to get out.

Fast!

Her heart was pounding so hard she thought it might give up.

Backing up, she felt a hot rip of pain slice through her hip.

The demon! He was tearing at her!

Scared out of her mind, she saw the fires of hell flaming in her brain, and she tried to run. Failed. Tripped.

"Help me!"

She tripped again, falling backward.

Thud! Her head banged against the floor.

Her walker toppled.

Her jar of spaghetti sauce went flying.

Smash! It crashed into a wall.

Glass shattered.

Red gravy streamed down the plaster walls.

Still Constantina screamed, over the horrible music, loud enough to wake the damned dead.

The nearest corpse being Gracie Blanc.

Praying, screaming, knowing that the Devil was somewhere in the room, Constantina threw off the metal beast that was her walker, untangled her skirt, and clawed her way over the green shag toward the doorway.

It seemed miles away.

"Help!" she cried again. "For the love of Mother Mary, someone call the police!"

Her old heart was pounding, her leg shrieking in agony.

For just a second, she thought she saw God, a powerful, brilliant light appearing in the doorway. "Father..." She raised her hand, lifting her outstretched arm, hoping that he would save her pious soul.

Then she realized the brilliant beam was from a flashlight trained on her. Beyond the glare, holding the long handle, was that horrid, lazy super for the building.

Harold Horwood.

"What the fuck's going on here?" he demanded.

"Call nine-one-one," she ordered, gasping for breath, trying not to see Satan in every corner. She clutched her heart. "Get the police and an ambulance."

"What the fuck for?" he said.

"For Grace."

"What's wrong with her?" Walking to the bedroom, stepping around the overturned walker, he skidded to an abrupt stop in a pool of Rubino's Pure Old Country Italian Spaghetti Sauce.

"Shit!" he half screamed. "Jesus H. Christ!"

"Just call nine-one-one!" she repeated sharply to the moron of an apartment manager. "And watch your language!"

CHAPTER 38

Bentz was beat, and he felt it in each of his muscles as he sat in the passenger seat of the department's cruiser and listened to the police band radio squawk.

Montoya, true to form, pushed the speed limit as he drove. Neither detective was in the mood for conversation; both were processing what they'd learned at St. Marguerite's.

Traffic was thick, the Crown Vic as hot as the surface of the sun, the humidity sweltering, Bentz's mood deteriorating with each passing stop sign. He was just too damned old for this shit. No two ways about it. The lack of sleep caused by a colicky baby on top of the all-night interrogations brought out the worst in him. Add to that his sticky shirt, compliments of the heat and humidity, and the frustration of getting nowhere on a case that was quickly attracting statewide and national attention.

The case was getting to him. Someone was getting off on killing nuns, for God's sake... *nuns!* Why?

The evidence was all over the place, too. Sexy, sadistic diaries, self-flagellation, orphaned girls who eventually joined the order, priests who were all too absent and one who would have been better suited as a gigolo. Then there was the secretive mother superior and one of the nuns disappearing in San Francisco. Two convents were involved so far; he wondered how far the horror would run. Were St. Marguerite's and St. Elsinore's the only two involved, or were they just the tip of a very heinous and far-reaching iceberg? Would the Catholic Church take another hit?

He didn't like the odds against it, and that worried him. Though not particularly religious, at least not in the traditional, organized manner, Bentz believed in God and he trusted that most churches and the people within them—clergy and parishioners—were good souls with all the right intentions.

But this case, and his job in general—where he saw the ugly underbelly of society and was faced with the utter depravity, evil, and psychoses of sadistic criminals on a daily basis—made him sometimes second guess the goodness of the Almighty.

His wife and two daughters, one a headstrong twentysomething, the other not yet crawling, always brought him back to center, to believing in good and, in so doing, squared him up with the Man/Woman/Being Upstairs.

"More company," Montoya muttered, and reached for his pack of recently purchased Marlboros. He nodded toward the street where, just across from the parking lot, a news van with the WSLJ insignia emblazoned across its white sides was parked.

"Great."

"Leave 'em to Sinclaire."

"Ya got that right."

They climbed out of the vehicle, and Montoya paused to light up.

"Abby know you're smoking again?"

"I'm not," Montoya said, "but, yeah, that woman's got the nose of a bloodhound. Soon as this case wraps, I'm done with these cancer sticks."

"Yeah, right."

"Seriously!"

Bentz sent his partner a we've-all-been-there-before look and rubbed the back of his neck as he walked up the steps of the station. Montoya took two more long drags, then crushed his cigarette into the canister of sand near the entrance.

It was late, just in time for shift change.

Cops in uniforms and plainclothes coming and going, voices

buzzing, heels clicking, laughter ripping through the hallways as Bentz shouldered open the door.

Bentz made eye contact with a few people he knew, even threw out a rare smile when he spied Vera, from Missing Persons, hurrying in the opposite direction.

He was still thinking about his day. He and Montoya had spent a lot of hours being stonewalled by the priests at St. Marguerite's and not getting much further with the staff at St. Elsinore's, which, really, was another jurisdiction, not that it mattered much. The crusty old reverend mother, Sister Georgia—though outwardly much more modern and, well, maybe not exactly "hip" but appearing more worldly than Sister Charity—wasn't going to give them any more information than she had to. Mentioning that Sister Camille's sexually graphic diary had been found at St. Elsinore's had only made her more tight-lipped and stiff. Sure, she wore no habit, but in her slacks, blouse with its big bow of a collar, and more fashionable glasses, she was just as rigid as Sister Charity.

Great.

They'd gotten nowhere.

The priests had been no better. Father Paul had been nervous to the point of chewing on the corner of his lips and fingering the folds of his cassock. Father Frank wouldn't speak without a lawyer, so that interview had been postponed, and Father Thomas of St. Elsinore's had been conveniently indisposed. Again.

Bentz was beginning to think that Thomas Blaine was little more than a figment of Sister Georgia's imagination, her "beard" for lack of a better word. She, at least to Bentz, appeared to be running the show at the deteriorating parish.

He walked into his office where the AC was struggling and tossed his jacket over his coat rack before sitting in his desk chair. What he'd learned today was that both Sister's Camille and Asteria had been adopted out of St. Elsinore's. As had quite a few of the novices and nuns at the convent.

An important connection?

Maybe.

Then there was Camille's room and the mattress. Nothing else had been found, just the single envelope slipped into the stuffing. A note never sent to her lover.

Frank O'Toole?

Or someone else?

He slid his holster and sidearm off his shoulder and hung them on the back of his chair. The fact that he'd worn his weapon at all through the hallowed hallways and offices of two churches and convents told him just how nuts this case had become.

And what about the missing dresses? His gut told him that was not good. Not good at all.

Hell.

Sister Charity had provided names of the nuns who had been orphaned and left in the care of St. Elsinore's orphanage:

Sister Asteria McClellan

Sister Camille Renard

Sister Dorothy Reece

Sister Maura Voile

Sister Irene Shikov

Sister Devota Arness

Sister Zita Williams

Sister Louise Cortez

Sister Angela Peterson

Sister Edwina Karpovich

So different. Their only links being St. Marguerite's and St. Elsinore's. Most of them were from the Gulf states, but not all, and certainly they were not all in love with Father Frank O'Toole.

Maybe he was jumping to conclusions.

Maybe St. Elsinore's orphanage had nothing to do with the murders.

Maybe involvement with Frank O'Toole was just coincidence, actually. As far as he could tell, Sister Camille had been the only victim who had consummated an affair with the priest. Sister Lea De Luca and Sister Asteria had only had fantasies about the man. Perhaps flirtations. There was no proof that they'd actually had sex with him.

Yet, the guy just wasn't the kind of man who should be wearing a priest's alb.

And who would be that right individual?

Remember your brother? James? Not exactly a shining example of a man who took an oath of celibacy and held tight to it.

Disturbed, his thoughts traveling along dark roads he'd rather avoid, Bentz made some calls, checked his e-mail, read over the final autopsy report on Camille Renard and her unborn child. She'd died by asphyxia due to strangulation, and the deepest abrasions and contusions on her neck were in a singular pattern that Bentz had seen before: a rosary, the beads sharp, the wire holding the strands strong enough to resist any attempts by the victim to break it.

There were scratch marks on her neck where she'd tried to yank the garrote off her neck, abrasions made by her own fingernails in the wild attempt to free herself.

His stomach soured at the thought of her frantic, terrified, and ultimately doomed struggle as she gasped for air, kicked at her attacker, her eyes bulging.

"Who did this to you?" he asked as the air conditioner wheezed. Through the window, he heard a semi's engine growl as the big truck rumbled down the street. He would have bet his pension on Father O'Toole, the lothario disguised as a priest.

However, the blood tests of Camille's fetus cleared him as the father.

But not necessarily of the murders, he reminded himself as his cell phone jangled. The caller ID indicated it was his daughter.

"Hey," he said, cradling his cell between his shoulder and ear.

"Hey back atcha," Kristi said, and her voice was a little weak, muffled by the sound of air movement, as if she were driving and trying to speak over her obstinate headset. "I just thought I'd call and offer a little moral support."

"Really?" he asked, unable to mask his doubt. Kristi had just finished her first true-crime book. It hadn't been picked up yet but was being looked at by several agents, one of whom had suggested Rick Bentz, as the homicide cop who had helped solve the case of a killer with vampire leanings at All Saints' College, write an intro.

He passed.

Didn't like the fact that his daughter was dabbling anywhere near a killer.

"Yes, really, though if you wanted to talk over the case with me, I'd be glad to listen."

"I'll bet."

"Oh, Dad, come on."

The battle they'd had all her adult life. Headstrong and as beautiful as Jennifer, her mother and Bentz's ex-wife, Kristi had given him most of the gray hairs that were silvering his head—and prematurely, he thought. "How's married life?"

"Oooh. Smooth segue," she said, but wasn't really pissed that he'd abruptly changed the subject. "I'll tell you all about it this weekend. I thought I'd drop by and see Ginny...uh, you and Olivia, too."

He grinned; she was needling him. "We'll look forward to it. Bring Jay along."

"I intend to." She laughed. "You know me, Dad—I never go anywhere without my husband."

"And you probably pump him for information, too."

"Only when he wants sexual favors."

"Ouch! TMI, Kristi. I'm your dad, remember?"

"My dad who has an infant. Don't pretend you don't know anything about sex, but, okay, let's change the subject."

He laughed and his eyes fell onto the list of names from St. Marguerite's. Orphaned girls who'd been adopted from St. Elsinore's. All young and full of life. All potential murder victims.

"I'll call Olivia and set something up, okay?" Kristi said, and he nodded.

"Great. She'll love it."

"Okay, Dad. I'll see ya."

She hung up, and he held the phone for an instant. Kristi's life had been in danger more times than he wanted to think about, times when, because of who he was, the cop, she'd come into a killer's sites.

He hoped to hell that was all over now.

Troubled at the thought of his daughter and her penchant for mystery and crime, he noticed that the tox screen for Camille Renard had come through on his e-mail. He scanned it and scowled when he recognized that she'd had Rohypnol in her bloodstream. Rohypnol, or "roofies" as it was called on the street, was the date-rape drug. Slipped into food or drink, the strong sedative could render a victim more than pliable, could even induce memory loss.

He wasn't surprised.

Now at least he understood why the victims went along with their killer's need to have them in bridal dresses. It explained why Camille was found in the chapel, apparently of her own free will, and why Asteria died in the cemetery. But it didn't tell him who had drugged them and forced them into being an integral actor in his bizarre play.

Drugs were easy to get these days. They could be bought on the street, stolen, or even purchased on the Internet. How many times had he, a cop for crying out loud, been bombarded with offers for GHB, another date-rape drug, in his personal e-mail account. "Son of a bitch," he said under his breath.

It was hours later, and he'd gotten through the last of his paperwork and was no closer to figuring out what had happened to the victims than he had been.

Stymied, he stared at the images on his computer screen. Camille lying dead near the altar and Asteria in the cemetery, her gaze fixed on the night sky and the angel over the tomb where she lay.

Both orphans from St. Elsinore's.

Both enamored with the same priest.

Both joining the convent because of trouble with men. He tapped his fingers and hadn't noticed that beyond the window, night had fallen, darkness above the glow of city lights.

"Hey!" Montoya appeared in his doorway. Without his jacket, stubble darkening the usually shaved area of his face, looking as rough around the edges as Bentz felt.

"Yeah?"

"Look what I got in the mail." He slid a prepaid cell phone wrapped in an evidence bag across Bentz's desk.

"Camille Renard's?"

"Yep."

"Who sent it?" Gingerly, Bentz picked up the bag.

"Anonymous."

"You check it out?"

"The info on the phone? Yeah."

"Anything good?"

"Not sure yet, but it's something."

Bentz nodded. "Yeah, it's something." The trick was to find out just what.

"The lab's going over it, see if they can come up with prints or even DNA from the saliva used to seal the packet, but that'll take time."

Which was fast escaping, Bentz thought. Still, it was something. "You think the killer sent it in? For attention? You know, playing games, showing how smart he is, smarter than us?"

"Could be."

At that second, Brinkman poked his head through the doorway, forcing Montoya aside. "Just caught a call," he said. "Homicide. Single white female. Working girl."

"Prostitute."

Brinkman offered a smug little sneer. "See, Montoya, you are smart after all. She's been picked up before. Gracie Blanc, aka Grace La Blanc and Grace Lee Blanco. One and the same." His grin was hideous. "As if an alias would throw anyone off track."

"Any sign of the killer?"

"Nah. She's been dead for a while. The neighbor, an old lady who lives down the hall, found her first and freaked out, fell down and started screaming, and the super, whom I'm making as her pimp, heard the screams, found the old lady and the vic, then made the call. When the officer who took the call arrived, he found our girl Gracie dead as a doornail. Now the ME's on his way; another couple of uniforms are there already."

And probably the press, Bentz thought.

"I'm in," Montoya said, and Bentz was already reaching for his jacket and holster. It looked like the long day wasn't going to end soon.

"Good." Brinkman's eyes narrowed and his lips thinned into that cat-who-ate-the-canary smile Bentz hated. "Cause here's the kicker. The old lady? Turns out she's a bit of a snoop, and guess who she saw leaving our dead girl's apartment last night?"

"Who?" Montoya asked.

"A priest."

"What?" Bentz froze.

"That's right." Brinkman was eating up Bentz's surprise. "The old lady was definitely not minding her own business and was looking through her peephole, and she saw a guy she described as a young priest leaving the vic's apartment around midnight."

CHAPTER 39

As the radio plays softly, I file the edges of the glass beads, carefully honing them to perfection, making certain each edge is as sharp as a razor, each facet able to slice through flesh cleanly.

At the thought of the tiny, glittering beads doing their deadly work, I smile. The rosary in my hands, strung together with heavy wire, seems to wink at me.

The swamp is still tonight, water lapping quietly, the smell thick with the odors of rotting vegetation and fish. Crickets are singing their nightly chorus, and a bullfrog supplies the bass notes.

The music, a tune from the eighties, stops and Dr. Sam's voice fills the airways with her sick psychobabble as callers dial her up and ask inane questions about their relationships, or their children, or their dying parents.

Fools! Don't they know she's a fake? Can't they tell all her pseudo-psychiatric advice is nothing but poison?

My blood boils within my veins, and I remember how close I once got to destroying her . . . and then I look up at the gator head mounted over my cot. It stares down at me, big eyes gleaming red as a demon's, his wicked teeth exposed, reminding me of the dozens of stitches in my leg, the work of an incompetent veterinarian, and the pain I still feel. I've named him Ipana, a nod to my grandmother's favorite brand of toothpaste.

"Nice try," I say to the stuffed reptile, and hear Dr. Sam's voice, smooth as silk, tell some poor girl to get out of an emotionally abusive relationship, to ditch her boyfriend of two years, the father of her infant son.

Another piece of garbage.

"Stay with the guy, Lola," I can't help but mutter. "Give him another chance. Let the boy know his dad. And give the guy what he wants in bed!" Stupid bitch! Has a kid with the guy, then decides he's no good. Probably plans on holding him up for ransom in the form of child support.

Something Camille would never do. She was nothing if not obedient and submissive. Oh, she had her hot streak; there was fight in her, just enough to keep the sex hot, the fire bright. Just at the thought of her, my dick twitches.

Never had a lover been so willing. So ready. So wickedly divine.

And now she was gone.

A mistake.

An evil, vile mistake.

I nick my hand with the beads, causing blood to bloom on one finger. I'd lost just a little of my dexterity along with a piece of my thigh in my unfortunate tussle with my pal Ipana.

Of course, Ipana lost that battle. I suck my finger, then find a bit of surgical glue before I finish filing. I tie off the last bead and I give a hard tug on my handiwork, a rosary like no other.

It holds.

Again I pull hard against the beads and the fastenings, but it's strong.

And unforgiving.

Perfect.

I slip it into the pocket of my backpack, right next to my sunglasses.

The cassock is zipped safely inside.

As a fish jumps in the water far below my cabin, I know I'm ready. I snap off the radio, open the trapdoor, and carefully step down the ladder to my waiting canoe.

* * *

The boxes belonging to Camille were a bust.

At least as far as Valerie could see. All five were opened, their contents strewn over the living room floor.

Nothing out of the ordinary.

If anything, the memorabilia, clothes, and few pictures were examples of a very normal life. No burning love letters, no vivid diary of a woman who confused pain with pleasure, sex with torture.

Camille's confirmation dress, the old pom-poms from St. Timothy's where she'd been a cheerleader, even a framed photograph of their parents, but nothing that indicated a life that was anything out of the ordinary.

"You're disappointed," Slade said as he flipped on a light, the gloom of the evening seeping in through the windows.

"Extremely."

"What did you think you'd find? A message with the killer's name scrawled in blood?"

"I guess," she admitted with a half smile. "Or something that pointed us in the right direction." She discovered a rosary and picked it up, staring at the glassy beads and letting them slide through her fingers to pool, like a holy snake, on the floor, the cross as its head, the twined ropes of beads its body. "My money's still on Frank O'Toole."

"Even though he's not the baby's father?"

"Maybe because of it."

"Let's give it a rest. I'll take you to dinner, and we'll come back and look at this with new eyes." He stepped over a pile of Camille's clothes and offered her his hand.

She didn't want to give up. Knew the answer was right before her eyes but couldn't think straight any longer. He was right. "Fine," she said, accepting his outstretched hand and climbing to her bare feet. "First, though, I'd better check in with Freya. Help out with turning down the beds." Each night they left plates of cookies in the dining room, along with a variety of drinks. On each of the beds they left truffles that Freya made herself.

"I'll meet you in the foyer in"—she checked her watch—"forty-five?"

"Got it." He whistled to the dog, and together they walked

through the back door and across the yard where a few bumble-
bees still buzzed over fragrant clumps of lavender in the twilit herb
garden.

Freya was on the back porch hanging up her hat, a basket of
picked herbs tucked under one arm, mosquitoes humming, one
moth flitting around the porch light. "Find anything?" Freya asked.
Earlier Val had told her that they were opening the boxes Cammie
had left in the attic over the garage.

"Nothing earth-shattering." Val leaned against the porch rails
and noticed the neighbor's cat slinking through the hedge of crepe
myrtle. Bo, despite having some bloodhound in him, didn't seem to
notice. Val said, "Thought I'd help you with the turndown."

"Too late," Freya said, glancing at Slade. Questions darkened
her eyes, but she didn't ask any of them. Instead, she said, "I already took care of it, *and* I've put out the brandy, port, and decaf
with the pralines and napoleons." She glanced at Slade, then back
at Val. "Turned down the beds, too." With a smile, she added,
"Just call me Ms. Efficient."

"And proud of it," Val said.

"Hmmm. You can return the favor."

"Never," Val teased.

Freya said, "So it's official. You can have the night off."

"Hey, whoa. Time-out." She tapped the fingers of her right
hand against the palm of her left, making the time-out signal. "So
now you're the boss?"

"Not just now." She grinned. "I'm always the boss."

"Yeah, right."

"Sounds good to me," Slade interjected. "I'm gonna run
through the shower and meet you in the foyer."

"Ooooh," Freya said as he walked through the kitchen, the
door slapping shut behind him. Bo stayed behind, tail wagging,
eyes on Freya. He'd learned who was in charge of all treats. "Hot
date, huh?" she asked.

"If that's what you want to call it."

"You know me, I only call 'em as I see 'em." She glanced at Valerie's wrinkled T-shirt and capris. "So what're you wearing?"

"Whatever I want. We're divorcing, remember?" But she was

already down the steps and heading toward the carriage house, Bo at her heels.

Freya's voice followed after her. "I wonder about that," she said.

Val wondered, too, but she didn't let herself think about it too much as she left the dog on the back porch of her cottage. He was sloppily lapping water from his bowl when she stepped inside.

Cammie's things were still strewn over the table, and Val picked up a long-forgotten brush. Something had to be here, right? Something important. Something she and Slade had missed. But the items were still the same: her baby shoes that had been bronzed, several report cards, old CDs, even some cassette tapes from the eighties, a set of mini-cassettes from the summer she'd spent learning Spanish, a boy's class ring she'd never given back, and a Barbie doll, her first from the looks of it. Barbie's hair was mussed and frayed, and her face had grayed with dirt. She could definitely use a scrubbing.

So what was it? What was it she was missing?

Val set the brush down, rocked back on her heels, and glanced at the items. She got nowhere. Even after looking them over for another ten minutes.

Her cell phone rang, and she swept it out of her pocket. "Hello?" she said, but no one was there. The only message left was labeled **Missed Call**, with no caller ID.

"Huh." She thought the person might call back, but the phone didn't ring again. Telling herself it was a wrong number, she silently perused Camille's belongings one last time and saw nothing out of the ordinary. Calling herself a really poor excuse for a cop—check, make that *ex*-cop—she stripped off her jeans and T-shirt and headed for her phone booth of a shower tucked into a corner of a tiny bathroom.

The pipes groaned as she turned on the water, then pulled her hair into a small bun that she secured on the top of her head. She cranked the window open, as the steam from the shower was as thick as the fog in San Francisco Bay, then stepped through the opaque glass door.

Once under the spray, she washed off the sweat and grime of the day. Lathering up, she rubbed the kinks from her neck, letting the hot needles of water massage her muscles as she wondered why in the hell she'd agreed to go to dinner with Slade.

It wasn't really a date; Freya had gotten that part wrong.

But... it might be more intimate than was a good idea.

And what's the problem with that? she asked herself. *Slade has been nothing but supportive since he rolled into town and blocked your car in the driveway. And face it, Val, you're still attracted to him.*

God, it was complicated.

Is it, is it really? The voice again. *Now you know for certain that Cammie was the liar, the seducer, that Slade didn't cheat. So are you going to blame him forever? Remember your wedding vows? Would it be so hard to start over? To trust him again? To allow yourself to love him as you so want to do?*

"You're pathetic," she whispered, but felt the little fissures in her resolve begin to crack, allowing herself to let him into her heart again.

Refusing to think about her crumbling marriage or any thought that it might possibly be repaired, she shampooed and rinsed her hair. Turning under the showerhead, she let the warm water run over her shoulders and down her spine.

You love Slade! You always have. Don't punish yourself or Slade because of the lies of a dead woman.

"Oh, Cammie." Val closed her eyes, and images of her sister ran through her brain.

Cammie as a child, chasing their little calico kitten and climbing high into a tree where power lines cut through the branches. Valerie had been frantic, screaming for her to climb down, but both Cammie and the cat were trapped. Cammie frozen and crying, the kitten glued to the bole of the tree, tiny claws digging into the rough bark. The little calico had finally scrambled down the willow's trunk, and Valerie, fear pounding through her ten-year-old heart, had climbed up and hauled her sister back to safety. She'd scolded the five-year-old, but Cammie, already stubborn and independent, hadn't cared. Once the danger was over, she'd acted as if it had never existed.

Then there were the high school years, when Cammie, an A student, on the girls' soccer team and cheerleading squad, had begun dating boys. Older. Younger. It didn't matter. Their mother had said only two words: *Boy crazy.*

Which had summed it all up.

She'd stolen her best friend's boyfriend—maybe he was the kid who had given her that gaudy class ring with the winking red stone; then, while still "in love" with Ben, she had been caught with a student teacher. It had been Cammie's senior year at St. Timothy's, and Val had already moved away and graduated from Ole Miss, had already taken the job in Texas, but she'd heard about it. Since Cammie had already passed her eighteenth birthday, no charges had been leveled at the teacher's aide, who was in his last year of college, but he had been sent packing.

Years later, after Cammie had finished a two-year course in accounting at a junior college, she had had several jobs as well as boyfriends.

Eventually, she'd come to visit Valerie and Slade, and the rest was history. There was the blowup at the ranch, and the next thing Val knew, her sister had decided to become a nun and landed at St. Marguerite's.

How odd they'd both ended up back in New Orleans.

Or was it destiny?

They'd patched things up as well as could be expected, and Cammie's things had wound up in the attic over her garage. "What will I do with them?" Val had asked her as she'd helped Cammie stow the cartons under the rafters. It had been hot as hell that day, the small space sweltering, spiders and wasps already claiming space.

"I don't know."

"You're sure you won't want anything?"

"Not now, and if I do, I can come and get it."

First Cammie, then Val, had climbed down the rough ladder that was built into one side of the garage. Val had pulled the trapdoor shut.

"You'll be in the convent."

"I know, but it's not a prison. I can come and go as I please."

Val had dusted her hands as they'd walked out the garage door and into the bright Louisiana sun. "I kinda got the idea that once you were in the convent, that was it. There wasn't much getting out."

"Maybe back in the Dark Ages. But Sister Charity has told me I can work in the clinic at St. Elsinore's or with the kids there, if I want to."

"Do you?"

Cammie had shrugged. As if it hadn't mattered. "I haven't the faintest idea. But trust me, Val, if I want to leave, I will. It's God's house. There are no locks on the doors."

Now Val wondered about her sister's insistence that there was freedom at St. Marguerite's. It seemed unlikely since Camille herself had referred to the mother superior as "the warden."

So the locks were all in the minds of those inside the cathedral and convent's walls. Is that what Camille had inferred?

Valerie wasn't convinced.

What was the often quoted line? She stood under the shower, and the old pipes moaned again as it came to her. "Stone walls do not a prison make, nor iron bars a cage..."

As she rubbed the kinks from her neck, she thought of Camille's diary, the graphic images of sex and submission. Was it possible that she'd confused her obedience to God with submission to men? Had sex and religion been all mixed up in her mind? Were sin and sex synonymous? No, that didn't make any sense. But what did? Those cryptic notes to herself?

The heart shape with the single word *CALLED* inside?

And what about *TO BF 2 M&M*? To best friend two Em and Em. So why didn't the message read 2 BF 2 M&M. Why was "to" not put in numerical form like the rest? And wasn't it BFF? Best friends forever?

She didn't really know the lingo.

The other message bothered her even more.

"C U N seven, seven, three four R M C V," she said aloud, the water spraying around her. It meant nothing. Just weird letters put in front of numbers. She repeated the message again as steam filled the room. Her mind kept turning the message over and over and...

Wait! She repeated the scribbled note again. When she said the numbers aloud, she remembered something from her childhood, something from the orphanage at St. Elsinore's. One little girl, the one who had barred Val from the slide—hadn't her name been something like Darlene or Eileen?—had said slyly, "You know what seven-seven-three-four is, don't you?" She looked sideways at her curly headed friend with the massive overbite. "It's hell."

The other girl had giggled wildy. "No."

"Sure." Glancing over her shoulder to make certain the old nun on the playground was looking the other way, the snotty girl had drawn the numbers with a stick. "Read them backward!"

Overbite had whooped, then placed her pudgy fingers over her mouth and curled her shoulders inward. "You're right!" she'd whispered, reading the letters in the dust just as the nun, Sister Anne, the kind one on playground duty that day, had looked over.

Quickly, the snotty girl had scribbled through her naughty little note. "Seven-seven-three-four," she'd said to Valerie, then run off, dropping her stick as the horrid loud bell had clanged that recess was over.

"Hell," Val said now, and heard Bo give out a sharp, gruff bark. She barely noticed as she remembered the weird notations in the diary. *C U N hell, C V.* So... "See you in hell?" Was that what Camille meant? "See you in hell a hundred and five?" What did that mean? In a hundred and five years? No, that wasn't right.

But it was close.... She just had to think hard. She took the loofah to her shoulders, sudsing up, rubbing hard against her skin. "What, Cammie? What were you—"

Bo barked again. More loudly.

And then...

Val stopped scrubbing, the loofah tight in her hand, water raining over her. Her ears strained over the sounds of rushing water and the gurgling drain.

Did she hear something?

Her wet skin crinkled.

Her muscles tightened.

Was the sound *inside* the house?

Her throat closed.

There it was again. A soft scrape. Footsteps?

Lather and warm water ran down her back, and she felt a needle of fear prick her brain.

It was probably Slade.

"Hey, I'll be out in a sec!" she called.

But hadn't he said to meet him in the foyer of the main house?

Creeaaak.

Definitely the floorboards groaning with someone's weight.

"Hello?"

She waited, water dripping from her chin and elbows.

No answer.

Nothing.

Just the shower's spray hitting her body and the tile walls.

She swallowed hard, listening.

Had she locked the back door?

Even latched the screen?

She couldn't remember.

She rarely locked it during the day, running back and forth to the main house, but at night, throwing the dead bolt was usually automatic... except that she'd left Bo on the back porch. Oh, God!

She hadn't even latched the bathroom door, probably even left it ajar.

Heart pounding, she reached for her towel, and through the frosted glass of the shower, she saw a movement—a shadow in the doorway. A figure in black, not unlike the demon of her dreams, the one with its tiny rodent teeth and malicious eyes.

What!

The hairs on her nape rose.

She shook her head to dispel the image and sucked in her breath, taking in moist, hot air. She wished to hell she had her sidearm. The steam in the room was so thick, but it was beginning to clear and...

She heard the shuffle of feet. Definitely feet running, hurrying away, a quick, disturbing gait scurrying through her small house.

Oh, no, you don't, you bastard!

Throwing the towel around herself, she started to slide through the door.

Bang!

She ducked automatically, expecting the bullet to whiz past her head, and nearly slid into the pedestal sink in the corner. But no bullet bored into the wall or shattered the mirror as she cowered near the toilet.

Heart thudding, she eased toward the door. In here she was trapped. No other exit than the door. The tiny window over the toilet was far too small to slide through. Crouching, she pushed open the door just as she suddenly realized what she'd heard wasn't the crack of a gun but the hard clap of the screen door slapping against its frame.

"Damn!"

Clutching the towel between her breasts, she hurried into the living room where the gloom of the evening had settled, darkness gathering in the corners.

The room was empty.

Quickly, leaving a trail of wet footprints across the wood floor, she walked through the kitchen to the back door where the screen was now closed and the yard empty, a few lights glowing near the pathway leading to the main house. She stepped out onto the porch and looked around, but she saw no one, just darkness gathering over the city.

Had her imagination, and the conjuring up of a nightmare, gotten the better of her?

Or had someone really been inside, peering through the crack of the bathroom door that she'd left ajar?

She saw Bo, sniffing the grass, getting ready to find the perfect spot to relieve himself, and wondered if he'd barked at the neighbor's cat or a squirrel, or...

Or what?

Why would someone be snooping around the house?

"Come on, boy," she said when he was finished watering Freya's favorite clump of daylilies. Tongue lolling, he trotted to the porch and climbed up the steps. "You really should find a better place," she reprimanded as she patted his head. "Or Freya might cut off your backyard privileges."

He barked once, a deep rumbling sound, while his tail swept the floorboards of the porch. This bark was different than it had been earlier, and wanting more attention, he shoved his head against her thigh.

"Well, come on in!" Getting goose bumps where her skin was still wet, she let the dog into the kitchen, latched the screen, then retraced her steps, pausing in the living room where Camille's things were still where she'd left them. A quick look convinced her that Cammie's memorabilia hadn't been disturbed.

What the hell had just happened?

Who, if anyone, had been inside?

Why did she feel violated, spied upon?

She glanced toward the window. For a split second, she saw the demon who appeared in her nightmares, the black beast with its tiny, sharp teeth, always ready to pounce.

"Don't be silly," she told herself, but double-checked the locks before she made her way to the bedroom to get dressed.

Her cell phone rang again.

She found it on the desk and clicked the TALK button before the third ring.

Once again, no one was there.

CHAPTER 40

"Don't freak out. It's spaghetti sauce," one of the uniformed cops explained to Montoya as he, Bentz, and Brinkman signed into the crime scene and noticed the sticky red stains sliding down the wall just inside Grace Blanc's bedroom door.

The living room was small, not a lot in it. Furniture that had been modern and cool in the seventies now looked tired and worn, a couple of metal tables surrounding a low, green couch and a garage-sale rocker in the corner.

"Good thing," Brinkman joked with an ugly laugh as he surveyed the oozing red stain. "I was beginning to think it was really bad-smelling, maybe bloody brains or something."

"Nice," Bonita Washington, the crime scene team leader, remarked, her voice dripping with sarcasm. "What are you, in the fourth grade or something? Grow up, Brinkman."

"Just trying to lighten things up."

"Oh, sure." She was having none of his lip. Then again, she didn't take crap from anyone. "You know, Brinkman, you might try to show some sensitivity for a change." She was all business as usual.

"Look, it's tight in here. See what you have to see and leave the rest to us. Okay? The sooner the body is removed, the better for everyone."

Click! Eve Marsolet was snapping off photos.

Another guy from the crime lab was dusting for prints, another measuring stains.

They picked their way to a bedroom where all of the action had taken place.

Someone from the ME's office was already examining the body of the victim—a redhead who lay on her mussed bed, as if she were staring up at the ceiling. Had she been alive. Half dressed, her face contorted in horror and pain, a bloody ring around her neck, scratch marks on her throat where she'd tried to tear off the garrote.

Montoya imagined her last minutes and looked away. Helluva thing. Maybe Abby was right; maybe it was about time he retired.

The room smelled of vanilla and garlic and death—a bad combination, one that had Bentz looking green around the gills. Then again, tough a cop as he was, Bentz always fought nausea at a homicide. He tried to hide it, but Montoya had caught the guy puking just outside a crime scene more than once.

"Time of death?" Montoya asked as the examiner took the body's temperature.

Frowning thoughtfully, the assistant ME studied his thermometer. "I figure she died sometime around midnight, maybe one o'clock this morning." He nodded to himself, as if silently confirming what he'd come up with. "Amount of rigor concurs."

"That's about the time Mrs. Snoop saw the priest leave," Brinkman observed.

To the room in general, Montoya said, "Be sure to bag her hands."

"Yeah, like we wouldn't." Lowering the clipboard onto which she'd been scribbling notes, Washington cast an irritated look his way. "Do your job, Detective. I'll do mine."

Brinkman's eyebrows bucked upward. "Ouch," he mouthed.

Montoya didn't give a damn. He just wanted to see what was under the vic's nails.

Bentz was quiet, and Montoya figured he was just battling the urge to purge when his partner said, "Look at this." He was in the living room, and his face was white as death, his jaw so tight the bone was bulging.

On the table in front of him was a radio and a hundred-dollar bill, the eyes of Ben Franklin blackened by a felt pen.

"Oh, hell and she's—"

"A red-haired prostitute. Check the station on the radio."

Montoya knew, deep in his gut, that the digital readout would be the numbers for WSLJ.

"Dr. Sam still does her radio show, doesn't she? You know, the one where she gives out advice in the middle of the night?" Bentz asked.

"*Midnight Confessions.* Yeah, Abby listens to it sometimes when she's up feeding the baby."

Samantha Leeds Wheeler was still on the air, still giving out advice despite the fact that she'd been the target of the insidious killer the police and press had dubbed Father John. A killer who raped and murdered his red-haired victims while listening to her show. He'd always left a hundred-dollar bill with the eyes of Ben Franklin blackened.

Montoya's gut clenched, and he felt that spooky sensation, a premonition that things were going to get worse before they got better. "Someone better call the radio station and talk to Dr. Sam, see if she's been getting any strange calls."

"I'm on my way," Bentz said, his jaw still set. It had been his shot that had nailed Father John, his bullet that had sent the guy into the depths of the swamp to become, they'd all hoped, gator food.

Since his body had never been recovered and it had been years since his last rampage, they'd all thought—police, press, and populace—that Father John, the serial killer who dressed as a priest to gain his victims' trust, had died in the brackish waters of the bayou.

Now, it seemed, they'd been wrong.

"Call Dr. Sam? What the fuck for?" Brinkman asked, always a little slow on the uptake; then, as if the light were slowly dawning, he muttered, "Holy shit!" when he spied the defaced C-note on the table and put two and two together. Shaking his bald pate, he added, "Well, ladies and gentleman, it looks like he's baaaaack."

"Or someone who knows his MO well enough to be a convincing copycat," Montoya said, though some of the details of the original crimes the cops had kept from the press. This guy, whoever he was, was informed.

"Five to one it's Father John," Brinkman said, biting his lower lip and narrowing his eyes on the defaced hundred-dollar bill.

No one took him up on the bet.

Val had nearly convinced herself that her mind had been playing tricks on her.

Nearly.

But the tight muscles at her nape and the goose pimples running up the back of her arms told her otherwise. Who would trespass in her house? And why?

It had to do with Camille's death.

In all the time she'd lived here in the carriage house, there had been no intruder, and now, with Camille dead only a few days, someone had intentionally crept inside.

Why?

"Val?"

She nearly jumped out of her skin.

Whirling, almost losing the damned towel as she spun toward the screen door, she spied Slade, freshly showered on the other side of the mesh. Bo was on his feet, tail wagging slowly, nose pressed against the mesh. "Oh, God . . . It's late. I'm not ready."

He slid a glance down her body, her fingers coiled in the rough terry cloth that swathed little more than her torso. "You look great to me."

"Thanks." Some of her fears dissipated. It was still somewhat light out, warm . . .

She felt his gaze lingering at the cleft of her breasts where her fist was clenched, white knuckled, over the towel.

"Are you gonna let me in or what?" He lifted an eyebrow, and she let out a long sigh.

"Or what," she said, automatically joking with him as she had in the past, though she wasn't in the mood for any kind of humor. Her nerves were still strung tight, the cottage seeming to have its own electrical current running through it. She walked swiftly, her bare feet slapping through the puddled footsteps still on the kitchen floor. "Sorry," she said as she reached the door and flipped open the latch.

"Something wrong?"

"I..." Was there? Really? Or was it her imagination? The old demon of her dreams returning to haunt her? "I don't know..."

"What?"

"It seems kind of silly now, but...I think someone might have come in while I was taking a shower, although that doesn't make any sense. I mean, I think I saw someone and heard him, but..." She threw up her free hand. "Oh, I don't really know. I've been jumpy lately."

"We all have." Slade walked into the kitchen, and as he slid onto a bar stool, he said, "Tell me."

She did. Wrapped in the damned towel, she told him what she'd felt, what she'd heard, and finally ended with "But who knows? It could have been the wind, I suppose, catching the door."

"And the footsteps?"

She sighed. "I don't know. My imagination, I guess. Just like the shadow passing by the door. Bo had barked, but it wasn't really a warning....Oh, hell, I don't really know," Val admitted, frustrated. She thought about telling him of the dream that kept her up at night, of the nightmare with the horrid demon dressed in black and chasing her down rainy alleys and slick, humid streets, holding its glinting chain and whispering, "Hussssssh." Hissing like a snake.

But she didn't.

In the light of day, the nightmare sounded silly, a terrifying dream that had no bearing on anything and only made her question her sanity. She, who had once been so strong. Fearless. A woman who had worked her way up the ranks to become a detective with the sheriff's department, a spot once reserved for good old boys. She'd made it!

And now...now she was shivering in the heat of the night, and Slade, damn him, reached around and placed an arm over her bare shoulders. "It's okay," he said. "We're here." She trembled again; this time it had nothing to do with the cold. The strength of Slade's arm around her, so familiar yet so foreign, so wanted and so un-wanted, caused the trembling deep inside.

"We?" she managed.

"Bo and me."

"What would I do without the two of you?" she mocked, and he let out a huff.

"I don't know, woman," he said. "But it wouldn't be pretty."

"Right."

He slapped her on the rump, his hand connecting with her towel. "I hate to say this, but get dressed." His lips curved into that irreverent smile she'd hated because it was so damned irresistible. "Bo and I are going to check out the grounds, run the perimeter, find out if we see any evidence of an intruder."

Or a ghost, she thought, for that's the sensation that had slid through her—that something unworldly had crossed the threshold to her home, intent on doing harm.

She quivered inside again and glanced over at the desk, where her notes were spread and the copies of Cammie's diary... "Oh, no!"

"What?"

But she was already moving to the small nook where her desk was tucked. Across the surface, phone bills, receipts, unopened mail, and reservation slips were stacked in neat piles. The flyer for this weekend's auction at St. Elsinore's was still pushed into the pages of the paperback she'd been reading, but that was it.

What was very obviously missing were the copied pages of Cammie's diary.

The scrawled, lined pages describing Cammie's most intimate and darkly sexual thoughts were gone. With a sickening thought, she wondered what would happen if someone from the press got Cammie's notes and printed them in one of the tabloids: CONFESSIONS OF A MURDERED NUN, with Cammie's photograph, one of her in a dark habit with a solemn, reverent expression.

"Oh Lord." Her eyes scoured the desk and floor, everywhere nearby, though she'd remembered leaving them on her desk. The spot was empty. "Damn it all to hell," she muttered under her breath; then Slade walked to the desk, asking questions, and she noticed the small black device tucked into the corner of the bookcase near the desk. In the very spot she placed her coffee cup when she was working. "What in the world?"

"What?" Slade asked.

"I'm not sure."

Barely visible, the thin electronic device was positioned in front of a picture of Cammie, taken during her senior year of high school.

Valerie felt a chill as cold as a Canadian winter.

Slade was next to her in an instant. "What is it?" he asked, his voice laden with worry as she picked it up. "A cell?"

"Uh-huh. A BlackBerry," she said, and knowing she shouldn't, she clicked it on. "I think it might be Camille's."

Within seconds, the small screen glowed and a picture appeared.

An image of Cammie in the throes of death.

"Nooooo! Holy Christ!" Valerie let out a disbelieving scream as she recognized the image.

Her blood turned to ice, and she dropped the phone as if she'd been burned. "Oh, God, no," she squeaked as the phone hit the top of the desk, faceup, and she found herself watching a three- or four-second video of her sister, taken just moments before her death.

Cammie stared into the camera, her eyes round with a sheer, horrid terror, her lips blue, her skin white. She gasped, unable to speak, blood oozing from her throat where the garrote, what looked to be a dark-beaded rosary, was cutting off her breath, her very life.

The towel slipped to the floor as Val's knees gave way, and she started to crumple, would have fallen to the floor except that Slade grabbed her. His strong arm surrounded her waist, and he drew her naked body close, drawing her to her feet, not allowing her to fall.

"I'm so sorry," he whispered against her ear, his hands tangling in her hair.

Tears rained from her eyes. "What kind of a monster would do this?" she asked, her voice thick, the pain of grief shredding her soul. "What kind of a sick, twisted son of a bitch would do this?" She was clinging to Slade with one hand, pummeling his shoulder with the other. "It's just not right, just not right."

"Shhh. I know," he said, but didn't try to stop her as she struck him in frustration. "I know."

"It's so damned wrong!" She squeezed her eyes shut and wilted against him. For once in her life, she couldn't be strong, wouldn't try to fight the pain, but just give in to it. Was it her fault? Had she been too hard on Cammie? Thrown her out when she'd thought—believed—that her sister and her husband were having an affair?

It seemed so petty now. A ridiculous bit of history. *I'm sorry,* she silently sobbed. *Oh, Cammie, I'm so, so sorry.* She was older; she'd always thought she could protect her baby sister, and she'd failed. Oh, God, how she'd failed.

"Come on," Slade said, and guided her to the bedroom. "We'll go out another time."

"You... you expect me to sleep?"

"I just think you need some time to work through this," he countered.

She wanted to fight him, needed to do something, *any*thing to find Cammie's murderer, but she couldn't battle him, the ghosts, the murderer, the whole damned world—not right now.

She let him propel her into the dark bedroom, didn't resist as he tucked her, naked, between the sheets, then left to get her a glass of water.

"Don't," she said as he set the tumbler on the bedside table, then claimed the cane-backed chair in the corner, kicked off his boots, and propped his crossed ankles onto the foot of the old queen-size.

"Rest."

"I can't... There's so much to do." Her mind was spinning in circles. Who had left the BlackBerry? Was it Camille's? What else was on it? She needed to call the police.

"I'll take care of it. Now, rest," he said again, folding his arms over his chest. "Just for twenty minutes. Think if you want to, but just... take a deep breath."

"And pull myself together?"

"Yeah," he said, and for once she didn't fight. "That would be a good idea."

Reluctantly, Val closed her eyes and sank back into the downy depths of her pillow. She let the darkness close in on her, willing the horrible images of Cammie dying from her brain.

She felt a thump as Bo jumped onto the bed and nuzzled close beside her, as if to give her comfort. Absently, tears burning behind her eyelids, she patted his head, soothing both herself and the dog.

Don't fall apart! You can't! Not now. You owe it to Cammie to be strong, to find her killer.

Surely, if she just thought long and hard, she could figure this out; she knew she could. But there was so much. Beyond who had killed her and Sister Asteria, why had Camille been looking into her own adoption? And who was the father of her child if not Father Frank O'Toole? Why did she, Valerie, feel like everywhere she went, someone was watching? Why was Cammie found in a bridal dress? What was it Sister Charity was hiding at St. Marguerite's? What were the meaning of the notes scribbled in Cammie's all-too-graphic diary?

And Lord, oh, Lord, what was she going to do about Slade?

"I can't do this," she said into the darkness. "I have to get up and do something."

"We will." Slade's voice was close. Now he was probably seated in the only other chair in the room, the one near the foot of the bed.

"No," she said, unable to fight the need for action. "We need to do it right now." She had the feeling that time was slipping away from her, that any second that wasn't used to try and find Camille's killer was a second wasted.

She threw off the covers, grabbed the sheet to cover her nakedness, though he'd seen her thousands of times before, then swung off the bed. He was seated in the chair with his heels propped on the end of the mattress, his legs blocking her path. He looked up at her. "You're sure about this?"

She nodded. "Ab-so-frickin'-lutely. It's time to stop being a wimp and get something done. Whoever's doing this is really ticking me off."

He grinned, offering up that untrustworthy slash of white. She thought he might try to stop her, but he nodded and swung his feet to the floor.

"I'm with you," he said, and her heart nearly broke.

"The date—it'll have to wait."

"I know."

"You want to give me some privacy?" She was still clutching the damned sheet over her chest.

"No." His grin stretched and was absolutely wicked. She arched an eyebrow and he said on a sigh, "But, being the gentleman I am, I will."

"Another bad line, Houston."

He chuckled, and, standing, he whistled to the dog. "Come on, Bo, the lady wants to be alone." He walked through the door and called over his shoulder, "We'll check the perimeter, but I'm sure whoever was inside is long gone."

"No doubt." As she heard him leave, she dressed—underwear, bra, T-shirt, and jeans. She scraped her hair back but didn't bother with any makeup other than a slash of lip gloss, then walked into the living area again.

There was the damned BlackBerry, right where she'd dropped it. She was careful as she picked it up, using a plastic bag as she stared again at the short video of her sister's death.

"You sick son of a bitch," she muttered, then hit the keys to play another one. Her heart dropped as she recognized Sister Asteria, in a bridal gown, a rosary over her throat, gasping for breath, tears rolling down her face as she, too, died before the camera.

What kind of psychopath were they dealing with?

Valerie's hands were shaking. She could barely touch the buttons for another video, and this one was blank, a black screen, but there was a voice, a harsh, hissing whisper, the same one that haunted her dreams.

Her scalp prickled and her mouth turned to sand as she listened.

"You're on the lissssst," the horrid voice intoned smugly. "There is no esssscape."

Valerie had no doubt the message was meant for her.

CHAPTER 41

Of course he found nothing.

Slade walked around the grounds of the Briarstone bed-and-breakfast and discovered nothing more dangerous than a possum, nine or ten babies on her back, lumbering toward the chokecherry and milkweed that grew in profusion near the picket fence.

Whoever had left the damned BlackBerry had disappeared like a wraith, leaving no footprint or any disturbance that Slade could see. Nor was there any scent that caused Bo to go out of his mind with barking.

Then again, the old dog hadn't seen the possum, so he couldn't be counted on for too much help. "Come on, boy," he said, and tried to stay calm.

No one had gotten hurt.

But the thought that someone had been prowling around the house while Valerie was inside alone bothered him, and despite all her tough, ex-cop act, he knew she was vulnerable. The creep had been *inside!*

What if, instead of slamming the screen door, the intruder had actually had a gun and fired? What if even now, Slade were in the emergency room of the local hospital, waiting at Valerie's bedside, hoping she would survive the attack? What if the attack had been deadly, a bullet straight to the heart?

"Don't go there," he warned himself as he climbed the steps to the back porch and swept his gaze over the main house and outbuildings one last time.

By now it was really dark, only the gray-blue illumination of the solar lights casting their eerie glow over the grass and flowers, their blooms already closed for the night. A few cars rolled down the side street, and there were none parked that shouldn't have been there.

Nonetheless, he was going to call Montoya.

Someone had wanted Camille's diary.

Why?

And who?

He stopped at his pickup, unlocked the glove box, and pulled out his pistol, a thirty-eight. Not a lot of firepower, but enough to deter an assailant. Tucking the weapon into the back of his jeans, he returned to the house and hurried up the back steps.

Inside, he found Valerie waiting, the damned BlackBerry in a plastic bag. Her face was white as death, her eyes round with a quiet fear, her pointed chin set.

"What've you got?"

"A little present," she said. "Left by our friend."

"Our friend? Oh." The intruder. "More than what we saw earlier?"

"Oh, yeah. Take a look." She handed him the BlackBerry in its see-through skin.

He stared at the tiny screen, once more saw Cammie draw her last painful breath, her terrified gaze beseeching.

"Son of a bitch," he muttered, sick inside all over again at the image.

"The show's not over." Val's voice was devoid of any trace of humor.

A second video appeared on a small screen, the woman, he knew from the news reports, being Sister Asteria. This victim, too, a beautiful woman, battled for and lost her life. Her eyes were bulbous, her lips moving, blood oozing at her throat as she lay helplessly on the ground.

"Dear God," he whispered, horrified. "Don't tell me there's more," he said, watching as Val pressed another set of keys.

"Nope. This time it's only audio." She pushed the key for speaker, and he heard the voice, a harsh, rasping sound, obviously disguised. He couldn't tell whether it was male of female; all he knew was that it was deadly.

"You're on the list," it said in a sickening hiss, then paused for effect before adding, "There is no escape."

The hairs on the back of his neck lifted. Fear crystalized in his brain, while anger that anyone would threaten Val fired his blood.

"This was meant for you."

"Apparently."

"We need to call Montoya."

"Already left him a message," she said, too calmly for his satisfaction.

Suddenly, this tiny little carriage house, the one he'd thought was so homey and cozy, smelling of Val's perfume and potpourri, now felt like a death trap, open to any twisted bastard who decided to take a potshot at her. A phone rang. Letting him hold the ziplock bag with the BlackBerry, she snagged her cell from the counter and looked at the caller ID.

"Montoya," she said.

"Tell him to get the hell over here!"

She was nodding as she answered, and after a short conversation, she hung up. "He's on his way."

"Good. When he gets here, I'll go get my things."

"Your things?"

"Until whatever is happening is over, until the madman who's doing this—and now targeting you—is dead or behind bars, preferably dead, I'm sticking to you like glue! Bo and I are moving in."

"But—"

"No arguments, Val. I'll camp out on the couch, but you're too important for me to just sit by and let some maniac walk into your house whenever he wants! Holy Christ, no! We'll change the locks on all the doors, even at the main house. Call Freya and tell her what's going on. I'll go double-check everything at the main house as soon as Montoya arrives. And when he gets here, we're going to demand police protection."

"Whoa! Hey, slow down," she said. "I don't think I need that. If the guy wanted to kill me, he could have easily. I was in the shower, for God's sake. I *saw* him and he probably saw me, but there was no attack."

"Yet."

"He just wants to terrorize me, and yeah, he has." She was nodding, twirling her cell phone in her fingers nervously.

"He didn't just terrorize two other women."

"Who were nuns at St. Marguerite's." Slade could tell by the way her eyebrows puckered together that she was thinking. Hard. Piecing it all together. "The killer just knows I'm nosing around, and he wants me to back off."

"The threat was pretty damned specific." Slade wasn't going to take any chances. "He wants to terrorize you, yeah, maybe convince you to stay out of it, but now that you've seen Cammie's diary, been poking around St. Marguerite's and St. Elsinore's, he's out for blood."

"What the hell is it he wanted from the diary?"

"Who knows?" Slade's mind was racing over the pages filled with sexual adventures written in a flowing hand—all true? Or were there fantasies involved? They may never know, but they were important to someone. "Maybe the police have found something," he said.

He saw her shudder, knew she didn't like anyone, even detectives from the Robbery/Homicide Division of the police department, prying into Camille's personal life. "I hope."

"And maybe," he pushed, "we should just leave the investigation to the police. That's their job; we could be getting in the way."

"No way." She leveled her gaze at him. Stepped closer. "It's not that I don't trust the police. For God's sake, I *was* a cop. But I know how thin a department can be stretched, how many man-hours it takes to work a crime like this. I believe they're throwing all their muscle into Camille's murder and that they'll probably be creating a task force, getting help from the FBI, and that's all well and good. But this is Cammie we're talking about, my only sister." She was now facing him, her bare toe pressed against the tip of his cowboy boot. "I'm not backing off, Slade." Her eyes were earnest, the pupils large. "And you know it. You know me. So don't waste your breath."

Her gaze held his, and in that instant, all he could think about was kissing her, dragging her into his arms, pressing the length of her to him, and making love to her until dawn. Only afterward, when the ghosts of the night, the phantoms that haunted them, receded into the shadows and the light of the new day streamed through the windows to warm their naked, sweat-soaked bodies, would he release her. But that, of course, was impossible.

"Okay," he agreed with more than a little reservation—oh, hell, he didn't want her getting hurt or putting herself in danger. "But the deal is I'm staying. Right here!" He pointed to the floor. "With you! Until I know you're safe."

For once, thank God, she didn't argue.

He considered that a minor miracle.

The call came on Montoya's cell phone just as they were wrapping things up at Grace Blanc's apartment.

"Let's roll," he said to Bentz after giving him a quick rundown of what he knew, that Valerie Houston's house had been burglarized. They jogged across the parking lot of Grace Blanc's building to the cruiser they'd taken from the station. Bentz, despite his age and extra pounds, kept up with him, and they climbed inside the Crown Vic, Montoya at the wheel.

Traffic was thinning, but still he darted around slower vehicles.

"Our guy's busy," Bentz said.

"Working overtime, it seems." He cut in front of a low-rider pickup, then headed toward St. Charles, where the dark street cast an eerie glow under streetlamps, the leaves of the large trees lining the avenue seeming to glisten. A solitary streetcar passed, traveling in the opposite direction, few passengers inside.

Straight out of a horror movie.

On either side of the broad avenue divided by the streetcar line were expansive mansions, as architecturally diverse as the city itself, but all grand and huge, with cultured grounds and many with wrought-iron fences.

Definitely how the other half lived.

"So what do a prostitute and two nuns have in common?" Bentz thought aloud as he stared out the window.

"That sounds like the start of a really bad joke." Montoya

scowled as he took the final corner too fast and saw Briarstone House lit up like the proverbial Christmas tree on the left. "The obvious answer is they all knew a priest who was very bad news."

"The question is, then," Bentz said as Montoya wheeled into the drive, stopping the Crown Vic a few inches from the bumper of an old, beat-up pickup, "who's the priest?"

"Yeah, that is the question." Montoya cut the engine and thought of the possibilities: Father Frank O'Toole, the priest who admitted to an affair with Sister Camille but who was not the baby's father, according to the blood work; Father Paul Neland, the older, tight-lipped priest at St. Marguerite's; the missing Father Thomas at St. Elsinore's; or someone else? What about Father John, the would-be priest who seemed to have risen from the dead to kill yet another prostitute? He was a possibility. But what did he have to do with the deaths at St. Marguerite's? He'd always gone after redheads. And then there was the missing nun, Lea De Luca. So far, the SFPO hadn't found hide nor habit of her.

He felt like he should be able to pull some mental strings and figure out what the connection was. The orphanage? The religious order? What?

He stepped out of the car and was halfway up the walk when he was greeted by Valerie Houston's husband, the guy who just happened to have shown up on the night his sister-in-law and would-be lover had been slain.

Coincidence?

Or not?

"Glad you're here," the husband said, shaking hands with Bentz, then Montoya. A tall, raw-boned man, he looked worried as hell. "I think my wife told you what happened. Come on inside."

"Inside" meant inside of the smaller cottage on the property, a building that, because of its tall, narrow build, looked to have once been the carriage house to the main mansion. Valerie Houston was inside, standing in the kitchen, a big dog at her feet. The hound's eyes followed Montoya and Bentz, and his tail, which had been sweeping the floor, became motionless.

And the husband was packing heat, carrying a weapon in the waistband of his pants.

"You licensed for that?" Montoya asked, motioning toward the gun.

Houston nodded and Montoya didn't ask to see the paperwork; he'd check himself. Later.

"Here's the BlackBerry," Valerie said without so much as a greeting. She'd caught the exchange between Montoya and her husband.

The device was wrapped in a plastic bag that she pushed across the counter. "I don't know if it's Camille's. I assume that it is and that the killer stole it from her on the night she died, then used it whenever he needed it. And, yes, I did touch it before I realized what it was." She met Montoya's gaze. "I looked through it, too, because I couldn't help myself."

Bentz got out his notebook, Montoya his digital voice recorder. "Let's go through this again," Bentz said. "What happened earlier?"

She launched into her tale of the break-in, if you could even call it as such. Neither of her doors had been locked when she'd thought she'd seen the intruder and had heard what she'd first thought was a gunshot.

They asked questions and she answered; the husband backed her up. They admitted that the scattered items in the living room belonged to Camille, the contents of boxes they'd found in the garage; then they played the first video on the BlackBerry, and every muscle in Montoya's body tightened as he watched Camille Renard, dressed in the tired bridal gown, struggle for her dying breaths. Panic rounded her beautiful eyes as they bulged and she finally, painfully, let go of life.

Fury invaded his bloodstream. What kind of sicko would kill someone and film it? A poor man's snuff film. Of a nun.

"Jesus," he muttered as the next video played.

His guts twisted as he watched Sister Asteria in another bridal gown, the darkness of the cemetery and whitewashed tombs surrounding her as she seemed to beg for her life as she was being garroted, blood circling her throat, the dress not yet decorated with its drops of blood. That must've been done afterward, after the video session was finished.

For a second, after the video was over, he couldn't speak, could barely think. The ticking of a nearby clock seemed to echo through his brain.

He thought of Grace Blanc, displayed on her bed, half dressed, her throat bruised and bloodied from a garrote. He glanced at Bentz, whose color had drained from his face.

"You said there was an audio message."

"Yeah," the husband said, his eyes dark, his eyebrows slammed together in worry.

Through the plastic, Valerie pressed another button, and soon a voice was hissing through the room. "You're on the list." The words were drawn out. Then there was a pause and the rest of the message: "There is no escape."

The voice was obviously disguised and not only threatening, but also smug. "I take it you don't know who it is?"

"No." Valerie shook her head.

"So why would you become a target? You're not a nun," he thought aloud.

"I wish I knew, but maybe it has something to do with Camille's diary. He took it. Maybe there's something condemning in it, something that would tie him to her."

"Maybe," Bentz said, taking notes. "But I agree. You're the target of his threat."

Montoya nodded. "We'll put a detail outside," he said, "to watch the place."

She was nodding.

He continued. "And we'll want to go through all of Camille's personal items, take 'em with us."

"Okay."

"I want to take a look in the attic," Bentz interjected. "See for myself, in case she left anything that wasn't boxed up."

"I'll take you out there," Slade said, and he pulled a flashlight from a drawer. For a man who'd come to New Orleans to patch things up with his wife, he seemed to know his way around her house. And the antagonism Montoya had sensed between them in their first interview, here at the house, then at the hospital, that invisible current of discord, seemed to be missing.

"Anything else you want to add?" Montoya asked. "Anything else unusual?"

He wasn't surprised when she nodded again. "Yeah. I got a couple of calls this afternoon. Hang-ups. No caller ID," she admitted.

"We'll need your phone."

"But—" she started to argue, then said, "Sure."

"And we'll need to take this." He motioned to the BlackBerry, but Valerie was already nodding. She looked Montoya straight in the eye. "You knew my sister, Detective," she said, her chin quivering despite the fire in her gaze. "Get the guy who did this to her. Nail his hide to the wall."

"I will," he said, knowing he was promising what might turn out to be the impossible but saying the words anyway. He caught a warning glance from Bentz but ignored it as he scooped the Black-Berry into his pocket and headed out the back door and into the night.

They asked more questions, checked the grounds, talked to Valerie Houston's business partner, Freya Martin, and five groggy guests. A married couple from Maine were in their seventies, and the wife claimed she never heard anything but her husband's snoring as he had dozed off. Three women from Oregon, all in their late forties, were on a "girl-cation away from the husbands and boyfriends" and hadn't noticed. Freya had heard the dog bark, but that was it. No sound of footsteps, revving engine, screaming . . . no one looking out the window and seeing someone dash across the lawn.

All in all a bust, Montoya thought as he returned to the Crown Vic. Over the echo of his own promise to "nail the bastard" who had killed Camille Renard rattling through his brain, he heard the eerie peal of distant bells, the midnight chimes tremulously counting off the hours.

CHAPTER 42

Like the calm before the storm, for the next few days, things were quiet. Too quiet, Montoya thought as he jogged through the streets at dawn. His legs were beginning to cramp, evidence that he'd pushed aside his exercise regimen in the last two weeks. The five miles he usually jogged seemed longer today, his breathing more difficult, though Hershey ran along beside him effortlessly.

Montoya, to keep up with the dog, would have to give up even his occasional smoke. Besides, Abby was on to him, not saying a word, just giving him the evil eye and wrinkling her nose when he came in from his "walk" and probably reeking of smoke. Normally she would tell him exactly what she thought, but when he was eyeball deep in a case, she usually gave him a little leeway. And he took advantage of it.

"The price of being a hotshot detective's wife," she'd tease. Although, since the birth of Benjamin, she'd been a little more cutting with her remarks, more fearful for his life. "It's not just you and me, anymore, Detective," she'd remind him.

As if he didn't know.

He rounded a corner, running through the Quarter, the chocolate lab beginning to lag a bit as they passed the buildings with their wide second-story balconies decorated in intricate patterns of wrought iron. Steam seemed to escape from the manholes, and he passed few people at the street, saw only a smattering of lamplights in the windows of the apartments over the storefronts at street level.

He pushed it, kicking up his pace a bit.

Reaching the river, he ran on the sidewalk flanking the water and took in deep breaths of the air, which was thick with the scent of the Mississippi. A flock of pelicans rose before him as his feet slapped the ground, and Hershey, though he looked longingly at the birds, didn't stray.

"Good boy," Montoya said with more than a little effort as he turned his mind to the case and the fact that the killer, thankfully, hadn't struck again.

At least not that anyone knew about.

The Feds were sniffing around, the task force pulled together, the press demanding answers, and everyone in the department on edge, expecting yet another homicide, another novitiate found with her throat garroted, or another prostitute strangled with a rosary, raped and left with a defaced C-note.

Yet, so far, there had been no reports of any such thing. Bentz had questioned Dr. Sam, the psychologist with the radio program *Midnight Confessions* on WSLJ, the target of Father John during his original rampage a few years back. She'd sworn that she'd had no out-of-the-ordinary calls or requests to the station, which was saying something, because Montoya thought anyone who picked up a phone and called a psychologist who was on the airwaves had a serious screw loose. Who in his right mind would talk about the most intimate of problems while all of New Orleans could listen in? Then again, weren't there a plethora of shows like *Jerry Springer* or even *Judge Judy* where people came forward with their most private matters?

"I don't get it," he admitted to Hershey as the dog loped at the end of his leash.

Montoya jogged through the dawn light, the fog rolling in from the river, his thoughts jumbled, sweat running down his body.

Sister Camille Renard's diary had been eye-opening, but other than offering up a few notes that didn't make any sense and describing her sexual encounters—all with anonymous partners—hadn't held much else. He'd winced when he'd read about her first experience, especially when she'd admitted to the diary that it had been less than what she'd anticipated; at the time, she'd expected so much more than a horny high school boy had given her.

It seemed that her other lovers had been more to her liking. He'd sifted through the diary, trying to place names with events, linking several experiences, because of the dates, to Brandon Keefe, a man to whom she'd once been engaged and who was now married with a couple of kids in California, and another to a man who had become a parishioner at St. Marguerite's, Joshua Lassiter, but that had been before she'd taken her vows. There were others still unnamed, then more recently, the entries that were most recent, Father Frank, certainly. Could there possibly be someone else?

Who, they didn't know.

The BlackBerry that had belonged to Camille Renard had not given up any clues that were easily evident, but the techs weren't finished with it, even though all of the messages, contacts, and old calls had been erased. Except for the last audio message and the two videos of the dead nuns.

The son of a bitch had been careful, and he was irritating the hell out of Montoya.

The lab was still trying to match blood types and so far hadn't come up with a serious candidate for the baby's father. Even the men who worked at the parish—Elwin Zaan, the janitor; Clifton Sharkey, a maintenance man; and Neron Lopez, the groundskeeper—were being checked.

The one glaring omission was Father Thomas. No blood had been taken from the priest, as he'd been away from St. Elsinore's more often than not.

Odd, that.

Still, Montoya thought wryly, he was doubting Thomas as the father. He smiled at his own little joke, then angled off toward the coffee shop where he usually picked up his regular cup of joe. At the coffee stand, he paid for his black coffee, got a cup of water for the dog, and left change in the tip jar for Jessica, the barista, a pillowy African American woman with silver hair. He sipped from the steaming paper cup as he walked back to the house and stretched his muscles. Hershey, finally tired, his tongue lolling out of his mouth, followed.

All part of his usual routine.

Except that now a killer was stalking the streets of New Orleans, his town, once again.

First Sister Camille and then Asteria McClellan. The two, as far as Montoya could tell, were only linked because of two parishes: St. Elsinore's, from which they'd both been adopted, and St. Marguerite's, where they lived and planned to take their vows.

As different as night and day, his mother would have said. Sister Camille, outgoing, spontaneous, a flirt, and, it turned out, someone who didn't take her vows of chastity seriously. Sister Asteria had no tell-all graphic diary. No pregnancy. Was still, according to the ME, a virgin.

Both women, though, had been drugged, traces of Rohypnol in their bloodstream. The date-rape drug—used on nuns. What the hell was that all about?

There wasn't any info yet on Grace Blanc, and the testimony of the old Italian lady, Mrs. Rubino, about seeing a priest through her fish-eye peephole was sketchy at best. She was partially deaf, and her eyesight wasn't near 20/20, so if she were ever put on the witness stand, assuming the police made an arrest, her testimony would be torn up by any defense attorney worth the cost of the ink on his diploma.

What a mess! Montoya drank his coffee and cut across the lawn to the house. On the porch, he stretched his hamstrings and quads, then finished the last swallow before crushing his cup. The neighbor's dog, Apollo the dalmatian, whined from the front porch, wriggling at the sight of the Lab.

"No!" Montoya said before Hershey even looked up at him or dashed inside. "Sit!"

He stripped out of his T-shirt, then wiped the Lab's paws with it while Hershey wiggled impatiently on the porch. "Hey! Give me a break." Once the Lab's feet were a little cleaner, he opened the door and the dog streaked inside.

"Trying to win brownie points?" Abby asked. She was in her bathrobe, her hair piled onto her head, standing at the kitchen sink and cutting up fruit while the coffee brewed and Benjamin slept in his infant seat on the counter.

"With you?" Montoya asked, then winked at her. "Always, baby."

"Oh, jeez, Montoya, so smooth! Be still my heart." Using her fingers, she made a fanning motion near her face, as if she were suddenly so hot she might faint; then she giggled and went back to slicing up strips of cantaloupe and watermelon. The baby let out a soft little sigh that touched Montoya's heart. He grinned and placed a finger on Ben's chubby cheek, watching as his son's tiny lips moved.

"Is Cruz around?"

"Still sleeping," she said, casting her husband a knowing smile. "It is only six-thirty. The only sane people awake are nursing mothers and type-A detectives."

"Yeah, right." His brother had crashed there for the better part of a week, spending time with Abby and Reuben, visiting their mother and other siblings, and generally hanging out. He hadn't said as much, but Montoya thought that Cruz might be trying to find a way to see Lucia Costa again, the girl he'd known in high school and someone the department was interested in; after all, she'd somehow discovered both Sister Camille and Sister Asteria as they'd died.

Montoya thought Lucia wasn't being completely truthful, but so far, he hadn't figured out what she could be holding back. Cruz's interest in her wouldn't help the investigation; in fact, it could bloody well harm it.

"I'm serious. It's too early to be up and around."

"Yeah, yeah. But you know how it is."

"When you're wound up in a big case, you can't sleep. So that means neither can I." Sighing, she sliced another cantaloupe in half, then started digging out the seeds.

Montoya, on his way to the back of the house, paused to snap his sweaty, now-dirty T-shirt against her buttocks.

"Hey! You're asking for trouble," she warned, waggling the knife.

"Oh, I like the sound of that."

"Really?" She was smiling as she twisted her head to look at him.

He couldn't resist and wrapped his arms around her, the cotton of her robe shifting beneath his fingers. "Really."

She glanced at the baby sleeping on the counter, as if considering. "I thought you had to be to work early."

"I think you could change my mind." He kissed her full on the lips and felt that hot, familiar rush, the liquid fire in his blood just as he did every time her mouth opened to him. Sometimes he wondered if it were possible to get enough of her.

He slid his tongue between her teeth and slipped one hand into the folds of the robe, searching out her breast, full and hard, filled with milk, covered in lace.

"Mmmm...," she murmured just as his damned cell phone rang.

He ignored it, but she pulled away. "Duty calls."

When he was about to argue, she arched a brow, reminding him of their argument several nights earlier—the one about his responsibilities of being a father and husband as opposed to being a cop. "Damn," he muttered.

"Right," she agreed, with more than a hint of sarcasm. "Damn."

He gave her a quick buss on the cheek, then answered. "Montoya."

"We got a hit," Bentz said, his voice rough, as if he'd just been awakened.

Montoya's muscles tensed. All of his attention was on the phone. "Yeah?"

"The maintenance guy. Clifton Sharkey? Seems as if he's had a prior. Assault."

"How'd we miss that?"

"Twenty years ago, in Canada. It's not enough to do anything but haul his ass in for more questioning, but it's something."

Finally! A break.

Maybe.

He felt a rush of adrenaline stream through his blood, that familiar buzz he loved when a case was beginning to fit together. Yeah! He was already heading down the hall toward the bathroom. "I'll be at the station in twenty," he said.

"But, Montoya," Bentz said through the receiver, "just for the record?"

"Yeah?"

Montoya kicked the bathroom door closed and twisted on the faucet.

"My money's still on O'Toole."

"We can't ignore our responsibilities, even though we're all still in mourning," the mother superior said during another meeting after breakfast, the third this week. Lucia, seated with the rest of the nuns and novices, sat in the stiff-backed chairs of a room down the hallway from the cathedral, a room used for seminars, meetings, or prayer groups. It smelled slightly stale, the windows closed, the whiteboard behind Sister Charity wiped clean.

Father Paul and Father Frank stood near the door as the reverend mother spoke, the older man forcing a smile that had all the warmth of a Siberian snowstorm. His hands were folded, soft, his pink fingers laced.

Father Frank seemed to have aged ten years in the past week. His dark hair, usually combed and clipped, was disheveled, showing a few strands of gray, his jaw colored by a dusting of beard shadow, his eyes hollow and sunken, as if the life, and perhaps even his faith, had been sucked from his soul. His fingers moved constantly. Nervously. Evidence of a man haunted by his own sins.

Sister Louise, her eyes sad, tried to meet his gaze, Lucia noticed, but he was a man caught in his own world. He was in the room physically, but his heart and soul were somewhere far, far away.

It wasn't just the priests. Everyone at St. Marguerite's was on edge, Lucia surmised, second-guessing their appointments to the parish. And not just those who wore the holy garb. The lay workers, too, were affected.

The janitor, Elwin Zaan, now leaning on his broom, was as somber as death.

Neron Lopez, the usually happy-go-lucky groundskeeper, hadn't been able to scare up a smile this past week. Lucia had caught him continually crossing himself and glancing up at the church spires, as if expecting to be struck down as he raked the gardens and pulled weeds.

Regina, the sour-faced cook, had quit yelling, keeping to herself, the cross at her neck more visible in the past few days, glinting on its chain as she'd rolled out pie crusts and ladled soup. Her barking of orders in the kitchen had become less pronounced, and there was talk, scuttlebutt, that she was considering resigning. Eileen, the receptionist with frizzy blue hair and color-coordinated pantsuits, had spent most of the past week dabbing at her eyes. Only Clifton Sharkey, the maintenance man who went about his job repairing everything from shoes to machinery, seemed mostly unaffected, though he was sweating a lot. Lucia glanced his way and saw him mopping his brow yet again.

"It's a time for us to unite and band together. Do not let fear into your soul...," the mother superior was intoning, all eyes on her as she walked past a desk near the windows.

All of the nuns at St. Marguerite's had been nervous and on edge, the feeling of safety within the hallowed walls of the convent shattered.

They had talked when they'd been gardening or driving to St. Elsinore's or while doing their chores. All the time between their scheduled prayers, meditation, and services to the needy, they had whispered their own fears. Just yesterday, in the garden, just before vespers, several of the women had met. Lucia had stood in the group, felt the nervousness of all the nuns, and carefully studied the glinting streaks of gold as the fish in the pond darted beneath the water's surface.

"Why Asteria?" Sister Dorothy had asked, worrying the beads of her rosary with her pudgy fingers. "She was so...good, so pure."

"Oh, please. Really?" Sister Maura had whispered, skewering the shorter nun with a dark stare. "Do you think that's what it's all about, that she was killed because she was impure?" She had shuddered, as if a cold breeze had swept through her, though the heat of the day had lain heavy on the gardens, where honeybees droned and a hummingbird hovered near the fragrant blooms of a magnolia tree. "No way."

"But she was," Sister Angela had agreed, peering through her narrow glasses and nodding.

"You think purity will save anyone from a madman?" Maura had demanded. "Because that's what's happening here."

Lucia had thought about the voice in her ear and held her tongue, but silently she agreed with Dorothy and Angela.

"But I'm just saying," Dorothy had said nervously, "that there could have been reasons Sister Camille was killed. . . ." She let her voice trail off and sketched the sign of the cross over her chest.

"Maybe we shouldn't discuss it," Sister Zita, ever the voice of reason, had said calmly, then flipped a stray piece of lint from her sleeve.

"She's right," Devota had agreed. "We can't begin to understand God's punishment."

"God's punishment?" Maura had repeated as two crows started squawking from the roof of the chapel. "You think that's it?"

Dorothy had said, "Well, she was... you know." She blushed, probably to the roots of her hair, though her short brown locks were completely covered by her veil. "With Father O'Toole."

"But no one's struck him down," Louise had said emphatically, her cheeks flushing, her hands sketching a frantic cross over her chest.

"Yet." Angela's voice had been hushed and worried, and the word echoed through Lucia's brain.

"Never!" Louise had shaken her head. "He's...he's..."

"He was involved with Sister Camille."

"I know, but..."

"But what?" Sister Maura had demanded. "It was all Camille's fault? Really? I know we live in some kind of throwback, archaic world here, but Sister Camille was no more to blame than Father Frank. He's a priest, Louise!"

"Shhh," Sister Irene had said with her slight lisp. She had to crook her neck to meet Louise's upturned gaze. "This isn't helping." She placed her long fingers on Louise's shoulder.

"That's right," Devota had said. "It's best we not gossip. We should take our concerns to the Holy Father in prayer. He'll advise us and help us to see what's right, what we should do."

Maura had rolled her eyes and rubbed the spine of her prayer book in agitation. "Step into the twenty-first century," she had advised.

"Remember your vows," Devota had rebuked, her pale lips turning down. "We all chose this profession, this life. We need to honor it."

"And atone if we have sinful thoughts," Sister Edwina had agreed somberly. "There are ways to seek atonement."

Sister Lucia remembered that this woman, so graceful and beautiful, was rumored to believe in self-flagellation. At least that's what Sister Camille had admitted, and hadn't Lucia herself witnessed Edwina walking the halls late at night, red stains on the back of her nightgown?

Sister Louise, rebuked, had let out a long sigh. It was obvious that she, like so many of the others, fancied herself in love with Frank O'Toole. Did he pursue them? Was he aware of his charm and just let it flow? Or was it subconscious and the thoughts in the heads of some of the nuns all just fantasies?

Not that it mattered now, she'd thought. It was horrid how what was happening at the convent was tearing them all apart.

For a second, Lucia had thought she should tell the others about the evil presence she felt, about how she sensed that the demon wasn't finished with his deadly work, when she looked up and met Sister Devota's troubled gaze.

Better not to worry them all.

Better not to let them think you're crazy.

"I don't think we should speculate," Lucia had said.

Zita had said, "Sister Lucia's right. We can't begin to understand the Holy Father's ways." Her dark gaze had moved to each of the nuns gathered in the courtyard. "Maybe we should just pray."

"And pray hard," Dorothy had said earnestly, "because we don't know who'll be next."

"Or if there will be another." Angela had adjusted her narrow glasses under the band of her wimple, a bead of sweat running down her face.

"Let's hope so," Louise had agreed, and for the first time Lucia had missed her soft humming throughout the hallways of St. Marguerite's. For the better part of a week, the corridors had been silent, quiet and as dark as tombs.

Everyone at St. Marguerite's had been affected by the terror.

Now, Sister Angela's cheeks were pale and wan, Sister Maura's scowl even deeper, her fingers running over the worn edges of her prayer book. Sister Louise's songbird of a voice was stilled; she didn't hum in the hallways any longer. Sister Edwina, usually tall and straight as an arrow, had drawn into herself, and even Sister Devota, as pious as her name implied, seemed pensive and dark.

It was chilling, really.

St. Marguerite's was suddenly thrust into the limelight, and it was uncomfortable. Vans from television stations were parked outside the gates as reporters stood, holding microphones, backdropped by the commanding edifice that was St. Marguerite's, retelling the story of the two dead nuns, bringing the horrifying murders of Sister Camille and Sister Asteria to the fore, reminding the residents of Louisiana of the terror that stalked the historic hallways of St. Marguerite's Convent.

The church had seen an influx of parishioners who actually attended Mass out of morbid curiosity, as well as a swelling in the amount of pedestrians and cars that passed by the cathedral and surrounding grounds.

The police cars that cruised by the gates at all hours weren't much comfort, nor were the added locks on some of the doors. Because, Lucia knew, the evil was from within. She felt it as surely as if she could see dark, crouching beasts with glowing eyes, snarling lips, and long fangs dripping with blood.

Even in the sanctity of the chapel, while on her knees, her hands clasped as she prayed, the whisper of evil remained, breathing hot against the back of her neck, causing her heart to pound in terror, keeping at bay sleep and the feeling of peace that usually overcame her as she prayed.

Was she the reason the evil oozed through the hallways of the convent? Was her shaken faith the cause of two horrible deaths already?

No! Of course not! That was crazy thinking.

But hadn't she been sought by the evil one?

Hadn't she been the only person to hear its vile hiss? Listen to its malevolent voice? Follow its depraved instructions as it urged her to find not one, but two dying women? She'd been the chosen one, picked by Satan himself.

The only way to ensure that no one else was harmed was to leave this safe haven, the home she'd run to for all the wrong reasons.

If she needed any other proof that she was supposed to leave, something more tangible than the voice she heard in the night, it was the glaring fact that Cruz Montoya had found her here, then sought her out.

Her reaction to him had been all wrong.

So physical. So mental. So...sexual. Just being near him again was a vow-breaking experience. Hadn't their one shared kiss, a meeting of the lips that had brought back a rush of memory and a torrent of desire, been evidence enough? Cruz Montoya was temptation.

Danger.

The word she'd whispered to him so long ago.

On the first night she'd heard the beast's horrid, hissing voice and smelled his dank, nauseating breath.

"So...it's imperative that we follow our hearts and our vows, our dedication," Sister Charity was saying, and she was staring straight at Lucia as she walked back and forth in the front of the room, in front of the whiteboard, like a teacher trying to get through to a disinterested class of thickheaded students.

Lucia tried her best to appear rapt; she couldn't allow the reverend mother to know her true intentions.

"We need to go on with our lives as usual. That's what Sister Camille and Sister Asteria would have wanted, and it's what the heavenly Father wants as well. That doesn't mean that we'll forget them or that they won't be heavy on our minds; it just means that we keep moving forward, giving praise to God, doing his work here on earth. Sister Asteria and Camille are with the blessed Virgin Mary and Jesus now."

At this point, Father Paul nodded. He and Father Frank stepped forward to join her at the front of the room. All eyes were upon them, and it seemed Sister Louise's face was nearly radiant when she looked at the younger priest. They all noticed it; Sister Devota cast a glance at Lucia and shook her head.

Still, Sister Louise beamed as Father Paul said, "Sister Charity's right. We must go on about our tasks here, for we do God's work. Whether you teach children, work with the homeless, or hold the hands of the sick, your job is important. We need to stand together, to be unafraid. Our work here will continue and we will persevere. We will let no henchman of the dark angel drive a stake of fear into our hearts." He looked at each and every person in the room, daring them to defy him.

Once satisfied that he had everyone's attention, his voice softened. "We will go about our duties, and I expect all of you to attend the auction at St. Elsinore's tomorrow night. Father Thomas is dedicating the event to the memory of Sister Camille and Sister Asteria. It's a beautiful gesture, and we at St. Marguerite's will support it." His gaze brooked no argument. "Now . . . together," he said, offering a smile that was intended to warm the coldest, most godforsaken heart. He lifted his hands as if in supplication to heaven. "Let us pray . . ." Then he clasped his hands together in front of him and bowed his head. "Heavenly Father . . ."

Lucia, too, bent her head but slid a look at Sister Edwina, who met her gaze for just an instant. And in that moment, Lucia realized that all the calming words in the world were of little help.

Edwina, like the other nuns, was scared to death.

CHAPTER 43

"I think this message"—Valerie pointed a finger at the notes she'd scribbled on the flyer for the auction at St. Elsinore's, the one that said C U N 7734 C V—"means 'See you in hell, Charity Varisco.'" She leaned back in her desk chair so that Slade, who had been making a sandwich in her kitchen, could take another look at the note. It wasn't the original, of course, nor even the copy, but what she'd written from memory and thought about for the past three days.

"Maybe." He was noncommittal as he carried over a plate with a tuna sandwich complete with pickles and set it in front of her. "Here, this is for you."

"Thanks." She cast a smile up at him as he leaned over her, so close she smelled his aftershave, a clean, brisk scent that brought back unwanted memories of making love to him in the morning, their naked bodies entwined in the sun-dried sheets, the Texas morning sliding in through the open window. The songs of the warblers getting interrupted by the chatter of jays and underscored by the low bawl of a lonely calf.

Her throat thickened as she realized how much she missed the ranch. How much she'd missed Slade.

If he noticed her reaction, he hid it, his eyes studying her scribbled note.

She cleared her throat. "I, uh, think part of it's in her little code, and then she just put the mother superior's initials down because at the time she wrote it, she was really ticked at Sister Charity."

"Then what does the other one mean?"

"I'm not as sure." She'd written it down as well. *TO BF 2 M&M.* "But I've been working on it," she admitted. And that was the truth. In the past few days, whenever she wasn't busy working at the inn, or trying to figure out a reason why Camille had been killed, or looking over her shoulder, she'd been thinking about the puzzle, and remembering the items she'd found in the boxes in the attic, she'd mentally gone through the things that were her sister's life. "I can't get off the 'best friend' thing, and though 'M and M' could mean anyone, I think she was thinking about our parents—I mean our birth parents. Mike and Mary Brown."

"Whom we've never found."

"Maybe they didn't exist. Maybe that's what it's all about."

"So then who is 'T O'?" he asked.

"I'm pretty sure it's Thelma O'Malley," she said.

"Not Tom, as in the priest at St. Elsinore's."

"Uh-uh. I can't think of anyone else, and Thelma was the widow who brought us to the orphanage and claimed our parents had died...but I can't find her. I've looked for Thelma O'Malley, Mrs. Stanley O'Malley, S. O'Malley, and T. O'Malley. I've even called people with the same last name, but so far I've struck out."

"Have you told the police?"

She shook her head. "No, because I'm not really sure. All I've got is a gut feeling and maybe some convoluted logic. The police have Camille's diary." Frustrated, the start of a headache niggling behind her eyes, she leaned back in the chair, pushing her shoulders against Slade's chest. He straightened as she said, "I just wish I had a way to find Thelma."

"If she's still alive."

"Yeah." Her gaze landed on the flyer for the auction at St. Elsinore's. "Maybe the answer is here," she said, thumping a finger on the glossy picture of the orphanage. The flyer contained a list of some of the donated items, including a trip to Las Vegas. Also there was mention of some local celebrities who were planning to attend, including the quarterback for the New Orleans Saints, the archbishop, and the radio psychologist Dr. Sam, to name a few.

"At the parish?"

"Uh-huh. Probably in the records the mother superior wouldn't let me open," she said, thinking of Sister Georgia, all warm and fuzzy on the outside but hard as granite under her friendly exterior. "I just have to find a way to get at them."

Slade set a big hand on her shoulder. "Seriously," he said, "this is a matter for the police." He'd been worried since the day of the intrusion, and, really, Val didn't blame him. She'd been more than concerned and hadn't argued when he'd changed every lock on both the main house and her cottage, tightened all the window latches, and parked himself in her living room day and night.

Despite the tension of the investigation, the worry and fear that had been an undercurrent in their daily lives, they'd gotten along. They'd worked together at the house, then gone out so that she could show him a little of New Orleans, everything from a notorious bar on Bourbon Street to a tour of one of the expansive and genteel plantations located on the river not too far out of town.

If she let herself, Val could imagine falling in love with him all over again, but she couldn't go there. At least not yet.

Cruz Montoya was starting to feel like a loser.

Never one to let the moss grow under his feet, he was beginning to sense the urge to move on, find greener pastures, face the rest of his life.

He threw the striped duvet that had been his blanket for the past week into some semblance of order, then headed for the shower. His excuse for staying was his family, of course. He got on with Abby, adored Reuben's new son, and spent time with his mother and other siblings, but the real anchor holding him to New Orleans was Lucia Costa. He could tell himself all kinds of lies, make up stories, pretend that there were other stronger ties to the city, but the truth was, he was fascinated by her, just as he had been over a decade earlier.

Even though she was a damned nun. Christ, his mother would be pissed if she could read his thoughts.

Good thing she wasn't clairvoyant.

Like Lucia?

Oh, hell, that was probably what drew him to her. It wasn't her shiny black hair, her flashing eyes, or stubborn chin. Nor was it her tiny waist and breasts just large enough for a man to take a second glance, or her sharp wit. Nuh-huh, it was her damned ability to see into another person's mind that really caught his attention and wouldn't let go.

Sure.

Now who're you kidding, Montoya?

He stepped out of the second bedroom and nearly kicked the damned cat . . . Ansel, he thought its name was. Something like that. It turned, hissed, and, gold eyes glaring, slunk away.

"I see you've made a friend for life," Abby observed. She was in the living room, sorting through photographs of the baby. A professional photographer, she'd taken off a few months while Benjamin was an infant, but she'd still found the time to take what looked like hundreds of shots of the newborn.

Hershey, lying at her feet, lifted his head and thumped his thick tail. "At least the dog likes me."

"Don't get too excited; he's not very discriminating. Loves everyone, from the crabby garbage man to my sister Zoey, who a lot of people can take or leave." She glanced at him. "Me being one."

"So I heard." Zoey was Abby's older sister who lived in Seattle. The sisters' relationship was, from what Reuben had confided to Montoya, difficult and strained at times.

"Don't get me wrong, I love her to death, would do just about anything for her, but sometimes she just rubs me the wrong way."

"I get the picture." Cruz got along with most of his siblings, some better than others.

"There's coffee in the pot. You might have to warm it up, though. Been there a while. Your brother left at the crack of dawn."

"I heard." Cruz poured himself a mug and set it in the microwave, then played with Benjamin, lying in his infant seat, his dark eyes following Cruz's movements. "You look too much like your daddy," he whispered to the boy, whose skin was as gold as Reuben's, and his hair, nearly black, curled a bit.

Abby laughed. "So I've been told."

"You'll survive," Cruz advised his nephew, and was rewarded with a wide, toothless grin.

"The ladies will love you."

"Geez, give it a rest, will you? He's just a little over three months old. The 'ladies' will just have to wait. Like twenty, no, make that thirty years!"

The microwave dinged and he grabbed his cup, nearly burning himself on the hot handle. Gingerly, he carried it to the bathroom, where he managed to take three swallows before he stepped into the shower and let hot, sharp needles massage his skin. As the steam surrounded him, he remembered that foggy night so long ago, the one in which his vehicle had slid off the road, and Lucia, it seemed, had been lost to him forever.

Now, maybe, he had a second chance.

Then again, odds were against it.

What was it their grandmother used to say? "You make your own luck, Cruz. Don't you forget it."

Grabbing the bar of soap, he decided it was long past time to take his *abuela's* advice.

The station was a madhouse. The Feds had shown up, two agents Bentz had known in L.A., but so far they weren't taking charge, just going over the case to date. The newspeople were camped outside, hoping for more information. Tips were coming into a hotline at a phenomenal rate, and then there was Clifton Sharkey, one of the new front-runners in the suspect race.

Montoya was pumped, going over the information at his desk, talking to other detectives in the lunchroom or task force area. He barely paused for lunch as he double-checked information, read his e-mails, finished reports, and all the while hoped to hell that they could nail Clifton Sharkey as the killer and get him off the streets.

He wouldn't lie to himself. He'd love it if somehow O'Toole were proven innocent of anything but breaking his vow of celibacy. It was just too damned hard to imagine the boy he'd known in high school, the athlete who had taken him under his wing, to be a killer.

As much as he wanted to be objective, he was hoping someone else would be proven to be the monster.

It was afternoon before he walked into Bentz's office and saw the information on Sharkey spread upon his partner's desk. The guy had already been hauled in, and they wanted to discuss how they were going to handle the interrogation.

"The charge is ten years old," Bentz reminded him, as they'd spoken briefly earlier on the phone. "Assault charge. But dropped. A domestic violence case. The wife." Seated at his desk, his eyebrows slammed together, his shirt already unbuttoned at the neck, tie askew, reading glasses on the end of his nose, Bentz was looking through copies of old reports. "Looks like he broke her wrist. She went to the hospital, but when it came time to press charges, she refused to testify against him."

"Typical." Montoya had seen it over and over again, the cycle of abuse that kept rolling through the generations.

Bentz looked up over the tops of his reading glasses. "So he and the wife have six kids, a couple of grandkids, and they're still married but separated. Have been since this." He pointed to the report on Henrietta Sharkey's injuries. "They've had separate residences."

"No divorce?"

"Catholic to the bone." Bentz scratched the side of his face as he thought. "No other incidents. And ever since, he's been sending her the lion's share of his paychecks."

"Atonement," Montoya said.

"Could be." But Bentz didn't seem convinced. "Hard to say."

"Anything else?"

"Yeah, his alibi didn't hold up. For the night of Camille Renard's murder. He claimed he was with son number two, watching the game, but when I called the son this morning, pressed him a little, he admitted that old Cliffie Boy was at home that night, watching the Astros getting their clock cleaned."

"Let's bring him in."

"Brinkman's already giving him the good news."

"But you don't like it." Bentz shook his head. "The other alibis, for the night of Asteria McClellan's murder and Grace Blanc's, stand." Again he met Montoya's stare. "That doesn't make sense, does it? Unless we've got another killer running around, drugging nuns and forcing them into bridal gowns before killing them with what seems to be a rosary and painting their necklines in the same pattern as the rosary beads." He was shaking his head. "I can buy that we might have a second killer for the prostitute. But the nuns?" His eyebrows elevated to his hairline. "No effin' way."

"Effin'?" Montoya repeated, and Bentz threw him a sheepish smile, then nodded to the recent picture of his baby, framed in silver and positioned on the credenza behind him.

"Yeah, Livvie said the swearing's gotta stop, that Ginny will pick up the bad language." He nodded. "Can't argue with that."

Page three?

The story about the murdered prostitute was buried on page three?

"Idiots!"

I can't believe the ineptitude as I read the evening paper, the kerosene lantern giving off an uneasy glow, the wind blowing hot over the bayou. The story of that whore Grace Blanc's death should be splashed all over the front page.

What kind of imbeciles decide where to place an article?

Ridiculous!

My blood is on fire at the disgrace, and I toss the paper aside, will burn it later.

Crickets and bullfrogs are again making their evening racket, and somewhere far away, a train chugs along, its whistle lonely and sharp, rolling through the forest of spindly, white-barked cypress.

Realizing how late it's become, I turn on the radio, listen to the program, *her* insidious radio show committed to helping all the restless souls worried about their current conditions. I hear "Jo"— or is it "Joe?"—in Aberdeen, Washington, complain about her husband's lack of attention, how he spends more time on the computer in a simulated, inorganic life on the Internet than he does with his family. Then there's Karen from some unpronounceable town in

Ohio complaining that her teenage daughter is sneaking out at night, possibly to meet her boyfriend, who is definitely part of the "wrong crowd." And there's Ozzie from Birmingham whose wife wanted that third kid and threatened to divorce him if he didn't agree. He saw no reason to add to the brood; two sons were enough for him—she could live without a little girl.

Through it all, Samantha, Dr. Sam, is cool and clear, as if she knows what she is talking about.

Fools.

They are all fools.

I glance up at the alligator staring down at me with its glassy, knowing eyes, and as I listen to Dr. Sam, I know my job is not yet finished.

I pick up the crumpled pages and spread them on the old, scarred wooden table, once a door, now propped on sawhorses. I read the story for a fourth time, noting the mistakes, wondering where the joke of a reporter got his "facts." Had the police intentionally duped him? Or was it a case of sloppy journalism, not even decent sensationalism? Where the hell was the editor, demanding more information, forcing the story of the prostitute's death onto page one?

No one is professional anymore.

That's the problem with this country! A pervasive lack of integrity to one's job.

Page three isn't acceptable.

Things will have to change.

I'm so irritated I actually see red in the eyes of Ipana, his toothy smile seeming to mock me from his position high on the wall. "They're morons," I tell him. "Cretins!" My skin itching with disgust, I flip through the pages and notice the moon riding high in the sky, shining a glimmer of silver light through the tiny window. I close my eyes and listen to the soft, sure cadence of her voice.

"This is Dr. Sam," she says easily. "Take care of yourself, New Orleans. Good night to you all and God bless. Remember, no matter what your troubles are today, there is always tomorrow."

A pause.

I wait, hearing the sound of water lapping at the poles supporting this cabin. A fish jumps.

Then: "Sweet dreams," she says, her voice vibrant and soulful over the radio waves as the music swells behind her in her signature sign-off.

I feel the corners of my lips twitch into a grin.

Sweet dreams?

Unlikely.

Is there "always tomorrow"?

I really don't think so.

In fact, I'm going to prove it.

CHAPTER 44

The nightmare came again.

Late at night, as determined as Satan's henchmen, it returned.

On silent footsteps, slipping into Val's subconscious, the looming, malicious beast appeared, black and tall, a silvery snake coiling through its hands.

The serpent's forked tongue flicked in and out, vibrating as it tested the air, its reptilian eyes sheathed with opaque lenses, the pits in its arrow-shaped head seeming to pulse with the cold blood that slid through its veins.

"You're on the lisssst," the viper hissed evilly, eyes unblinking. "There is no essssscape!" And it hung closer, slithering through its master's talonlike hands, coiling in the air, hanging so close to Val's face that she could feel its hot breath.

Frozen, she couldn't move, couldn't bat the evil head away. It seemed to smile, showing a near-white mouth and fangs that dripped with pearly drops of venom.

"Val, no—watch out!" Camille warned her, and Val caught a glimpse of something black, a wraith, rushing past, a cold breath of air in its wake.

Wait! Camille wait for me! she mouthed, but the words remained unformed over her tongue.

"Too late," the creature holding the snake croaked, its voice having the raspy timbre of an ancient crone. "She's gone."

"No!"

"She only got what she deserved," the demon-monster said. "And you know it."

"No! Cammie! Come back!" Val was searching everywhere, her heart pounding wildly, Camille's doom reverberating through her soul. "Don't leave me." She was crying now, sobbing. "Please, Cammie, come back. I didn't mean it. I didn't mean to send you away...Cammie!" Hot tears flowed from her eyes.

"Too late. Sssshee's gone! Dead!" This time it was the snake who spoke again, vile, horrid reptile.

Val tried to scream, and the creature holding the snake threw back its head and laughed, a shrill, shrieking sound like claws on a blackboard.

Val's skin crawled, and when she looked down, she saw it, too, had become shiny, her flesh turning to gunmetal-gray scales.

Again the hideous laughter and the looming beast showed its tiny teeth, no larger than those of a rat, in black gums that dripped poison.

"You're on the lisssst!"

With glittering, hungry eyes, the snake struck.

Val screamed, bracing for the sting of the bite.

"Valerie! Valerie!" Slade's voice sounded far off and echoed, as if he were on the far side of a long tunnel and was yelling at the top of his lungs. "Val! For God's sake, wake up!"

She blinked.

The darkness was gone, and in its stead was the soft glow of the bedside lamp. Slade was leaning over the bed, his strong hands on her shoulders as he shook her, forcing her to the surface of consciousness, pushing the horrifying nightmare back to the shadows of her mind. "Oh...God."

"You're okay. It was only a dream," he whispered.

"No...it was too real." But even as the words passed her lips, she knew she was lying. Already, in her tiny bedroom where rational thought wrestled with implausible fears and won, she was beginning to calm, her tense muscles relaxing, the fragments of her dream scurrying away.

"Shhh." Slade's arms enfolded her then, and he slid onto the bed beside her, on top of the covers while she lay beneath. "It's okay," he said into her hair, and kissed the top of her head.

Her face was damp with the tears still streaming from her eyes.

Thankful for his strength, for his calm while her emotions were a tempest, she clung to him and cried. For the sister she'd lost years before; for the woman Camille had become, the nun with her tainted vows; for the niece or nephew she would never meet, never know; and for the marriage she was hell-bent on destroying.

Long, soul-wrenching sobs broke from her throat. She'd denied it for so long, but the truth was that she would never see Camille again. They would never laugh together until they gasped, unable to catch their breaths and cry joyous tears, never fight tooth and nail, each so stubborn she wouldn't break down.

"Oh, Cammie," she wept aloud. "Oh, God."

Throughout the storm, Slade held her. Never saying a word, his arms strong, the beat of his heart steady, his breath ruffling her hair.

"I–I'm so sorry," she forced out.

"Shhh."

"No, Slade, I'm so damned sorry," she said when most of the rage that propelled her grief had slipped away. "For us and the way I treated you, for blaming you when I should have known..."

"It's over," he said, still attempting to calm her.

"Is it? For us? Is it too late?"

He paused and then whispered, "I don't know."

Neither did she. *Be careful what you wish for.* Hadn't she heard the saying a thousand times in her life? And hadn't she wished that she and Slade could divorce quickly? Hadn't she rued the day she'd met him? Hadn't she regretted getting married so quickly?

And now...

In bed, with only the ashes of the nightmare and Slade's strength, his resolute iron will, his once-vibrant love, she knew she'd been mistaken.

"I...I love you," she admitted brokenly.

"I know."

She waited a bit, sniffing. "You do?"

"I've always known. I was waiting for you to catch up."

"What?" She pulled her head back and looked up at him. "You're kidding, right? When someone bares their soul and says they love you, the normal response is, 'I love you, too.' "

"But you already know that. I've told you over and over."

She took in a long, shuddering breath. "Wait a second. Something's wrong here—why not now? Why can't you say it now?"

"Because it would be just the normal, expected response." His eyes darkened just slightly. "And I don't ever want us to get into that rut. To do what's expected. The common. When I tell you I love you, I want it to be heartfelt."

"Every damned time."

"Yep," he said. "At least." And then he kissed her. Long. Hard. With the passion that she remembered so vividly. She closed her eyes and didn't know how he managed to kick off his jeans and T-shirt, or how the bedside light was turned off, but all those things happened.

And she was with him again.

His hands sculpting down her rib cage, his mouth tasting as she remembered. His lips pressed urgently to hers—warm, demanding, and she responded, opening her mouth and feeling his tongue slip familiarly against her teeth.

Warmth rushed through her veins, and more, that special tingle that started at the base of her spine, grew upward and blossomed at the back of her neck.

He kissed the side of her face, then the curve of her neck, and she lolled back her head, the room fading into her subconscious, all sensation centered on him, this man who was her husband.

He slipped lower, tracing the hollow of her throat, laving the thin stretch of skin across the bones, concentrating on the pulse she knew was pounding there. She closed her eyes, lost herself to him as his hands found her breasts, strong fingers kneading gently at first and then more urgently as she began to breathe hard, short, and fast breaths that matched his.

"Slade," she whispered into the darkness as he found one nipple with his mouth and lazily rimmed it.

She wriggled in anticipation, warmth beginning to throb deep inside. Sweat breaking out across her skin. Desire throbbed through her brain, and she was filled with the scent and feel of him.

He breathed across the wet areola, and she thought she might scream with the want of him. Her fingers threaded through his hair as she pulled his head tight to her and he began to suckle.

Oh, God!

Desire, undulating through her, coursing in white-hot waves through her blood, caused her to move with a gentle but heated rhythm. She dug her fingers deep into his shoulders as he continued his quest, sliding ever lower, parting her, touching her and tasting her.

Hot, arcing thrills spasmed through her veins. Hotter and faster as his fingers and tongue explored her. Her mind was filled with the want of him, her body demanding more as he slid upward, keeping her legs parted with his body, kissing the perspiration from her skin.

With a moan, she touched the strident muscles of his shoulders and arms, her fingertips brushing his skin, causing the flesh to tighten.

"Careful," he warned as she skimmed her hands lower, across the washboard of his abdomen and along his hips.

"Never." She kissed him with wild abandon, savoring the salty taste of him on her tongue, drinking in the fresh scent of him, rediscovering the planes and angles of his body. The corded, long muscles of his arms, the thick strength of his shoulders and chest, the tight bunch of his buttocks, and the hard flesh of his thighs.

She touched him everywhere, kissed him where she could, pleasured him as long as she dared before he pulled her upward into his arms. Then, holding her fast beneath him, he levered himself upon his elbows and, looking into her eyes, slid her knees farther apart with his own.

She gasped as he hovered over her.

Then she waited.

Licked her lips in anticipation.

But he didn't move.

Just stared down at her.

"Slade?" she finally said.

"Yeah?"

"What is it? Why aren't you...?"

His smile stretched wide then, a white slash caught in the moonlight streaming through the open window.

"I am. In time."

"In time?"

"Uh-huh." He smoothed the hair away from her face, and she felt his hands tremble. "I love you, Valerie," he said, his voice gruff with sincerity as he thrust deep into her. "Goddamn it all to hell, I love you!"

Could she do it?

Really?

Leave St. Marguerite's forever?

Lucia swallowed hard and skimmed down the darkened hallways of the convent on her tiptoes, making certain she didn't create any sound whatsoever. Her hastily conceived plan that harkened back to the waywardness of her youth, rather than to her time at St. Marguerite's, had been forming in her brain for the past twenty-four hours, gelling. Perhaps if she left now, before the voice became louder, more insistent, she could save the life of another nun.

Maybe even her own.

Heart thudding, sweat collecting between her shoulder blades and on her palms, she hurried past the sconces, set low, her shadow passing like a ghost behind her, the long hallways seeming endless and narrow, closing in on her.

Around every corner, she expected to run into someone or some*thing*, though she didn't know what. Didn't want to know. The voice in her head was quiet tonight, but she was scared out of her mind that she would hear it again and that it would force her toward another gruesome death scene where one of her friends, another woman who had pledged her life to God, would be dead, skin cold, eyes lifeless.

She shuddered and kept moving, down the stairs, her feet as quiet as moth's wings. Along the corridor past the chapel and farther to the back door of the mother superior's office she hurried.

Over her own shallow breathing and the clamoring of her heart, she thought she heard the drop of a footstep, the scrape of leather against the old, hard floors.

You're just imagining things. No one is up. No one is following you. You're the only one stalking around in the middle of the night.

But that wasn't true, was it? Sister Camille had been walking the halls around midnight, and so had Sister Asteria, right? The police thought they had made it to the crime scenes on their own two legs. And hadn't she herself seen someone escaping the chapel on the night of Camille's death? Then there was Sister Edwina—hadn't Lucia seen her walking the halls late at night?

They weren't the only ones.

Lucia stopped.

Held her breath.

Closed her eyes and listened, her ears straining.

Was that a footstep?

Or not?

Had whatever she'd heard stopped?

Opening her eyes, she looked over her shoulder to the long, dark hallway where she saw only blackness between the thin pools of light cast by the low-lit sconces. Was the demon lurking there? Were his red eyes hidden in the murky umbra? Was he waiting, teeth glistening?

Her heart was beating a thousand times a minute, sweat sliding down her face. She swiped it aside with the sleeve of her habit and, telling herself that she couldn't let fear paralyze her, continued quickly on, her feet barely skimming the floor as she finally reached the back door to Sister Charity's office, which she knew was always unlocked.

Biting her lip, she twisted the handle, pushed on the panels, and stepped over the threshold.

She shut the door behind her with a soft click and made her way to the mother superior's desk.

In the dark, she stubbed her toe on the sharp corner of a bookcase.

"Ssss." She sucked in her breath and bit back the urge to cry out.

She couldn't let anyone at the convent know what she was up to.

Never.

Slowly, her eyes adjusted to the darkness and the moonlit shadows in the room where the sparse furniture was cast in shades of gray. She crossed stealthily to the desk, then waited, forcing her breath to slow, her heart to calm.

She listened as she reached for the phone.

Was that a footstep in the hallway?

Her hand froze over the receiver, hovering in the still air.

No... nothing.

Quit freaking yourself out! Just do what you have to do!

Without making the slightest noise, she plucked the receiver from its cradle and, while the dial tone buzzed its loud, flat sound into her ear, dialed the number she'd memorized:

Cruz Montoya's cell.

Her heart was hammering, tiny prayers going through her mind as the phone rang somewhere far away.

Hail Mary, full of grace...

Ring!

The Lord is with thee...

Ring!

Blessed are thou—

"Cruz Montoya." His voice was gruff, thick with sleep.

Lucia's knees went weak, and she braced herself on the edge of the desk. Her heart pounded crazily in her ears.

This was a mistake!

"Hello?" he said, angry now. "Hello! Oh, for the love of—"

"It's Lucia," she whispered quickly, trying to pull herself together. Her voice sounded too loud. Surely someone would hear her.

"Lucia?" he repeated.

"Yes! Can you meet me?"

"What?"

"I said—"

"I know what you said, but now?" He sounded less groggy, as if he was finally awake.

"In about half an hour."

"Do you know what time it is?"

"Of course. But I need to see you. It's urgent."

A pause. "So you changed your mind about never wanting to see me again, is that it?"

She'd forgotten just how maddening he could be.

"Please, Cruz. I need your help."

A pause. She counted the seconds. At five he said, "Oookay," as if he wasn't certain.

Her heart nearly fell through the floor. "I wouldn't have called if it wasn't important!" she whispered, worried that he wouldn't do as she asked. Then what? She didn't have a plan B.

"So then where? At the convent?" His voice was wary, as if he expected there to be some trick to her request.

"No!" Panic flooded through her. "Not here. Meet me at... There's a gas station and mini-mart on Rampart, near the park."

"You're serious?" Doubt had crept into his voice.

"Yes," she said, looking over her shoulder, feeling as if this very room had eyes and ears all its own, as if she were being observed. She shivered, suddenly cold as death. "I'm as serious as I've been about anything in my life."

She heard it then.

The pad of footsteps.

Heart in her throat, she slowly replaced the receiver and, careful not to stub her toe again, slid into a dark corner that would be behind the door as it opened, in the corner by the bookcase.

She held her breath, the tread coming closer, her heart's thudding cadence in counterpoint.

Don't come in here. Please, please, please... don't—

Then, almost automatically, as she heard the footsteps pause outside the door, she grabbed the door's knob and held fast.

On the other side, someone tried to twist it open.

Lucia strained, put all her muscle into it.

The pressure released.

She didn't give up. Held tight.

Again, the doorknob tried to turn.

Sweat rained down her forehead, dampening her palms. The knob slid a bit but didn't give.

She heard a snort of disgust on the other side; then the pressure released.

Lucia bit her lip. Didn't move.

But the footsteps moved on. Threading down the hallway. Which direction?

Lucia's throat was as dry as the Sahara. Her skin wet with nervous sweat.

Did she dare try to leave, to stick her head out of Sister Charity's office? So what if someone caught her?

No! No one can see you or you won't be able to meet Cruz! Time is passing.

She counted off sixty seconds and was about to open the door when she heard another lock click softly.

What?

From where?

She whipped her head around, searching for the sound.

Again the soft tread of footsteps, but this time coming from the other side of the main door to Sister Charity's office, in the outer reception area, where Eileen Moore's desk was located.

Oh, sweet Jesus!

In a few seconds, whoever it was would be inside. There was no time to leap across the room and try to lock the door now! Nor did she have the option of holding it in her hands as she had this one. Not unless she wanted to be exposed.

Lucia figured she had no option but try to escape. Holding on to her fraying nerves as best she could, she waited half a second; then, just as she heard the doorknob twist on the main door, she opened the back and slipped through, closing it without a click.

She took off like a shot. Running away, her footsteps light as a butterfly's wings, the hem of her habit swooshing against the floor.

She rounded the corner just as she heard the door through which she'd just passed open again.

The intruder would know it hadn't been locked.

He'd figure out that someone had been inside.

Oh, dear God!

Lucia only hoped she could get away before whoever it was realized it was her. Sending up a quick prayer, she hurried up the stairs, and as she reached the landing, turning toward the next floor, she heard the voice again, that vile, rasping snarl as loud as it had ever been:

Pssssssstttt.

This time she wouldn't listen.

This time she'd break the cruel chain that had been tethering her.

This time, just maybe, she'd save a life, but in her mind's eye, she already saw the images, quick black and white snapshots of a woman, in a bridal gown, grasping the tightening chain at her neck, her mouth moving beneath her veil like a fish out of water, desperately trying to take in air through gills that wouldn't function.

Was it too late already?

She cast a worried look over her shoulder, seeing nothing but darkness.

Psssssst! the voice sibilated as the midnight bells began to toll mournfully.

Under their dulcet peals, chasing after her in the night-shaded hallways, was the creeping hiss of indecent laughter.

CHAPTER 45

Montoya couldn't sleep.

The case was getting to him, and even after a long lovemaking session with Abby, he tossed and turned, unable to find the peace of mind to drop off.

He'd rolled toward her one last time, and as he'd slipped his arm around her waist, Abby had sighed contentedly, wiggling her rump into his crotch and causing him to get hard all over again.

She felt it, too, and said, "Not again, Detective. Our little guy is going to wake up soon."

"Well, my little guy is interested."

"Tell him to give it a rest." She scooted away and sighed deeply into the pillow, so he rolled over and told himself to slow down, think hard, work out the kinks in the murders.

Clifton Sharkey was still in his sights because of the bad alibi for the Camille Renard murder. He'd sworn that he'd only lied to protect himself, that he was afraid that the cops wouldn't buy the fact that he was home alone, not with his record.

Frank O'Toole was still on the radar, too. The fact that he'd cowered behind his father's three-piece suit and law degree wasn't helping his case, not with Montoya.

Father Thomas Blaine was due back in town tomorrow. Montoya meant to meet him at his office first thing in the morning.

Then there was Father John.

The real deal, back from the supposed goddamned dead? Or a copycat?

Montoya felt that the murderer was just toying with them, whoever the hell he was, that the murder of the prostitute might be meant to throw them off the case.

Where the hell were the missing bridal gowns? Was it significant that two of the victims, the nuns, had been adopted out of St. Elsinore's? Not so with Grace Blanc, the working girl.

There were too many loose ends in this case and no way to tie them up.

Tomorrow night was the auction at St. Elsinore's.

Montoya planned to be there.

He heard a noise.

The baby?

He listened, his father radar on alert.

No. It was Cruz. Probably getting up to use the crapper. Sure enough, he heard the toilet flush, and then damned Cruz walked down the hall and out the back door.

Montoya glanced at the digital clock.

Twelve-seventeen.

What the hell?

He rolled out of bed just as he heard the sound of Cruz's Harley roar to life, then a tire chirp.

Montoya walked to the back door and stared out to see the red taillight of Cruz's motorcycle wink bloodred, like the eye of a dying Cyclops. "Hey!" he yelled, but it was far too late, and the sound of the motorcycle winding through its gears slowly faded.

He turned to walk into the house again and nearly ran into Abby, her hair mussed, her eyes squinting. "What's going on?" she asked around a yawn.

"I wish I knew," he said, and closed the door. "I wish to hell that I knew."

She offered him a bit of a grin. "Can I buy you a drink?" she teased.

"A little late for that, but . . . ?" He arched a suggestive eyebrow.

"But?" she replied, responding in kind.

He grabbed her and hauled her off her feet. She let out a squeal of surprise. "You're bad, Montoya!" But she was laughing.

"That I am, woman, and I intend to show you just what it means."

"Oh, God, save me from the husband with bad come-on lines," she said, but giggled as he kissed her more roughly than usual, growling against her neck. She laughed outright at his tough-guy tactics, and they tumbled onto the bed together while Cruz took off for who knew where.

Cruz waited under the flickering fluorescent lights of the gas station.

Lucia was late.

Or wasn't coming at all, had just pulled his leg.

No, that thought didn't sit well. He lit his last cigarette, crushed the pack, and told himself he'd give her five more minutes. No more.

And what then?

Just leave?

No way, tough guy. She's in trouble. You'll wait.

Disgusted with himself, he took a long drag and told himself no matter what, this was his last smoke. He'd quit years ago, only bought a pack a couple of days ago because of Lucia. He'd gone a little nuts seeing her again.

Stupid reason.

The gas station was open. An all-nighter. One pimply faced kid in a stocking cap and mechanic's suit with his name, "Al," on a patch sewn between the zipper and shoulder was manning the pumps and till. In Cruz's estimation, Al couldn't be more than nineteen, maybe twenty, but there he was, head bent into his cell phone, texting like mad but available if someone drove up and needed service.

He smoked in silence, feeling the thrum of the city, despite the fact that it was quiet, the middle of the night.

New Orleans was never asleep. Along with the humidity, the heavy air on his skin, and the wash of neon lights on the streets nearby, there was an underlying current of energy that throbbed just beneath the surface of the night. Invisible but palpable.

A car slowed for a red light, an old Chevy rattling and wheezing as it idled, the single guy behind the wheel eyeing the gas station for a second. But the light changed and the Nova rolled noisily away.

Cruz checked his watch and jangled the keys in the pocket of his leather jacket. Where the hell was she?

From the corner of his eye, he saw movement, a woman crossing the empty street.

If he hadn't been looking for her, he wouldn't have recognized Lucia. Dressed in jeans, a long-sleeved T-shirt, and a cardigan sweater, her hair braided and slung over one shoulder, a large pack strapped to her back, Lucia Costa looked more like a coed on a backpacking trip than a woman who'd so recently sworn she wanted to take her final vows to become a nun.

He crushed out the Camel and met her at his bike, its chrome pipes and black paint so shiny it looked wet as it gleamed beneath the glowing fluorescent tubes.

"Hey," he said, trying to sound casual, even though his pulse had kicked up just at the sight of her. "What's going on? What're you doing?"

"Escaping," she said, and flashed him a nervous smile that tore at his heart.

"From the convent." It was a statement.

"Yeah."

"How'd you get out?"

"We all know how. It's not a prison, not really, though lately..." She glanced anxiously over her shoulder. "Can we just go?"

"Where?"

"Somewhere we can talk."

"At one in the morning?"

"If that's what time it is now, then yes." Her big brown eyes implored him, and he figured, what did he have to lose? "Sure," he said, wondering where the hell this would go. "Hop on."

The honest thing to do, Lucia knew, as she sat in the all-night diner in the middle of the night, would be to ask Cruz to take her to the bus station, to tell him that she never wanted to see him again and ask him not to follow.

But that would only lead to more problems.

More lies.

More heartbreak.

And she wouldn't really be able to disappear.

No, she had to carry out her hastily conceived plan. There were holes in it, yes, she knew that, but she would rely on God to see her through this.

She had to dupe him.

And then atone like crazy.

Please help me, she silently prayed, then dredged an oily French fry through a pool of ketchup in her shrimp basket. Cruz had found the diner, located on the outskirts of town, the place nearly dead.

Paddle fans moved lazily over a long Formica counter with a metallic trim and a row of empty stools covered in red faux leather. The only waitress, a slim African American, was refilling the slowly turning pie display with thick slices of key lime, Dutch apple, banana cream, and Georgia peach pies, if the boxes stacked on the counter were to be believed.

The place reeked of well-used cooking oil, fried onions, and a thin layer of smoke, which Lucia was able to view through the opening between the back of the counter and the kitchen. Past the hanging pots and pans, she noticed the open door that led to the parking area.

A fry cook in a grease-splattered apron was standing in the shadows, shoulder propped on the exterior doorjamb as he sucked hard on a cigarette. With the cook was a busboy who was leaning on a broom while lighting up.

Cruz and Lucia were seated in a corner booth, toward the back of the long, narrow building, away from the plate-glass windows looking out onto the highway. She was eating the remains of her shrimp basket; he was ignoring his cheeseburger but working on his second beer.

His hair was mussed and shining black, his eyes a deep chocolate brown and rimmed in suspicion. The tiny scar slicing one eyebrow, reminding her of the accident that nearly took her life, seemed a little more evident today.

"So you're leaving the convent, and you think it's best if you run away?" he asked, his brown eyes slitted as he studied her.

"Yes."

"Why?"

"Because of the murders. It's... unsafe."

"You think the killer will come after you?"

She wanted to tell him about the voice, about her fear, about how she was compelled to do its bidding, whatever it was, but she couldn't—didn't want to sound as if she'd totally gone off her rocker.

Cruz knew enough about her ESP, or curse or whatever you wanted to call it, as it was.

"You found the bodies?"

She nodded.

"How?"

"I... I was up. I guess I heard something. I can't really say. I just know that I sensed something was wrong." That was downplaying the urgency she'd felt, the compulsion to go where her mind led her, the urgency with which the hiss had prodded her.

"You're the one who sent Camille Renard's prepaid cell phone to the police, right?"

"Oh. You... you know about that?"

"Put two and two together. Found you near the post office, then overheard my brother telling someone on the phone about the phone showing up."

She nodded, couldn't lie. "She'd left it with me. For safekeeping. She was afraid Sister Charity might find it, and she had the BlackBerry...then...then she was killed and...I didn't know what to do."

"You were close to her."

She thought of Camille, and a great sadness swept through her. "Yes." She met his inquisitive gaze. "The world isn't all in black and white, not colored like a nun's habit or a priest's vestments. There are shades of gray in it, and Camille, she was all about those hues. Sometimes pure as snow, other times black as sin, most often somewhere in between. But, yes, I was close to her, and I miss her like crazy." She fought a spate of tears and blinked hard.

Cruz shifted his gaze away, then downed the rest of his beer.

"I made a mistake in keeping it, so I sent it to the police department." She shook her head, looked at the door. "I should have given it up immediately."

"It probably would have made things easier."

Five more customers arrived, and unlike Cruz and Lucia, who spoke in soft tones, they were loud, probably half-drunk, and fell into a booth near the front of the building. There were three muscle-bound guys with shaved heads and skintight, sleeveless shirts to show off their tattoos and two women. One in a short skirt, tights, and cropped T-shirt, the other in a sundress and cowboy boots.

Reluctantly, the waitress sauntered up to them and scribbled down their orders in between questions and jokes, laughter, and, from one of the men, a demand for a "round" of beer.

"Make it light beer," Cowboy Boots insisted, and her friend laughed as the guys shook their shiny pates.

"So why me?" Cruz asked once he'd swung his attention back to Lucia. "When you were pretty damned sure you never wanted to lay eyes on me again."

She winced and for once tonight was honest. "I knew you'd come."

"Lucky I was still in town."

"I know." She nodded and sucked up the remains of her diet soda through her straw.

"So what now?"

"I want you to take me away."

That stopped him cold.

"I mean that literally. I've thought about it. I want to go to Houston. From there I'll figure it out."

"What's in Houston?"

"Not St. Marguerite's."

"You're giving up on your vows."

"I don't know. Probably. The archdiocese won't take kindly to me leaving in the middle of the night without telling anyone. I'll call as soon as it's light. Stop long enough to let Sister Charity know that I'm okay and that I haven't been abducted or...or anything," she added, thinking of Sister Camille and Sister Asteria.

She probably didn't have to be so devious. She could, she supposed, just have Cruz drive her somewhere and leave her. But was that really possible? If she spent more time with him, touched him, probably kissed him again, would she be able to let him go? Even now she was having second thoughts.

No...this was best.

"I just need to use the bathroom," she said.

"Me too."

"There's only one," she said. "Unisex."

"Ladies first." He drained his beer. "I'll pay up." He climbed to his feet, and as he did, she stood on her tiptoes and slipped one arm around his waist, her fingers sliding into the pocket of his jacket as she kissed him lightly on the lips.

"Thank you, Cruz," she said, seeing that he was stunned. Her fingers discovered his key ring. She closed it in her fist, then stepped away from him and hurried down the hall.

He stared after her as she pushed open the door to the restroom. *Don't let him search for his keys, oh, please.*

Heart hammering in her ears, she used the toilet, washed, and was out of the restroom just as Cruz was leaving bills on the table. Her throat was dry, her palms wet, and she felt as if she were drowning in her own perfidy.

Oh, Holy Mother, help me.

As she left the restroom, she met him in the hallway. His eyes were dark, flashing.

He knows!

Her knees nearly buckled.

To her surprise, he grabbed her and dragged her against him, pulling her tight, her body fitting to his. "I hope you know what you're doing," he said, breathing hard against her lips, "because I sure as hell don't." Before she could pull away, he kissed her. Hard.

Passion seething between them. She felt the brush of his whiskers and tasted the hint of beer and cigarettes.

The fever running hot in his blood seemed to seep into hers.

I want you, she thought wildly.

She sagged against him for a crazy instant, felt a moment's regret, and opened her mouth as he tasted her. The world seemed to melt away, the sounds of the diner disappearing over the thudding of her heart, the desire thundering through her blood.

No, no, no! But she didn't stop. Couldn't.

When he finally lifted his head and stared into her eyes, his were hot. Intense. Her skin was throbbing, tingling.

His voice was ragged as he said, "It's not a sin if you renounce your vows," he said.

"I... I haven't taken the final ones."

"Lucia, think about it."

Her heart cracked, and she wondered for a moment if she'd ever stopped loving him. For years she'd told herself her fascination with the man was a schoolgirl crush.

Now...?

But loving him would be an act of supreme idiocy.

Swallowing hard, feeling guilty as sin, knowing she was using him like the kind of women she abhorred, she said, "I will, Cruz," and though she meant it, that she would consider renouncing her vows, had already decided, in fact, she knew she couldn't, wouldn't, consider his underlying question. There was no future for the two of them. She knew it now; he'd know it in a few minutes.

He let her go and walked into the bathroom.

Lucia didn't wait an instant. She grabbed her backpack, put it over her shoulders, and pushed her way out the back door, past the busboy who was emptying the trash from a smaller can to the large bins near the parking lot. The smell of old coffee grounds, rotting vegetables, and bad fish soiled the air.

Lucia barely noticed as she jogged across the lot and told herself she could do this. She could steal a motorcycle; she could ride it without skidding into a ditch or hitting another vehicle.

It's just like riding a bike—once you learn, you never forget! Or so her cousin, Juan, had once insisted.

Oh, Holy Father, she hoped that just once Juan knew what he was talking about!

She was already fumbling with the keys as she reached the Harley. Her heart was pounding crazily, her hands sweating so badly that she nearly dropped the key ring.

Come on, come on, she told herself. It had been years since she'd driven a motorcycle, and then it had been her cousin's little Honda, half the power of Cruz's beast of a machine.

Adrenaline screaming through her veins, she threw her leg over the seat, started the bike, and took off. The Harley growled, tires chirping and laying rubber as it streaked forward.

Cruz's helmet flew off the handle bars to bounce behind her across the asphalt of the parking lot.

"Hey!" A man's voice followed her, and she looked over her shoulder to see Cruz, feet planted shoulder-width apart, backlit by the diner, a tall, broad-shouldered, and far-too-sexy man. As if it finally hit him that she was actually taking off and leaving him, he started forward at a dead run, all the while yelling her name.

Too late.

Lucia lowered her head as the engine whined. She shifted, and the bike hit a pothole in the parking lot, shimmied, then straightened as she reached the street. She slowed slightly, then gunned it.

Hang in there. You can do this, she told herself, but sent up a quick prayer, just in case God was listening.

The headlamp burned bright as the thick Louisiana night rushed by, the wind catching her braid so that it streamed behind her like a long black snake.

She roared past a park and told herself to obey the traffic laws, to not push the speed limit and risk being pulled over. Not until she reached the freeway. Then she could let the Harley out, run it through its gears, and ride, as her cousin would say, "hell-bent for leather."

She rounded a corner, sweeping through an amber light as she headed northwest.

Was it her imagination, or did she hear the hiss of sibilant laughter over the roar of the Harley's big engine?

Heart in her throat, she closed her mind to the images of a dying nun, her throat rimmed in blood as she lay over a bed of glinting metal, the blood dripping onto her tattered gown, her face blurred beneath the veil.

"Psssst!"

"Leave me alone!" she cried to the rising wind. She saw the signs for the freeway and stepped on the gas to leave New Orleans and Cruz Montoya behind forever.

CHAPTER 46

So I slept with my husband, Valerie thought. *So what?* No big deal, right?

Then why did it feel massive? As if Val's life had shifted on its axis?

Oh, for the love of God, she was starting to sound like some starry-eyed heroine in a chick flick. *Stop it,* she told herself, and rolled over.

Slade was lying on his stomach, arms folded under his squashed pillow, his head twisted in her direction. The sheets were tangled and bunched over his buttocks. He slept soundly, snoring softly, his face relaxed, his tanned skin in contrast to the white sheets. A shock of hair fell over his eyes, and dark lashes rested against his cheeks. Her heart filled at the sight of him as it had so long ago. She stared at the width of his shoulders and the slope of his spine, all taut muscles covered with smooth, golden skin.

Why had she been resisting him so long?

What was wrong with falling in love with her own husband?

Especially one she felt now had been vindicated, falsely accused by yours truly.

With a sleepy groan, he rolled onto his back, his entire torso exposed, his erection evident.

"Gettin' an eyeful?" he asked in a voice rough with slumber.

"You're awake?" she said, and couldn't help the heat that washed up the back of her neck.

His smile slowly stretched from one side of his beard-darkened jaw to the other. "Like what you see?"

"You're incorrigible."

"I love it when you talk dirty to me." He rolled off the bed and, as stark naked as she, wrapped his arms around her and pressed his mouth to hers.

"Oh, for the love of—"

Still kissing her, he walked her backward into the small bathroom, reached into the shower, and before it warmed, pushed her through the tiny opening and under the bracing spray. She squealed, with him laughing, and as the water temperature heated, so did she, her blood pounding as his hand moved across her slick skin. Using a bar of soap, he washed her, kissed her, and pinned her against the tiles where he lifted her onto his thick erection, sliding her easily onto him as the water cascaded over them.

She blinked against the spray and gasped at the depth of his penetration, the breath squeezed from her lungs, her breasts flattened and soapy.

"Oh...oh...oh, God, Slade," she cried as the first wave of orgasm crashed over her. Convulsing, sputtering, feeling spasm after spasm of release, she clung to him, arms wrapped around his neck, legs surrounding his hips as he thrust upward, his breathing as rapid as her own, her back sliding against the wet tile. Melting inside, she dug her fingers into his shoulders.

Again he plunged deep into her.

And again.

And again.

Until she closed her eyes and let out a deep-throated sound she didn't recognize as her own voice.

"Oh, God," he ground out, then shuddered a release, his head thrown back, the cords of his neck distended as he came inside her, stiffening, every muscle in his body contracting.

For several seconds the water washed over them, and slowly their breathing slowed. She was eye level with him, staring deep into his smokey gaze, watching drops drizzle from his hair and off the tip of his nose.

"You're incredible," he said, and she laughed.

"Uh, you did all the work."

"My pleasure, ma'am."

"I told you that aw-shucks, country-boy charm doesn't work with me."

He laughed then, still holding her, still inside her. "No? God, I'd love to see what happens when something does work. I might just have a heart attack!"

"I hope not. Think of all the fun we'd be missing." She kissed him soundly on the mouth then, the shower still spraying them, then disentangled herself and grabbed a towel. "What a difference a few days make." She was thinking of earlier in the week when an intruder had been in her home as she'd stood under the shower's spray.

"Hey!" He grabbed her arm. "About last night—"

"Pretty damned great, right?" she teased.

He didn't smile. "Yeah, it was. But before. You had a nightmare..."

"The same one I've had for years. I had it as a child, and for a long time it was gone...then..." She thought for a moment and didn't want to dwell too deeply on the monsters of her subconscious. "It's returned."

"Since when?" he asked, and she didn't have to think too hard.

"Since I came back to New Orleans," she admitted, but didn't add, *Since I left you back in Bad Luck.*

"You want to talk about it?"

"No." She was certain of that. Thinking of the dream would only shatter the peace of mind they'd found together, ruin it all. "Maybe later."

"Seriously?"

"Yes." She looked straight into his eyes, where drips of water were still starring his lashes. "In time." She slipped out of his grip and steadfastly shoved all thoughts of the nightmare from her mind.

Once she'd toweled off and thrown on her robe, she started coffee and let an anxious Bo out as the warm Louisiana sun began to warm the day. Lights were on in the main house, and birds were already chattering, though traffic was sluggish, as it was the weekend.

Slade, dressed only in low-slung jeans, walked into the kitchen. "You could get lucky today," he said with a wink.

"I thought I already did."

"That was me. But I could take you out to breakfast. What about beignets down by the river? I'd even spring for some fancy coffee drink—you know, the kind those people in the Northwest are so nuts about."

"A latte?"

"Or whatever."

"Sure, but first I have a few duties here. Let me help Freya and then we'll—"

Her cell phone rang and she picked it up. She didn't recognize the number on the caller ID but answered anyway. "Hello?" she said as Bo whined to be let in and the coffeemaker gurgled.

Nothing.

"Hello?"

Her heart froze.

"Is anyone there?"

"You're nexxxxxxt," the snakelike voice hissed. "And there is no essssscape."

As the sun crested the eastern sky and fingers of gray light slipped through the streets and alleys of New Orleans, Montoya found his brother outside. Cruz was seated on the back stoop, Hershey lying at his feet, his battered motorcycle helmet at his side, a cigarette burning, unsmoked between his fingers.

To top things off, Cruz smelled like a brewery.

The motorcycle was conspicuously missing, probably lost in an all-night poker game.

"Trouble?" Montoya asked as Hershey climbed to his feet and nudged his leg for a pet.

"Nothin' I haven't faced before." Cruz looked up and sighed. "Boy, did I fuck up," he said.

"Want to talk about it?"

"Hell, no!"

Montoya sat on the stoop beside him and waited. Cruz crushed his cigarette under the heel of his boot; then reluctantly, pissed as hell at himself, he told his brother about his night.

* * *

Sister Charity was beside herself.

Two nuns missing this morning? *Two?*

She swept down the hallway, the skirts of her habit rustling, her rosary beads clacking, her hem brushing across the floor.

Oh, Holy Mother, be with me.

They had searched the grounds and the rooms, but nowhere could she find Sister Lucia and Sister Louise.

Where could they be?

Worry ate at her, causing her stomach to burn with acid and her mind to travel to dark places inhabited by Lucifer himself. *Don't go there,* she silently reprimanded herself as she walked through Sister Lucia's room one last time. It was empty, all her earthly possessions gone, the bed neatly made.

Sister Louise's room, however, was just the opposite. It looked very inhabited, the impression on her mattress visible still, the sheets rumpled, the covers thrown off. But the bed was cold to the touch. Cold as death.

Charity's heart constricted. Fear seeped into her soul, and even the corners of her eyes felt tight, as if pulled by imaginary strings.

Thankfully, she thought, no bodies had been found.

Maybe they left.

Together.

The difference in their rooms mere indications of their different personalities.

Perhaps fear had driven them away. And what part of that fear could she ascribe to herself, forever clucking after them like a mother hen or guarding over them like a hawk? Had she been kinder, wiser in her administration, more loving and less rigid, perhaps she wouldn't be looking for them now.

Forgive me.

She'd spent the very early hours of the morning praying, searching and telling herself she was panicking for no reason, that the frantic drum of her heart was an overreaction; but now she was convinced. All her rules, the extra security, the new locks and police driving by St. Marguerite's was to no avail.

She walked into her office and realized she'd received a message, one that came in, according to the recorder, a few minutes after five a.m., a time she was never at her desk.

Clicking the PLAY button, she heard a voice she recognized, one she'd prayed she would hear again.

"Reverend Mother, this is Lucia. Lucia Costa. I want you to know I'm fine. I left the order this morning, and I'm on my way to a new life. I realize you might not trust this message, that you might think I'm being coerced into leaving it, but please, trust me, I'm safe. May the Holy Mother's grace be with you."

Click.

The message was over.

Sister Charity sank into her chair and replayed the message twice, telling herself she didn't hear a sound of distress in the girl's voice, that Sister Lucia wasn't lying.

Where had she gone?

Why didn't she say?

Because she's tired of your meddling.

Because she's afraid.

Because she doesn't want to be found.

Sister Charity bowed her head, felt all of her sixty-seven years, not old by any means, she'd told herself, but this morning she was weary. Her joints ached and she felt ancient, the relic she'd heard more than one novitiate call her. Not yet the dinosaur that Sister Irene thought she was.

She placed her elbows on the top of the desk, cast one quick glance at the picture of the Pope, and prayed to the Holy Father for guidance, for help. She was humbled. Afraid. Didn't know what to do.

In her mind, she heard the voice of God.

Follow your heart, Charity, my child. You know the truth. You know what you must do. Be obedient yet vigilant, firm yet kind. Trust yourself and those around you. Believe in me and in my Son and in the Holy Spirit. Trust the Holy Trinity.

When she whispered a soft "amen," she realized her eyes were filled with tears and that she'd been weeping in both sorrow and joy. Her cheeks were damp, salty drops falling onto the top of her desk.

She tried to pull herself together. Her grief would not over-shadow her faith; her fear would not thwart her courage. She, as the handmaiden of God, would prevail.

Yet her hand was shaking when she reached for the phone and dialed St. Elsinore's parish. Though it was barely seven, someone answered, probably due to the fact that tonight was the auction for which the parish of St. Elsinore's had been planning for over a year.

When she was finally connected to Sister Georgia, Charity forced herself to murmur a few pleasantries she didn't feel and imagined the mother superior at the orphanage without her wimple, veil, and habit. A modern woman was Sister Georgia, a nun with both feet securely set on the sod of the two-thousands, and yet, deep in her heart, she was as staid in her ways, as structured in her beliefs as was Charity.

She had to be.

They both learned their lessons from Sister Ignatia, together at St. Elsinore's, as orphans. Both Georgia and Charity had grown up within the crumbling walls that were now, for the first time in nearly two hundred years, being emptied of their charges, eyed for possible demolition.

A travesty.

"So, what can I do for you?" Georgia asked after they got through trivialities.

"I want to speak to Father Thomas," Charity said, girding her loins for battle. She and Georgia were like competitive siblings, always trying to outdo each other.

"He's not in right now. But I'd be glad to give him a message."

I just bet you would. "Is he ever there?" Charity asked, unable to keep the bite from her words.

"He's a busy man. The Lord's work is never done."

"I'm well aware of that," she said, and decided she had to tell Georgia what was happening. "I'm hoping he'll consider rescheduling the auction," she said, knowing she was asking the impossible. "We have a . . . situation here at St. Marguerite's. Another one of my novitiates has gone missing . . . well, maybe even two, and as it is, I think it would be disrespectful to go on with any kind of festivities."

There was a long pause and then a sigh on the other end of the line. "I understand," Georgia said, surprisingly accommodating, "but you know, it's too late. The invitations have been sent, the tickets sold, the hotel ballroom booked, the caterers and women of the church who have gone to all the trouble to get the refreshments and dinner ready. Oh, Charity, you and I both know what Father Thomas's response will have to be. I'm sorry," she said.

"Me, too, Georgia." There was no reason to press the issue. Even before her request had been presented to Father Thomas, wherever in the world he was, Georgia had squelched it.

Of course.

"I'm not certain that the choir will be able to perform."

"Surely they will. For their lost sisters. For the Holy Father. I know this is a time of great trouble for you, Charity, but this auction is for the good of the very place we called home for so many years. Even Sister Ignatia, bless her heart, is going to attend. Father Thomas is going to wheel her in, though she'll have an attendant, of course."

Just how old was Ignatia, the woman who had helped raise her and yet terrorized her? Ninety-five? A hundred? Even older. Sixty years ago, she'd been a miserable woman in her forties, and the years surely hadn't improved her sour, almost cruel disposition.

In Charity's opinion, Sister Ignatia had scarred more children than she'd helped.

"It's going to be grand," Georgia said on a sigh, as if she were a debutante going to her first ball.

"If you say so," Charity whispered, but didn't believe it for a moment, not with two of the novitiates confirmed dead—murdered, here on the hallowed grounds of St. Marguerite's Cathedral—and two more missing.

"I do. You'll see."

Charity took in a long, deep breath as she hung up. She rubbed her fingers across the smooth, worn surface of her desk, her heart heavy.

Why was she being tested?

She glanced at the crucifix hung on the wall over her door. Jesus's gaunt frame was etched in dark wood, but even so, the scars of his wounds, the crown of thorns, the nails pounded through his hands and feet, were visible.

How could she possibly think her own pain was anything when she thought of his agony? She crossed herself, closed her eyes, and whispered several prayers.

Then, squaring her shoulders, she picked up the receiver again.

This time to call the police.

CHAPTER 47

Montoya stormed into the station. He took the steps two at a time and strode directly to Bentz's office without bothering to drop his sidearm at his desk or grab a cup of coffee from the kitchen.

He'd forgone his run this morning and was itching for a fight.

Bentz was just reading his e-mail while the rest of the department came to life. Cops chatting, keys rattling, phones jangling, air conditioner wheezing, the weekend staff already arriving. The smells were there, too, fresh coffee mingled with floor polish, a burning smell from the overworked copy machine, and the stale odor of human sweat, left over from a recent booking.

All part of the ambience.

"We need to find my brother's Harley!" Montoya announced, irritated beyond belief. "Right now it's probably heading northwest on the ten, heading toward Houston or Texas or Arkansas or goddamned Oklahoma! And it's being ridden by our star witness."

"Slow down," Bentz suggested, waving him into a side chair near the corner of his desk. "What the hell are you talking about?"

Montoya preferred to stand and took a spot near the window. "My son of a bitch of a brother," Montoya said, fury singing through his blood. "What a fuckin' idiot!" He glanced at Bentz and said, "Don't even start with some joke about it running in the family."

And then he launched into the story that Cruz had told him on the stoop a couple of hours earlier. He explained that Lucia Costa, Sister Lucia, who was romantically involved with Cruz as a girl, had called him, begged for his help because she wanted to leave the convent in the dead of night. She hadn't wanted to face Sister Charity or something, was scared, she'd claimed, then stolen his bike and left Cruz to walk back to Montoya's house. She'd also admitted to having mailed Camille Renard's prepaid cell phone to the police—in an act of contrition or something, which Cruz might believe but Montoya didn't.

Then again, Cruz was pissed. Furious that he'd been played for a fool, he'd stopped at a couple bars on Bourbon Street before he'd returned, tail between his legs, and waited for Montoya to wake up to give him the great news. "The last thing he saw was the taillight, heading, he suspected, to the freeway. The only reason he knows she was heading west was that she mentioned Houston, but hell, that could be a lie! She could be heading to California or New York City or the fuckin' Yukon! Sheeeeit!" He kicked at Bentz's metal wastebasket, bending it with the toe of his boot, then shoved a hand through his hair, wanting to wring his brother's neck. "Dumbass!"

"Careful with the government-issued office equipment!"

"That trash can has 1965 written all over it!" And, from the looks of it, had been kicked a time or two before.

Bentz, Montoya noticed, wasn't feeling the same ire that fueled his blood.

Bentz asked calmly, "You put out a bulletin on it?"

"Yeah."

"Good, 'cause we have another problem."

"It's not even nine a.m. and the hits just keep coming," he said, some of his rage ebbing. "What?"

"The reverend mother at St. Marguerite's called this morning. She already reported that Lucia Costa was missing; though, supposedly Lucia called and said she was okay, which I guess your brother just verified. But she's not the only one missing. Louise Cortez, another novitiate, is gone, too."

"Jesus H. Christ!" Montoya threw up a hand and stalked in front of the desk.

"There's already two units at the convent. I was just waiting for you to show up so we could head over there."

Montoya was already walking through the door. "You know I've been inside the church more in the last week than I have been in ten years."

Bentz snorted a laugh as he reached for his jacket and holster, checking to see that his service weapon was snapped in. "Guess we're lucky the walls haven't fallen in on us."

"Yeah," Montoya said, "real fuckin' lucky!" He was out of the office first, returning the way he came, his boots clattering down the steps. He nearly ran into a cop urging a man in handcuffs down the hallway to an interrogation room. The guy smelled like he'd slept in his own vomit, and his hair was matted, his face scratched and pimply, his eyes blinking, his teeth clenching and grinding.

Definitely tweaking. Probably meth.

Montoya signed for a car and walked outside again. The sun was shining, but a thickening layer of clouds was beginning to cluster, the humidity already intense. What was with the nuns at St. Marguerite's? He thought of the missing bridal dresses and the list of novitiates and nuns who had at one time in their lives lived in the orphanage at St. Elsinore's.

Sister Louise Cortez's name was on the list.

Sister Lucia Costa's was not.

Lucia was alive.

He had serious doubts about Louise.

"We gotta get this guy," he said as Bentz slid into the Crown Vic's already-warm interior and buckled his seat belt.

"The sooner the better."

Montoya lead-footed it across town. Traffic was light, as it was Saturday morning, and the trip fairly easy. Bentz told him that he'd caught the report on Grace Blanc's family—a brother in Duluth, Minnesota, her mother, finally giving up the cold northern winters, now lived year-round in Miami. Both Grace's relatives seemed shocked and saddened at the horrid twist of events.

Montoya pulled into a parking spot near the back door of the cathedral. He noticed the spires stretching upward, seeming to puncture the gray bellies of the clouds rolling over the city. The cathedral was dark and somber, no parishioners scurrying in and out, no nuns making their way to the garage to pick up a car and drive to the hospital or St. Elsinore's, no priest stopping to chat with pedestrians as they strolled by.

No, the huge edifice looked dark and foreboding, an empty fortress that was unwelcoming, hardly a sanctuary for those with troubled souls.

This morning, he observed as he walked across the lawn to the back gate, there was no yellow tape strung across the entrance, no news vans parked nearby, no one from the medical examiner's office, no crime scene investigators.

At least not yet.

No telling what they would find when they started searching.

Would they locate the body of Louise Cortez, or would she, like Lea De Luca and now, perhaps, Lucia Costa, disappear forever?

Montoya had a bad feeling about Louise.

A real bad feeling.

"The police have released Camille's body," Valerie said as she clicked her cell phone shut, and a cold wave washed through her body. She was in the passenger seat of Slade's truck, returning from their breakfast of beignets and café au lait at the long, low restaurant in the French Quarter. They'd sat beneath slow-moving paddle fans, listening to the buzz of conversation while watching the Mississippi roll slowly toward the Gulf.

Water fowl had cruised the shore, smaller birds hopping along the sidewalk hoping for crumbs.

Slade had insisted that they go, so, after she'd called Rick Bentz at the police department, helped Freya with the breakfast and dishes at Briarstone, and met with an officer who came out to take her statement, she'd agreed.

Getting out of the house and into the bustle of the city had helped elevate her mood and stopped her from dwelling on the sibilant voice's threat.

You're nexxxt. Breathy pause. *There is no essscape.*

She and Slade hadn't talked about it during all of their time away from the cottage. They'd agreed the subject was taboo and had enjoyed their time together. It was almost as if they were falling in love for the first time.

Except, she reminded herself as the truck hit a pothole and bounced, this was round two.

And the peaceful morning that they had managed to restore had been shattered, the call from the funeral home bringing Val back to earth, to reality and the soul-scraping truth that her sister had been murdered, the victim of a psychopath whose thirst for blood was yet unquenched.

Her jaw tightened at the unfairness of it all. Who was this creep, and how the hell were they going to catch him and throw his ass in jail? She wanted revenge; she wanted the bastard to pay, and she was frustrated that he hadn't been identified.

If not that swine of a vow-breaking priest, O'Toole, then who? she thought idly as Slade braked for a woman pushing a baby carriage, then turned the corner onto St. Charles Avenue. On one side of the avenue, they passed Audubon Park, on the other the circular drive of Loyola University, one of the buildings looking like a medieval fortress built of red brick. Next to Loyola were the groomed lawns leading to the pale bricks of a massive edifice that was part of Tulane University. "The Harvard of the South," according to some of her friends who had graduated from the school. That was up for debate, though, she knew, as she looked at the arched windows and the smooth grass, the beauty of the campus.

Two schools Camille would never have a chance to visit.

"You know," Slade said as he turned down the side street leading to Briarstone. "We don't have to go to the auction tonight." He'd been worried all day, ever since the morning telephone call.

"I wouldn't miss it for the world. Everyone involved in this case will be there." She thought of Father Frank O'Toole again. Would he show his face? "And Camille would want me to attend."

"You don't know that." He rolled to a stop across the street from her garage.

"And that's the problem, isn't it?" she said. "I never will."

"So what have we got?" Bentz asked as he and Montoya picked up ribs from a takeout place a few blocks from the station, then found a park bench where they could talk, pick at the bones, watch the storm roll in, and generally work out the day.

"You mean besides diddly-squat?" Montoya's mood hadn't improved much. Talking for hours with nuns who they were getting to know well enough to send Christmas cards to, being stonewalled by the priests, and trying to get a bead on the reverend mother had been draining for them both, Bentz knew, and Montoya, always more volatile, a "young buck," wasn't taking it well. Though he'd mellowed a little over the years—marrying Abby and becoming a father had helped—he was still explosive and impulsive. Working with Reuben Montoya was always a challenge and always exciting. Bentz bent rules; Montoya broke them.

They picked at their ribs, the sauce tangy and gooey, and watched ducks floating on a pond where the water was turning a worrisome shade of gray, reflecting the clouds rolling in. A woman was feeding them, and they were gathering around her, quacking and demanding bits of bread.

On the far side of the pond, a woman was trying to walk a black dachshund. He was straining on his leash, barking insanely first at the ducks and then at a squirrel that scurried up the bark of an oak tree.

"Stop it! Charlie! Come on," the scrawny woman on the other end of the red tether commanded.

Charlie paid no attention, as disinterested in what she was saying as a teenage boy with a new video game.

"Why did Sister Lucia take off when she did? Why last night?" Bentz thought aloud.

"Maybe she knew that something was happening with Louise Cortez; she was the first one to find both the other bodies."

"You think she was involved?" Bentz asked.

"With the murders?" Montoya sucked on a rib but shook his head. "No way. But she could have seen something that put her at risk. Cruz says she's got some kind of ESP going on." Montoya rotated his hand and shook his head, as if he didn't really understand the phenomenon, but Bentz did, at least partially; his wife, Olivia, was either blessed or cursed with her own little bit of woo-woo, though it seemed to have died or gone dormant for a while. He hoped to hell it stayed that way.

Using a plastic fork, he dug into his coleslaw, barely tasting the tang of spices or the sweetness of the honey in its dressing.

"Sister Louise, the nun who's missing, she was an orphan at St. Elsinore's. Adopted out to a couple in Maine, but she came back."

"Sister Charity searches for them," Montoya said. During the interview process, Sister Devota Arness had let it slip that the reverend mother was in constant contact with all the women who had at one time or another been orphaned and stayed at St. Elsinore's.

"But Lucia Costa had family."

"So if the connection between the victims was living at St. Elsinore's, then she would be safe."

Bentz finished his coleslaw and wadded the waxed paper that his ribs had been wrapped in. "Lucia Costa probably didn't know that; hell, we just came up with it. All she sees is fellow sisters being killed." He tossed the wadded paper into the trash.

"We know that Camille Renard was involved with Father O'Toole. But the others weren't." That lead, the one that kept nagging at him, was going nowhere, he thought, like the squirrel he was watching, the one who had taunted Charlie the dachshund. It was now scampering from one tree to the next, only to be dissatisfied and hurry, tail puffed and flicking, across the lawn again.

"Except for the missing nun. Sister Lea," Montoya said, biting into his corn bread, then brushing the crumbs from his goatee. He scowled, not liking his train of thought.

"Right." But it wasn't enough. The connection to Father Frank O'Toole wasn't strong enough. Even if he had been involved with Lea and Camille, what about Asteria, Lucia, and Louise?

His thoughts in a tangle, Bentz finished his lunch, draining his Diet Coke and tossing all the remains into a trash can while he considered the fruitless morning. Uniformed cops had scoured the grounds and buildings of St. Marguerite's convent, cathedral, and cemetery and had come up with nothing. Nada. Zilch. No signs of a struggle, no dead body, nothing on Louise Cortez. And who the hell knew where Lucia Costa and Cruz's motorcycle had ended up.

The neighbors, as usual, hadn't seen or heard anything unusual. Father Frank had an alibi: Father Paul. They had spent the night talking, working on sermons, and praying until long after midnight.

Louise could have been kidnapped in the morning, so O'Toole wasn't completely off the hook, but still...

Montoya finished his ribs, ignored the slaw, and took two more bites of his corn bread before tossing the remains into the trash. Together, each lost in his own thoughts, they returned to the station.

"And so I agree with Father Thomas. I feel it's our duty to attend the auction tonight," Father Paul insisted. Once again, he'd asked Sister Charity to round up the novitiates, nuns, and laypeople so that he could lecture them on what was expected, his version of a pep talk. With a solemn-faced, quiet Father Frank O'Toole at his side, Father Paul was trying to convince everyone who had gathered in the meeting room to go about his or her business—no, *God's* business—as normal.

As if they could!

Was he out of his mind?

After what had happened here?

His was the-show-must-go-on mentality.

Sister Charity listened and nodded her agreement, though her commitment to the auction was waning, and she had to force her lips into a curve of accord. She'd done it all her life, of course, followed the rules, obeying the church's law, trusting in the Trinity, in her church. She'd accepted that only men became priests, and most of those men were good, God-fearing men whose faith was unshakeable. The few bad apples, and there seemed to be more of them than she had ever thought, were tarnishing an institution that had existed for more than two millennia and that would stand until the end of time.

For those who dismissed organized religion as unhealthy, as taking away one's right, one's individual opinions, she said, "Bah." The church was good. The people within it were good.

But Father Paul, right now, standing near the windows, was pushing her to the limits of her patience in insisting they partake of the festivities at St. Elsinore's tonight.

Outside, visible through the panes, a storm was brewing, dark clouds smoldering overhead. The rain was predicted to start around four, a storm unleashing all its fury around six, just in time for the festivities at St. Elsinore's.

Sister Charity's heart twisted. To the depths of her soul, she loved St. Elsinore's, and she'd been giving her heart, mind, and body to the upcoming auction, had been excited to be a part of it, not only as someone who had grown up there, but also as a member of the church.

However, things had taken a tragic and dire turn.

With two of her novitiates missing and two more murdered, it hardly seemed right to leave the convent and partake of any of the celebration tonight.

Why not? What good has staying here done?

A deep sadness settled in her chest. Though she hated to see the orphanage at St. Elsinore's moved, the building marked for the wrecking ball, she had thrown her heart and soul into helping with the transition.

How the choir would perform without Sister Louise was beyond her. But they would make do. She was a firm believer in God giving a person only what he or she could handle.

Father Paul was leading them all in prayer, though the nuns and staff were nervous, had been on tenterhooks all morning, with the search of the convent and property and then the inevitable questions from the police.

All the women were worried about Sister Louise and Sister Lucia, as well they should be.

She glanced down, saw she was wringing her hands, and caught a warning glance from Father Paul. Today, she thought, he was insufferable, unbending and pushy, when he should have been kind. Understanding.

Couldn't the same be said of you, Charity? Haven't you always run a "tight ship"? Haven't you always been the captain? While the priests might have been the admirals, working from a distance, you have been the stalwart leader, the person directing these nuns to their paths. Have you always been kind? Or understanding? Or has your rigidity become your Achilles heel, the weakness that will eventually bring down your ship? And who will pay? You? Or those you have trusted with the oars, the women who have come to live here under your guidance, who have trusted in you to steer them straight, the very young innocents you saw and recruited? Truly they are your "sisters," Charity, for you have no others. You never have.

She swallowed a sudden lump in her throat and stiffened her spine. This was no time for retrospection or second-guessing.

Her gaze returned to Father Paul, a desperate priest gathering his flock. Beside him, Father O'Toole stood, white-faced and stricken. Unlike the impassioned Father Paul, the younger priest was just going through the motions of his profession, his expression slightly dazed.

Father Frank O'Toole's mind, it seemed, was several thousand light-years away.

CHAPTER 48

"Just for the record, I think this is a big mistake," Slade said. He was futzing with his tie, scowling into the mirror and trying to talk Val out of attending the St. Elsinore's auction.

She wasn't about to be dissuaded.

"I know. You've said—oh, about a hundred times." She was already dressed in a black silk sheath and heels, her hair twisted onto her head. "Let me do that," she said, and fixed his tie, then saw their reflection in the full-length mirror she'd propped into a corner of her bedroom. "Oh, God, look," she said, and grinned at their reflection. "It's so *not* us!"

"Thank the good Lord for small favors," he mocked, but grinned at the image—she in the floor-length dress, black because she was in mourning, he in dark slacks and a white shirt, tie, and jacket, his hair combed, his jaw devoid of even the smallest beard stubble.

A far cry from the dusty jeans and faded work shirts they'd both worn on the ranch. Though, she reminded herself, she'd already packed a small bag filled with a flashlight, her tennis shoes, and a change of clothes. She intended to look around the old school tonight, to find out more about her birth parents and whatever it was that Camille had found, while the auction was in progress.

She hadn't mentioned her plan to Slade, didn't want to hear his arguments. Not that he didn't have legitimate concerns; ever since she'd received her latest threat, she'd been edgy. Somehow she'd become a more pressing target. From *You're on the lisssst* to *You're nexxxt!*

As Slade said, she was coming up in the world, at least from the killer's perspective, and it gnawed at her. Big-time. Then there was the worrisome fact that two more nuns had gone missing. She'd talked to Bentz earlier, and he'd informed her that Sisters Lucia and Louise were missing. So far, no bodies had been located, and no one was certain whether they were alive or dead—though Bentz had hinted he believed Sister Lucia was still with the living.

Slade, upon hearing the news, had flat-out refused to attend the auction, but when she'd told him she was going with or without him, he'd been forced to agree. "No way are you going there alone!" he'd said, and hadn't accepted her offhanded remark about being with hundreds of people.

The bottom line was that people were being killed. People attached to St. Elsinore's and St. Marguerite's.

Nuns, she reminded herself, and didn't want to think about the prostitute who had also been killed. The press had tried to link the murders, but so far the police hadn't indicated that they were connected.

Any way around it, the citizens of New Orleans were worried.

And, truth to tell, so was she.

A part of her wanted to run and hide, but the other part, that section of her that had become a cop, was ready to track down this sick, anonymous coward and nail his ass.

Slade's gaze met hers in the mirror. "But you do look amazing," he admitted. "You know, we could order in and spend the night in bed."

"No way." She gave his tie a yank. "We're going!"

"I love it when you're bossy," he said, and grabbed her, pulling her tight, and there in front of the mirror kissed her hard.

"Uh-uh, you're not convincing me," she said with a grin when she pulled her head back and looked him square in the eye. In heels, she was nearly nose to nose with him.

Nearly.

"I'm on to you, Houston," she warned with a wink, then before he kissed her again slid out of his arms and hurried out of the bedroom. Bo, who had watched the entire dialogue, trotted after her to the living room, where she noticed the rain had begun to fall, thick drops drizzling down the windows. "Summer storm," she thought aloud.

"An omen."

She glanced over her shoulder as he walked into the room. "I don't believe in omens.

"No? Well, I do." And with that, he found his pistol and shoved it under the waistband of his slacks before throwing on his jacket.

"We're going to a church auction," she reminded him.

His smile held no fraction of amusement. "Exactly."

The call came in just before five.

Cruz's motorcycle, none the worse for wear, had been located, parked and locked at the bus station in Baton Rouge. A state cop had seen it, called in the plates, and discovered that it had been reported stolen, Montoya's name listed as the contact person at the NOPD.

"We need it. Part of a homicide investigation," Montoya told the officer. "The bike was stolen by a witness."

"Records say it belongs to a Cruz Montoya."

"My brother." Montoya sketched out an abbreviated story for the cop and made arrangements for the Harley to be secured and brought into the garage at the crime lab. Maybe there was a clue as to where Lucia Costa had run to left on or around the bike.

He hung up the phone and got online to check the bus company's routes and schedules. The earliest Lucia could have arrived in Baton Rouge was around three in the morning, so Montoya checked all the buses leaving from two-thirty on. It took almost an hour for the company to double-check records, but there was a bus that left for Houston at 7:00 a.m.

Did he believe she headed west?

Not really.

Her mission was to ditch Cruz, to fool him, so she wouldn't have played her hand so carelessly. Nuh-uh.

Montoya was sweating as he rolled back his chair, the air-conditioning unit on the fritz again. The St. Elsinore's auction was scheduled in an hour, and he intended to be there, to look through the crowd, see who was there. Maybe the killer would show his face; then again, probably not, but Montoya had the gut feeling that the homicides of Camille Renard and Asteria McClellan had been conceived earlier, perhaps starting at the first place they had crossed paths, if only fleetingly, and that was St. Elsinore's orphanage. The connection was there, but not complete, like a train whose cars were on the track, one after the other, but not hitched together.

So some of the women who had been orphans at St. Elsinore's had ended up as nuns and novitiates at St. Marguerite's. Was that so odd?

He picked up his paper coffee cup, its few swallows of java staining the inside, cold and nearly congealed from the morning. He tossed it into the trash under his desk and realized that the noise in the department had lessened, most of the staff having left for the day.

But not Bentz.

As Montoya stepped into the hallway, he noticed that Bentz's desk lamp was glowing through the open doorway of his office, soft light spilling into the corridor.

Montoya poked his head inside and found his partner, shirtsleeves rolled over his forearms, elbows on the desk, a clump of hair falling over his eyes. He had jotted notes all over a yellow legal pad, but his gaze was focused on his computer monitor, a split screen with two victims visible. Grace Blanc, the prostitute, was on one half, and another, a woman he didn't recognize immediately, filled the second half of the monitor. She looked familiar in the crime scene and was splayed in the same position as Grace had been left.

Shit, he realized, it was a picture of Cherie Bellechamps, one of Father John's victims back when he was terrorizing the city a decade earlier.

Both women were half dressed, their red hair mussed, their eyes those of the dead, the purple scars surrounding their necks sporting the deep cuts from irregular beads—in the case of Bellechamps, a rosary.

"What gives?" he asked, taking in the two, nearly identical images.

"Father John," Bentz spat out angrily. "I didn't want to believe it, but I think he's back." Bentz tossed a sheet of paper across the desk to Montoya. "Just got the blood type back on the sperm found in Grace Blanc," he said. "Guess what? It matches that found in the sperm left in all of Father John's victims ten years ago." He reached into his desk drawer, found a pack of Juicy Fruit gum, and silently offered Montoya a stick. When his partner declined, he unwrapped a piece and tossed it into his mouth. "It's not DNA, but..."

"I was hoping that son of a bitch was dead."

"You and me both, but look." He pointed to the monitor with its grisly photos. "The crime scenes are nearly identical. I suppose they could be copied, but would the new killer have the same rare blood as John?" He was shaking his head.

"Well at least we know who he is."

"Do we?" Bentz clicked the pen in his hand. "Probably has a whole new ID, maybe even a new goddamned face." From the file, he withdrew a photo of the killer, one from ten years prior. "I've already requested computer enhancement on this. What would he look like with a beard, without, as a blond...Oh, crap, who knows what he looks like now? Damn it all to hell!"

Montoya studied the old photo, and his stomach soured. "So you think he could be one of the priests that we've been talking to?"

"Or not talking to. Father Thomas has been pretty damned shy, and Camille worked at St. Elsinore's in the clinic. You know, I bet if we looked hard enough, we could find a pharmacist attached to St. Elsinore's. They've got pharmaceuticals there."

"Look, even if you're right and Father John has come back and assumed some new identity, he can't have new fingerprints and certainly not DNA...or blood type."

"Yeah, well, here's the kicker," Bentz admitted in disgust. "That blood type?" He snorted. "It's the same as Sister Camille's baby's. He's the fu—effin' father!"

* * *

Slade held the umbrella over Valerie's head as they dashed across the hotel parking lot of the boutique hotel to the dinner part of the auction.

The hotel was built in the early eighteen hundreds and recently refurbished to its antebellum charm. Huge white columns supported a wide front entrance flanked by rows of paned windows over ten feet tall. Each window was framed by black shutters and gas lanterns that were blazing against the gathering storm.

Beneath a covey of umbrellas, guests of the hotel funneled through the main doors, their raincoats shedding water, their jewels and smiles flashing in equal splendor. A news team had arrived, the van parked across the street, the reporter Brenda Convoy and her cameraman nearby, filming the arrival of the guests—everyone from the mayor to local television personalities, sports figures, and businessmen and women who were a part of the Crescent City's populace and culture. There were rumors that Trey Wembley, son of one of the city's richest men and a current Hollywood heartthrob, would be in attendance.

Brenda Convoy, Valerie thought sourly, wouldn't want to miss that interview.

"I hate these things," Slade whispered, already tugging at his tie as Valerie greeted Sister Simone, who was serving as a hostess.

Tonight the nuns from St. Elsinore's and St. Marguerite's were wearing traditional habits, and Sister Simone was no exception. Her wimple and coif were stark white against the flowing black serge of the holy habit, a wooden rosary hanging from her belt.

"Good to see you again," Simone said with a smile.

"You, too."

"So here you go." She handed Valerie a manila envelope printed with the symbol for St. Elsinore's. "There's a program in this packet, along with a list of the items you can bid on and a paddle with your number on it, just in case you find something you can't live without."

"Thanks!" Val said, though she had no plans to bid on any of the items.

With Slade's hand steadfastly at her back, they moved inside, along with a rush of other guests, through a foyer of mirrors, marble, and potted palms. In the center stood a massive table, upon which an ornate display of tropical flowers—anthuriums, birds-of-paradise, and torch lilies—bloomed in bursts of vibrant color.

A string quartet played soft music at the foot of a grand staircase. Wide steps with a deep floral runner wound upward before splitting to the second floor. With gleaming mahogany rails and white balusters, the staircase was reminiscent of the most beautiful of plantation homes.

In the foyer were black-and-white photographs of St. Elsinore's, propped up on easels, a veritable history of the buildings, showing how the church, orphanage, and grounds had changed with the years. Hundreds of children and scores of teachers, nuns, and nurses and a few priests were caught in long-ago fragments, tiny instants of time.

So many of the people had passed on, Val thought, eyeing the displays and noting the change of fashion in the children, the addition of electrical and telephone wires in the shots, the growth of trees, the morphing of the vehicles in the street from carriages and wagons to Model Ts, the big boats with fins of the cars of the fifties, then increasingly sleeker vehicles.

In one of the more recent pictures, the 1960s or '70s, judging from the vintage of the cars, Val caught a glimpse of the spire of the cathedral and an oak tree. A solitary nun, dressed in a dark habit, her sleeves voluminous, was reaching for the hand of a small child.

Val froze, her eyes on the image of the nun's face, young and unlined, yet still harsh, her dark eyes glinting. In her other hand she held the links of a rosary, a silver cross dangling through her slim fingers.

"What?" Slade asked.

Val's heart hammered wildly at the sight of the black-and-white photograph.

In her mind's eye, pictures of her youth flashed in painful, sharp fragments. She remembered entering the stark, glistening hallways of St. Elsinore's. Losing sight of Baby Camille. Crying at night for her parents. Wishing Mrs. O'Malley would return and save her.

From what?

Val blinked hard and smelled, for just a second, the same scents she had as a child:

Floor wax.

Ammonia.

Pine cleaner.

Fear.

A tremor passed through her.

"Are you all right?" Slade's voice brought her back to the present just as he was taking hold of the crook of her arm and herding her away from the stark, mind-jarring picture.

"Y-yes," Val said, though she was lying as she tried desperately to pull herself together, back to this bustling hotel, back to a night in the twenty-first century.

She took one final glance at the easel but stopped. Her heart nearly dropped through the floor. "Wait!" she said, and stared at the young nun in the still shot. If she layered on the years, weathering the nun's skin, adding wrinkles and the harshness that decades of disappointment can etch upon the skin, she recognized the nun as a young Sister Ignatia.

Val's nerves stretched thin. Her heart raced. Not just a nun, not just the woman who had grasped her five-year-old arm in her strong fingers with their sharp nails, whose rosary reminded a child of a silvery snake, but also the monster who haunted her dreams— the demon that besieged her subconscious, a being that had, over the years, transformed from a cruel witch of a woman to a creature with her tiny teeth, slithering silver rosary, and talonlike hands.

"Oh, God," she whispered, a chill that brought a rash of goose bumps to her skin running through her. All these years, the terror she'd felt was because of a nun who yelled, a nun who slapped at her fingers with a ruler, a nun who seemed to enjoy inflicting pain.

Val shuddered, told herself it was silly, when so many of the people at the orphanage had been kind.

"Valerie?" Slade asked, his eyes darkening with concern, his fingers still strong around her elbow.

"I'm . . . I'm fine," she managed, forcing a weak smile. In truth, she knew that the images from her youth, the fear and the pain, would probably be with her for the rest of her life.

"We don't have to stay." It wasn't just that the situation made him uncomfortable, she saw, but that he was seriously worried about her.

"I said I'm fine. Come on." She headed for the dining area where they took seats at one of the many tables scattered throughout the cavernous room and waited as others joined them and drinks were brought. Beer and wine were available, though no hard drinks were on the menu.

Before they were served, Father Thomas, a tall, dark-haired man with an easy smile and sharp eyes, walked to the microphone and introduced himself and his staff on the raised dais.

Sister Ignatia, an honored guest, was wheeled in. She was shriveled and humpbacked, her face thin and drawn, etched with wrinkles that made it seem she was a wax figure melting into her habit.

This was the woman who had caused so many of Val's nightmares? This tiny, withered piece of flesh in a nun's habit? How could this poor old woman still permeate Val's subconscious and bring on the night terrors?

Unable to get out of her chair, Ignatia was parked at one of the closest tables to the dais. She barely moved, just huddled in the chair, a handwoven afghan tossed across her lap, a silver cross danging from her neck.

Maybe now, Val thought, her nightmares would finally fade.

As soon as Ignatia's wheelchair was situated to her cranky specifications, Father Frank and Father Paul joined Father Thomas at the microphone. Enthusiastically, Thomas suggested everyone bid on the items that were on display at St. Elsinore's, in the old gym. The donated items were incredible, everything from a trip for two to the Belvederes' beach home in the Carolinas to a "one-of-a-kind" white grand piano donated by Arthur and Marion Wembley, lifelong citizens of New Orleans and members of St. Marguerite's. The Wembleys, he noted, were both orphans at St. Elsinore's over eighty years earlier.

With that piece of inspiring information, he asked everyone to join him in prayer before dinner was served.

As soon as the last "amen" was whispered and most of the guests made hasty signs of the cross over their chests, the dinner service finally began.

Val had no appetite. She was too keyed up, her focus on what she had planned at the orphanage. This might be the only time she would be able to search St. Elsinore's records, search for the information that had set Camille on her doomed path. While everyone was in the gym at the auction, Val would, with a little luck, sneak into the archives and find out just who the hell she really was.

Her identity, she felt certain, was connected to her sister's murder; she just didn't know how.

She pushed her shrimp and melon salad around on her plate. She felt as if she were being watched, every movement observed, but who, in this crowd of six or seven hundred people, was watching her? Scrutinizing her.

The hairs at the base of her scalp lifted, and she looked over her shoulder.

She saw no one singling her out.

But then, what better place to hide in plain sight but in a sea of unfamiliar faces?

CHAPTER 49

From his position near a side door, Montoya surveyed the crowd in the hotel's dining area. Over five hundred people, all dressed to the nines, all ready to open their wallets for the new orphanage, but no one he recognized as Father John.

A waiter passed, carrying a huge silver tray and rustling the fronds of a palm tree. A spiky leaf brushed against his face, and he shifted, moving a little closer to the front of the room, where he had a better view of the crowd.

And one of them, he thought, could be a killer.

Was the son of a bitch in their midst?

With enough plastic surgery to hide his identity?

Or disguised as what? The priest's garb during his last killing spree would be a dead giveaway. So, then...? His gaze scraped the crowd.

He noticed a few other cops in plainclothes, mingling with the crowd, some even subtly taking photographs and videos from hidden cameras; it was so easy to do these days with cell phones and pocket cameras.

Montoya caught Bentz's gaze and nodded when the priest, the often-missing Father Thomas, now standing at the mic, had mentioned the Wembleys, the couple who had been Father Frank's alibi on the night of Camille Renard's homicide. Arthur and Mar-

ion, solid parishioners, had made a generous donation of their beloved Steinway piano.

Montoya had done his research on the devout couple. They
were giving most of their earthly possessions to charity, as they'd
recently moved from a four-thousand-square-foot mini-mansion on
the Mississippi to a small apartment in an assisted-living complex.

Montoya had talked to the couple. After spending most of their
lives amassing material possessions, the Wembleys were now more
concerned with the hereafter than their collection of classic cars,
art, and their beloved Steinway Louis XV, now up for auction.

And there was something more he'd seen when visiting the
aging Wembleys at the hospital, where the old man was fighting a
losing battle with the Grim Reaper. Though they played the part of
the loving, dedicated couple, there was something that didn't sit
quite right with Montoya, as if the wife wasn't as dependent upon
Arthur as he was on her. Probably because of the old man's declin-
ing health, Montoya told himself, but he didn't quite buy it.

It was almost as if a lie had been flitting around Wembley's hospital room, the truth chasing after it.

Or was he imagining things, seeing falsehoods because he expected them?

Tonight there was a buzz of excitement in the dining area, a
charge of electricity. Unfortunately, he thought, it wasn't only because of generous and giving souls ready to pay far more than items
were worth for a good cause. No, there was more going on here;
the newspeople were here en masse, hoping for a story, one tied to
the macabre murders at St. Marguerite's.

Sick freaks!

And the fact that the auction had sold out was no doubt due in
part, not to the local celebrities who were donating their time, nor
the good feeling of donating to a worthy cause, but to the bit of
scandal associated with St. Elsinore's.

The two women who had been killed had been orphaned themselves, put up for adoption from within the very walls that were
now scheduled to be sold and probably demolished. Camille Renard, a novitiate, had been pregnant, rumored to have been involved with Father Frank O'Toole, the handsome priest who was
here tonight.

Free publicity, gruesome though it may be.

Yeah, there was a current of electricity moving through the crowd, and some of it could be attributed to the heinous crimes that Montoya was investigating.

It was intriguing though thankfully the public knew few of the details of bridal dresses, bloodied necklines, orphans, secretive religious orders, and a madman on the loose again. A dead prostitute and a nun's diary that read like a guide to kinky sex, the scenes so graphic he'd nearly ignored the little scribbles that had accompanied the text, notes he'd not understood.

Important?

He shrugged, as if someone had actually asked him the question. Weird numbers and symbols, hearts and arrows, like cupid encrypting a special message. All wrapped up in death.

A helluva thing when you thought about it.

The wheels of the bus go round and round,
Round and round, round and round.
The wheels of the bus go round and round
All through the town....

The childhood song ran through Lucia's mind as the Greyhound's tires sang over the pavement. How many times had she sung the lyrics along with making the hand movements with the kids at the orphanage at St. Elsinore's?

She sighed, leaning her head against the window as the night rushed by. Tonight, she knew, was the auction for the building of the new orphanage, and a part of her longed to be there; just as a part of her longed to be with Cruz again.

Idiot!

That part of your life, with the orphanage, and certainly with Cruz, is over.

The bus was nearly empty. Besides Lucia, there was just an old woman with a child of around eight two seats back from the driver. The child was nestled in the woman's arms; both were asleep. In the back was a twentyish man with a scar that ran down one side of his face and tattoos visible on his big arms. He was leaning back in his seat, plugged into an iPod, his eyes closed.

Lucia sat in the middle of the bus, on the opposite side of the aisle from the others.

Tonight she was dressed in street clothes again, though her hair was cropped short, compliments of her own hack job with a pair of scissors she'd stolen from the convent. She was traveling courtesy of Sister Camille, who had left her, along with her cell phone, a wallet filled with hundred-dollar bills. Fifty of them, to be exact.

A fortune to Lucia. She sighed, her breath fogging the window as she remembered Camille giving her the money.

"Just in case," Camille had said when she'd tucked the thick leather billfold into the pockets of Lucia's habit just two days before she was killed. "The Holy Father may want us to give up worldly possessions, but he surely doesn't want us to be stupid."

"But where did you get this?" Lucia had gasped, intending to return it to Camille.

"It doesn't matter," Camille had said, but her smile had faded. "I guess some people might say it's hush money." She'd squeezed Camille's hand. "But rich people, you know, people like Marion Wembley, they call it a 'donation.' "

"To what?"

Camille had grinned again. "To ensure their future is never ruined. That some secrets are never revealed," she'd said cryptically, with a naughty little smile. "Just take it, okay?"

"I can't."

"Then keep it for me. Please." Her eyes had clouded. "I might need it."

Lucia had swallowed hard and slowly nodded, even though she'd known she was somehow compromising her values, committing some vague sin. "Just for a while..."

And now Camille was dead, murdered, and Lucia had thrown away all of her promises to herself. She was using the cash to put as many miles as she could between herself and Cruz.

She closed her eyes and wondered where she'd be in the morning.

Her route had been a zigzag course to nowhere.

She'd gotten aboard a westbound bus in Baton Rouge wearing exactly what she'd had on when she'd left Cruz; then, once the bus had crossed the state line into Texas and stopped at the first station, she'd bought a ticket heading south. In the restroom, she'd donned her holy habit. She'd worn it for as long as she was on the bus rolling toward Mexico, so if anyone saw her, they'd remember the habit—that a young nun was on the bus to a border town.

Two stops later, the one before the border, she doubled back, taking a northbound bus and wearing street clothes again, this time adding a pink sweater that she had in the backpack. At each stop in her circuitous route, she changed something about her appearance. She had sunglasses and a scarf she tied over her hair that she wore with a blouse and jeans or with a T-shirt and skirt.

Now, as rain began to fall, the bus was climbing hills. With the bus speeding by long stretches of dark countryside, she thought about the East Coast, but not north—no, she was a Southern girl.

The names of the towns along the coast went through her mind, and she settled on Savannah—a big enough city to get lost in, yet small enough to feel like home. Yes, she thought, Savannah.

She noticed the driver, a portly man with a buzz cut and red face, switch on the windshield wipers.

The wipers on the bus go swish, swish, swish
Swish, swish, swish, swish, swish, swish.
The wipers on the bus go . . .

At the hotel, the salad plates were removed by the waiters. Val, nerves strung tight, scanned the dining area and eyed the patrons. She recognized many of the nuns from both parishes. Conversation and laughter, rattling dishes and clinking glassware created a rumbling cacophony that rolled through the room as steaming plates of jambalaya, crawfish étouffée, red beans and rice, and stacks of biscuits and corn bread drizzled with butter and honey arrived.

Though she and Slade tried to avoid small talk, they were forced into conversation with the three other couples seated at their table. It came out that each of the couples had been married for at least ten years, and they all had grade-school-age children. Two of the men had been adopted out of St. Elsinore's. One couple had adopted both of their girls through the orphanage. All of them were intrigued with what was happening at St. Marguerite's.

"It's a real reunion here tonight," the taller of the men, redhaired Ned, enthused.

His wife, even-featured with a pile of blond hair, agreed while a pinch-faced woman, Connie, couldn't quit talking about the horrible goings-on at St. Marguerite's as she drank two—or was it three?—glasses of wine.

It was all Val could do to hold her tongue, especially when Camille's name came up.

"I heard she was pregnant, you know," Connie said, her eyebrows rising at the scandal.

"Really?" the third woman, a brunette with wide doe eyes, said, shocked.

"Shhh." Connie's husband, Vince, scowled.

"I will not! They claim the father is the priest, and I don't blame her—look at him!"

"Connie!" Vince rebuked, his face suffusing with color. "Please." But Connie, tipsy, was eating up Father Frank with her eyes. "I wonder about that other nun who was killed. Maybe she was having a thing with the priest, too!" Connie laughed and nearly fell off her chair. "And now I heard from my friend who works there that another couple of the sisters are missing. What kind of a convent is that? They're dropping like flies over there!"

"Shhh!" The husband was angry now. Embarrassed.

Val couldn't stand it. Despite a warning glance from Slade, she said, "Camille Renard was my sister."

"Of course she was. She was everybody's sister," Connie said, her eyes a little glassy as her fingers held up a wobbling glass of Chardonnay. But Vince stiffened, and the other couples went completely silent, setting their forks on the table.

"No, I'm not talking about her being in the convent and taking vows. She was my blood sister," Val said evenly, and saw the shock register in six pairs of eyes. Slade looked as if he wanted to throttle her, but Val wasn't about to back down now. "We both were brought to St. Elsinore's when our parents died. She was a lovely woman, and I miss her terribly."

"Oh, dear God," Ned's wife whispered.

The other crossed herself.

"But she was preggers, right?" Connie had lost all sense of propriety.

"I'm so sorry," her husband said, and to his wife, "Come on, honey, let's go."

"But the auction hasn't even started." She was slurring her words now, and Val, irritated and ready for a fight, wondered how many drinks she'd had before she'd walked through the hotel doors.

"I'll be good, I promise," she said, trying to appear cute.

Her husband wasn't having any of it, and he herded his tipsy wife out of the room. They wove their way to the doors while the rest of the people at the table picked at their food, a silent, awkward table in the midst of noise.

Slade placed a hand on Val's knee and warned her with his gaze to not make a scene. He was right, of course. Especially when she considered what she planned to do later. She didn't want anyone to notice her. Or miss her.

Her gaze skimmed the crowd again, and she noticed several people from the police department. Her gaze locked with Bentz's for a second, and she saw Montoya leaning against a post and eyeing Father Thomas, who, just as dessert of Bananas Foster was served, introduced Sister Charity and the St. Marguerite's choir.

The reverend mother seemed to have shrunk in the past few days, her skin paler than Val remembered, the starch drained out of her.

"As you know," Charity said into the microphone after she'd tapped it to see that it was still live, "we've suffered some terrible losses at St. Marguerite's lately." Her voice was clear and strong, even over the feedback of the mic. "Our choir, too, has been affected, but in honor of those who have passed and those who are missing, for the glory of God and this great cause, we will perform." The corners of her mouth tightened a bit as she paused, then said, "But first, I'm going to ask you all to pray with me and observe a moment of silence for Sister Asteria and Sister Camille, who were called home so recently, and for those who are missing from our order." She glanced at Father Paul, who led the prayer; then, after a quiet moment when nothing so much as ice cubes clinking disturbed the silence, Sister Charity led the smaller group in song.

Val watched, listened, and wondered what it would have sounded like if her sister and the novitiate who had the beautiful voice, the one who was always humming, Sister Louise, were still in the group. As it was, the hymn was melodic and, to Val, melancholy, the nuns sad as they raised their voices.

Val glanced at her program and saw that it had been printed too early to erase the names of all the members of the choir, and as she studied the names, listed one after another, she saw something she'd missed earlier. Or was she nuts?

The sopranos were listed as:
Sister Camille
Sister Asteria
Sister Lucia
Sister Louise
Sister Edwina
Sister Devota
The altos were:
Sister Zita
Sister Irene
Sister Maura

When she took the first letters of the sopranos' names and listed them, they spelled out C A L L E D. If she drew a heart around the letters, like a noose, she'd get one of the messages Camille had left in her diary.

So what? she asked herself. *That's kind of random.* Still she felt a bit of a buzz run through her nerves, the sense that she was on to something—something important.

What had Camille said so long ago—that the sopranos all had a crush on Father Frank. Was it possible?

Val's mind was racing with possibilities, and the conclusion she drew was too bizarre to consider:

Camille had known which nuns had a crush on Father Frank.

Of the six, two were dead and two were missing. Both Sister Lucia and Sister Louise were nowhere to be found.

Val's insides turned to ice. Were they dead? Already dressed in bridal gowns, their throats sliced by the horrid garrote?

If so, she thought, looking over the list of names again, it meant that Sister Edwina and Sister Devota were his next victims!

Valerie turned her attention to the small choir, singing the Lord's praises, lifting their voices in song.

Sister Devota's gaze moved, slid across the room. For half a heartbeat, she stared straight at Valerie.

As if she knew.

As if she, too, felt the evil that was hiding in the corners, noticed the tremor of premonition that ripped though Val's soul.

Or was Val wrong?

Hadn't the killer told her differently? Hadn't he singled her out?

You're nexxxt, he'd rasped into her phone, telling her that she would be his victim. *There is no essscape.*

Sister Devota's gaze had shifted again, and Val drew in a long, calming breath.

She decided she wouldn't be played as a victim. *Bring it on, you twisted bastard,* she thought angrily. *I'm sick and tired of playing games.*

So this is it, I think from my spot on the upper landing. I stare down at the patrons of the orphanage as they gather, a teeming, glittering crowd, all eager to partake of the festivities.

A tribute to the whore...

A joke.

And yet, don't I feel her presence here? Don't I hear her laughter? A wave of regret passes through me as I think of Camille with her naughty smile and bright eyes.

"Teach me," she'd pleaded, so willing.

And I had.

But I hadn't been alone in her education, I realize.

There had been many teachers.

That was why she'd been so unique.

I've lost at love before, of course.

But this time... this time I cannot stand the pain.

I feel the rosary, deep in my pockets, the sharp beads clicking softly, and I smile as I find a back staircase, the one used by the hotel staff, and step inside.

I push the button with the arrow pointing downward, and it lights brightly.

With a groan, the old car shudders into motion and I descend.

As if to the very bowels of hell.

CHAPTER 50

Val had to tell him.

There was just no getting around it; she had to let Slade in on her plans.

"Let's get out of here," she whispered before the final prayer was intoned.

"Why?" Slade asked, but she was already pushing back her chair. When he caught the determination in her gaze, he followed suit. They weren't alone. Other patrons were leaving the hotel, hoping to dash the few blocks to the orphanage and start bidding on the items on display in the old gymnasium.

"I want to poke around in the records of the orphanage," she said under her breath, "before the whole place is torn down." She didn't have time to explain her urgency; it was just a feeling she had, stronger since seeing the picture of Sister Ignatia with the child. Soon the orphanage would be torn down or sold, the old records, those not on computer, lost or buried, the secrets they held gone forever.

"You can't just go digging through the old records."

"Not even if they're about me?" she whispered as they crossed the main foyer, past the stools where the string quartet had played earlier, and through the glass doors into the night.

Rain was coming down steadily now, the wind whipping up.

Slade battled the umbrella, then walked toward the church and orphanage. She sidestepped puddles as water rushed in the gutters, gurgling down the street, and though the air was warm, the drops falling from the sky felt cool and heavy.

As they made their way, she told Slade about what she'd seen in the program, how she'd tied it to Camille's notes. He listened, holding the umbrella, but shook his head.

"You don't think it's anything?" she asked.

"Anything significant? I don't see it."

"You think I'm grasping at straws?"

"You tell me."

She didn't have time to argue with him, as they'd reached St. Elsinore's.

Lights blazed around the cathedral, washing the old bricks with an eerie illumination that seemed to magnify the decay, showing off the crumbling bricks and cracks in the whitewash. While Spanish moss danced and swayed in the gusting wind, gargoyles stood guard of the cathedral. Perched on the gables and downspouts, the tiny demons appeared to ogle the flow of humanity streaming into the heavy doors of St. Elsinore's.

It was silly to think that anything evil lurked here, Val knew, especially with all the patrons filling the building. Wasn't there safety in numbers?

You're nexxxxt, the gargoyle situated on the corner of the nave seemed to hiss from his roost. *There is no esssscape.*

"Bull," she said under her breath, refusing to freak herself out.

"What?" Slade leaned forward, obviously trying to hear her over the rush of the wind.

"Nothing," she said as they walked through the hallways lined with tables covered with items that were available for bidding, the silent part of the auction that would last until the verbal auction ended. The bigger items like the trips, a vintage carousel horse, and the Wembleys' piano would be offered once the silent auction was declared over, in this case in two hours.

People were already bidding on items, signing their names to bidding sheets, adding amounts to the dollar column. Around each table, someone from St. Elsinore's or St. Marguerite's was stationed.

Sister Simone and Sister Georgia, the reverend mother for St. Elsinore's, were already in the building, but Val also glimpsed several of the nuns who were in the St. Marguerite's choir. Sister Maura, Sister Devota, and Sister Zita were walking around the hallways and gymnasium, though she didn't see Sister Edwina. She told herself not to worry, that Edwina had been in the choir less than an hour earlier and that her theory that *C A L L E D*, the message left in Camille's notes, wasn't anything. Even if the notation indicated that the sopranos were half in love with Father Frank, it all had been just in Camille's mind.

Right?

At that moment, she saw Sister Edwina appear, walking swiftly out of the restroom.

Nothing to worry about other than her own case of nerves.

And what she had planned.

More and more people arrived, and the throng became louder, the halls more packed, the fever of bidding running hot through the crowd. Val felt her nerves tightening. Just being here brought back unwanted memories, and every time she caught a glimpse of Father Frank, she felt the pain and loss of Camille's death all over again . . . Camille's and her unborn child's deaths.

Bastard, she thought when she caught him leaning forward and talking to a little girl who was with her parents. It was nothing, a friendly gesture priests did all the time, but it made Val sick. The man was a fraud.

As if Father Frank felt her gaze, he turned his head and looked at her. She expected to see a smarmy, smug smile; instead she saw eyes without life, dead and haunted.

She turned away.

As the bidding was closed on the silent items, the staff and volunteers for the parishes collected the bidding sheets. Most of those attending worked their way into the gymnasium, a cavernous room with high ceilings and open rafters. If she closed her eyes, she could smell old sweat from soiled jerseys at basketball games and the teen angst and worry, even disappointment, of girls standing at the sidelines of a Friday-night dance. The old memories hung in the air, left over from the years when, off and on, the gym had been attached to a school.

Now the crowd was excited, enthralled, the buzz of the festivities, lubricated by a few glasses of wine, evident. Rain slanted against frosted windows high over stacked bleachers, but the room was stifling and hot, too many bodies giving off too much heat.

If a fire marshal had been around, Valerie believed he would have closed the place down. As it was, people were jockeying for position, and Father Thomas had climbed to the auctioneer's platform, a few steps higher than the crowd.

At his side was Sister Georgia, in her habit, and a slim woman with dark red hair that was almost auburn and a smile that lit up her face. She was introduced as Dr. Sam, the radio psychologist for WSLJ. Her program, *Midnight Confessions,* Father Thomas insisted was one of the most popular in not only New Orleans, but also most of the Gulf Coast.

Another couple of introductions were made before one more prayer, this time led by Father Paul, and finally the oral auction was officially open. Sister Georgia made the announcement.

First up, a trip for two to Las Vegas. But that wasn't all—there was a pair of matching wingback chairs donated by a local furniture store, a carousel horse that had been owned by a famous actress, and, of course, the grand piano. . . .

Montoya was on Valerie Houston like glue. He'd seen her leave the hotel early, and with a quick signal to Bentz, took off after her. She was with her husband, so that was good, but he was still worried about the message she'd received earlier, the threat claiming she was to be the next victim.

Was it possible that it was a prank?

Sure.

But he didn't think so.

His gut told him to follow her, so he gave Bentz the high sign, then called him on his cell. Bentz was on Father O'Toole, while Brinkman, Zaroster, and several other undercover cops were watching the group as a whole.

Everyone in the department thought the killer wouldn't be able to stand it, would be lured out of the shadows by all the festivities and media attention. If he was going to go after Valerie Renard Houston, Montoya intended to be there.

He followed her and the husband to the church and watched as they mingled with the other guests; he even went so far as to hang out in the gymnasium where the oral auction was beginning. One of the guests of honor was Samantha Leeds Walker, the radio psychologist and original target of Father John ten years earlier.

As he watched Dr. Sam step up to the microphone, he felt a tightening in the back of his neck, the foreboding that something bad was about to happen. If Father John was truly here, if he was the monster they were chasing, the killer who'd strangled Grace Blanc with a rosary, wouldn't he turn his attention to his original target?

Ten years ago, that sick son of a bitch had killed women who looked like Dr. Sam, who he made to look like her. Was she the primary target, or was Valerie Houston? Was the call to Valerie a way to throw the police off his real target?

Val, standing near the back of the gymnasium, took it as her cue. She'd already scoped out the building and knew that stairs leading to the basement were located in the office and on either end of the building. The office was being used by volunteers from an accounting firm to tally up the bids of the silent auction, so that was out. The south entrance was too close to the gym, it would be too easy to be spotted, so she would use the stairs to the north.

"Did I mention that this was a bad idea?" Slade said as they ducked beneath a velvet rope and slipped quietly along the hallway leading away from the gym.

"Only about a thousand times."

"Make it a thousand and one, okay?"

"Duly noted." She hurried around a corner to the staircase, which, of course, was locked. "Damn," she said, pounding a fist upon the door. She'd thought—well, hoped really—that it would be easier than this. Of course, she'd figured that might not be the case.

"Okay, let's take that as a sign."

"To give up?" She was shaking her head no way. "Maybe the door at the south end..." But what were the chances? The grounds were locked tight. Disgusted, she let out a frustrated sigh. "I know this might not be a big deal to you," she said, disappointed, "but it is to me. I think that somewhere in the archives down there"—she hooked a thumb at the basement door—"is the answer to a dozen questions about myself and about Camille, maybe even a clue as to who killed her. I tried going through the church, and Sister Georgia stonewalled me. And if you tell me to talk to the police, it will take forever. By that time, this place could be a pile of rubble."

"The archdiocese won't destroy the records," he argued, but she saw him wavering.

"Not on purpose, maybe, but someone definitely doesn't want me to know the truth." She leaned her head back against the panels of the door. "Oh, hell," she muttered, and Slade touched her on the shoulder.

"I've got a Pomeroy lock-pick set in my truck."

"Not on you?" But she felt a rush of adrenaline; they could actually get through this blocked passage.

"No." His grin was a slash of white. "I really didn't think I'd need one."

"You were wrong."

"Again, apparently." He shook his head. "I'll go get it and will be back in ten minutes, so don't go anywhere."

"I won't."

"I don't know . . ." He glanced nervously down the darkened hall.

"I'm here with five hundred people and police everywhere," she said, reading the worry in his eyes. "And I was a cop."

"*Was* being the operative word in that sentence. And you don't have a weapon."

"I'll be fine."

"Why do I think I'm making a mistake?" he muttered, then to her surprise grabbed her around the waist, drew her tight against him, and pressed anxious lips to hers.

When he lifted his head, he rested his forehead on hers. His breathing was as ragged as her own, his heart beating hard enough that she could feel its restless cadence.

"You think you're making a mistake," she said breathlessly, trying to make light of the situation, "because you're the husband. That's what husbands do."

"Yeah, right." He snorted his disbelief and pulled the pistol from the waistband of his pants. "Take this."

"We're at a charity event at an orphanage, for God's sake!"

"And you're chasing a killer."

"You didn't think you'd need lock picks, but you thought a gun might come in handy?"

He glowered at her and pressed the .38 into her palm. It felt good. Solid. Reminded her of her days as a detective. "Take it, or I won't go."

"Fine!" She tucked the gun into her purse.

"Use it if you have to."

"I won't have to."

He wasn't listening to any excuses. "You owe me, wife." He pulled away and started jogging for the main doors. Tall and athletic, his jacket flapping, his boot heels ringing in the hallways, he disappeared around a corner.

"Oh, don't I know it," she whispered, her heart twisting a little.

Sister Charity slipped from the gymnasium after the bidding had begun on a premier item, a trip for two to Las Vegas. That's what all her devotion and sacrifice had come to; it felt like pawning Jesus for "two fabulous days and nights" in Sin City, an expensive penthouse hotel room, complete with a hot tub big enough for six and complimentary tickets to some concert—Wayne Newton—or Cirque du Soleil.

All in the name of the Holy Father.

Heart heavy, worry propelling her, she slipped through the hallways of St. Elsinore's, the ghosts of the past giving chase as she embarked on her mission.

And you, are you so much better? Silently reproaching the selling of vacations, but you, skulking through the hallways, intent on doing anything you can to ensure your secrets are safe. Who are you to judge, Charity Varisco? A fine reverend mother you are!

She shut her ears to the nagging voice in her head, pasted on a smile she hoped looked genuine, then nodded to a few straggling parishioners who were still hanging in the hallways. But she didn't stop to speak to any of them and made her way straight to the restroom and into a stall. She waited a few seconds, and once she was certain no one was inside, drew a deep breath and slid into the hallway unnoticed.

She didn't return to the gymnasium but hurried away, in the opposite direction, under the ropes that indicated that the rest of the building and the south hallways were off-limits and restricted. Nearly running, her skirts rustling, the beads of her rosary clicking, she found her way to the door of the basement in the south wing. She was concentrating on withdrawing her key ring, one she'd kept for decades, and silently praying that the locks of the ancient building hadn't been changed when she thought she heard something.

A footstep?

A sharp intake of breath?

She paused, looking into the dark corridor, toward the end of the building, the darkened, silent end. Was that a movement, near the far window? Her heart clutched, but as she squinted, she saw nothing lurking in the shadows. And she didn't have time to investigate. Fifteen minutes, she told herself. She could only be gone fifteen minutes, twenty on the outside, before someone would notice or start asking questions. She could cover for herself for that short span of time, but not much longer.

At the door, she paused only to make a quick sign of the cross. Then she inserted her key into the lock, twisted, and with a welcome click, disengaged the bolt. "Thank you," she whispered, feeling that God was guiding her as she slipped through the doorway and snapped on the light switch as her footsteps clattered loudly down the stairs.

God? Or a demon straight from Satan's legion?

She thought about the mistakes she'd made in her lifetime, the falsehoods she'd spun all in the name of vanity and pride. She'd atoned for years, slapping herself with that sharp riding crop in the mirrored room, sucking her breath as the leather straps bit into her flesh, mortified that Father Paul was watching, the old lech.

She'd had no choice but to allow his perversity, his ogling of her torture as he did God only knew what in his hiding place. But then he'd wanted more than just her nakedness to "admire," as he'd called it, when she knew it was more that he was interested in watching the suffering that comes with self-flagellation—the mortification.

Oh, she'd been a fool.

And here she was still covering up. She snapped off the lights to the stairwell, thought she heard something above but told herself it was just the crowd in the gymnasium, the old timbers of the building creaking with the weight of hundreds of excited people moving around on the floor above.

Snapping on another switch, the one that allowed the dim, hanging single bulbs to illuminate this rabbit warren of corridors, she walked unerringly through two hundred years of stored junk—everything from chairs and bed frames to old pictures, artifacts, desks, and mattresses. No doubt the rats were nesting in the alcoves where boxes were disintegrating, and she didn't want to think about the spiders . . . or the snakes. She heard the drip of rusting pipes, saw pools of condensation, and refused to consider the vermin that made the basement of St. Elsinore's home.

Though it was a shame that the buildings were being sold, possibly for demolition, she reminded herself that everything has a life span. Perhaps St. Elsinore's, with all its dark secrets, was rightfully in its death throes.

She found the area she was looking for. Cages of a sort. Areas walled off by chicken wire, beyond which were shelves of wooden crates, metal boxes, and plastic tubs, all labeled by date.

The combination lock was already open, the dial already spun appropriately to spring the shackle that held the door closed.

"Huh," she whispered to herself. *That's odd.*

She didn't have time to wonder about it. Seconds were clicking off quickly. She heard some noise from overhead—screaming? No, probably yells of delight. She walked into the wire room and studied the boxes until she found the one she wanted. She pulled it down from the middle shelf and was going to riffle through the files, to find the one she wanted, when she heard a noise again and looked up.

Her heart jolted and she dropped the tub as she saw a figure in the doorway, a figure she recognized, one with an evil smile and hard eyes.

In one hand was a file, in the other a wicked, long-bladed knife.

And on the floor, pooled near the door, a yellowed bridal gown.

* * *

Montoya watched as the bidding on a pair of chairs ended with Dr. Sam announcing, "Sold to number 514!" and the wingbacks were rolled to one side of the gym, while a white grand piano was pushed into the spotlight.

"Here's a gem," Father Thomas said with a wide, happy grin. "Donated by Arthur and Marion Wembley, a genuine Steinway Louis XV grand piano!" From his position on the auctioneer's platform, he allowed Dr. Sam to rattle off some of the finer points of the Steinway and looked proudly down on the piano as the volunteers lifted the lid and propped it up.

Dr. Sam was watching the action and was nearest the piano. "This rare, incredible instrument is rumored to have been played by..." Her voice trailed off, her eyes rounded, and she let out a scream that curdled through the gym. The attendant who had been propping up the piano's lid dropped it.

Bang!

"Holy Christ!" he said, backing up. "Holy...Oh, God!"

The shriek echoed through the gymnasium. Everyone else went silent. Staring.

Fear rippled through the cavernous room.

Montoya didn't wait a beat. He ran toward the stage, along an aisle, while the crowd, stunned, sat transfixed. The volunteer who had pushed in the piano, a large Asian man, was backing up and staring at the gleaming white Steinway as if it were the yawning gates of hell.

"Someone call nine-one-one," Samantha, finding her voice, yelled into the microphone. Still on the stage, white as a sheet and visibly quivering, trying to compose herself, she, too, couldn't take her eyes off the piano.

A collective gasp went up.

Confusion reigned.

Dozens of patrons were already reaching for their phones, digging in their pockets, searching their purses, ready to jam the lines to the emergency number.

Father Paul's face was a mirror of Dr. Sam's. White and filled with terror. "If we could all stay calm..."

But the voices of the crowd were already reaching Montoya's ears.

"What is it?"

"For the love of God, what did she see?"

"Look at Jim, would you? Yes, yes, he's the attendant. The one backing off the stage. Looks like he saw a ghost!"

"Oh my God, Chuck, we have to get out of here...."

Montoya pulled his badge from his jacket pocket, flipped it open, and held it high while running for the front of the gym. "Police!" He vaulted up the two steps of the stage and jogged to the piano. "Everyone stay calm." He caught Bentz's eye and those of several of the undercover guys. "Stay in your seats. We'll sort this out."

No one, he sensed, believed him.

At the piano, he lifted the lid and propped it up, then backed up a couple of steps as the stench of rotting flesh reached his nostrils.

It was the stench of death.

Inside was a woman's corpse. Dressed in a tattered bridal gown, her throat circled with a ring of dried blood, her face a mask of horror, the woman was sprawled upon the tuning pins and strings. Blood had pooled beneath her. Coagulated on the silvery strings. A rosary glittered darkly in her plump fingers.

"God help us," Father Frank, standing near the piano, said as he peered inside, then quickly made the sign of the cross and looked away.

Montoya's gut twisted and his jaw clenched in frustration. He wanted to retch as he stared into the terrified and very dead face of Sister Louise Cortez.

CHAPTER 51

Val eased down the darkened stairway. She'd propped the door open with one shoe so that Slade could catch up with her, then walked barefoot toward the light at the end of the stairs.

She'd heard Sister Charity approach as she'd waited near the basement stairs and had hidden in a small alcove that had once housed a water fountain. When the reverend mother had slipped through the door, she'd dashed across the hallway and caught the heavy door before it had latched.

Once the light to the stairs had been turned off, she'd slipped out of her shoes and into the stairwell.

She'd brought the gun, and feeling foolish, she'd taken it out of her purse and left the safety on. She was following a nun for God's sake, the reverend mother, so the weapon seemed ridiculous, yet she kept it in her hand as she moved silently down the stairs, biting her lip to keep from crying out in case she stubbed a toe in the dark.

She didn't want to chance discovery by turning on the lights over the steps; better to stay in the shadows, not alert the mother superior that she was being followed.

Why was Charity Varisco sneaking through the locked corridors of the orphanage during the auction? Shouldn't she be upstairs, part of the festivities? Then again, Val remembered the note

Camille had left: C U N 7734 R M C V. Val had come up with no other meaning than *See you in hell, Charity Varisco.* But that didn't make any sense, was no explanation. The other note with the arrows surrounding the words *Reverend Mother,* as if she were a target.

Down she went. In the hallway that was lit, she waited, seeing no one, stepping into the light. Heart in her throat, skin crawling, bare feet stepping across the dusty cement, she moved forward slowly.

She heard a nasty little squeak and the scrape of tiny nails, then saw a rat's beady eyes reflecting the light as he squatted in a corner. At the sight of her, the rat shot forward, diving into a hole, its scaly tail slithering after him.

Val, clenching her teeth, kept inching forward, and as she did, she heard the sound of voices. Angry, threatening voices.

The skin at the back of her neck prickled.

Her throat tightened, and she kept her gun out in front of her as she moved closer to the argument, her ears straining.

She recognized the reverend mother's voice, but there was someone else's, someone she should identify. Oh, God! It was the raspy, disguised whisper she'd heard on her phone.

"Is thissss what you're looking for?" it asked, and Val's heart thumped wildly, spurred by adrenaline and pure, crystalline fear. "Her birth certificate?"

Birth certificate? Whose birth cer—And then she knew that it was hers, the record of Valerie Renard's birth. It had to be. Her stomach became a fist.

"Give that to me." The reverend mother was insistent. Panicked.

"Why? So you can dessstroy it? No way. Come on, move it! Let's go!"

"I'm not leaving."

"You don't and I kill her. Got it? Like the others. She's nexxxt."

Val's knees threatened to give out. She flipped off the safety of the .38.

"You wouldn't."

"Of course I would!" Pure conviction. Determination. Evil intent. "You should know that by now. Aren't the others proof enough? Now get moving!"

For some reason, the mother superior was bargaining with the maniac for Val's life.

She heard a movement ahead, then walking, an uneven tread, Sister Charity's unwilling gait, probably, as she was being forced deeper into the bowels of the basement.

Somehow Val would have to stop this insanity. She had a gun. Did the killer? Could she take that chance? She stepped forward, ready to confront the murderer and his victim, when a switch was hit.

Click!

Darkness, stygian in its blackness, rained down on her.

Damn! Now what?

She could turn back, wait for Slade, find a cop in the gym, but she would lose time and probably the trail of the reverend mother and the killer in this rabbit warren that seemed to go on endlessly.

Who knew where the hallways and tunnels that made up this basement would lead? No, she had to follow. Not just for the knowledge on that birth certificate, but also for the mother superior's life!

Surely Slade would catch up with her...right?

Val didn't second-guess her instincts.

Hardly daring to breathe, her skin tight over her muscles, she followed the bob of a flashlight's beam as it wended its way deeper into the darkness.

"Everyone stay where you are!" Montoya was working crowd control, the rest of the force who had attended the auction keeping the patrons in the gym. The scene was a madhouse, panic threatening to overtake everyone inside.

The smell of Sister Louise's corpse had escaped, and a doctor had been called up to confirm what was so patently obvious: Sister Louise was dead.

The word was spreading like wildfire through the patrons. Some were weeping, one woman fainted, and some men wanted to give chase—but after whom? And to where?

Father Paul was trying to maintain some control, with Father Thomas, too, reaching out to their flock, reminding them to "stay calm and pray, seek God's counsel."

Father Frank was shell-shocked, leaning on the rail of the raised podium, looking as if he would keel over. Dr. Sam had managed to compose herself. Ty Wheeler, her husband, who had been in the crowd, ran forward to stand next to her, placing a strong arm over her slim, bare shoulders.

Montoya took the mic and reconfirmed what he'd tried to yell out earlier as he raced to the stage. "Everyone, listen up! I'm Detective Montoya, NOPD. Several of us are here, and we want you to know that we're handling the situation, but we need your help. Everyone stay calm. Return to your seats. We've got a... situation here, but as long as we all work together, it'll be okay. More officers and emergency workers are on their way, and as soon as they get here, we'll start talking to each of you, taking statements and letting you leave. Until then, please, just sit tight." He glanced over at Father Thomas and Dr. Sam, then added, "The auction will have to be postponed, and the staff at St. Elsinore's will handle it and get in touch with all of you. For now, please, everyone just sit down."

Fear was palpable, evident in the round eyes and white faces. The woman who had passed out was being attended to by a doctor.

Montoya and Bentz had managed to keep everyone but those onstage, and briefly the doctor, away from the body and had called for more backup, but the place was a nightmare.

Some people were craning their necks trying to look inside the piano. Others were at the doors trying to escape, while still others huddled together, worried and afraid, their night ruined, all concerned that a killer could be in their midst.

Montoya didn't doubt it for a minute. He closed the lid of the piano while Bentz talked to the guy who pushed it into the display area.

How had Sister Louise, a big woman, been lifted inside and no one knew? Where had she died? When?

A dozen questions would have to be answered if they could, but for now he had to deal with crowd control, help keep the panic at bay.

Father Frank, who heretofore had been quiet, almost paralyzed, gathered himself, straightening his shoulders as he took a step toward the podium. "I suggest we pray again," he said, and before anyone could argue, he bowed his head and made the sign of the cross over his vestments. In his deep baritone, he began, "Holy Father..."

Most of the crowd followed suit, and for the first time since the investigation into Camille Renard's death had started, Montoya felt as if the real Frank O'Toole was finally emerging.

As the parishioners lowered their gazes, Montoya also noted that Valerie Houston and her husband weren't in the gym, and other people he'd seen earlier were missing, though some could be in the restrooms and the office adding up the bids from the silent auction.

Brinkman was covering the office, Zaroster and two undercover cops the hallways. He, Bentz, and the two priests were keeping the crowd in the gym, but he knew around any nook or corner, in any corridor or bell tower, Father John could be lurking.

Waiting.

And there would be more victims who would suffer his deadly wrath.

While Father Frank O'Toole led the congregation in prayer.

Slade found her shoe.

Dripping wet from his mad dash outside, he raced to the north staircase, and just as a collective gasp went up from the gymnasium, he located the open door propped by a sling-backed high heel belonging to Val.

Damn!

How the hell had she opened the door? And why were the lights out? Hadn't he told her to stay put, made her swear she'd wait for him?

Well, it figured...

A bad feeling stole over him, but he stopped himself from yelling out to her, sensed that there was trouble. Serious trouble.

Soaked to the skin, he kept his lock picks in his hands and noiselessly descended the stairs just as he heard the sound of sirens, screaming through the stormy night, their shrieks piercing and getting louder as emergency vehicles approached.

Good!

Get the hell here, he thought frantically as he reached the bottom of the stairs. Rather than risk the overhead lights, he found a lighter in his pocket and switched it on, the tiny flickering flame casting the gloom of the basement in shifting, uneasy shadows.

Again he heard the wail of sirens.

Get here fast! For the love of God, get the fuck here fast!

Heart trip-hammering, nervous sweat prickling her skin, Val managed to follow the beam of the flashlight as it washed across crates and cement walls. The weak beam showed in trembling blue light the cracks in the foundation, the collection of forgotten artifacts, furniture, and memorabilia as they descended even farther, through an archway and two sets of doors.

At every turn, she thought she would be discovered, and she wondered, as the temperature lowered and they walked down yet another set of stairs, where they were going.

Deeper and deeper beneath the orphanage, to a point where the corridors became tunnels, the cement of the walls changing into roughly hewn rock.

Val tamped down her fear, but as the temperature dropped, she began to sweat even more, her nerves strung as tight as piano wires, her heart beating a nervous, irregular tattoo, the pistol clutched in her fingers.

Where was Slade? Oh, God, could he please show up and bring the damned cavalry with him? Or would she have to face the killer alone, perhaps shoot a priest?

Down a narrow set of steps where the walls felt as if they were closing in on her, she followed the dim blue light. Cobwebs hung from the lowering ceiling, clinging to her hair, brushing against her face. The air smelled as if it hadn't been fresh in decades, with dust and rot combining to form a dank odor that caused her skin to crawl. It was all she could do not to cough as they opened a final door.

"Why are we here?" Charity asked, her voice quavering with fear as it ricocheted hollowly back through the tunnels to Val.

The light had stopped moving, shining thinly against the stone walls.

"There's someone I want you to meet."

Oh, God, Val thought worriedly, *the killer has an accomplice!* She glanced over her shoulder and strained to hear, listening for any sound of another person. . . . Were there footsteps following her? Did she hear the sound of labored breathing? Had she walked into a trap? She whirled quickly, the .38 pointed into the dark, her finger sweating on the trigger.

In her mind's eye, she saw the demon from her nightmares, the rat-eyed monster with the silvery chain. *That was only Sister Ignatia. You know it. Don't let your imagination get the better of you!*

Her heart felt as if it might explode.

But no one, no *thing,* leaped out at her.

Swallowing her fear, Val turned back to the light and edged closer, staying in the shadows, her eyes adjusting to the weird light. She realized with sickening disgust that they'd made their way down to a tomb of sorts, where coffins were tucked into pockets cut into the stony walls, a few, old and rotting, standing on their narrow ends, propped against the dusty wall. Charity was standing in front of a single casket, the lid of which gaped, as if it had never been sealed. As if it were waiting.

It was still too dark to see the killer's face, but she caught a glimpse of a knife, a long, sharp blade that glinted in the half-light. There was a pool of white at the madman's feet—the once-white lace of a bridal gown.

Oh, God, no!

This psycho was going to kill Sister Charity, strangle her with a sharp garrote and squeeze the life from her as soon as he forced the nun into the damned dress.

Val had to stop this madness. She had to!

"What do you want from me?" Charity asked, glancing nervously at her captor.

"To atone for your sins—and none of that flogging you do for that old pervert Father Paul. No, I want you to admit that you're a liar and a fraud," the killer said, sneering, "that you're unfit to be a bride of Christ. Just like the others."

"Oh, Dear Father," Charity whispered. "You know?"

"That you had a love child with Arthur Wembley?" the killer sneered.

Now, without the voice's rasp, Valerie thought she recognized it; she'd heard it before. A soft voice...

I'm sorry, Reverend Mother, the voice had said as Sister Charity's lips pinched in silent rebuke.

Valerie's heart froze.

It was the same voice she'd heard in the garden at St. Marguerite's, the same, she now realized, as the snotty little girl with the cast thirty years earlier, who had barred Cammie from the slide and said slyly, *"You know what seven-seven-three-four is, don't you? It's hell."*

Sister Devota?

She was the killer?

A woman?

A nun?

No! That was nuts...too crazy...

As if the killer had read her mind, she sprang into action. Val, still gripping the gun, heard a frantic quick shuffling of feet, shoes sliding over the floor. A scuffle of sorts. A struggle.

No!

Val took a step forward as a woman, Sister Charity, mewled pitifully.

Then all became suddenly quiet.

Deathly quiet, the tomb feeling like death itself.

Goose bumps rose on the back of Valerie's arms, fear wrapping cold talons over her soul.

Save her...you have to save her.

Slowly she crouched, glancing behind her into the inky folds of darkness, feeling as if she were about to be ambushed.

Someone coughed.

Val whipped her head toward the sound, toward the eerie wash of blue light just as a grating voice slithered from the murky dead air. "Come on out of the shadows, Valerie. Oh, yes, I know you're there. I know you followed me. I waited for you. So come on out."

Val's stomach dropped. She didn't move a muscle.

"You heard me," Devota said, angry now. "Come out from your ridiculous hiding place. Don't you know you can't hide? You're on my turf now, Val. Mine and God's."

Val still didn't move. She could still get the drop on this psycho!

"Oh," the raspy voice said, as if suddenly remembering some small detail. "And drop the gun, or I will, right here and now, in front of your eyes, slit your pathetic mother's throat!"

Slade heard voices.

Not from the auction overhead but from the dark space in front of him, the words garbled and soft as they slid from deep in the tunnels that he'd found, a complicated series of tombs that smelled of death and decay. A place where rats scurried, pipes dripped, and he felt as if he were walking through the smoldering ashes of long-forgotten lives.

He was moving as quickly as he could, images of Val facing off with the killer filling his mind. He saw her struggling, a garrote at her neck, the strong hands of the killer twisting tighter and tighter, cutting off her air, the sharp noose cutting through her beautiful neck.

Don't go there! Just keep moving! Save her, for Christ's sake!

His lighter was little illumination, and he took another wrong turn, then doubled back. Breathing hard, fear sizzling through his body, he forced himself to stop and listen, his ears straining to hear over the fear pounding in his heart. The sounds of the auction had long disappeared, and here, several stories beneath the building, he moved forward.

He thought of Valerie, and his insides turned to water when he imagined losing her, that some maniac might wrap a flesh-slicing garrote around her throat and squeeze the life from her. He thought for a moment of what his life would be like without her, how empty the world would be.

No, he thought, his jaw turning to granite. He'd do anything to save her.

Anything!

God help him that he still had enough time.

CHAPTER 52

The crowd in the gymnasium was restless, but backup had arrived, the officers taking charge, EMTs on hand to help with those who were feeling ill.

Bentz, eyeing the restless throng, gave up his position to Zaroster and approached Montoya with the bad news. "There's a door open to the basement in the north wing," he said. "Zaroster discovered it and we've got a uniformed guy standing guard."

"Why?"

"It was locked earlier. I checked with Sister Georgia, the reverend mother here." He was fidgeting, his eyes searching the crowd, chewing gum like a fiend, feeling that something was going down. Something bad. "And we've got some people missing."

"Valerie and Slade Houston?"

"And Sister Charity and Sister Devota, that I can come up with off the top of my head." His gaze roved the crowd. "Who knows who else?"

Father John!

"Son of a bitch."

Bentz nodded. "My thoughts exactly."

"He's here!" Montoya was certain of it. He had only to think of Sister Louise's dead body stuffed into the piano... "Shit a brick! You think he's got them?"

Bentz didn't answer. But, yeah. He did. But he wasn't going to voice it. Not yet. "I don't know, but let's find out." Bentz was already heading out of the gym, cutting past people in their fancy clothes and worried expressions, hoping to get one more shot at Father Fucking John.

This time, the bastard wouldn't survive.

Devota had lunged, grabbing Charity from behind, twisting one arm back so painfully that Charity heard her tendons popping. She'd cried out as the younger woman had drawn a knife to her throat, but she'd known her scream was useless.

Charity had tried to fight but had lost the battle before it had begun. She was sweating and scared, her heart beating so frantically she thought it might explode.

What could she do?

How could she save herself?

How could she save her daughter?

Oh, Sweet Mother Mary, why had she spent her life holding on to her lies, spinning more, compromising her soul?

Devota had barked out a threat: "And drop the gun, or I will, right here and now, in front of your eyes, slit your pathetic mother's throat!" and Charity's knees had buckled.

Valerie couldn't be here! Oh, dear Father, no, not after all the years Charity had so rabidly tried to protect her only child.

"Did you hear me, whore?" Devota snarled, her breath hot against Charity's ear, the thin blade at her throat, slicing into her skin, cold and wicked as it split her flesh.

Charity whimpered as she felt her warm blood begin to flow from a wound already stinging. How could this be happening? Why would Devota, the girl she'd met at St. Elsinore's when Charity had worked there, the poor child who had broken her leg and had always walked with a limp thereafter, turn on her? How had she become this vile monster? Surely, as God would see to it, there was an ounce of reverence, of piety, of goodness still within her soul. "Devota, please... think of the Blessed Mother. Do not give into Satan's calling."

"Shut up, you old hypocrite!" Devota hissed. "What do you know? Always hiding your own sins and judging others for theirs.

Your time is over, *Mother*," she snarled. "You can take it up with God when you see him." Then, to the surrounding darkness, "You! Valerie Renard! Sister of the whore! Step forward!" She wrenched Charity's arm, and the older woman squealed in pain. She couldn't fight—the knife blade was too sharp—and if she complied, perhaps Valerie would be saved. . . .

But she knew better.

Weren't Camille and Asteria proof enough of that, and probably Louise and Lucia as well? Her knees crumpled.

Devota yanked her to her feet. "I said, step forward!"

To Charity's ultimate horror, Valerie complied. *Blessed Mother of God, please, stop this madness.* But she watched in terror as Valerie stepped into the cruel, frail light.

Tall and beautiful, as strong as her father had once been, Valerie leveled her gun directly at Devota's head. "She is *not* my mother."

"Of course she is! Don't you know that this is what it's all about? That you were the love child of this old lady and that wheezing skeleton who donated the piano?" Devota seemed amused at that. "That's where they'll find Louise, you know, in the piano, but no longer singing, I'm afraid. She's sung her last solo."

"Oh, for the love of the Holy Mother." Charity's worst nightmares were confirmed.

"And your dear old daddy, Wembley, used his money to pay off everyone, including Mike and Mary Brown, so that no one would know. Everyone kept the secret, just as long as the money kept flowing. Sinners, every last one of them!"

"Don't listen to her," Charity said, and was rewarded with another sharp tweak to her left arm. Her right was free; she could swing back and hit Devota in the face, but that would probably ensure that she would die as the knife blade found her jugular or carotid.

"But I'm not lying, am I?" Devota whispered with a kind of horrid, dark glee. "I found out the truth that you worked so hard to hide all these years . . . your secret love child."

"Please," Charity whispered, her head thundering, the truth hammering away at her brain, chipping at her pride and exposing her self-loathing as warm blood slid down her neck in this musty, dark tomb.

"Wasn't too hard to do," Devota bragged. "All I had to do was shadow the whore. She was on to something, found out about the adoption papers being altered when she worked at St. Elsinore's. And then she came down here and verified everything she'd put together."

"I don't believe you! Let her go!" Valerie insisted, unflagging, her eyes directed on Devota.

"Then again, you always were dull. I remember you from the orphanage."

Charity could feel Devota's bitterness curdling through the dusty air. She, the unwanted one, the lame girl, the one always passed over.

Valerie took another step forward. Her voice was low. Threatening. "I said, let her go!"

"Not just yet."

"Now." Valerie didn't drop the gun.

"You're not in control," Devota reminded her.

But Valerie, as tough as Charity had been in her own wasted youth, didn't back down. "Why are you doing this?" she asked, verbalizing the questions that had formed in Charity's mind.

"God's work," Devota said again, with that drip of satisfaction at finally explaining herself, her mission.

It scared Charity to death.

Devota tightened her grip. "Someone has to get rid of the harlots who shame the church, who defile the order. So you see, your 'sister,' she really wasn't any blood relation to you. Oh, yeah, she looked like you, but there was nothing between you. Nothing! It was a lie. Anything that said otherwise, about how you resembled each other, was pure coincidence...or fantasy. People see what they want to see, you know, but Camille, she found out."

Charity felt her captor tense at the thought of Sister Camille, as if the prettier woman had been her rival. "Everyone bought into her act, but she was dark below the surface. Pure evil."

Val's face, in the weird light, remained impassive.

Devota went on, almost as if the words that had been bottled up in her for years were now bubbling upward, like froth from some ruined, bitter champagne finally uncorked. "She couldn't wait to stick it to Old Man Wembley. I followed her, witnessed the old woman, the *wife*, paying the blood money to Camille, and you know what she did with part of it? She gave it to that witchy little Lucia. That twit! I saw it with my own eyes, and it didn't take too long to put two and two together."

"You don't know what you're talking about!" But Valerie was wavering, her voice not as strong.

"Of course I do!" Devota snapped, suddenly angry all over again, spittle flying as she added, "True to her nature, that Jezebel was blackmailing the Wembleys, and the missus, she wasn't too happy about it!"

Charity couldn't stand to hear another word. "What do you want from me?" she demanded, reeling from the mortification of her life, her secrets, being exposed—to the very daughter she'd tried to save.

She realized that she was about to lose her life, now, when she had so many sins to atone for.

"What do I want from you?" Devota repeated, unafraid of the gun that was trained on her. She was breathing hard, furious, as she sneered into Charity's ear, "I think you know, *Reverend Mother*. I want you to pay, of course. Like the others. They, too, were whores, all of them in love with Father O'Toole."

"No!" Charity shook her head. She wouldn't have the sisters vilified.

But Devota was convinced of their sins. "I know that probably only Camille had actually lain with him," she said, and a shudder ripped through her body. Charity could feel it. As if the thought of Camille and Frank together was so vulgar Devota could hardly stand it, was nearly to the point of vomiting. Yet, she wasn't finished.

"But the others, they wanted to. I saw it in their eyes, those pious little hypocrites. Every last one of them." She was breathing hard, as if she'd walked up fifty flights of steps, her rage seeping through her blood. The fingers around Charity's wrist gripped harder. "All of those pretty little girls who had all the advantages, who had been adopted to homes...with...with parents. And brothers and sisters." She was nearly panting with her rage. "They shared Christmas Eves with the grandmothers who baked apple pies and filled their stockings with hand-knit caps and dollies and little tins of chocolate," she said bitterly, the girl always left behind. "They believed in Santa Claus and had siblings to fight and play with, boyfriends in high school. They had crushes and friendship rings and ... and some of them were cheerleaders or athletes before going to college with men meant to be their husbands." She was spewing her anger, nearly choking on the unfairness of it all. Her fingers clenched so tightly Charity cried out, but Devota, in her rage, didn't notice, didn't care. She was reliving all the injustices thrust upon her. "They had first kisses and first loves, and they wrote in diaries...." She glanced at Valerie. "Oh, yes, they wrote all their lurid thoughts in diaries. All their sinful acts recounted and detailed..."

Charity saw her daughter wince, and for the first time the gun wobbled, if only just a bit.

"You blame the girls who were adopted?" Valerie whispered, disbelieving.

Why didn't Valerie leave? Charity thought desperately. Val could just run away, hide in the dark and save herself. But staying here, arguing with Devota, was of no use. She would only end up getting herself killed. "You should go," Charity said, trying to hold her daughter's eyes. "Quickly..."

Valerie glared at Devota, moved a little to the left but didn't turn tail. "The others were innocent."

"Innocent?" Devota repeated in revulsion. "Those idiots? They didn't know the meaning of the word! Only when they'd had their fill of their normal lives, when their parents or a boyfriend or life didn't give them what they wanted did they come running back, crying out that they wanted to be nuns. To be pure of spirit. To become brides of Christ!"

She squeezed Charity. "And you took them in, didn't you, Reverend Mother? Every last pathetic one of them, especially your pets, those who came from St. Elsinore's. You gave them a new life, instruction, and showed them the way, but all the while you were a scheming, lying fraud! A whore who slept with a married man, bore him a child and hid it all!"

"No," Charity squeaked, feeling blood slide beneath her collar. *Please, Valerie, leave. Leave now!* She tried to stall. "I believe—"

"I don't care what you believe. It's all a lie anyway. And God knows!" Devota said. "He sees you for what you are and the rest of them, too, when their vows got too difficult. All of them were ready to jump into the first handsome priest's bed." She leaned closer, her spit touching the shell of Charity's ear, her rancor oozing through the old tombs. "I saw them, Reverend Mother, and so did you, but you allowed it, didn't you? You let them flirt. You let them dream. You let them fantasize and imagine sleeping with him. Because you knew of their hunger, their desire, their evil, vile desire."

This was going so badly. And Valerie...*Holy Father, please make her leave. Don't let her blood be spilled.* "They...they may have had fantasies, but—"

"But they were supposed to be devoted to Jesus, the son of the Holy Father!" Devota nearly screamed, her voice cracking, the depth of her fanaticism showing.

Charity remembered her as she was: Darlene, a half-crippled, unwanted, and never adopted child, and the girl had embraced the life of the convent with open arms. There had been a darkness to her, too, a cancer in her soul that Charity had hoped would shrivel with her faith. She'd renounced her given name of Darlene and taken Devota, but the cancer, that blackness planted by Satan, had taken over, and the woman before her, a monster bent on her own vision of righteousness, was no better than Lucifer himself.

Fear pounded through Charity's brain as the blood trickled from her neck. Despite her pain, she stared straight at her only daughter and silently prayed that Valerie would have the good sense to run into the darkness, to never look back at this monster Charity had helped create. "Leave," she ordered desperately. "Leave now!"

Val only took another step to that same side, as if to get a better angle for her shot, as if she hadn't heard a word Charity said. With incredible calm, she stood in the wavering light. "I said, let her go." Valerie was firm, her eyes trained on the sick woman holding the knife.

"No."

"I'll shoot."

"Of course you won't! You can't shoot that in here," Devota said in disgust, as if Val were a complete moron. "You'll miss and hit your mother, or the bullet will ricochet and kill you both." She paused a moment, taking in little short breaths, as if a finger of excitement had slid down her spine, a new, thrilling energy passing from her body to Charity's. "I think there's someone you both might want to meet."

Oh, dear God! Charity, the blood from her neck spilling onto her shoulder, felt a new dread. The tone in Devota's voice was triumphant.

Smug.

Devota shifted then and, letting the knife slip a little, yanked open one of the coffin doors, the one that had never really been sealed.

To Charity's absolute horror, a corpse, rotting and desiccated, tumbled out of the coffin.

"Son of a—!" Val gasped, and jumped back.

Charity let out a bloodcurdling scream. Her knees gave way as she stared at the dead body of a woman who was little more than bones, pieces of dried flesh, and scraps of hair. The woman's skin had shriveled, her eye sockets were empty and black, and she was wearing the remains of a stained and threadbare wedding gown, its faded ribbons and tattered lace fluttering in the dim, eerie light.

"Recognize her?" Devota demanded.

Oh, yes. Of course she did. With sickening clarity, Charity knew she was looking at the body of Sister Lea De Luca, the nun who was supposed to have left for San Francisco years ago, the one who had sent her cards.

Devota gloated, "It's amazing how easy it is to find someone to send mail from another city. And all the while you"—she wrenched Charity's arm and she nearly cried out—"thought you knew what happened to her. You thought that you'd dealt with 'the problem.'"

"You're insane," Val whispered, the gun no longer steady. "You killed this woman."

"Punished her," Devota corrected. "Sent her soul to hell. Just like the others. It was so easy. I just told her that Father Frank was waiting. For her. Down here. And she fell for it. Put on her pretty little dress."

"Because you drugged her!" Val accused.

"I *helped* her."

"By luring her down here and killing her?"

"She was a slut. A whore! She didn't deserve him."

Devota was so enraged she was starting to tremble.

"Frank O'Toole?" Val's lips curled in revulsion.

"And," Devota ranted, "she didn't deserve to wear the holy habit, not with all her impure thoughts, her dreams of whoring with him! Lea deserved what happened."

"You can't play God," Charity whispered.

"Didn't you? Every day, Mother? *Pretending* to do his work, to do what was best, to lead us all on the righteous path? And all the while you were holding your precious secrets. I just wonder how many times you let that old man take you to his bed, how many times you slept with him, how many times you touched him, kissed him, did what he begged. Is that what this is all about?" She took her knife and sliced it downward, ripping through the fabric of Charity's habit. Charity felt the cold steel tip of the blade slice into her skin, running down one side of her spine, like a fish about to be filleted.

"Stop!" Val ordered.

But the knife slit the habit in two.

Tears filled Charity's eyes.

She stared at the rotted corpse.

In that moment, she knew that both she and her daughter were doomed.

God help me. Help us.

She had to do something. Try anything. To save her daughter and her own black soul.

Gathering all her strength, Charity let out a scream of fury and rage, of hate and defiance; then, closing her eyes, she forced her knees to go slack, to unhinge.

She collapsed.

And a startled Devota tumbled with her to the floor.

"Valerie!" Slade yelled out her name, and it came echoing back to him, tumbling through the tunnels, over a heart-stopping shriek that bounced off the walls.

"Hell!" He ran toward the sound, frantic with fear, certain that the maniac had Val in his clutches.

Goddamn it, why had he left her alone while he retrieved the damned picks for the lock? He knew she wouldn't stay put, not if given the chance. He'd been a fool. And now Val was paying the price.

Dread thundering through his skull, he blundered through the darkness, not caring if anyone knew he was in the tombs.

It didn't matter.

Let the killer be distracted from his heinous act.

Let the son of a bitch focus on Slade.

Bring it on, you bastard!

He only prayed that he could get to Valerie in time. If he didn't... if Val was already dying at the hands of that maniac, then Slade would personally send the son of a bitch's soul straight to hell.

No!

Val saw the reverend mother, *her* mother, sink to the floor. Blood slid down skin that was bared, the flesh of Sister Charity's back scarred and covered in welts, as if she'd been whipped over and over again.

As Charity fell, she clutched the killer's skirts and dragged Devota downward.

Valerie threw herself at them, lunging, ready to push the nose of her pistol against the monster's head and pull the damned trigger. She'd blow the psycho's brains out and to hell with the consequences. "You bitch!"

Devota was ready, wouldn't give up easily.

She kicked out with her good leg, her heel connecting with Val's shin.

Craack!

Pain splintered up Val's leg.

Another sharp thrust of Devota's good foot.

Bam! The heel of Devota's shoe struck hard.

Ricocheting pain as sharp as a serpent's bite screamed through her bones, sending her reeling.

The gun spun out of her hands. She scrambled for it, juggling it, sucking in her breath, the agony ripping up her leg, causing a blackness to pull at the edges of her eyes.

She couldn't pass out! Not now!

She lost control of the pistol. It spun into the dark.

Clang!

Steel hit the hard rock floor, then skidded away.

No! No! No!

Desperately, Val flung herself at the .38. Her toe snagged on the outstretched, bony legs of Sister Lea's corpse.

Val fell forward.

Bam!

Her chin bounced on the stone floor.

Her teeth jarred.

Her palms scraped along the rough stones, scraping skin, breaking fingernails as she scrambled for the damned gun.

Her legs tangled in the lacy folds of the wretched wedding dress, and she looked up to see Devota, breathing hard, eyes glittering with hatred in the faded light, a looming figure draped in black, struggling to her feet.

Like the monster in her dreams. More evil and callous and malicious than Sister Ignatia. The bloody knife dripping from her hand.

A murderer dressed as a nun . . .

Fear coiled through Val.

"It's over," Devota said, smiling with a crazy, off-kilter grin that stretched her lips thin, snakelike, over her teeth. "You're nexxxt!"

Oh, God.

Horror curdled her blood as she kicked free of the yellowed folds of stained lace, her ankle and leg throbbing. "No, you stupid bitch," she whispered, her voice just as deadly, her hands searching, grasping for the gun. One fingertip brushed something cold and metal. The pistol! "You are. You're next!"

"Valerie!" Slade's voice echoed through the tombs.

"Here!" she yelled desperately, her fingers stretching over the .38's grip.

Too late.

With a scream of fury, Devota kicked the pistol away. It skittered across the floor. So incensed she nearly lost her balance as she dropped to her knees, she grabbed Sister Charity's veil and yanked hard, pulling back her head, exposing the mother superior's white throat. A tiny gold cross dangled and winked from a tiny chain around Charity's neck, where blood was already running.

"Stop! Don't!" Val yelled, horrified.

Sister Charity closed her eyes and started praying, her vulnerable throat working as she whispered, "Hail Mary, full of grace..."

In the smokey blue light of the flashlight, Val watched in horror as Devota drew back her knife, then, with a quick stroke borne of hatred, sliced the soft tissue of Sister Charity's throat.

"Oh, God, no!" Val cried.

Blood spurted from the reverend mother's throat, showering Devota and spraying against the coffins and walls of the crypt, bloody drops hitting the fleshless corpse of Sister Lea.

The flashlight went rolling, its beam spinning crazily against the tombs. Val caught glimpses of the hollow-eyed skeleton and Sister Charity's blinking, terrified face as she clutched her throat. Blood, dark and red, seeped through her old fingers, the silver wedding band on her finger disappearing in the ooze.

Their gazes met—mother and daughter. Val, her soul shredding as her mother bled, tried to stand, but her leg gave way and she fell, at the mercy of this beast....

"Don't," Charity whispered, pleading with Devota. "Please don't harm her..."

"Shut up!" Devota's nostrils flared in outrage. "I'm done listening to you!" She kicked the mother superior away.

"Leave her alone," Val said.

"And I'm not listening to you either!" Devota glared at Val. "You're as bad as the lot of them. All those stupid women. The girls in this damned orphanage. I tried to point them out to God so he could punish them, but he didn't seem to listen! Turned a blind eye to their sinful deeds. I meted out punishment, even back then, showed him the sinners. I even broke one girl's arm as she tried to steal from the bakery, but did he punish her? No! It was all up to me."

"She was only three," Charity whispered.

Devota grinned. "Too young to talk."

Damn it all to hell!

Val had heard enough. This monster had been hurting others, trying to destroy them, since she was a child. She'd probably been building to this point, bit by bit, and if anyone looked hard enough, they would find other victims who had been "punished" by her over the years. She'd escalated, her deeds getting more cruel as time passed. But what had finally pushed her over the edge to murder? Seeing Sister Lea with Father Frank? Falling in love with him herself? Hadn't Camille's cryptic message, a heart encased *C A L L E D*, included Devota as the *D*? Who really knew? Probably not even the murderess herself.

Eyes focused on Devota, Val slowly inched her way into the direction the gun had skidded.

But it was far too late.

"There is no essscape," Devota hissed, blood splattered all over her twisted, hateful face. She stood slowly, her bloody knife dripping over the bridal dress she'd brought with her. Like a monster from a horror movie, a hideous beast maimed but still bent on its hellish mission, Devota walked forward, dragging the damned dress.

Where's the pistol? Where?! Val's hands scrabbled over the rocky floor.

"Don't...please...love of God...Valerie...she's not...she isn't taking vows," Charity gurgled. Devota whirled on her.

Frantically, Val reached around her, searching for the .38, silently praying her fingers would encounter the barrel while her eyes were trained on Devota's twisted face. She tried and failed to ignore the hideous dripping blade dangling from Devota's blood-drenched fingers.

"I know she isn't a nun!" Devota said to the crumpled form of Sister Charity. "But she was adopted out, wasn't she?" Devota's expression filled with hatred. "She and the whore of a sister of hers, taken in by a family..." In the half-light, Devota returned her attention to Valerie. "And he fancied you, too. I saw him lay his hand on your shoulder when you talked to him, just as I saw the light in his eyes when Asteria handed him a rose in the garden, or the way he smiled at Sister Lea...Yes, even I fell for his charms, but I was stronger than to give in to my evil thoughts. God helped me see the truth, that I was stronger than those weak, quivering, lusting idiots.

Satan tempted them, you know. He lured them into falling for Father Frank, and they all willingly surrendered whatever piety, whatever courage, whatever devotion they'd once thought they'd had. They gave in. I didn't!" Her voice actually shook for a second. "And he, too, was to blame. God tested him, and Frank...Father Frank failed." She swallowed hard and hesitated for a second, collecting herself.

In a moment of striking clarity, Val knew that Frank had rejected Devota. Sometime, somewhere, she'd been passed over in his affections, just like she'd been passed over and never adopted to a family. Maybe it was real, maybe it was all in Devota's twisted mind, but the result was the same: one more strike to her battered, malevolent soul.

As if reading Val's thoughts, Devota shuddered and spat, "But he *liked you*, didn't he? Frank *lusted* after *you*!"

"No." This was taking a turn she didn't understand.

"Just like all those others who twittered and giggled, laughing and sighing at the sight of him, starting with...that!" She curled her lips in revulsion as she pointed her knife at the grisly remains of Sister Lea.

Val thought of the heart symbol with the letters inside. *C A L L E D*. She'd made a mistake. One of the Ls was not Sister Lucia, but Sister Lea. Camille, Asteria, Louise, Lea, Edwina, and Devota... How right Camille had been. They all, including Devota, had been in love with the priest.

"Did you see her last moments?" Devota demanded. When Val didn't respond, she clarified. "I'm talking about that whore of a woman you thought was your sister. The only child of Mike and Mary Brown."

The BlackBerry. And the horrid pictures of Asteria and Camille dying, struggling for breath, bleeding, their fingers scraping their own bloodied throats...

Rage boiled inside Val. "You sick, twisted bitch," she accused as Sister Charity let out a wheezing, gurgling breath. "Who do you think you are?"

"God's servant."

"What?" Val couldn't believe her ears. "Oh, for the love of— You sanctimonious, self-aggrandizing bitch! You killed those women because they were adopted? Because Frank O'Toole liked them? You're out of your mind!"

"Oh, but they were happy," Devota argued. "You should have seen them smile blissfully as they put on their ridiculous gowns."

"Because they were drugged!"

"High on love."

"Bull!" Val knew that they'd been drugged. Devota might have been able to get what she needed through the clinic where she worked or from some of the people she was supposed to be helping, some of them drug addicts. Val felt sick when she thought of Cammie and how she'd been duped, used by this twisted, vengeful woman.

In the flashlight's beam, she caught sight of a glint, a bit of metal. The gun! Fifteen feet away.

"Nuh-uh-uh!" Devota warned, as if reading her mind. She raised her brutal knife high overhead, its dripping blade ready to strike again.

"Go to hell!"

Val rolled toward the weapon.

"Val!" Slade yelled, his deep voice reverberating through the halls.

Surprised, Devota glanced toward the sound.

Val touched the barrel of the gun with the tip of her fingers, but it spun away again, skittering over the stones.

Devota turned back and saw Val's mistake. "Stupid Jezebel!" With surprising agility, Devota leaped forward, her fingers curled like talons over the knife, her shadow a hideous wraith. "Die!" She thrust her arm out. The wicked blade gleamed steely blue, slashing downward, bits of blood flying.

Val flung herself to one side.

Too late.

Hot pain seared down her shoulder.

"Die! Damned your heathen soul to Satan!" Devota hissed, and jerked her knife upward, determined to plunge it into Valerie's heart.

"Stop, you goddamned bitch!" Slade yelled from somewhere in the shadows, somewhere behind the killer's back. "Drop the knife!"

From the corner of her eye, Val saw him step into the light, his face drawn, his eyes blazing, ten feet from Devota's back. Fury twisted his features, but he didn't give Devota a second to think.

Throwing himself across the tomb as if to tackle her, he shot forward, airborne.

Devota spun, twisting the knife.

Oh, God!

With insidious delight in her eyes, the she-devil intended to rip Slade from his neck to his crotch, spilling his guts.

"No! No! No!" Val cried, and threw herself toward the gun just as a horrible, wet, rasping scream issued from the bloody lips of Sister Charity.

In one last, desperate act, as if propelled by God, the dying nun flung her body upward, knocking Devota down onto the bed of the tattered wedding dress, Charity's half-dressed body pinning Devota to the floor as she gasped for breath.

Swearing, Slade skidded across the floor on his shoulder.

Devota reacted. "Why can't you just die?" she screamed at Charity, then plunged the knife deep, burying the blade between the older woman's breasts.

Blood from Charity's neck poured over Devota and dripped onto the wedding dress.

"Get off me!" Devota ordered, trying vainly to free herself. Val reached the pistol just as Charity Varisco, her biological mother, died holding down Camille's killer.

Slade scrambled to his feet.

"Don't do it, Val," he warned, but he was too late.

With dead calm, ignoring the pain in her shoulder and ankle, Valerie crawled over to the two nuns and placed the muzzle hard against the younger woman's temple.

She would have pulled the trigger, but Slade's fingers wrapped around hers. "No," he said, shaking his head, drawing her close. "It's over."

The sound of footsteps, thundering wildly, resonated through the tomb.

The police.

Finally.

Val sagged against her husband, her emotions ragged, her heart dark. This, the crumpled form of a woman with scars crisscrossing her back, was her mother, the woman who had given her life and, in the end, saved it. Tears filled her eyes, and she blinked hard, clinging to Slade, wondering how she had ever doubted him, silently swearing she would never let him go again.

"It's all right," he said, his voice a whisper in the unused air of the musty room. "It's all right." One arm held her fiercely to him, infusing her with his strength.

Flashlight beams wobbled and crisscrossed before landing on the carnage.

"Stop! Police!" Bentz ordered.

"Drop your weapons!" someone else shouted.

"Joseph, Mary, and Jesus. Oh, God, what a mess!" Montoya's voice, seeming to come out of a mist of pain.

With Slade's help, she let go of the gun. Her fingers unclenched and it fell, slowly. The barrel clanged noisily against the floor.

"Help me!" Devota cried. "Help me. They tried to kill me. Please..."

"Don't believe her," Slade said to Montoya, his breath ruffling Valerie's hair.

"I don't," Montoya said. "Then again, I don't trust anyone."

Slade wrapped his arm more tightly around his wife and said again, "It's over."

She clung to him and bit back tears. She knew she'd never let him go again... but she also knew he lied.

This horror, the breadth of Sister Devota's madness and cruelty, wouldn't be over for a long, long time.

If ever.

CHAPTER 53

"You're sure about this?" Val asked Freya on Monday, after she'd returned from a two-day stay in the hospital. She was sore as hell but glad to no longer be in the care of Our Lady of Mercy's staff. If she never saw an IV line or a blood-pressure cuff or red jello again, it would be too soon.

Freya, standing in Val's kitchen, scraped her gaze down Val's body, taking note of the cast on her leg due to a hairline fracture of her tibia, thanks to Devota, the killer nun. God, that sounded terrible, but at least she was behind bars, unable to hurt anyone else.

And the secrets of Val's birth were out in the open; she now knew who she was, though it wasn't a happy thought. How many mothers could she bury before she turned thirty-five? It was hard to think of Sister Charity as her mother—that stern old bat of a nun who turned out to be loving in her own distant way, and Arthur Wembley, her father? The guy had to have been in his sixties when he'd had the affair and ended up fathering a child he didn't want. Now he, too, was dying. Val didn't think she'd make the trip to see him in the hospital, nor did she want a face-off with his wife, the elderly woman who had paid off Camille rather than allow details of her husband's illicit affair to come to light. No scandal at the bridge table for Mrs. Arthur Wembley.

Devota had actually helped out good old Marion by killing Camille and ending the blackmail. That still bothered Val a lot, that Camille would use Val's birth as a means to extract money—for what?

Probably herself and her child.

As soon as her pregnancy was discovered, Camille would have had to leave the convent and she'd have to provide for her baby...

Just thinking of her sister brought a lump to her throat. God, Val missed her. True, Camille hadn't been the most rock-steady of sisters, but there had been many and variegated shades of gray to Camille. Never black, rarely white, Camille had always been a mystery, but a fun one. Val considered Camille's child. Who was its father? If not Father Frank, then who had impregnated her? Val decided she would never figure out the answer to that one. As far as she knew, Camille hadn't divulged the child's paternity to anyone.

Maybe she didn't know. Maybe she thought the baby could be Frank's. Maybe the father doesn't even know about it....

Val wondered vaguely if Sister Lucia, Camille's best friend, had known the truth. According to the police, Lucia Costa had skipped town. No one believed she was dead, but then, who really knew?

"Yeah," Freya was saying, nodding, her red curls catching in the sunlight streaming through the windows. "I'm sure. Sarah said she'd come and help me for a while, until you decide."

"I thought you never hear from your twin."

"Well, unless I call her...and she's 'between gigs,' whatever that means." Freya's mouth spread into an easy grin.

Boot steps rang on the porch, and Val looked toward the back of her little carriage house. Slade, Bo following him, walked through the door, the screen slapping behind him. "You've made up your mind, right?" he asked her, smokey blue eyes sparking with humor. "We're giving this pathetic marriage of ours one more shot?"

Val couldn't help but laugh. "I suppose. If you mind your p's and q's."

"Oh, God, don't get cute on me," Freya begged, holding up her hands as if to fend off an attack. "I might just throw up my cheese blintz!"

"We're never 'cute,'" Valerie insisted. "I abhor all that kind of stuff."

"Good." Freya's eyes said she didn't believe a word of it. "Then keep it in mind. And we'll talk about you selling out your interest at the end of the year—see where you are."

"Barefoot and pregnant," Slade said, then laughed and winked at his own joke. "As if that would ever happen."

"As if you would ever want it to happen," Val said.

"The pregnant part is good."

"Hmmm. Maybe. I think I should get out of my cast first."

"It's kinda sexy." Slade was pulling her roller bag from the bedroom. "And I've always had a foot fetish—barefoot would be all right."

Freya looked stricken. "Enough!"

"He's kidding!" Val said. "See why he drives me crazy?"

"Yeah, and you love it." He was out the door again, and Val sighed.

"Thanks for everything," she said to Freya.

"No thanks needed. The added notoriety of what happened here has only helped business. Sick as it is, I've had to turn people away. We're full up for the rest of the summer, which isn't usually the high season around here."

"I'll miss you," she said, and it was heartfelt.

"Ditto. And I'm leaving everything just as you left it in here. While Sarah's with me. But"—she wagged a finger at Val—"if you ever say you're not coming back, I'm putting all your stuff on craigslist and selling it. I'll turn this room into an apartment for the guests—it'll make me a fortune." Her eyes lit up at the prospect.

"I changed my mind. I won't miss you at all."

They laughed and hugged, and then Val, with Slade's help, limped out of her little house and into the truck.

They were going to start over, to pick up the frayed threads of their marriage and weave it back together.

He started the engine and, with Bo between them, pulled into traffic.

They were on their way to the ranch outside of Bad Luck, Texas. She was going to forget that she'd ever mistrusted him, and she had already forgiven Cammie.

Val closed her eyes and prayed it would work out. As she did, she felt Slade's hand close over hers, as if he'd read her thoughts.

"This is gonna be good, wife," he said with this cowboy grin. "Just you wait and see."

And in the distance, they heard the bells, pealing through the summer air, counting off the next few minutes of the rest of their lives.

"So that's it, case closed?" Montoya asked as he walked into Bentz's office Monday afternoon, then flopped into one of the chairs in front of the desk.

"It'll never be closed," Bentz said, "not as long as Father John is alive." He was tired, his shoulders ached, and he was pissed off that the fake priest had slipped through their fingers again.

"You don't know that he is alive," Montoya said, playing devil's advocate again. "Grace Blanc could have been murdered by a copycat."

"Blood type says it's the same guy."

"DNA isn't back yet. Come on, I'll buy you a beer."

Bentz shot him a look. He rarely drank.

"Okay, a Diet Coke or whatever it is you like." Montoya was on his feet again, and Bentz grabbed his jacket as they walked out of the office and down the stairs to the main level.

Outside, the day smelled fresh, the air clean, a breeze tossing around the fronds of a few palms that were planted near the street.

"Grace Blanc won't be the last one," Bentz said, irritated.

"But at least the nuns at St. Marguerite's are safe again."

"At a price." Sister Charity Varisco hadn't made it. From what he'd heard, she'd dived onto the knife-wielding Sister Devota in order to save Valerie Renard Houston, her biological daughter.

But Devota had survived and would go to trial. Her wounds hadn't been deep, and the DA was putting together a case that would ensure that she be locked up for life.

Which, in Bentz's estimation, wasn't long enough. Too many women, good women of faith, had died at her hand. She was, as Montoya had commented, "a real nut job."

"Hey, wait up!"

He didn't want to look over his shoulder, knowing he'd see Brinkman jogging up, sweating out his shirt, wheezing.

Montoya turned and frowned as they reached the door to the bar.

Brinkman caught up with them and reached into his shirt pocket for his pack of cigarettes. To Bentz's surprise, he shook out several and offered them each a smoke.

Bentz shook his head. "No, thanks."

Montoya hesitated, then said, "Naw, I'm off 'em. The case is over, and Abby's on to me."

"Pussy-whipped." Brinkman snorted, lighting up and shooting smoke through his nostrils.

"Yeah, well, I'm still married."

Brinkman started to bristle but instead shrugged off the dig at his multiple marriages and divorces. "Lucky you," he said, and Bentz opened the door.

"I'll be right in," Brinkman said as Montoya slid inside. "Order me a light beer."

"In your dreams, Brinkman. You can order it yourself."

Bentz let the door close and let the darkness of the bar seep into his bones. He felt the urge for a beer—light or otherwise—but thought better of it and walked up to the bar, where Montoya had already claimed a stool.

The barkeep turned and set two glasses in front of them. A frosted glass of beer for Montoya, a Diet Coke for Bentz. They should be celebrating, the case of the killer who'd stalked the brides of Christ no longer at large, but he was still bothered because of Father John slipping through their fingers.

Then again, Bentz probably always would be. Father John, that bastard, was the one who got away.

EPILOGUE

Some deaths are worth great risk.
But they are necessary, if revenge is to be served.

It takes time, and patience, of course.

I had to wait for five months, had to be quiet, to tamp down the most basic of my urges while each night I listened to the radio and listened to *her* give out her pathetic advice.

But I did.

I waited.

I planned.

I checked schedules, shift changes, routines, and how one could get into the prison.

It wasn't as hard as I expected.

For priests still travel to other parishes, and they give counsel to inmates, so with false ID I was able to walk through the doors of the prison where Sister Devota, née Darlene Arness, is incarcerated.

With the same ID and a confident smile, a little glint in my eye for the woman guard, and my hands folded over my Bible, it's an easy matter to gain access to Devota, in her cell, where she wants to make confession.

Of course, it's all on camera, but I'm not worried. She opens her arms and heart to me, confessing all, even the murder of my beautiful and wicked Camille and the others. She's not worried, as I am a priest; her confession is safe with me. She doesn't see the rage, the telltale tic beneath my left eye, the way my knuckles turn white as I hold the Bible. She not only murdered my child, but also the woman I loved. And I loved Camille, make no mistake. My love for that witch was insatiable.

But, of course, I try to look calm, to act the part of the understanding priest and hear her confession. I'm here to mete out my own special justice, and when she explains about Camille and the baby she was carrying, my child, I feel the need rise.

I remember first spying Camille at St. Elsinore's, when I was searching the old ruins for items I could use, and she mistook me for a traveling priest. I saw the glint of interest in her beautiful eyes, the tiniest of smiles, and I felt her desire, one quickly hidden but, over time, elicited. Even when she realized I wasn't a priest.

She never knew my true identity, of course, just thought I was a rogue priest, one who wanted women too much not to have been cast from church to church.

And she didn't ask too many questions, perhaps suspected and didn't want to know the truth. Besides she was too smart, had lived in New Orleans too long not to have speculated on my true identity.

But she didn't check; or at least she never told me she did.

Maybe my sordid reputation, if she even considered it, only added fuel to her already unquenchable fire, the heat of her sexual needs.

The nunnery was not for Camille.

But I miss her, wretchedly so, and it is all I can do not to scream at this lump of twisted womanhood who so blatantly killed her—using my own technique, no less!

Insidious bitch.

It's all I can do to hear her confession and to know that after this night, I will have to submerge again, become invisible, tamp down my needs. Though this idiotic copycat has stolen my thunder, I will rise again, but not for a while, not until this night, too, has passed and I have become but a legend.

To everyone but Rick Bentz.

My teeth grit as I think of him, and the pain from his bullet seems to sear my flesh again as the pathetic nun mumbles her confession. Yes, I will become a ghost again, and only reappear when the time is right.

As Devota breathes her last vile words, I bless her, but then, before she looks up to my face again, as her head is bent, I place one hand over her mouth and quickly snap her neck.

I prop her up in the chair, and then, while the cameras are rolling, knowing Rick Bentz will review the footage, I slip out of the prison.

I'm not far away when the sirens begin to screech, but it's already too late.

Dear Reader,

When I first started writing *The Night Before,* I had no idea that Nikki Gillette would leap off the page and demand a story of her own, which became *The Morning After.* Then, of course, I couldn't leave well enough alone as she and Pierce Reed's story still hadn't been told. Hence, the following book, *Tell Me,* which involves Nikki, her guilt over a good friend's murder, and her need for the truth.

But the series doesn't end with *Tell Me.* I'm currently finishing the fourth book in the series *The Third Grave.* This time Nikki finds herself eyeball deep in a mystery and cold case that has fueled speculation and gossip for years. Twenty years earlier the Duval sisters vanished and the police have been baffled ever since. Now, in the aftermath of a severe hurricane, three little graves have been discovered, two with bodies, one empty. Has the final resting place of the Duval sisters been found? Will the old case be finally solved? If so, why is the third grave empty? Had the third grave ever had an occupant? Had the intended victim managed to get away? Or are the graves part of another macabre crime?

The exposure of the unlikely burial spots has all of Savannah on edge. Even so Nikki, despite warnings from the police and most especially her husband, can't stop from investigating. And the more she digs, the more danger she uncovers. Far too late she realizes that she, too, is caught in the cross-hairs of a twisted killer.

Will there be more stories in the Savannah series after *The Third Grave*? At this point I don't know, but with Nikki Gillette, it seems, there's always a tale to be told, so we'll just have to see.

You can find out more about all of my books at www.lisajackson. com or follow me on Facebook and connect with me on Twitter!

Keep Reading!

Lisa Jackson

Lisa Jackson, #1 New York Times bestselling author and a master of heart-pounding suspense, returns to the beautiful city of Savannah, Georgia, where crime writer Nikki Gillette and her husband, Detective Pierce Reed, find a cold case leading to a new nightmare . . .

The old Bonaventure mansion is a rotting shell of its once-grand self, especially after a disastrous hurricane sweeps through Georgia. The storm does more than dislodge shutters and shingles. It leads to a grisly find in the cellar. Three graves. But only two skeletons . . .

For Nikki, the discovery is a gift, the perfect subject for her next crime book—though Reed has made her promise not to keep involving herself in dangerous police business. But despite the increasing tension between them, Nikki can't stay away from this story. Rumors are widespread that the burial site is the resting place of the Duval sisters—three young girls who went to the movies with their older brother, Owen, twenty years ago, and never returned. Forensics confirms that the remains belong to Holly and Lily Duval. But where is the youngest sister, Rose?

Owen Duval was, and remains, the prime suspect, alibi or no. But as Nikki and Reed delve deep into the mystery, fractures in the case begin to show. There is more to the sisters' disappearance than anyone ever guessed. Far from an isolated act, those deaths were just the beginning. And there will be no rest, and no relenting, until the killer has buried the twisted truth along with his victims . . .

**Please turn the page for an exciting sneak peek of
Lisa Jackson's
THE THIRD GRAVE
coming soon wherever print and e-books are sold!**

CHAPTER 1

Bronco Cravens was sweating bullets.

Not only because of the heat from an intense Georgia sun.

But from his own damned case of nerves.

He rubbed his fingers together in anticipation, but didn't move, just searched the undergrowth through narrowed eyes one last time. He tuned into the sounds of the lowland: The lap of water against the muddy banks, the whir of dragonfly wings as the narrow-bodied creatures darted along the shore, and the tonal croak of a bullfrog hiding somewhere in the reeds.

The air was still and thick. Sultry enough to paste his shirt to his body.

His nerves were stretched thin, his blood running hot at the thought of what he was about to do. He searched the heavy undergrowth for any kind of movement and licked his already-chapped lips. Sunlight and shadow played through the Spanish moss draped live oaks, but he saw no one, no flicker of movement, felt no eyes boring into his back.

Squinting, he tried to distinguish sunlight from shadow through these dense woods. The swollen river moved quickly in a soft rush, mosquitos buzzing near his head, but he heard nothing out of the ordinary.

No sounds of footfalls or twigs snapping. No murmur of hushed voices or the crunch of tires on old gravel just over the rise. No whine of a distant siren.

No, it seemed, he was all alone.

Good.

No time to lose.

He patted his pockets, had the keys, his cell phone, a flashlight and his pistol, a Ruger LCP, a lightweight automatic that was forever with him. All set. "Let's go," he hissed, glancing over his shoulder to his boat where the dog he'd inherited sat at attention, ears cocked, waiting for a command. Fender had been a gift from Darla, a pure breed blue tick heeler if the previous owner were to be believed. But that was before Darla had left suddenly, slamming the door behind her while screaming, "Don't you ever call me again, you fuckin' loser! And you can keep the damned dog."

He had. Kept the dog, that was. And yeah, he'd never phoned or texted again. Nor had she. Fine with him.

Today, bringing the heeler along may have been a mistake. Sleek coat glistening in the sun, Fender leapt over the edge of the boat to land in the shallows and followed as Bronco took off, running, his boots sinking into the thick mud. Fleetingly Bronco remembered playing on the grounds as a child, fishing, catching snakes and bullfrogs, skipping stones across the pond, watching dragonflies skim the surface, their wings crackling, sunlight catching on their iridescent bodies. He'd run this path often as a kid, but it had been years since he'd taken out his father's fishing boat or stole some of his Camel straights, or hid a six pack in the old culvert. Back then, those had been the worst of his sins.

Now, of course, there were others.

More than he wanted to count.

Now the stakes were a damned sight higher than pissing off his old man and risking Jasper Craven's considerable wrath. But he wouldn't dwell on that now, couldn't dare thinking about his run-ins with the law. Just the thought of prison, of being hauled back to a cement cell, made his skin crawl. He couldn't go back there. Wouldn't.

And yet, here he was. Trespassing. Tempting fate. Intending to break into the Bonaventure mansion where his grandfather had once been caretaker and had sworn the old lady who had lived there had secreted a fortune. His blood ran hotter at the thought of it. Wynn Cravens had admitted he'd seen the rare gold and silver coins, some dating back to the Civil War, along with a cache of jewels and silver certificates and thousands of dollars that old Beulah Bonaventure had secreted in the basement of the once-grand home. Beulah had been mad as a hatter, Gramps had claimed, but he'd sworn the valuables were there—viewed with his own eyes.

Bronco was about to find out.

And change his life.

He grinned at the thought.

No time to lose.

Sunlight was already beginning to fade.

Yesterday's hurricane, a goddamned category five, had torn through this part of Georgia, leveling homes, splintering trees and flooding the city. Telephone and electric poles had been uprooted, the power was out for miles and cell phone service patchy at best.

A disaster for most of the citizens of Savannah.

And a blessing for Bronco.

He crested a rise, a natural levee that had kept most of the flood waters surrounding the old home within the river's banks. From the corner of his eye, he caught a flash. Movement. His heart nearly stopped. But it was just his stupid dog taking off through the tall grass, startling two ducks. Wings flapping noisily, quacking loudly, they took flight.

Shit!

His heart leapt to his throat, but he heard no footsteps, nor shouts, nor sirens, nor baying of hounds.

Good. Just keep moving.

Get in.

Find what you're looking for.

Get out.

No more than fifteen minutes.

Twenty, tops.

He saw the sagging fence with its rusted *No Trespassing* sign dangling from the locked gate and vaulted over what was left of the mesh then spied the house, built on a rise, surrounded by live oaks, the once-manicured lawn surrendering to brush. The white-washed siding was now gray and dimpled, paint peeling, roof sagging and completely collapsed around one of four crumbling chimneys.

For half a beat, Bronco stared up at the house, its windows shuttered and boarded over, graffiti scrawled across the buckling sheets of plywood, the wide, wrap-around porch listing on rotted footings.

His grandfather's voice whispered to him: *"Don't do it, son. Don't. This—what y'er contemplating—is a mistake, y'hear me? It'll only bring you trouble, the kind of trouble no man wants."* He set his jaw and ignored the warning. He'd waited long enough. Now, finally the old man was dead. As if Wynn Cravens's had heard his thoughts, his raspy voice came again: *"Boy, you listen to me, now."*

Bronco didn't.

"Y'er gonna get caught," Wynn Cravens cautioned from beyond the grave. *"Sure as shootin'. And then what? Eh? Another five years in prison? Hell, maybe ten! Could be more. Don't do it, son."*

"Oh, shut up," Bronco growled under his breath. Something he would have never said to his big, strapping grandfather if the man were still alive. Of course, he wasn't. Wynn Cravens had given up the ghost just two weeks earlier, his big heart stopping while the old guy was splitting wood.

With Wynn's passing, Bronco's fortune had changed.

This was his big chance, maybe his last chance and Bronco was going to make the best of it. After all of the bad breaks in his life, finally something good was coming his way. He took the hurricane as an omen. A sign from God Himself.

Right now all of the cops and emergency workers were busy being heroes.

Which gave Bronco some time.

From the corner of his eye he caught a glimmer of movement, a blur through the trees. Not the dog this time. Fender was right on his heels.

He felt his skin crawl. There had always been rumors of ghosts haunting the grounds, lost souls who'd found no escape from the tarnished history of the Bonaventure family. Bronco, though he hated admitting it, couldn't help believing some of the old stories that had been whispered from one generation to the next. Even his grandfather, a brawny no-nonsense Welshman, had believed that tortured spirits moved through the stands of live oak and pine and had sworn on the family Bible that he'd seen the ghost of Nellie Bonaventure, a seven year old girl who drowned in the river in the 1960s. Bronco knew nothing more than that her death had devastated the family. Glimpses of the girl had always been reported the same: A waif in a dripping nightgown, dark ringlets surrounding a pale face, a doll clutched to her chest as she forever wandered along the edge of the water.

And the sightings hadn't stopped with Gramps. His father, too, and a man of the cloth had sworn he'd seen the ghost, though Bronco thought Jasper Cravens's glimpse of the apparition had been the likely result of his affection for rye whiskey rather than an actual viewing of a bedraggled spirit. And hadn't he once, while sneaking through these very woods thought he'd caught sight of a pale, ghost-like figure darting through the underbrush?

He'd told himself, the apparition had been a figment of his imagination, but now, the thought of any kind of wraith caused the hairs on the back of his arms to ripple to attention.

"A crock," Bronco reminded himself just as he spied a deer, a damned white-tailed doe, bounding through a copse of spindly pine.

He made his way toward the back of the house, through weeds and tall grass to the listing verandah that stretched across the rear of the house and offered a view of the terraced lawn and bend in the river. Quickly, across the rotting floorboards he walked to the side door, the one his grandfather and the rest of the staff had used. He slid the key from his pocket, sent up a prayer for good luck, then slipped the key into the lock. A twist of his wrist and . . . nothing. The key didn't budge.

"Shit."

He tried again, forcing the key a bit. Shoving it hard.

Once more the lock held firm.

"Goddamn it!" Just his luck. After waiting all this time, after planning and hoping and . . . this always happened to him! In an instant he saw his decades long dream of wealth disintegrate into dust. Maybe he'd have to break through the old plywood covering the windows. But that would take too long, be too noisy.

"Fuck it." He wasn't going to give up. Not yet. Setting his jaw, he jammed the key in again, then suddenly stopped. This was all wrong.

He'd watched the old man do this a hundred times.

He remembered his grandfather babying the lock.

Bronco tried again, but didn't force the key in hard, "gentled it" as Gramps used to say. *"Like dealing with a hot-headed woman, son, you got to tread softly, touch her gentle-like."*

"Come on. Come on—"

Click!

The bolt gave way and the door creaked open.

He was in! Quickly, his heart hammering, his nerves strung tight, he stepped into a small vestibule with a narrow set of stairs running up and down and a door leading into the kitchen. He headed down the curved steps to find another door at another landing. Unlocked, it swung open easily to reveal yawning blackness and horrid stench that seemed to waft upward in a cloud. Nearly gagging, he pulled a rag to cover his mouth from one pocket and a small flashlight from another. God, the smell of rot and decay was overpowering. He switched on the flashlight and descended the final flight to step into three or four inches of water, black and brackish and thick with sludge.

This better be worth it.

He skimmed the standing water with the beam of his flashlight and tried not to think of what creatures might nest down here— rats and gators and water moccasins or black widows hidden in dark places.

Don't go there. Don't think about what could be living down here. Concentrate, Cravens. Find the loot and get the hell out before you get caught.

Ducking beneath raw beams black with age, rusted hooks and nails protruding, he slogged through years of forgotten furniture, books, pictures, all ruined and decaying. The flashlight's beam skated over the water and mud, across broken down chairs and crates stacked atop each other.

A spiderweb brushed his face and he felt a skittering of fear slide down his spine.

This place was getting to him. Too dark, too smelly, too . . .

Scritttcch.

He froze at the sound.

What the hell?

His heart went into overdrive, thudding wildly.

He whirled, swinging the beam of the flashlight past a listing armoire to . . . oh, shit! A dark, disjointed figure stared back at him!

Bronco jumped backward, startled. Automatically he reached for his Ruger. Someone was down here! A weird apparition that, too, was staring at him while scrabbling for a weapon and pointing a beam of a high-powered flashlight at his face. Reacting, Bronco fired just as he realized his mistake.

Blam!

The dirty mirror shattered!

His own distorted image splintered into a hundred shards of glass that flew outward, glittering crazily in his flashlight's beam. "Shit!"

A rat squealed and scurried between several stacks of boxes.

Freaked, Bronco took aim at the rodent, but stopped himself before pulling the trigger. The damned rat was the least of his problems. If anyone had heard the gun go off they'd come and investigate. *Shit, shit, shit!*

"No way," he said under his breath. He just had to work faster.

Get in. Get out.

That was the plan.

Gramps had said there was some sort of hiding space at the southeast corner of the foundation, a deeper cache where he'd seen Beulah Bonaventure hide her valuables.

So find it already.

Pushing aside a bike with flat tires propped against a post, he kept moving, still bent over as he stepped around a pile of empty bottles that had been stacked near the brick foundation. He ran the beam over ancient bricks stacked nearly four feet tall that made up the foundation. Carefully he eyed the mortar, searching for any cracks and—in a second he saw the seam. Partially hidden by an ancient armoire, he noticed a flaw in the design where the pattern of the bricks changed.

The old man hadn't lied.

With renewed effort, he held the flashlight in his teeth and shoved one shoulder against the armoire, shoving the heavy chest to one side, wedging it tight against a stack of stained boxes. Sure enough, the seam was the outline of a small door cut into the bricks.

He just had to figure out how to open it. He had no more keys, no crowbar, but as he shined his light over the seam in the bricks, he ran the tips of his fingers over the rough edges of the mortar.

No knob.

No pull.

No handle of any kind.

Damn.

There had to be a way.

More carefully he touched the edges of the seam again but . . . nothing. "Come on, come on," he muttered in frustration.

No one said it would be easy, but he could use an effin' break.

Thump, thump, thump, thump!

The noise thundered through the basement.

Bronco froze.

What the hell?

Oh, shit! Someone was running across the porch!

No!

Had he closed the outside door? Locked it behind him?

Hell, no!

Crap!

Why was anyone out here after the damned storm?

In one motion, he ducked, dimmed his flashlight, and raised his gun, his eyes trained laser-sharp on the foot of the stairs where only the faintest shaft of illumination was visible. Sweat drizzled into his eyes.

Could he really do it?

Kill a man? Or a woman? Or a damned kid?

Crap, crap, crap!

Heavy breathing, more thumping as whoever it was rounded that final landing.

Oh, Jesus. Someone heard the shot! That's what it was!

Bronco's finger tightened over the trigger.

In a blur of motion a shadow leaped from the final steps.

He fired—*Bang!*—and caught a glimpse of shiny fur as an animal yelped in pain.

No! His stupid dog! Jesus Christ, he'd just killed his damned dog! The shot was still ringing in his ears but still, he heard a pitiful whine and scrambling paws. "Boy—here, boy."

The heeler was at his side in an instant, unhurt, just scared and shaking, brown eyes bulging. But no blood. Bronco checked with his flashlight, running the beam over the dog's coat. "You idiot," Bronco muttered, but gave the shivering animal a quick scratch behind his ears. "I coulda killed . . . oh, hell . . ." There was no time for this. Now there had been two shots fired. No telling who might've heard them. One could have been dismissed, but two? Nope. No way. He had to work fast. To the dog, he whispered, "You stay. You hear me? Don't move a muscle."

Fender whined, his tail tucked between his legs. his body trembling.

Shit!

Bronco couldn't worry about it. He had less time than ever. He had to find the release for the door. And fast.

He swept the light over the beams, searching for electrical wires that would lead him to a switch for the small brick portal even though, if that were the case, if the catch on the door was electrically controlled, he was screwed. The power to the house had been shut off long ago.

Think, Bronco, think. This has to be simple. Something you're missing! What had Gramps said? Something about a combination?

He returned to the door, crouched beside it, ran the flashlight's beam over the dirty bricks once more.

From the corner of his eye he saw the dog nosing around again, but ignored him. Right now he had to concentrate. Crouching low, Bronco took a step backward, ran the flashlight over the door again and . . . he saw it. A chip on one of the lower bricks that was slightly different than the others. Smoother. A long shot, but he knelt in the muck, placed his finger in the small divot and waited for a click.

Nothing.

Yet . . . then he spied another, similar notch on the brick above. He touched it. Again, zilch.

Get in.

Get out.

Fender crept up to him. Curious. Nosing around.

Bronco ignored the dog and tried several times to open the latch. But nothing happened.

This had to be it. Right?

The dog whined, the hackles on the back of his neck bristling, but Bronco was deep in concentration before he noticed the third notch on a brick that abutted the other two.

Tentatively. Sweat dripping from his nose, he placed a finger on the notch. Still nothing. Damn. Maybe he was way off base with this.

Fender, muscles tense, let out a low growl.

"Hush!" Bronco muttered. He couldn't be bothered with the dog right now. He rocked back on his heels holding the beam steady on the small door. No more notches. Just the three in those abutting bricks. That had to mean something. Had to. He chewed on his lip. What if he touched all three impressions at once? What were the chances?

Again the dog let out a warning growl, but Bronco paid no attention.

He leaned forward, placed his fingertips into the holes one at a time. Nothing budged. He tried again this time touching all of the indentations simultaneously.

Over the low rumble of Fender's warning growl, he heard a soft but distinct click.

His heart hammered. He licked his lips. But nothing moved. "Damn." This had to be it. Nervously, knowing he was on the brink, he tried again, then on inspiration, pushed on the rough bricks, rather than waiting for the door to magically open.

It gave!

Scraping loudly as he shoved on it, the door slid slowly inward. The scents of dust and dry rot sifted out.

He was in!

Bronco could have shouted for joy!

All the years of waiting!

As Bronco leaned forward, shining his light into the dry space beyond, the stupid mutt gave out an eerie whine. "Shut up," Bronco said, leaning forward. He peered into the dark, tight cavern, sweeping the beam of his flashlight over the interior, expecting to find a cache of unimaginable treasure.

But no.

No glittering gems or stacks of bills.

Instead . . .

What the hell?

What the bloody hell?

The flashlight's beam landed on a skull.

A human skull.

With empty black sockets where eyes had once been, the jaw open, teeth visible in an eerie grin of death, the fleshless face seemed to stare straight into the bottom of Bronco's soul.

He let out a scream before he saw the second skull, next to the first, smaller and just as long dead. Their clothes were tatters, blouses, one with a bra, shorts, and sneakers.

Oh, fuck!

Kids!

Fuck! Fuck! Fuck!

Frantically, he scrambled backward, as if expecting the skeletons to stand and start chasing him. He stood quickly, his head cracking painfully against a rough beam.

His knees buckled, but only for an instant.

Then he ran. Knocking over boxes and bins, banging his knee against a forgotten chest of drawers, Bronco Cravens ran as he'd never run before.

Connect with U(s)

Visit us online at
KensingtonBooks.com
to read more from your favorite authors, see books
by series, view reading group guides, and more.

Join us on social media

for sneak peeks, chances to win books and prize packs,
and to share your thoughts with other readers.

facebook.com/kensingtonpublishing
twitter.com/kensingtonbooks

Tell us what you think!

To share your thoughts, submit a review,
or sign up for our eNewsletters, please visit:
KensingtonBooks.com/TellUs.